05/19

This book should be returned to any Lancashire
County Council Library on or before the date shown

- 2 OCT 2021

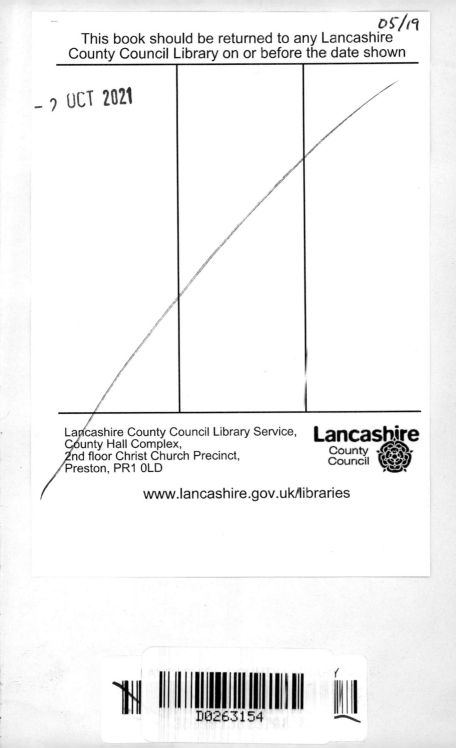

Lancashire County Council Library Service,
County Hall Complex,
2nd floor Christ Church Precinct,
Preston, PR1 0LD

Lancashire
County
Council

www.lancashire.gov.uk/libraries

Born in Chatham and partly raised in Dublin, Liz Lawler is one of fourteen children and grew up sharing socks, pants, stuffed bras and a table space to eat at. Liz spent over twenty years working as a nurse, and has since worked as a flight attendant and as the general manager of a five-star hotel. She now lives in Bath with her husband.

Also by Liz Lawler

Don't Wake Up

I'LL FIND YOU

Liz Lawler

ZAFFRE

First published as an ebook in Great Britain in 2019
Published in Great Britain in 2019 by

ZAFFRE
80–81 Wimpole St, London W1G 9RE

A CIP catalogue record for this book is available
from the British Library.

ISBN: 978–1–78576–603–9

1 3 5 7 9 10 8 6 4 2

Printed

Prologue

Courage abandoned her as she stared into the darkness. Her legs turned to rubber, as if she'd run long and hard, and her heart thudded as she dragged in air. Her mind froze with indecision. She needed to get a grip. To just get on with it and start searching, before the porter returned and caught her there. Her week of spying on him and following and noting down times of his every movement could change. His nightly routine of hanging up his porter's jacket in the staffroom, with keys still in the pocket, before getting into his car and driving off-site to one of three neighbouring takeaways was no guarantee he would not return any moment and catch her in the act. She needed to be quick.

She pressed her trembling hands together, attempting to squeeze away the tremors, and stiffened her legs to give them strength. It was not the fear of looking that stopped her taking this step, it was the fear of what she would find.

She reached out and patted the wall, feeling for the light switch, hearing the pings and buzz of electricity as each Perspex square on the ceiling above illuminated brightly. The noise filled her ears and in her heightened state she imagined it being heard outside the building. She listened intently, but the momentary sounds had already ceased, and she could find no more reason to abandon her mission. The place was silent except for the sound of her own breathing.

The room – rectangular, windowless and very private – looked like a bank vault with safe deposit boxes, where clients were taken and left in privacy to open a box and store their most valuable items. The difference here was in the size of the boxes. Each was big enough to take a body. The first and last were even bigger and were used to take the largest of the cadavers. On one wall she counted twelve doors – enough fridges for twelve bodies. That meant there were twelve spaces to check, not counting those on the facing wall. If she hurried she could be out of there in minutes, have the keys back in the porter's pocket with him none the wiser to her being there. It may only take the opening of one door to find who she was looking for . . .

The small terracotta floor tiles were worn and the black scuff marks told of the back-and-forth journeys of rubber-wheeled trolleys. Parked trolleys and a hydraulic lift sat at the far end of the room, the lift plugged in for battery charging. A single chair was set against a drab grey wall.

She would open doors from left to right, bottom to top so that she didn't miss any out.

She made her way to the nearest fridge and gripped the handle. The heavy door opened with barely a sound and cold air cooled her heated face. The cadaver was zipped inside a white body bag. She held her breath, not wanting to breathe in the air of the dead, the lingering scent of hundreds of bodies that had lain here before. The temperature was set to keep bodies cool, but could not prevent rot. When she finally took a breath, she was relieved to find that all she could smell were the harsh chemicals that the fridges had been sterilised with. Her fingers trembled as she eased open the zip, relief flooding her as she saw grey, wispy hair. Inside was a featureless old man or woman with hollowed-out cheeks. She closed the bag, shut the door and moved to open the fridge above. Her eyes fixed on a bald head, noticing wrinkles and liver spots. There were similar bodies in the next few chambers, with more grey hair on some, whispery white patches on others, a peach-coloured afro on another, then a shock of white-blonde hair tied back with a scrap of bandage. Someone young.

Resting for a moment, she tried not to imagine a face to fit that body. She unzipped the next bag, gagged and had to cover her mouth. The head was charred black with red congealed blood that had settled like jellied lava pushing through burst skin. She banged the door shut and gulped the air, trying not to imagine the particles of dead flesh that she could be inhaling. *The dead can't hurt you*, she whispered into her cupped hand. Only to discover a moment later that they could. Inside the next fridge was a tiny, cocooned shape wrapped in a white sheet. She felt an unbearable ache inside her throat. There was a pink teddy lying atop the shrouded baby. It may have been a gift from the parents, and she felt unforgivably intrusive for seeing something so private and precious.

She slumped to the floor and leaned back against the cold steel. She was torturing herself in this place. She should have requested this search in the presence of someone else; demanded that they show her the inside of every fridge, but she couldn't run the risk of being refused or seeing the pity in their eyes as they reluctantly agreed. They would think she had lost her mind to request such a search. As far as they were concerned the patient had simply absconded and was not one of the dead lying in this mortuary.

She crawled to the last two doors and reached up to open the top one first. Hardened by what she had already seen, she unzipped the bag fast and was surprised to see the soles of feet. The underside of the toes was pure white, the arches and heels dark purple. They were young feet, smooth and unworn by time. They could be male or female, though they were small. Using the door to steady herself she stood up and felt her insides buck as she saw the painted toenails. *Blue's so much prettier, don't you think? It shows off your tan better.* With fingertips, she reached in and touched the feet. They were cold. She cried out, unable to stop herself. It could be *her.* A white identity band circled the left ankle, the name hidden from view. She twisted the band slowly until she saw a printed name: Jane Doe. It was the name used for an unknown, the unidentified. Her breath felt ragged. Until she saw the face, she couldn't be sure.

The body was in the fridge but the wrong way round. She would have to pull out the tray to see the face. She gripped its rim and pulled, but it didn't slide out. She tugged harder, but it stayed put. She stared at the sides of the tray to try and see why it was stuck but could see nothing obvious. Maybe it just needed a stronger pull. She placed a foot against the door below, leaned back and pushed hard with her foot to put her weight behind the tug, but it was hopeless. The tray refused to move. Frustrated, she stared in at the body bag, staring at the space above it. Calculating. Thinking. Maybe there was enough room for her to climb in over it. The compartment was bigger than the others, and there was a further tray slot midway up the wall, room for a second body. She would have to unzip the bag as she went along so that when she got to the end the bag would be completely open. But fear filled her. The space looked so small, a narrow icy tunnel with only darkness at the end. She would have no room to turn around. She would have to get out of the fridge feet first, slide over the uncovered body and pray she held her nerve.

Placing her knee gingerly on the tray, she positioned herself; left foot on the left side, right foot on the right side. Keeping her head low and her weight off the body, she crab-crawled her way in. The air she breathed was dense and cold and it chilled her skin as it clung to her. Her thighs were already beginning to tremble as she held herself awkwardly on toes and hands, in a spread-eagled press-up. Arching her back to relieve the stress, she was startled as she felt the ceiling pressing down on her, reminding her how tiny the crawl space was. She gulped at the air, trying to quell her rising panic. She needed to use her knees to take her weight, so that she could rest on her elbows. She shook from the strain of her position and needed to get comfortable. Clumsily she moved one knee forward as the edge of the metal tray dug into the bone, before bringing the other forward to lessen the pressure. She brought her shoulders back and straightened her arms so that she was on all fours, and immediately realised her error. She was now higher, her back a solid plane fixed in position, a feeling of weight on top of her as she pressed against the roof. She had taken up all the space with her change of position and now she was stuck.

She struggled, instinctively, shaking her head like a rabid dog stuck in a hole, banging it against the steel, grunting with the effort to get free, but her hands and knees were locked and her inability to go backwards or forwards petrified her. She wheezed, a whistling sound as her airway closed, and then, spent, weak with effort, she flopped down, resting on the body beneath her. She touched the plastic bag, feeling its smoothness, its coolness, and slowly her limbs stretched out and she realised how foolish she was to have panicked. There was enough room for both her and this body.

Moving her hand beneath her, she reached down as far as her fingers could stretch, searching for the zipper. Her fingers fumbled as they touched the bag, and she felt a solid mass beneath, but no goddamn zip. Her face mashed against the plastic as she half twisted, pushing her shoulder down and straining her muscles to reach it. *Please, please just give it to me,* she chanted inside her head, and then let out a cry of victory as the metal piece slid between her fingers. Wasting no more energy she pulled the zipper towards her. The scratching of metal against plastic echoed loudly in the confined space. She stopped as she reached the neck, seeing the sudden strands of dark hair, her fingers becoming like boneless appendages as they touched its softness. Tears blurred her vision and she was thankful for the watery screen. She could view the face through a teary waterfall and climb back out of here and still not know if it was her. She could hold on to the hope that she wasn't dead.

She blinked away the tears and let her eyes adjust to the darkness. Slowly she brought the zip all the way up to see the top of the head, and somewhere in the region of where her heart lay, she felt a stillness. An absence of a heartbeat to match the one against her. The eyes were closed, lips pulled together and skin a washed-out milky grey. She gazed at the face. Then it came. A crushing, a squeezing, a pressing feeling right inside her heart. *She had found her.*

'Wake up,' she whimpered. Then, shoving the body hard, she yelled: 'Wake up, damn you. Stop fucking playing about!'

She wrapped her arms and legs around the unyielding form, trying to make it move. 'You're not dead,' she cried. 'You're just cold. People can be brought back to life when they're cold. You simply have to get warm. Come on. Wake up *Please!*'

Shuddering with grief she huddled into the still figure, placing her warm face against the cold face, her tears and mucus dripping down the neck of the body she held. Her cries changed from howls to sobs to whimpers as her mind slowly absorbed reality. Her search had finally ended. She could now lie there. She would stay for ever. She would not leave her in the dark. Stay there till—

The fridge began to hum, a healthy sound to indicate it was on. The air had suddenly become colder. Solid blackness filled the space where she lay. The square of light, from where she had crawled into the space, was now gone. While she lay there someone had entered the morgue. Someone had seen the fridge open. Someone had closed the door.

Chapter One

Emily stirred at the sound of the cries. Someone was calling for help. They sounded desperate. Terrified. In need of urgent care. Her throat felt restricted, clogged somehow, and she was unable to call out to reassure the person, to tell them she was there, that she was coming. She swallowed the heaviness from her throat so she could speak. 'I'm here,' she rasped, opening her eyes and gazing blearily up at the white ceiling above. 'I'm here,' she whispered, feeling desolate in the quietness of the room, knowing the cries she'd heard were hers alone. She was home, safe in her bed, not in an icy tomb. Her eyes and throat ached with the memory of her dream. Her face was damp with tears; tears that came when she slept – when she dreamed that Zoe was dead. The mortuary was the last place in the hospital she had searched for her sister. No one had been able to account for her disappearance. She had been a patient one minute, and a missing person the next. But when the days had become a week, when the police were no further forward with finding her, Emily had felt that she had no other choice but to look for her there.

In her dreams she always found her. In her dreams she held Zoe in that fridge. Not the body of a Jane Doe who had been deliberately placed in the fridge with her feet to the door out of respect, as she had been decapitated in a motorbike accident. Emily had been holding the head in her hands when they opened the fridge door and found her. She remembered nothing after unzipping that body bag, apart from the detached head. She had shut down after seeing something so horrible. Only the solid darkness, an awareness the door had been closed, had revived her enough to cry out and say she was there.

The day the call came, Emily had already been awake. She'd been up since the crack of dawn, in the middle of painting this room she was in now. The window had been open, and the radio was blaring as she tried to work off her annoyance with Zoe. She'd been startled to recognise the voice of one of the doctors she worked with and initially thought he was calling about a work-related issue. When he said it was her sister he was calling about, Emily had felt her gut clench, imagining a car accident, a fatal injury. He'd quickly reassured her and said that Zoe was on the observation unit and there was no need to rush. Her sister was sleeping soundly and had suffered no ill effects from the large quantity of alcohol consumed. She had a saline drip and would probably wake up bright and breezy in a few hours. If Emily had got herself to the hospital soon after that call had ended, her life now would be very different – or rather it would have remained as it was. But she hadn't rushed. Instead she'd showered to get the paint out of her hair and off her hands. She'd phoned her parents to let them know that she and Zoe wouldn't be over for Sunday lunch, a white lie told to prevent them from finding out about Zoe's admission to hospital, saying that they had both been called in to work. In the time that it took her to get to the ward, everything changed. Zoe was missing.

Those first few hours of looking for her hadn't really impacted on Emily. As she had turned each corner, she had expected to see her sister standing there tearful and feeling sorry for herself. The nurses on the ward hadn't been concerned; patients, especially those admitted for intoxication, frequently absconded without even signing the self-discharge form. It saved the embarrassment of the obligatory, well-rehearsed talk on the dangers of alcohol and the offer to see part of the alcohol liaison team before going home. Apologising on her sister's behalf, Emily had gone straight to Zoe's flat, expecting to find her there. When Zoe's flatmate, Jo, opened the door and told Emily that her sister had been taken to A&E, Emily had asked her to round up the other flatmates. The five other students had come out of their bedrooms slowly, walking like the living dead, eyes blackened from sleep-caked mascara, makeup smudged down their faces, hair wild and free, wearing vest tops and pyjama shorts. They'd looked like the backing dancers from 'Thriller'. They had all been out the night before with Zoe. None had gone to the hospital with her as they too were drunk and not allowed on board the ambulance. At Emily's insistence, each of them checked their mobiles for texts, missed calls and social media notifications, and all gave the same response. 'I've got nothing from her.' They suggested she would probably have gone to McDonald's for breakfast. Or rather, they hoped that this was the case so they could text her, asking her to bring them back food. Maybe she was lying low, Jo suggested.

It was this suggestion that Emily initially suspected was the most likely, until she replayed in her mind their conversation from the night before. Zoe had rung at nearly ten o'clock, her voice already slurry from drink. 'Hey Sis, really fucked up, failed all my exams. Don't suppose you wanna come out and party?' Emily had spent ten minutes on the phone reassuring her younger sister that she could retake exams; it wasn't the end of the world. 'But overspending my student allowance is. I'm in debt up to my eyeballs, Sis.' Again, Emily had reassured her that she'd find a way to sort out the problem. She hadn't joined her because she simply hadn't wanted to go out and drink with a bunch of students a decade younger than herself and be the one buying the drinks all night because none of them had any money. Instead, she'd encouraged her to let her hair down and told her that tomorrow her problems would look different.

It was the last part of their conversation that had caused her to think that Zoe would just turn up – the part where she lost patience with her, told her to grow up, told her to consider others for a change. She had refused to answer further calls. Her phone had vibrated beneath her pillow regularly throughout the night. This is what had made her behave the way she did the next day. Pure anger. She'd had enough of Zoe.

On the second day Zoe was missing, Emily returned to the hospital and called the police. A police constable had arrived soon after and taken statements and a description of Zoe. The hospital CCTV footage had shown Zoe wearing a long dark cardigan over her hospital gown, walking barefoot and dangling a pair of high-heeled shoes in one hand and a plastic carrier bag in the other. They were able to follow her movements as she walked towards one of the side entrances, a road usually used for hospital deliveries, which led out on to the main road. That was the last sighting of Zoe.

Emily had searched every patient's bed before she was convinced that her sister wasn't in one of them, even though the CCTV footage had showed her leaving the hospital. Emily had needed to believe that Zoe hadn't been readmitted, perhaps as a result of collapsing or being run over, perhaps unconscious and unable to say who she was. It was three days after Zoe went missing that she was officially declared as such and a detective inspector put in charge of her case. Geraldine Sutton's impressive title was what really put the fear of god into Emily. That someone so high-ranking was looking for her sister meant that the police were taking her disappearance seriously. As Emily began to think in terms of abduction and death, a paranoid thought consumed her: that her sister had died in the hospital, through human error, and that there was a cover-up.

Emily squeezed her eyes closed. She could not think about Zoe now. She must concentrate on the day ahead. She must focus on not eating or drinking, stay nil by mouth from midnight as of last night, remember to bring her overnight bag, her admission letter, mobile charger, a book to read. Today at least her mind could be free of Zoe, if only while she was anaesthetised for this minor operation. Zoe was missing. She was not dead. And while the police may have given up all hope of finding her alive, Emily refused to do so. Not that the police had voiced that opinion. Not yet, anyway. She must hang on to that and if necessary, remind them to keep searching. She owed Zoe that for what she had done. For what she could never undo.

Chapter Two

The private hospital had opened two years ago, close to Windsor Bridge, affording the patients a view of the River Avon. In a city famous for its Georgian architecture, the design of the building had passed through planning despite its bold and contemporary features of plated shiny steel and walls of black glass. Four storeys high, it offered both inpatient and outpatient care, eighty patient rooms, a state-of-the-art diagnostic and therapeutic suite, four operating theatres and a psychiatric wing that Emily liked to steer clear of.

A year ago she very nearly landed up in there. Only by acknowledging her foolish actions – 'not prudent' was the actual phrase she'd used – had she allowed them to see that they were not that of a madwoman, but those of someone desperate enough to search the mortuary on her own. In the end, as no physical harm had come to anyone – bar a hefty shock to the porter who had found her and who accepted the reprimand for allowing her to get into the mortuary in the first place – no charges were brought by the police. They may have viewed things differently if they knew she had spied on the porter for a week, to work out when he wouldn't be there so she could carry out the search. The psychiatrist who saw her discharged her back to her GP with the recommendation that she have counselling. Stress, grief and depression were an expected and acceptable excuse for her actions, given the circumstances. At the time Zoe's face and name were current national news, and Emily had seen the look of pity in the police officer's eyes as he questioned her about her behaviour. Still, the fear of being locked away in a psychiatric ward had unsettled her enough to haunt her. If she'd said the wrong thing or reacted in the wrong way her freedom may have been taken away.

Switching her gaze to the entrance of the hospital building, it felt strange to be walking into it as a patient and not a nurse. She'd only started working there three weeks ago and it still felt new to her. While not exactly at home yet in her new surroundings, she took comfort in the fact that that she knew most of the staff by face or name now, knew what was hidden behind locked doors and cupboards and where she needed to go. She made her way over to the lift which would carry her up to the surgical unit. It was the place where she worked five days a week. Only not today.

In the short time she'd been here she had come to know the routine requirements for surgical patients. Nil by mouth, followed by surgery, followed by post-op checks, followed by returning home. She wasn't simplifying the needs of these patients; in the aftercare anything could go wrong: a wound dehiscing, a sudden bleed, anaphylactic reactions to the anaesthetic drugs or blood transfusions. The ability to know what to do when these things happened was all part of post-operative care. Emily worried that the member of staff looking after her would not be as experienced as she was. Her mind grew anxious as the lift moved upwards.

The hidden enemy was the slow bleeder, sneakily leaking away so that the body was almost unaware of it until it was almost too late to undo the damage. The real skill in nursing was required in detecting the early-warning signs of deterioration – early being the operative word – or 'enemy' as she preferred to call it. It was why an Early Warning Score system had been introduced into hospitals to ward off medical failings. From her experience, the tool was only useful if backed up by clinical knowledge, with having an understanding that what is 'normal' for one patient may be different for another. The resting heart rate of the average person is 60 to 100 BPM, while in an athlete it could be as low as 40. Emily could still see the pallid face of the young jockey who'd been brought in to A&E; a young man she would always remember, a patient she had triaged as a Priority Two before handing over his care to the assigned nurse. Emily had seen the fear in his eyes because he knew something was very wrong with him. The first-year staff nurse caring for him had not alerted the team until it was too late, pointing to the monitor and arguing that his heart rate was normal as he lay there dying. Death from internal bleeding had been a harsh reminder to her to always look at the patient before the machines. If she had, she would have noticed the pallor of his skin and the cyanotic lips telling her that something was wrong.

Maybe she would speak to the nurses who'd be looking after her, test their knowledge, remind them of what to look out for.

She breathed deeply as the lift doors pinged open and deposited her onto the correct floor.

The healthcare assistant was staring at her in a way that was bordering on rudeness and Emily was tempted to poke out her tongue. She was used to people staring; taking a second look at a face that was familiar, trying to figure out where they knew her from. The woman was a member of staff she hadn't met before. She had a head of blonde curls and wore lots of mascara, which made her big blue eyes pop out. Pale pink lipstick made a cupid's bow of her mouth, and her face reminded Emily of a baby doll with painted eyelashes and lips. Her maroon trousers and tunic fit snugly around her hips and bosom, trapping the two pens in her breast pocket tightly and showing her shapely form. She frowned and then smiled uncertainly. 'Sorry, it's just that you look so familiar?'

Emily decided not to be helpful and point out that a face very similar to her own – Zoe's – was plastered on posters across the city. For a time, her image had been displayed on the front page of newspapers across the country and on news programmes on the television. 'I work here.'

The woman shook her head. 'I'm new, so I don't think we've met, but I still know your face from somewhere . . .'

'Emily Jacobs.'

The woman's expression froze before forming a polite mask. She looked as if she might run away for a moment and Emily felt a little mean. 'It's OK. I get it a lot. Just please don't call me Zoe.'

The woman shook her head hard. 'Of course not. Look, let's start again. My name's Shelly. I'm a healthcare assistant.'

Emily hid her amusement. She had just told the woman she worked there. She would know Shelly was a healthcare assistant from the colour of her uniform.

'You say you work here? As a nurse? Clerical? Catering?'

Emily felt like a smart-arse. The woman was new. She was being professional by identifying her role. Many patients would need that explaining to them. That a ward sister or charge nurse wore navy, a staff nurse a lighter blue and healthcare assistant, maroon.

'Staff nurse.'

Shelly smiled. 'Great. So you know the routine. I'll show you to your room and get you settled. Put a name band on you and so forth. Get a urine sample off you. It must feel strange being a patient here?'

Emily nodded, feeling less tense. At least Shelly was in tune with how she was feeling. She should be grateful that Zoe's face was so familiar. It meant she was still in the minds of people and she hadn't been forgotten.

Fastening the strings of the inadequately designed theatre gown together as best she could, Emily hoped her dignity was intact. Beneath the hospital gown she was naked. Freshly showered and devoid of makeup, perfume or deodorant, she stood in front of the narrow mirror. Her short black hair was tucked behind her ears and the trauma of the last year was evident in her face. The purple and grey smudges beneath her blue eyes were now a permanent blemish. Whether she slept well or not made little difference to their appearance; only concealer could hide them. Her face had taken on a narrowness that made her eyes seems bigger and her image more like Zoe's. She was ten years older than Zoe, but right now she could be mistaken for her. Emily thought she looked like a teenage boy, all jutting collar bones and gangly arms. Only recently her mother had said she looked like the poor cow that had her hair cut off and her teeth pulled out in *Les Misérables*. She stared at the blood she had spat in the sink. The pink foamy splatters in the basin worried her that she was physically falling apart. At twenty-nine she had a permanent ache in her stomach and suffered from headaches and sleep deprivation. Her GP had of course checked her out and told her to worry less, explained that they were symptoms of anxiety. A year ago, she'd been a fit young woman. Last month her counsellor had urged her to opt for part-time work or light duties, believing her unable to cope full-time with what she was going through. With no end in sight for the 'going through', she knew her mind was better occupied – at least some of the time – in caring for others. 'Light duties' would not cut it. She needed to be busy.

So she had chosen to work on the surgical admissions unit at a new private hospital with the hope of finding new challenges, the least of which was meeting the high expectations and demands of the paying patients. Having only ever worked in the NHS, she found the private setup was run more like a five-star hotel. There were en suite bathrooms, luxury toiletries, fluffy white towels, Sky TV, newspapers and daily visits from a chef to take menu orders. Every requirement was catered for. Emily sorely missed emergency medicine. She missed the thrill of the red phone screeching, the silence in those waiting seconds before resus doors banged open to allow fast-moving trolleys to rush in to deposit their critical patients in need of urgent care. She would never work there again. Never go home at the end of a shift and know her life was normal. The place held too many memories to remind her of what her life used to be like.

Gathering her toiletries and holding the back of the gown together, she made her way back to her bed.

Chapter Three

There were two beds in the room and the other bed was now occupied. All other rooms in the private hospital were single occupancy, and that is what the patients paid for. Room 31 was unnumbered but was referred to as 31 for want of a title. Some referred to it as 'the side room'. The two-bedded ward was mostly used as an overspill for NHS patients; 'waiting list initiatives' booked for elective surgery and paid for by the NHS.

A young woman who was perhaps in her late teens or early twenties lay curled on her side with her eyes closed. She had a slight build and was wearing, at a guess, size eight jeans with room to spare. Judging by the length of her shape in the bed she was barely five feet tall. Her hair was dark and lustreless and her skin pale beneath the olive tones. A thin silver bracelet circled her right wrist. It looked big enough for her hand to slip through, like a child's would if wearing her mother's bracelet. On her feet were well-worn leather flip-flops. Even on her slight form the yellow T-shirt was too small, barely covering her midriff – unless the small size of the T-shirt had been intentional, to show off a flat tummy? Emily silently put away her things and heard the rustle of movement. The young woman, or girl, as Emily thought her, was awake.

Emily smiled at her neighbour but was greeted with an anxious stare. She smiled again and said hello. The brown eyes were wary and they scanned the room, full of fear. Emily was beginning to suspect that perhaps her neighbour didn't speak English or was prevented from talking by pain. She pointed at the girl and then at herself and mimicked the action of someone being in pain, clutching at her belly. The girl briefly shook her head.

On her bedside locker was a theatre gown and cap and Emily was about to suggest she help her get ready when common sense prevailed. The patient beside her didn't know she was a nurse and would think it very strange if she started to try and undress her. She may even think she was being assaulted.

'Do you speak English?' The girl looked more anxious and edged to the side of the bed. Emily held up her hands in an attempt to show a calming manner. 'It's OK.' She pointed at her hospital gown. 'I'm going to theatre too.' She indicated the clothes on the bedside locker. 'Those are for you to put on.' She touched her wrist and then pointed at the silver bracelet. 'You'll have to take that off.' The girl immediately covered the bracelet with her other hand as if in fear of it being taken.

Clearly not in any pain, the girl shot nimbly off the bed, took the clothes from the locker and scurried from the room. Hoping that she hadn't chased her nervous neighbour away, Emily settled on her bed and waited.

She was anxious about the procedure she was having – and embarrassed about having to take time off work after only just starting at the hospital. Four weeks ago she had found a lump in her left breast. But she had not expected to be seen in clinic so soon. The ultrasound scan and needle biopsy were taken at the fast-track 'two-week wait clinic'. She was surprised to receive the results on the same day, making up for the agonising four hours she had hung around the breast care centre. The breast registrar, who was clearly in a hurry, had read the results without looking up: a 'likely benign' lesion, but due to 'a small degree of uncertainty' it was decided best to remove the lump. When she received a confirmation letter to have the surgery she was pleased to see that it was to happen here. It would at least prove she wasn't skiving.

A nurse came into the room pushing a trolley while steadying a white plastic tray on top of it. She was the ward sister, wearing navy trousers and a navy tunic instead of the lighter blue tunic worn by staff nurses. Emily had not met her formally yet. The woman had been on annual leave when Emily came for her interview and she'd only seen her in passing since starting her new post. 'It's Nina, isn't it? We haven't worked together yet, but I've seen you around.' Emily felt her face become warm as Nina stared at her sternly. 'Sorry, I meant Sister Barrows.'

The ward sister went to the end of the bed and picked up the clipboard holding Emily's medical chart. She frowned as she read and then asked, 'Who put you in this room, Miss Jacobs?'

Emily shrugged. 'Shelly. The healthcare assistant who met me at reception.'

Nina Barrows tutted. 'Well, she shouldn't have.' Then, seeming to realise that her manner was abrupt, she adjusted her sharp tone. 'Sorry. I didn't realise it was you in this room. They should have given you room twenty-nine.'

Room 29 was a single occupancy, and Emily felt grateful that they thought she deserved a room to herself. She hoped Shelly wasn't in trouble for not putting her there. 'It's fine in here.'

Nina Barrows held up a finger. 'Just give me a minute. I want to make sure that our new staff member hasn't put any other patients in the wrong beds.'

When she returned, Emily was pleased to see her looking less cross. Her manner was more caring as she quickly took a set of observations and helped Emily put on some very tight and unattractive white anti-embolism stockings.

'How are you settling in?'

'You mean now as a patient, or here as a nurse?'

'As a nurse. Do you find the pace slower than you're used to?' The question suggested that the ward sister thought Emily had come straight from emergency medicine without a break in her career. She hoped that was the case and that all of her new colleagues were unaware that she'd had time off sick for a whole year. On her application she was able to truthfully write the date her last employment ended as six months ago. It had been her decision to leave after receiving six months full pay, and she hadn't wished to eke out another six months at half-pay when she knew she would never return. At the interview they hadn't asked about the gap in her employment history but she'd been prepared to say, if called on to explain, that she was looking after her unwell parents, which wasn't a complete lie.

'It's a different kind of pace, but no less challenging.'

The ward sister eyed her speculatively. 'I only managed a year in A&E. To be honest, I really couldn't stand seeing so much pain.'

Nina moved over to the sink to wash her hands, patting them dry before wetting them again with an alcohol hand rub. 'In the staff room, you may call me Nina, but out on the ward I prefer Sister Barrows. I think it makes for a better working relationship.'

Emily frowned. Nina – or rather, Sister Barrows – was coming across as a bit priggish. She was glad the woman had her back to her. In her old hospital, everyone was on first-name terms, even when addressing a doctor, unless it was in front of the patient, and *that* made for a better working relationship. She suspected that Sister Barrows had trained during the days when nurses wore frilly hats and capes to hide their uniform when off the ward, and where doctors were only ever addressed as 'doctor'. Her auburn hair, most definitely dyed, was up in a sleek bun and had probably been worn that way for the last forty years. It was impossible to imagine what her face was like when she was younger because of her stern features, and her whole bearing seemed tense. Emily couldn't imagine her relaxing, eating junk food or sprawling out on a couch in front of the telly. She imagined high-backed, uncomfortable armchairs, with lacy armrests and a tea tray laid out precisely with a cup and saucer and tea strainer. Emily hoped she hadn't got off to a bad start with her.

'Sister Barrows, thank you for looking after me today and I'm sorry to be taking time off so soon after starting here.' Emily wondered if her nose had just gone brown and despised herself for seeking approval. It made her come across as weak.

Fortunately, her wheedling seemed to do the trick. Barrows actually smiled. 'You have nothing to apologise for. You didn't choose for this to happen. Mr Dalloway will sort you out and you'll be back at work before you know it. You're in very safe hands.' Her reassurance was meant kindly, but Emily couldn't see the woman ever being demonstrative, or showing real warmth to someone in need. She was pleased, though, that she was in the hands of Mr Dalloway.

The surgeon worked in both the NHS and here in this private hospital and she'd seen him a few times in the emergency department, though she hadn't spoken to him. Tall and lean, with smoothed-back fair hair that was turning grey, he had a regal and private air about him that warded off the inclination to start up a conversation. His lofty reputation as a surgeon put him somewhere up there with the gods. When she had first met him, a decade ago as a student nurse, he'd been referred to as a 'dying breed', an old-fashioned general surgeon who could do anything from remove breast cancer to fix a bleeding aortic aneurysm, and Emily knew she was lucky to be having the consultant attend her. Her operation would be carried out by the main man himself, the clinical director of the hospital, and not by one of his underlings.

'Now, I must get on. The anaesthetist will be in to see you shortly. Then we'll be back to take you down. You know you have nothing to fear? This is merely procedural.'

Emily nodded and Barrows departed. She knew what Barrows was referring to. Fear of breast cancer. In truth Emily had given no thought to the lump in her breast, other than that it had come at an inconvenient time. Her new job had just restarted a future that had been put on hold during the last year. It had given purpose back to her life. Something to hold on to. She had dropped most of her friends, having no time to offer them. She had dated no one in the last year and avoided any opportunity to do so. Searching for Zoe had taken up all her time, and fleetingly she wondered if by coming back to work she was subconsciously giving up hope of finding her. Putting obstacles in the way to make her life busier, to ward off thinking that Zoe would never be found.

There was a knock at the open door. Emily raised her head off the pillow. The woman standing in the doorway was wearing blue scrubs and had sun-kissed hair scrunched up in a loose ponytail. Her tanned arms and face suggested a holiday in a warm climate. 'I've been looking all over for you. Nurse Ratched told me you were in room twenty-nine.'

'Nurse Ratched?' Emily replied.

'You're either too young or you haven't seen enough movies. Where I come from we call ward sisters like Sister Barrows, Nurse Ratched. You know, from *One Flew Over the Cuckoo's Nest*?'

Emily hadn't seen the film, but she'd heard of it. She smiled. 'So, you're American?'

The anaesthetist shook her head. 'Nope, married to one and after being over there for fifteen years I decided to adopt the accent. It kind of makes me feel cute.'

Emily instantly liked her and hoped that behind the goofi- ness she was good at her job. 'So, let's get down to business,

Emily Jacobs. It says here that you've never had an anaesthetic. Is that correct?'

Emily nodded.

'Your bloods and obs are all good. You have no past medical history, no allergies and you last ate and drank last night? So now just scoot forward and let me have a listen to your chest.' Taking the stethoscope from round her neck, she rubbed the metal disk briskly and placed it below Emily's right shoulder. 'OK, nice deep breaths in and out.' With each intake of breath, the anaesthetist moved the stethoscope right to left, up and down Emily's back. Then she sat on the bed. 'All good. So now all we need is to go through our checklist and look at your name band.' Emily held up her wrist so that the details on the ID band could be inspected and matched against her paperwork. 'And we're good to go.'

'Fifteen years? You don't look old enough.'

'Forty,' the anaesthetist said, then put a finger to her lips and whispered, 'Did I just say forty?'

Emily grinned.

'You tell anyone and I'm liable to kill you.'

Emily laughed. 'That's not the most appropriate thing to say to someone you are just about to anaesthetise.'

The quirky anaesthetist stood up. 'True. But it's effective.'

'Are you back home for good?' Emily hoped she was. She was the friendliest face she had met here so far and she would look forward to working with her.

A sadness briefly dimmed the attractive face. 'Nope. Poorly relative. Managed to get some locum work while I'm over here. Then at least I can offer some family support.'

Emily was sorry she'd pried. As the anaesthetist made to leave, Emily stopped her. 'What's your name?'

She bowed playfully, placing one hand against her chest and giving a theatrical wave with the other. 'You can call me Meredith.'

Chapter Four

There was a high-pitched whine and then a kethunk and a zap. It was the sound of a defibrillator charging up and then discharging its electric current. Emily opened her eyes, disturbed, and saw curtains drawn around her bed. A light was switched on in another part of the room and she could see the shadowy shape of someone moving past. There was a person at her neighbour's bed. The defibrillator started charging up again, making a high-pitched humming noise as it reached crescendo, and then giving a brutal zap as it fired its bolt. She held her breath. The poor young woman was in serious trouble. They had tried to shock her twice, which didn't bode well. Mindful of her breast, she edged her way across the bed and leaned over, pulling the curtain aside to see what was happening.

Someone in theatre clothing was performing chest compressions. She could tell by the straight arms and downward movement of the shoulders. The cardiac monitor faced Emily. It had been put on silent mode, otherwise it would have been beeping madly. She could see the erratic peaks rushing across the screen. Her eyes lowered to the bed, but her neighbour's face was hidden from view by the person attending to her. One slim arm dangled limply over the edge of the bed, and Emily watched the small hand flick each time a compression was made on the chest. She jolted as someone touched her shoulder and then winced as the taped dressing pulled on her breast.

'Shit, you gave me a heart attack.'

In the near darkness whoever was beside her was shining a torch right in her face. 'Shush,' she heard.

Blinking as the light left her face, Emily saw its beam settle on her cannula. A syringe was quickly attached and fluid injected. 'Hey, I don't need any painkillers,' she protested.

About to object further, she suddenly felt floaty and her tongue felt fat. Her jaw was floppy and her eyes, unable to focus, closed as she descended into rapid darkness.

The rattling of china woke her and she squinted through heavy-lidded eyes as she spied the cup and saucer on her bed-side locker. Nausea filled her as she raised her head off the pillow. The movement set off a seesaw motion in her stomach. Shelly stood at the monitor beside her and Emily felt the squeeze of the blood pressure cuff inflating around her arm. A moment later the machine bleeped its findings and Emily saw her blood pressure was a little on the low side. No surprise there. That was normal, considering she'd had surgery and an anaesthetic the day before.

'There's tea beside you. How are you doing?' Shelly asked. Her face looked tired this morning, as if she hadn't had time to put on any makeup. Emily sympathised. Shift work made a fine enemy of your sleep pattern and early starts never got any easier.

'Thumping headache and feeling sick. Do you think I could have a couple of paracetamol?'

Shelly nodded. 'I'll tell Sister Barrows. She's just giving the medicines to the patient next door.'

Emily looked around the room, noticing her curtains were drawn back and the bed beside her was unoccupied, neat and freshly made for the next patient. 'What happened to the lady beside me?' she asked.

Shelly glanced at the empty bed, her expression blank. 'Guess she was moved in the night.'

Emily was relieved; at least she had survived. She hoped the girl was doing better. 'Good.' Her bladder was full. She got out of bed. 'Need the loo. Thanks for the tea.'

When she returned, a medicine pot with two paracetamol had been left for her. She swallowed them with a glass of water, then sipped her tea. It was too early to start showering and getting dressed. At seven thirty in the morning she knew it would be a few hours yet before she was discharged. She would get back into bed and try and sleep off the headache. It had probably been caused by whatever they gave her in the night. That was a bit naughty of them, to give her something without her permission. She certainly wouldn't have done it, unless the patient was unconscious. Even when a patient was crying out in pain she still told them what she was giving them and why. She would watch out for this type of practice when she was on duty, as it was not something she would condone.

Rupert Dalloway had aged since the last time she'd seen him. His fair hair was greyer than she remembered. He looked tired and his broad shoulders stooped slightly in a white hospital coat over blue scrubs. On his feet he wore navy leather clogs. Sister Barrows stood one step behind as if out of deference to the surgeon.

'Good morning, Miss Jacobs. Everything went fine. We excised a four-centimetre lump. It looked exactly like a fibroadenoma; nothing to worry about. The sutures under the skin are absorbable and the dressing is splash proof, it just needs to stay on until we see you in clinic with the histology results. You may experience some mild tenderness and have slight bruising. Other than that, you're fit to go.'

His summary was perfunctory and to the point. He had yet to look at her.

Emily smiled politely. 'Thank you, Mr Dalloway. I hope to be back at work by next week.'

He nodded briefly. 'Yes, well, I'm sure that won't be a problem. Do you need a sick certificate for your workplace?'

'Miss Jacobs works for us, Mr Dalloway,' said Sister Barrows. 'She started a few weeks ago. Miss Jacobs is a highly trained ED nurse. In fact, I believe she was a sister in her department? A nurse practitioner?'

Emily was surprised by the praise. Perhaps Barrows did like her after all. 'Yes, Sister Barrows, that's correct.'

Rupert Dalloway raised his head, his eyes more engaged until his gaze fell on Emily. The change in his expression was immediate. His eyes opened wider, his brows lifted, his mouth parted slightly. 'Aren't we the lucky ones getting someone so skilled? Welcome aboard, Sister Jacobs,' he said in a rush, as if trying to move past the moment.

'Staff nurse.' Emily corrected, guessing his expression of surprise was because her face was familiar. 'I'm no longer a sister.'

'But a title, my dear,' he said kindly. 'Welcome aboard anyway. See you when you get back to work. Any questions before we leave?'

Emily shook her head. 'None concerning myself. I just wanted to ask how the young woman beside me is? I know they had to shock her in the night.'

Dalloway stared at the empty bed, a frown between his eyes, and Barrows looked perplexed. 'What woman?' he finally asked.

'The one that was beside me yesterday morning,' Emily said louder than she intended. 'The one they were resuscitating in the night.'

Barrows' lips formed into the shape of a prune. Emily was beginning to wonder if the woman was permanently cranky. 'You have been the only patient in this room since you were admitted, Miss Jacobs.'

Emily stared at her, astonished. 'What? She was here beside me. Young, small, dark-haired. I was talking to her.'

'You need to calm yourself, Miss Jacobs.'

'I am calm. But I'm confused by what you're saying. There was a woman beside me!'

Dalloway stepped closer to the bed. His hand reached out to rest on her shoulder. 'Perhaps it was a dream, my dear.' Then he said, 'Has the anaesthetist been in to see you?'

'No. Not since yesterday. There's been no need.'

Barrows stepped forward. 'Perhaps if we could step outside and have a chat?'

Emily stared at her resentfully. 'Whatever you have to say to Mr Dalloway, please say it in front of me, especially if it's about me.'

A coolness entered the woman's eye and Emily suspected that she had just made an enemy, any previous liking merely imagined. 'As you wish. You had a nightmare. They had to calm you.'

Emily gaped at her.

'It's here in your medical notes.' Barrows tapped the folder in her hands, then opened it to a page and read aloud. 'One forty-five, patient calling out in her sleep, clearly distressed. In view of medical history, five milligrams of Diazepam given via IV to settle.'

'I didn't have a nightmare,' Emily said, even more emphatically. 'There was a patient beside me!'

'Do you think we should have the anaesthetist see you, Miss Jacobs?' Dalloway asked, and Emily looked at him in shock. He had turned away so she couldn't see his face, but she suspected he was no longer thinking that they were lucky to have her. He was thinking she had imagined this. One thought could lead to another and before she knew it, he would be suggesting a psych review. She needed to calm this situation down. To reassure him that there wasn't the need for anyone to check her over. Something was amiss about the patient beside her. Perhaps she had died and they simply didn't want her upset? Whatever their reason for not wanting to talk about it, Emily's instinct was to shut up and stop asking questions.

She let herself fall back against the pillow as if exhausted and her manner became flustered, her eyes blinking in confusion.

'Maybe you're right, Mr Dalloway. A dream, as you say. I . . . I have them sometimes. Nightmares. It must be the after-effects of the anaesthetic. I should know this, being a nurse. I'm sorry if I alarmed you.'

Dalloway did not seem reassured. He gazed at her sceptically and Emily knew she had to say something more. 'It's not just the anaesthetic. I have frequent nightmares. I should be used to them by now. You see, my sister is missing.'

He looked at her with compassion. He had figured out who she was. 'Your sister, Zoe Jacobs. The student nurse who went missing from the hospital.' He stared at her for several long seconds. Then, as if coming out of a trance, he nodded bleakly. 'I'm sorry for your loss.'

Angry tears filled her eyes. She stared at him resentfully. 'Don't say that! She's missing! Not *dead*. Missing. And I will find her.'

Chapter Five

Emily paid the taxi driver as the car pulled up beside Margaret's Buildings, a pedestrian street which the taxi couldn't drive along as it had been paved to allow for tables and chairs and billboards for the few shops and bistros. Around the corner from The Royal Crescent and The Circus, the businesses here were in a desirable location in this very affluent part of Bath. Her home was above one of the shops. She made her way to a blue front door.

Climbing to the second floor, she let herself into her flat, set down her overnight hospital bag and walked into the kitchen to put on the kettle. She pulled out her mobile, still fully charged, and scrolled through her few contacts. She stopped at Eric Hudson, her counsellor for the last year, who had in the last month reduced their meetings to fortnightly. She tapped his name and saw the red phone symbol appear. Then she heard his soft Bradford accent.

'Hey, Emily, how're you doing?'

'I'm good, thought I'd say hello. I've just got out of the hospital and wanted to hear a friendly voice. You know.'

A moment of silence went by and Emily could picture him staring at the phone and not being fooled for one minute. 'You want to meet up?'

She squeezed her eyes shut. What would she say? I saw a woman in the bed beside me who doesn't exist? 'No, you're alright. I just wanted to say hello.'

More seconds of silence. 'How about we bring our meeting forward and catch up tomorrow?'

Emily shook her head as if he could see her. 'No, seriously, everything's good. As I say, I just wanted to hear a friendly voice.'

'OK. And you're alright? Everything went OK?'

She laughed and said everything went fine. The last thing she needed was for him to be concerned about her mental health, and she didn't want to raise any doubts in his mind that she was not doing well. She had already raised those doubts in the minds of the people she worked with and she wouldn't be at all surprised if she were asked to not come back.

'Good. Well, if you need to hear a friendly voice again, give me a call.'

After she said goodbye she sent him a text message:

Thanks for the chat. See you at our appointment. E

She felt relieved that she hadn't told him about seeing a woman that apparently didn't exist and more in control. She relaxed, turned on the radio and set about making herself some lunch. Food was what she needed. Food, a bath and then more sleep. She would not think about that woman until she was more rested and the anaesthetic and other drugs she'd been given were completely out of her system. When she was more clear-headed she would re-examine her memory and piece together the day before. She now needed to empty her mind and forget the conversations with Barrows and Dalloway. When he suggested the anaesthetist see her again, she'd panicked at the thought of how quickly her state of mind was being called into question. At how easy it was for others to take control. She must guard against this happening again. She had a past they could use against her. One strike already. She didn't wish to add more.

Waking from an evening nap, she stretched out on her lumpy sofa and felt an achy tightness in her breast. The dressing had to stay on, but she could peel an edge of it away from her skin to relieve the tension and she should take some more painkillers. Emily gazed around her living room, her eyes drawn to test patches of various greys she'd imagined painting the walls and wondered if the paint she'd bought a year ago for her bedroom would still be usable and not have gone hard by now. Maybe it would be better to start again with fresh paint and a different colour. *Blue is so much prettier, don't you think?* She quickly tried to silence Zoe's voice in her head. Sometimes, snatches of remembered conversations could steal hours of her day. They came without warning, tormenting her. Then the unrelenting guilt would set in. She had never admitted feeling this guilt to Eric in case he wanted to explore it further. Nothing he said could change what she felt, but if she told him about these intrusive thoughts, it might make him think that she had something more to hide.

She must never admit what she had done on the day of her sister's disappearance to anyone. She had seen the evidence of her sister leaving the hospital, of her walking down the road used by business vehicles for deliveries to the hospital, just like the policeman had. This is the memory she needed cemented in her mind. Thinking back to yesterday, Emily now had to consider whether it was guilt and paranoia that had made her imagine that woman beside her. Was that why she never heard her speak? Because her imagination didn't allow her to hear a voice? She breathed deeply, feeling her heart race at the thought of her mind being this fragile.

She had come a long way in this last year and was now able to fully concentrate on other things in her life. These last three weeks back at work had shown her this. Her mental health problems hadn't stopped her doing her job. She knew her new colleagues regarded her as highly efficient. She needed no one to rely on, no hand to hold to show her the ropes of the job. She was highly trained. In emergency medicine, every form of illness and accident entered through the same door and there was no stepping back and waiting for others to come and do a job for you. She had gained a lifetime of experience in that department and had no anxiety about her ability.

Now she needed to listen to the warning signs of her own body or eventually she would be of no help to anyone. Especially to Zoe. Neglecting herself had to stop right now. She needed to be both mentally and physically strong. Working had so far been the best medicine and today she may well have jeopardised that. She needed to put that right and reassure Barrows that she was not a liability. She picked up her iPad from the small coffee table by her side and googled Staff Portal for The Windsor Bridge Hospital where she signed in and found Barrows' work email address, hoping the woman checked her emails regularly. Writing quickly, she thanked the ward sister for looking after her and apologised for her outburst that morning. She said that after sleeping well this afternoon she remembered having a nightmare in the night, which had almost certainly contributed, with the drugs she'd been given, to her believing that what she had dreamed was real. She assured her that her thinking was now straight and that she was looking forward to returning to work.

Once she had sent the email, she leaned back and closed her eyes, trying to imagine that it was her sister she had seen in the bed beside her, her sister lying there in a yellow top and jeans and leather flip-flops. Her sister, with her short black hair, blue eyes and toenails painted an aqua blue. Yet as hard as she tried to replace the face of the young woman, her sister's image would not stay. Brown eyes stared back at Emily. Brown eyes that were anxious and scared.

Chapter Six

The blare of the television could be heard from outside the house. Having already knocked on the front door and rung the bell twice, Emily made her way along the side of the property to the back door. Stepping into the small kitchen, the sour smell of the unwashed dishes and overflowing bin could not disguise the rancid smell of gone-off food. Placing the shopping bag and cool box on the table, Emily moved aside a loaf of bread and saw mould growing like green moss on top of a casserole dish. The dinner she had made her parents last week had spoiled. It remained untouched where she had placed it. It hadn't even been put in the fridge. The units and cooker and fridge hadn't been properly cleaned in a year. She would say her hellos and then give the kitchen a good clean. Though she suspected even that would barely remove the dank odour.

Turning into the narrow hallway, she spied the pile of unopened letters building up behind the front door. She would look through them later, check there weren't any outstanding bills.

She wished the closed living room door was at least ajar. To save her clothes, her hair from reeking. She held her breath, opened it wide and let out a cloud of cigarette smoke, using the door to fan it into the hallway and then escape to less polluted parts of the house. Her parents sat at either end of the brown sofa watching daytime TV, an ashtray balanced on each arm of the sofa. On a glass coffee table was her mother's tipple, white wine from a box, and down by the side of her father were cans of Stella.

Her mother looked up. 'What you doing here? Haven't seen hide nor hair of you all week.' Her father either burped or made some sound at the back of his throat.

'Been a bit busy, but I'm here now. To see how both of you are doing.' Emily hadn't told them she was going into hospital for an operation. She hadn't wanted them to think she was looking for sympathy.

'So you couldn't find time to visit us, then? Still looking scrawny, I see. Hope you ain't hoping to eat. We ain't done the shopping yet.'

Her mother's idea of shopping was a nip along to the corner shop for bread, butter, milk, tea and coffee, and wine and beer of course, if they ran out.

'No, I'm fine, Mum. I brought you two some dinner. Made you a cottage pie, got you a few groceries as well.'

Her parents were both in their late fifties, both on benefits, and they drank and smoked their days away with the TV on from morning till night. It amazed Emily that they never actually seemed drunk and could always hold a conversation – peppered with typically spiteful comments from her mother – and walk in a straight line across the living room. She wondered if bitterness kept you sober. A year ago she had believed their grief to be genuine and had supported them as they both quit their low-paid jobs.

She encouraged them to take their prescriptions of anti-anxiety drugs and sleep remedies, and she accompanied them to collect their benefits. When her mother suggested that they should get compensation for the disappearance of their daughter, Emily had been disgusted. They were savvy, that was for sure. Up to speed with everything they could get. *Surely that hospital should be held responsible*, her mother voiced loud and clear on several occasions, hinting that Emily should look into it, as she was part of the establishment. It wasn't genuine grief that stopped them from going back to work and trying to carry on. It was the entitlement to grief that they grabbed onto. How could they possibly do anything with their daughter missing?

Her mother seemed mollified for a moment and took a sip of her wine. 'So, what you up to then?'

Emily went and sat on the only other seat in the room, a leather footstool. 'I've gone back to work.'

Her mother looked at Emily's father. 'You hear that, John, she's back to work.'

Her father glared at his wife. ''Course I heard. I'm in the room, ain't I? Suppose she has to, otherwise she'll lose her job.'

'Actually, it's a new job—'

'Actually! You hear that, John, she's using them fancy words again, like we ain't got a brain between us. She can't just say "I got a new job".'

Emily gritted her teeth to hold back her resentment. She would never understand how she could have been born to these two people. From an early age, probably as young as five, she had felt alien to her parents. She had used the word 'love' on every card she had ever made them in school, but it was a feeling unfelt, a feeling that simply wouldn't grow. Ill-equipped to meet her emotional and intellectual needs, her parents tried less with her as they viewed the failure to bond to be Emily's fault. They could not love something that did not love them back. She had learned to not need them emotionally and simply accepted that she belonged to them – the two people who made her. She stopped trying to grow love until the day Zoe arrived. She was nine when her mother, then fat and forty, disappeared for a few days, returning slightly less fat carrying a wicker basket. Emily had gazed into it and seen a baby girl, kitted out in a pink knitted hat and matching cardigan. Her face was red and scrunched up and her tiny fist patted the air. Emily felt as if that tiny hand had left an imprint on her heart. For the first time in her young life she had felt love. She had looked at the pink bundle and been filled with a need to love back. Her life in that moment changed. Loving Zoe was all that mattered.

'So, you got time to work then?' her mother now needled.

'I have to, Mum. I'll go crazy if I don't do something.'

'So who's gonna be out there looking for her if you're working?'

'The police—'

'Police! Do me a favour. They ain't looking for her anymore.'

'It's an ongoing investigation, Mum.'

'You spouting that copper woman again?'

'Leave her be, Doreen. She's doing her best,' her father said. Emily glanced at him gratefully, but realised he was trying to settle for a sleep as she saw his slack features. He just wanted them quiet. She eyed him sadly. John Jacobs was a weak man and he took his lead from his wife. Any chance to develop a normal father–daughter relationship had been denied them long ago. He had no determination of his own. If his wife refused their daughter affection, so did he.

'Course she is. It's a pity she didn't do her best when her hospital rang her to come and fetch Zoe.'

'They never rang me to come and fetch her, Mum.'

'Course they didn't. Same as she never rang you the night before to ask you to come out with her. What was it you said to that copper woman?' Her mother frowned as if thinking hard. 'Oh yeah, that's right, you were bleedin' tired.'

She had held nothing back when questioned by her parents about the lead-up to Zoe's disappearance, and from that moment on Doreen Jacobs never let up reminding her that she had failed her sister.

'Not too bleedin' tired now, though. So I suppose you've given up?'

'Of course I haven't! I'm picking up my spare printer while I'm here so I can print more leaflets.'

'Leaflets?' her mother laughed scathingly. 'What the bleedin' good do they do?'

'They keep her in the public eye. They stop people from forgetting. What more do you want me to do, Mum?'

Her mother picked up the TV remote and flipped the volume louder. Over the noise Emily couldn't be sure if she heard her say, 'Your lot lost her' or 'You lost her'. Either way, she was still blaming her, as the TV was suddenly muted and she aimed her next barb. 'She followed you every bleedin' step you took. You encouraged her to go into nursing. She'd have been happier working in a shop or being a hairdresser, but you filled her head with being like you. And when she failed 'cos she found it too hard, you ignore her.'

The failed first year exams had also come out during questioning, along with anything that might be considered a reason for Zoe having gone missing. She closed her eyes to squeeze away the one memory she could never tell them.

'It's not your fault,' had been the opinion of everyone. The police, her colleagues, her GP, her counsellor. Not your fault. They had repeated it many times. But like her mother, Emily believed that it was.

Bagging up the dirty laundry in a black bin liner, she set it by the back door ready to take with her when she left. If she put it on to wash in her parents' washing machine, the chances were that it would still be in there next week and would end up going mouldy. She vacuumed upstairs and downstairs and gave both the bathroom and kitchen a thorough clean. Putting the cottage pie into the microwave, she set the timer for five minutes and pulled out two clean plates and trays and sets of knives and forks. On the kitchen windowsill was a faded photo of Zoe at the age of two sitting in a paddling pool. The silver-plated photo frame had come from Woolworths and was inscribed with the words: I Love My Mummy. Emily had wrapped it for Mother's Day as a gift from both daughters and her mother had loved it, though she had never asked why there was only a photo of Zoe and she had never swapped it for one with both daughters.

A short while later, with the spare printer on the back seat of her car and nary a wave of goodbye from her parents, she drove away. Wiping at the tears on her cheeks, she knew it was self-pity that was making her cry. After cleaning their house all day, and being made to feel unwelcome, she was achy and tired and just wanted to get home. She had moved out two years ago, virtually the same week as Zoe, who decided that she too wanted to become a nurse and follow in her big sister's footsteps. And for the first time in her life, Emily was free. Free of her parents and free of the responsibility of caring for Zoe. She had grown up on this council estate surrounded largely by good, honest, hard-working people. She had grown up in a house that she knew intimately: every blade of grass in the small back garden, every nook and cranny in each square room. She had grown up in a house that she then lived in for most her life, but she had never been able to call it home.

If she never had to go back to that place she wouldn't be sorry, but like a self-administered penance, she knew she would return. She would go back again and again and probably look after them for ever, or at least until Zoe was found. When that day came, she would stop visiting.

Chapter Seven

Emily pulled on her yellow hi-vis vest, hung her work rucksack over one shoulder and made ready to leave. The smell of new paint was strong, and she crossed over to the lounge window and opened it a few inches, not wanting to come back in the morning and have to sleep in paint fumes. The pale grey had lightened the room, making the white ceiling look whiter, and she was satisfied with the outcome.

She spent the last few days of her sick leave inside, putting her time to good use by turning her flat around. She rearranged furniture and switched pictures to other walls, replaced lamp bulbs and generally gave her home a makeover. The only room she hadn't touched was her spare bedroom, which she had turned into 'Zoe's Room'. To decorate it she would have to remove the dozens upon dozens of brightly coloured Post-it notes that she had stuck up on the wall to make her search for Zoe easier – scribbled notes with names, phone numbers, addresses of people Zoe knew, places she went. A map of the city dotted with multiple coloured pins marked off areas where Emily had searched or put up posters, or showed where friends lived, sightings where the public swore they'd seen Zoe during appeals made for her whereabouts. Emily had checked them all. From morning till night these past twelve months she had spent every day following up on any lead or snippet of news, mostly via Facebook from well-doers in her quest to find Zoe. Misinformation had caused the rise and fall of her hopes on many occasions, but it was worth the heartache to have Zoe's name out there. She'd chased up on dozens of false sightings in the hope that one of them was the real thing. She'd put up with the cruelty of people, the time-wasters, who thought it was OK to post comments on Zoe's appearance or rant at the police for not finding her in hope that someone had some real information on her. Alongside the map were newspaper cuttings, both local and national, telling of Zoe's disappearance. The room had been dedicated to finding Zoe and was filled with all her personal stuff as well. Boxes of clothes, shoes, bags and bin liners packed full of pillows and duvets and cuddly toys. Jo had contacted Emily a month after Zoe went missing and said that the landlord was happy to keep the room rented out to her sister, but that he would need payment. Emily managed to fork out for three months' rent before accepting that she couldn't afford to do it long-term, with the result that she was asked remove all of Zoe's stuff. She had spent less time in this room since starting back at work, and vowed not to let things slip. It was helping her stay strong being back at work, refreshing her mind to step away from it all so she could refocus on finding Zoe.

She had camped inside the walls of her flat for the last few days and felt, for the first time in over a year, more like her old self. Energised, organised and, if not exactly happy, settled. She was ready to get back to work. Beneath her bra she wore a light dressing to keep the nylon material from rubbing against the healing wound. She was twelve days post-op, and it looked clean and pink with no sign of infection. She was fit and well and was looking forward to her shift. And the email she'd received from Barrows reassured her that she was welcomed. Emily switched off the last light in her flat and closed her front door.

In the mirrored back wall of the lift Emily checked her appearance. Her face was flushed and her black hair fluffed up from the cycle ride. She was caught in the act of primping her hair as the lift door opened. Dalloway stepped aside to let her pass and gave a cordial nod, and she wondered if he recognised her.

The corridors on the second floor criss-crossed, leading into four areas with the lift at the centre. Arrow-shaped signs were affixed to each wall pointing the way to the wards: Nash, Austen, Allen, Sulis. The corridors were empty and quiet. Visiting time had ended and the patients, if still up and out of their beds, were probably now returning to them. On the door by the staff changing room she entered the four-digit code into the keypad and pushed the door open. A fresh smell of deodorant hung in the air, and a locker door banged shut. Then she heard voices and made her way round to her locker.

Two nurses were in the act of getting ready, one pulling a tunic over his head, the other putting on a pair of trainers. Shelly was sat on a bench, scrolling through her mobile, and was the only staff member Emily recognised. She wondered if the other two had permanent night shifts.

She gave a friendly smile, opened her locker and said, 'Hi everyone, I'm Emily. First time on nights. Here, that is.'

An attractive man in his mid-thirties stepped forward. His light brown hair was smoothed back in a short ponytail. 'Jim Lanning,' he said, shaking her hand. 'I'm agency.'

'Me too,' added the younger man beside him, fixing a fob watch to his tunic. 'Ricky. Work mostly days, but saving to do a road trip round America, so I'll take any shifts on offer.'

Shelly smiled at Emily in acknowledgement. 'Nice to see you again.'

The sound of locker doors banging shut reminded her that she still needed to change into her own uniform. Emily headed into the toilet. She was surprised that the hospital got away with only providing a unisex changing room. The area was certainly big enough to have incorporated two changing rooms. Instead, they had divided the room with four rows of lockers in the centre and a female and male area at each end, offering separate toilets, shower room and changing cubicles. She was not shy about changing in front of the others, but it was a good excuse to use the loo at the same time. When she came out of the cubicle five minutes later, the changing room was deserted, her colleagues already gone. Catching sight of the wall clock, she saw that she was a minute late for the start of her shift. Hurrying, she made her way to the staff room.

The nurses had pulled chairs close to a desk, forming a half circle, and behind it sat Sister Barrows. She peered over her half-moon glasses. 'Are we all here now?'

Emily slipped into the last seat and offered a quiet apology.

'We're short-staffed tonight, and we have a full house. Two of the healthcare assistants from the late shift are staying on to help out for a while. I want Shelly to work with them and circulate between the four areas. Those of you who were on last night work the same wards again. I'll take Sulis Ward. Nurse Jacobs, I'm allocating you Allen Ward, but I want Nurse Lanning there too.'

Emily felt her hackles rise. Was she being given a second pair of trained hands because the ward sister didn't think her capable?

'You've got the busiest ward tonight, three post-ops back in the last hour, one still in theatre, and one of the post-ops needs one-to-one care. I want Nurse Lanning to focus on her, please. She's a forty-four-year-old who has had a hysterectomy. Her blood pressure's a little on the low side.'

'Shouldn't she be transferred to the High Dependency Unit?' asked Shelly.

Barrows dipped her head a fraction and looked over the top of her glasses at the healthcare assistant. 'We're quite capable of monitoring low blood pressure. And in any case, HDU is full.'

'I'm on it,' Jim Lanning said in an overly loud, serious voice, as if the man were imagining giving care to a patient who'd had major heart surgery. Emily cringed a little.

'Indeed,' Barrows replied dryly. 'When she's stable I then expect you to give Nurse Jacobs a hand on the ward.' She stood up. 'Well, let's get started then, shall we? I'm sure the day staff are eager to get off home.'

The staff nurse who handed over to Emily was thorough. She took her through each patient's medical history – their operation, their vital observations, their pain score – and left Emily feeling confident that she knew as much as she needed to take over. The only patient she hadn't been introduced to was Mrs Harris, the patient with low blood pressure who Jim was focusing on. Emily was happy to unlock the medicine trolley and get started with the routine jobs.

An hour on, she had dispensed most oral medication, put up infusion bags, given intravenous antibiotics and inserted a new cannula into one of the patients, who'd winced when she'd flushed it with saline and said it had been playing up all day.

She stopped by the two-bedded room, the same one that she had occupied as a patient, and put her head round the door. 'Everything OK, Jim? Do you need anything?'

The patient in the bed was still and sleeping. Oxygen administered via nasal cannulas was secured by tubing fitted around her ears. 'All good. I'm on it. She's a little cold. Her temperature is 35.5. You can throw me another blanket if you're passing.'

'Her blood pressure still low?'

'Same, nothing to worry about.'

'You want me to take a look?' Emily asked.

Jim stared at her as if she'd just said something outrageous and gave a short answer. 'No.' Then added, 'Quite capable of assessing her, thank you.'

Emily stepped back, embarrassed. 'OK. I'll just get you the blanket then.'

The next couple of hours flew by and Emily was kept busy after receiving her last patient back from theatre, a forty-three-year-old woman who'd had her gall bladder removed. She was violently sick, probably from the morphine, but finally settled after Emily gave her an IV anti-emetic for the nausea.

The noises and call bells, the toing and froing to carry out tasks and see to patients, had ceased for a while. She listened to the silence and thought how different it was to A&E, where night and day merged into one and where it was never quiet. It was strange to be waiting for a patient to call.

Chapter Eight

It was 3 a.m. and all was quiet. Emily yawned. She had neither seen nor heard from Shelly all night, and suspected the others thought she didn't need help with two staff nurses working on the ward. She would have liked to have seen her, if only for a five-minute chat. She'd left Jim alone after her last visit and had only seen the back of him once earlier when he'd nipped along to the toilet. She'd called out to him, asking did he want her to watch his patient, but he'd waved his hand in the air and she saw the back of his head shake from side to side as he called out his laconic reply: 'No.' She wondered why he was still in with the patient and hadn't bothered to come out and help on the ward, so she got out of her chair, deciding she'd pop along and ask him if he needed a break or a cup of coffee or a pillow for his own head if he was nodding off in the room. He could even be lying down on the other bed for all she knew. She wasn't that bothered if she didn't see him, but she'd let him know she wasn't a fool either.

At first she didn't see him in the room, as she was expecting to see him standing by the bed or sitting in the chair. The other bed remained unoccupied, the covers pristine. When he raised his head off the woman's chest she saw fear in his face.

'I don't think she's breathing!'

Emily immediately switched on the overhead lights and advanced towards the bed. Placing her hands firmly on the woman's shoulders she spoke loudly, 'Hello, can you hear me, Mrs Harris? Hello. Mrs Harris! Hello!' The woman gave no sign of response.

'Shit,' Jim uttered, standing still as a statue, unable to move. 'I don't understand. I thought she was OK.'

'Get the crash trolley,' Emily said, and at the same time she took the brakes off the bed, moved it away from the wall, then reapplied them.

'Where?' he asked, his eyes desperately scanning the room as if hoping to see it there.

Emily kept her voice calm, and at the same time pulled the emergency call bell. 'Go out the door, turn left. It's between here and the next room. Unplug it from the wall and bring it here.'

He fled the room. Emily took the headboard off the bed and positioned herself at the patient's head. With two fingers beneath the woman's chin she tilted the head back and put her ear near the woman's mouth, watching for a rise and fall in the chest. The woman was making a feeble effort to breathe. From her pocket Emily pulled out her Tuff Cut scissors and quickly snipped open the woman's theatre gown. The dressing over the abdomen was intact and dry; but the belly was swollen.

When Jim returned she told him to move the bedside locker away from the bed and bring the crash trolley nearer to her.

Taking a Guedel airway from a drawer, she quickly inserted it into the woman's mouth to keep her tongue from falling back, and replaced the nasal cannulas with a bag valve mask, attaching the tubing to the oxygen outlet on the wall and turning the flow up high. She watched as the woman made another feeble effort to inhale, and she squeezed the rugby-ball-shaped resuscitator to push more oxygen into her.

'Jim, fast-bleep the RMO.' Resident medical officer was a term Emily was still getting used to. In private practice it was the title for the on-call doctor, whereas in the NHS she would have just asked for the senior registrar to be bleeped. 'And get the anaesthetist to come back in, tell them this patient is peri-arrest, and then bring back two litres of warmed Hartmann's solution and rapid infusion bags.'

While he rushed once more from the room, Barrows and Shelly arrived. 'Where do you want me?' asked Barrows.

'If you can take over ventilating her, I'll get the defibrillator ready and put another cannula into her.' Barrows took over, positioning herself at the head of the bed. Emily addressed Shelly. 'Shelly, I'm not sure Jim knows where to find everything. I want two warmed bags of Hartmann's and rapid infusion bags.' Emily suspected the woman would need a blood transfusion but until the doctor gave the go-ahead, Hartmann's solution would act as a substance to replace any blood loss. 'Can you also bring the HemoCue machine?' Shelly nodded and pelted back out the door.

Freed up, Emily hit the start button on the patient's monitor to get a fresh reading of vital signs. She grabbed two defibrillator pads, unpeeled their sticky covers and slapped them on, one above the right breast, the other below the left breast, then switched on the defibrillator. Quickly, she pulled out another drawer on the crash trolley and chose a large cannula. She strapped her tourniquet above the elbow of the woman's right arm and let the arm dangle over the side of the bed. When the hand had turned a reddish blue and a vein began to surface in the crook of the arm, she inserted the wide-bore cannula into the bulb of the vein and was glad to see the instant flowback of blood. Filling a syringe with saline, she flushed it to ensure its patency.

'What's the situation?' she heard a familiar voice ask, and was relieved to see Meredith come into the room.

'Feeble respiratory effort when I got here. Immediately commenced bag valve mask ventilation. She has a size four airway in situ. She has a distended abdomen and as you can see she's tachycardic and her blood pressure is eighty-five systolic. I don't know how long it's been that low as I haven't had a chance to look at previous recordings.'

Meredith picked up the observations chart, quickly scanning it. 'Christ, her systolic pressure's not risen above ninety-five for the last three hours. Why the hell wasn't I called?'

'I've only been in the room a few minutes. You'll have to ask Staff Nurse Lanning. He's fetching Hartmann's.'

'Good call, but she needs blood as soon as possible. So let's give her two units to start with.'

After quickly examining the woman, particularly around the abdomen, Meredith went over to the crash trolley and pulled out a longer flexible plastic tube which would go further down the back of the throat to replace the smaller airway already in situ. It would permit air to pass freely to and from the lungs and allow the patient to be ventilated during surgery. The procedure would require two people. 'You alright to help me, Emily? Sister Barrows, can you grab Mr Dalloway, he is just finishing in theatre two. And we'd better let Mr Davies know his patient's condition.' Emily nodded, as did Barrows.

Over the next half an hour Emily assisted Meredith, making ready and passing all the equipment required when needed. At the same time she instructed Jim to fetch blood and oversaw him and Shelly check it and put it up. The woman was deathly white, and while her blood pressure had dropped no lower, she had made no visible recovery. Whatever was causing the bleed inside her needed to be found quickly and stopped.

The patient trolley, loaded with drip lines, monitors, portable ventilator and a pale patient was pushed by a porter and escorted by Meredith back to theatre. Emily sank down on the empty bed and took a couple of deep breaths. She couldn't help but think about what a close call that had been. Any further delay and the woman could have died. It was still touch and go, and until she came back out of theatre stabilised they couldn't count their blessings yet.

'I'm going to make us some tea,' Barrows announced from the doorway. 'Nurse Jacobs, all your patients are fine so please take five minutes. The same goes for you, Nurse Lanning. We'll have a debrief in the staff room at four o'clock.'

Emily looked at her watch and was surprised to see that it was only a quarter to four. The last forty-five minutes had felt like hours. The two-bedded ward showed the aftermath of an emergency situation, with equipment and instruments left abandoned. The floor on the other side of the bed was splattered with spilled blood. In his haste to get the blood into the woman, Jim hadn't connected the transfusion set firmly enough to the cannula and blood had poured out.

Jim had not yet spoken about what had just occurred, even though he was probably desperate for reassurance, and Emily, from her experience of dealing with many emergencies, chose not to give it. She would give the facts and not her opinion when asked. It was up to Barrows to investigate why the patient's deterioration was not picked up on sooner.

Rolling her shoulders back, and mentally giving herself a shake, she stood up and began the task of putting the room back in order. She would start first with the crash trolley and ensure it was restocked and ready for use for the next time. Jim followed her lead and started putting the headboard back on the bed, his movements energetic, his breathing and sighs too loud. He was irritating the hell out of her by just being in the room. Angrily, she shoved the bedside locker and an injection tray slid off and fell to the floor, scattering used needles and syringes.

'I'll get that,' he offered.

She was already on her knees, ignoring him and gathering up the contents. 'Just pass me the sharps box, please.'

'I thought she was OK,' he said. 'I thought you—'

She glared at him and he shut up.

She dropped each unsheathed needle carefully into the yellow plastic tub and let her eyes wander over the area for any she may have missed.

A glint attracted her attention to the crevice where floor met skirting board. Using her fingernail, she carefully scooped it free and watched a chain of small links follow her finger. Her eyes fixed on her find and her heart beat uncomfortably. She had found a bracelet. A silver bracelet – too big to stay on a small wrist.

'Hey Emily, hold the lift!'

Emily turned around and saw Meredith running to catch her up. She put her hand out to stop the lift door from closing. The anaesthetist was dressed in pink and navy Lycra knee-length running shorts and pink short-sleeved polo shirt. On her feet she wore navy Skechers.

'*You* are one incredible nurse. Do you know that?'

Emily coloured self-consciously and tried to hide her face.

'No, don't look away,' Meredith said, touching Emily's shoulder till she looked back at her. 'I've just torn into Ratched after reading yours and Fuckup's statements and asked her how someone who is clearly as inexperienced as him can work here? Without you last night we would have had a dead woman on our hands. Do you know he hadn't even done a HemoCue test on her? A simple prick of the finger would have told him what was going on. He said he asked you to do one. Said you had said it was normal?'

Emily stared at her, astonished. 'Me? He wouldn't let me into the room! I offered to check on her!'

Meredith smiled in amusement. 'Easy does it. We know he lied. He knows you saved that woman's life. Dalloway is singing your praises right now to Mr Davies, so don't be surprised if you get a call from the man. It was his patient.'

'Thank you, Meredith,' Emily finally said, still feeling shocked at what Jim had said. 'I'm glad I could help.'

'Ditto, Emily. Big-time ditto.'

The lift reached the ground floor and both women stepped out. Emily swung her rucksack onto her other shoulder and it caught the side of her breast, making her wince. Meredith saw her face. 'Hey, are you OK? You need to be careful. It's alright coming back to work if you sit down for your job, but ours is a physical one, so take it easy with lifting and things.'

'I'm OK. It's healed nicely.'

'Tough cookie, aren't you?' Meredith remarked, and Emily smiled.

'What was the cause of the bleed?' Emily asked as they carried on walking to the exit. 'I haven't had a chance to find out.'

Meredith raised her eyebrows and sighed heavily. 'Nicked vessel. So Mr Davies is going to have to answer for it. Fortunately for him Dalloway was on hand to sort it out and, with luck, the woman will have no lasting damage, other than a delayed recovery time. It was a slow bleeder that should have been picked up on a lot sooner. I don't think we'll be seeing Nurse Lanning back here again.'

Emily gave a thankful sigh. 'Thank god for that. Not about him, but that the patient survived it.'

'Indeed. There but for the grace of god, and all that.'

Emily smiled. She felt tired. 'You know you're already losing your accent.'

'I know,' Meredith nodded, before pulling her right foot up behind her leg and holding it against the back of her knee to stretch. 'My colleagues back in the States will think I talk all posh when I return. Jeez, my husband won't be able to keep his hands off me.'

Emily laughed, then added a little shyly, 'Well, I for one am glad that you're still here. Though not if your family member is still poorly.'

Meredith shook her head. 'It's early days yet, but it's looking less grim. I'm hanging around just in case. Hey, we should go out for a drink some night. Let me talk you into coming to work in sunny California. You'd love it there, Emily.'

Emily felt a warm glow inside and the previous tiredness fall away. It would be so good to start afresh. To have a future to dream of. A life to start living. Then she remembered Zoe, and the small glow of warmth she felt turned to wet ashes. How could she begin again? She could not walk away from her sister. She had made an irreversible choice a year ago. She had to live with that. This life she had to bear was her punishment – until the day came when they found Zoe.

The anaesthetist jogged away, calling out to Emily to set a date while Emily looked for the key to her bicycle lock, searching her rucksack pockets, her tracksuit pockets and then her scrunched-up uniform. She felt metal through the material, but instead of pulling out keys she pulled out the silver bracelet, safe in the pocket of her uniform. She hadn't told anyone of her find as she had yet to decide who she could tell.

Chapter Nine

In reception Emily tapped the letters of her name and date of birth on the screen to sign in and was unsurprised to see that she was the next patient to be seen. Eric Hudson never ran over time and kept you waiting. She'd been given the last appointment of the day and the waiting room was empty. She walked to the water cooler and helped herself, refilling the paper cone twice to quench her thirst. She was hot from her cycle ride and felt out of sorts. She hadn't slept well after her night shift. Her usual harrowing dreams of Zoe were matched with equally disturbing dreams of this young woman. At one point both the woman and Zoe were riding tandem on a powerful motorbike, Zoe the driver, at breakneck speed on a motorway. She had felt their fear as they tried to escape someone chasing them, and she had not been able to warn them about the standstill of traffic further up ahead. She had woken from the dream drenched just as the motorbike hit an oil tanker truck. The discovery of the bracelet had played on her mind, and she knew that today's session was going to be taxing if she wanted to keep this new anxiety hidden. She had no wish to add more medical labels to her name. Depression, Anxiety Disorder,

Prolonged Grief Disorder and Post-Traumatic Stress Disorder were titles she was well versed with. These nifty little labels were all things that had been discussed with her over the last year, and by and by she accepted that she probably had them all to some degree. She didn't need a psychologist to tell her this. And in truth she was beginning to resent these labels. They were merely the names given to pigeonhole what she was experiencing.

Talking therapy was the treatment she was receiving. It was a way of dealing with negative thoughts and making positive changes, and she had adapted her thinking to prove it was working. She no longer stood for hours on street corners, staring at every female passer-by in the hope of it being Zoe. She no longer followed strangers, thinking them familiar, an old friend of Zoe's perhaps, and startling them with her behaviour. She behaved normally. She got up, washed, dressed, shopped, visited her parents, her therapist, kept herself to herself and got through each new day without alarming anyone. And now she was back at work, a major step forward to prove she was coping. So why was she still having therapy, she wondered, not for the first time in the last month? Surely Eric Hudson had other patients more in need of his service than her? Counselling sessions on the NHS usually lasted six to twelve weeks. Was it her GP or Eric who pushed for her to have more than the normal quota? She felt guilty for resenting his care.

He was a kind man and he had seen her through some dark times. When she first met him, she had been reluctant to talk to someone who was going to analyse her every word and watch for something mentally wrong with her. She had thought him solely as a counsellor, qualified in his field to offer counselling. It was on the business card he gave her with his contact numbers that she saw the letters PsyD after his name, and realised he was in fact a doctor of psychology. In that first hour of meeting him, hearing him speak openly about Zoe, about the devastating effect her disappearance had caused, she knew she had nothing to fear. He was there to help heal her and because it was an ongoing mental torture, he expected no quick fix.

Slim and a little taller than Emily, he looked younger today. She thought it was because of the lack of his usual jacket and tie. He'd no doubt discarded them due to the warmth of the room; the heat outside had turned the office into an oven. The blinds had been partially pulled to block out the sun, and a fan was switched on. She knew he was forty. It was the only personal information she had on him, as on his fortieth birthday a month ago when he'd said he'd passed a milestone, she'd teased him for being thirty. He'd then laughed and told her to add on another ten years. She regarded him as the closest thing to a friend, yet she knew nothing else about his personal life. He knew everything about hers.

Fixing his calm blue eyes on her now, he said, 'Are you ready to talk about what you couldn't on the phone last week?'

She stared at him warily. This wasn't what she had been expecting him to say.

She settled herself in the chair opposite him, a comfortable blue armchair with wide armrests, and placed her rucksack neatly on the floor, giving herself time to think.

'If you're not ready, that's fine, but I'm here to listen when you are.'

She swallowed hard and then began to speak. 'Something happened when I was in the hospital. As a patient, that is. There was a young woman in the bed beside me. Small, dark-haired and I think probably foreign. I spoke to her, trying to reassure her. She didn't speak back and she seemed scared.'

Eric nodded slowly. 'It stands to reason that you may be afraid when you're in hospital and you can't speak the lingo.'

'Yes, that's what I thought too. Only, during the night I was woken by the sound of the defibrillator. I heard the zap of it as it was being used. I pulled my curtain aside and hospital staff were at her bed trying to resuscitate her. A nurse or a doctor suddenly appeared at my side, giving me a fright, but I couldn't see them as a torch was shone in my face and the next thing I knew, they were giving me an IV injection and I blacked out.'

'Poor woman,' Eric commented.

Emily clasped her hands together, wishing she had something to hold. There had been a cushion in the chair the last time she had been here and now it was gone. Perhaps to be cleaned from tears spilled onto it by other patients. 'The next morning the bed beside me was empty and the healthcare assistant suggested she'd been moved in the night, so I was relieved she'd survived.' Emily repositioned herself in the chair, folding her arms and trying to make herself smaller. She closed her eyes and concentrated on her breathing. Eric let her sit quietly. He would allow her time to collect her thoughts without interruption or prompting. On many occasions they had sat in silence for several minutes.

Breathing out slowly, she opened her eyes and gave him a grateful look. 'When the surgeon and ward sister came to see me, to tell me that everything had gone OK and I could go home, I asked about the woman and they told me that I was the only patient that had been in that two-bedded room.'

He blinked in surprise. 'Really? They said you were the only one there?'

She nodded. 'The surgeon wanted me to see the anaesthetist.'

'I take it he's thinking it's a reaction to the anaesthetic. Have you had one before?'

'I've never had surgery before.'

'So, what are your thoughts on this, Emily?' His expression was curious.

'I don't know, Eric. A hallucination?' She laughed harshly. 'I am so tempted to let myself believe that. Until last night, I had almost persuaded myself that I had imagined her.' She reached for her rucksack and took out a folded white tissue. She placed it on the arm of her chair and unfolded it. 'She was wearing this bracelet. I saw it on her and I thought at the time that it looked too big and could slip off her wrist. I don't know what the hell is going on, Eric, and I don't know who to trust.' She stared at him, bewildered. 'Surely I couldn't have imagined this?'

He smiled kindly. 'It's possible that you did. You were, are *still*, actively searching for Zoe, and looking for similarities would be reasonable. You've thought other patients were her before. Both women bore a similar resemblance to your sister.'

Emily shut her eyes, trying to block the memory of those last days in her old job, when she'd barely been functioning. Zoe had been missing for three weeks when her job came to an abrupt end. Her colleagues had realised that she was using the place to vet every female patient who came through the doors. On her last shift, Emily had left her own patients unattended and went AWOL from the department, having heard a young female patient had been taken to theatre from resus. The nurse caring for the woman said she had nice black hair. It had only been a passing remark, but that was all it took to have Emily scarpering off at speed to see if it was Zoe. Something similar had happened the previous day. Emily was found on the other side of the hospital, seemingly in a trance, staring at a patient on a ward. Her sick leave was instated with immediate effect, and with it came the fear that she was leaving the last place where Zoe was seen alive.

She stared at him with tear-filled eyes. 'That was then. But I have never imagined seeing someone who wasn't there. They were real people. I may have imagined them being Zoe, but I didn't imagine them up out of thin air! I really don't know what to think. I'm scared half the time that if I say the wrong thing I'll get carried away in a straitjacket. I need my job because it's the only thing in my life that allows me to focus on something other than her and if I fuck it up by coming across as a loony, I don't how I'll cope. I have nothing else.'

'Breathe Emily,' Eric quietly instructed, clearly hearing her distress. 'Just breathe.'

When she was calmer and more in control, he spoke again. 'Is it possible you were dreaming?'

Emily made a despairing sound. 'That's the whole point. Apparently in the night I had a nightmare, which is why they say they gave me something to calm me, but the nightmares I have, as you know, are always the same: me stuck in a mortuary fridge with a dead body. Why dream up someone new who doesn't even look like Zoe?'

Eric pressed his palms together, resting his chin lightly on the tips of his fingers. 'Perhaps your mind has focused on trying to help another young woman, because of your frustration at not being able to find Zoe. You may have even seen this woman in passing, stored the memory and dreamed about her being a patient. She may even have been a past patient who you nursed. Emily, you're suffering with ambiguous loss; you have no answers and therefore no closure. Added to which your relationship to Zoe went beyond that of an older sibling.'

'But how can I have imagined her in that much detail? The clothes, the hair colour, an actual face and not just a blurry image?'

Eric pointed through the window to the small enclosed garden of the surgery. 'I can see you standing there right now. I've projected the image of you in front of me to be outside in that garden, but I have you standing, not sitting. Hope is a two-edged sword – a desire to see someone so strongly draws the mind into desperately believing it to be true. Which means your kind of grief renders you unable to find mental peace. It's called intrusive imagery, Emily.'

Emily looked at the empty garden and could see herself as he'd pictured her, just like she could imagine a soft sand beach, lapping waves and blue sky. 'I understand what you're saying, Eric. I really do. What I don't understand is how I can simply walk into that room and see a solid mass and not an image. Or how I could find her bracelet on the floor nearly two weeks after the event.'

'You could have seen it when you were a patient there,' he said simply. 'Your eyes could have clocked it at some point, harmlessly lying on the floor or beneath a bed. Or even in the spot where you actually found it. Then when back on duty, you remembered it being there.'

She glanced away, biting her lip. 'So you don't think I should look for her then?' She was aware that this would be the one question that might test his patience.

He slowly shook his head. 'That's not a good idea, Emily. As a patient you were out of your normal role in that room. You are used to being there as a nurse. Zoe went missing from a hospital. Maybe you needed to give yourself another purpose for being in that room, other than being a patient. Maybe your mind needed to search for somebody new.' Concern showed in his eyes. 'Be cautious, Emily. Don't lose sight of how far you've come, of what you have now. I still believe returning to work is the best step forward. It may have been wiser to go back part-time, but you're a stubborn one and I can't knock you for that. But don't give yourself more than you can deal with. I wasn't going to mention this, but it may be pertinent – I am aware that the date of your operation was Zoe's birthday. Special dates, anniversaries,

Christmases, are a particularly hard time to accept a loss. Your mind may have simply taken you away from dealing with it by focusing on something less painful.'

Tears pricked Emily's eyes and her face fell. 'Oh my god. How could I have forgotten? Her *birthday!*'

Emily cried properly when she got back to her flat. She was angry and confused that 30 June had come and gone and she had not remembered it was Zoe's birthday. A second birthday had passed by. Zoe had gone missing on 19 June, eleven days before her nineteenth birthday. She had now turned twenty and her parents hadn't mentioned it, but that shouldn't be a surprise. Six months ago they had tucked into their Marks & Spencer's Christmas dinner on trays on their laps watching all the best that Christmas TV had to offer, and had even put up a fake Christmas tree. Special days, without Zoe, were still celebrated in the Jacobs household.

Wiping her eyes, she picked up one of the many photographs of her sister that she had framed and glared at her. Taken in the evening, Zoe was wearing Emily's leather jacket because she'd been cold, sitting on damp grass in Parade Gardens, where she and Emily had gone to listen to the bands at a music festival. The photograph had been taken four weeks before Zoe went missing. It was the last photograph she had taken of her sister.

'Sometimes I hate you, Zoe, for putting me through this. Sometimes I wish you hadn't been born,' she whispered.

Emily squeezed her eyes to shut out the image of her sister. She was vulnerable right now, and if she allowed herself to think the worst could have happened, it would break her. She had to keep reminding herself that Zoe had disappeared once before, for three days, after going to Glastonbury festival aged seventeen. There had been no phone call or text from her to say that she'd hooked up with new friends, or that she'd gone to the coast to set up a fresh camp to carry on partying. It was selfish, thoughtless behaviour that had made Emily worried sick and unable to sleep until she returned home.

She'd regularly turned off her mobile and been uncontactable if Emily had refused to give in to her on something, usually loaning money, or told her off for advertising on Facebook that she was out all hours of the night when Emily knew she was on a shift the next day. It was these behaviours that allowed Emily to cling to the hope that this is what she had done now.

She had simply disappeared for a while.

Eric walked through Royal Victoria Park and enjoyed watching young families out in the early-evening sunshine; fathers kicking balls with toddlers and mothers sitting minding pushchairs. Through the trees he could see the vivid colours of hot air balloons and hear the whoomph sound of the burners inflating them. He brought his own children here most weekends, come rain or shine, because he believed that children should experience all elements of weather, should feel the rain on their faces, the wind in their hair, the snow with their hands. Being outside should feel natural and not something only chosen on a sunny day. He didn't want them growing up indoors, stuck in front of some screen, because it was raining outside. And they liked it here – they liked to feed the ducks.

So far he had spotted three posters of Zoe Jacobs around the park, protected by plastic sleeves and secured with cable ties to the lamp posts. They were new-looking; probably recently put up by Emily to replace ones that had been spoiled by the elements. He was aware she put a fresh load of posters up every few months. He had become used to seeing Zoe's image dotted around the city and was always reminded of how alike the sisters were, as both had very black hair, blue eyes and pale skin. When he had first met Emily her hair had been shoulder-length, unlike that of her sister in these posters. When she cut it off, Eric had initially thought she was self-harming until she explained that it was falling out and a bald patch had appeared behind one of her ears. He knew that the loss of hair was likely caused by stress. It had grown in the last few weeks and the pixie hairstyle now suited her gamine face. Though it made her look more like Zoe, which of course could be her intention. Maybe it made her feel closer to Zoe.

He sighed heavily as he thought back to their discussion half an hour ago. She was worrying him. She was doing so well, and had been these last few months, but now it seemed as if she was having a setback. Though she denied seeing someone who wasn't there, the reactions of the hospital staff members seemed to suggest that what she had seen hadn't been real. It wouldn't be the first time she had imagined someone. At the time she'd been taking a low dosage of amitriptyline for depression, and hallucination was listed as one of the side effects. She'd been convinced she'd seen Zoe as close as a metre away, standing right in front of her. Eric had to prove to her it was merely a tree with Zoe's face on a poster staring back. In those first few months he had seriously worried that long-term she would not cope if her sister remained missing. Emily had burned with energy, with the need to do something, anything, to help find Zoe. She had trawled the streets of Bath on a daily basis, first searching among the homes of old friends, school friends, friends of friends, in the hope that someone may have seen her. She had visited every shop, pub and public business, the railway station and the bus station with her endless supply of posters, refusing to leave until they put up a photo of Zoe in their windows. And she had camped inside the police station, sitting in the waiting area every day, to get a fresh update from Geraldine Sutton. DI Sutton had phoned him a couple of times in those first few months to come down to the station and talk to Emily, as she was concerned about her and didn't want to send her on her way with no good news.

Emily had been his patient for the last year and he had come to greatly admire her; her quiet dignity and inner strength had pulled her through this miserable time and he hated the fact that just as she had turned a corner, giving shape to her life again, she was causing him new concerns. He wondered if it was too soon for her to be back at work, especially in a hospital. He could not ignore the fact that her job was to care for others – people that were vulnerable, in need of someone that was capable. Many health workers suffered with mental disorders, as one in four of the UK population did, and they were able to function fully, with or without support. Some even fully recovered. Emily's GP had been satisfied that she was fit to work, and he had been too – until today. He had hoped that eventually their sessions could come to an end and Emily would be signed off as his patient.

He would now have to re-evaluate the situation and monitor her more closely. For starters, he would be keen to re-establish weekly sessions, even if it meant them taking place over the phone. If she was intent on searching for an imaginary woman it could lead her into all sorts of trouble, such as misunderstandings with her work colleagues who had no perception of her traumatic loss. He would hate for her situation to become unmanageable, for her to fail just when she had started living again. He had dealt with many forms of loss: survivors of car accidents that had been fatal to others, parents who had lost a child, people who had lost someone through illness. Recently he had begun counselling a woman whose husband had been diagnosed with early-onset dementia in his sixties. She was grieving ahead of time for the loss of what was yet to come; the loss of her husband's mind. Emily's loss was one of the worst kinds – to not know what had happened – possibly for ever.

Chapter Ten

Emily could see that the phlebotomist was having difficulty drawing blood from the man's fat arm. The woman had tried in the crook of his arm twice and at both attempts the needle had missed the vein and caused the two puncture sites to bleed. The problem with fat arms was that it was difficult to see or even palpate a vein. Now Emily watched her tighten the tourniquet on his forearm and could see that she was going to stab him blindly and fail a third time.

'Would you like me to try?' she offered. She had been in the middle of admitting Mr Patel, who was booked for surgery the next morning, when the phlebotomist had arrived with her trolley. Emily was surprised to see that they worked past five o'clock. In the NHS this role would be a nine to five job, Monday to Friday.

Mr Patel looked from one woman to the other. 'I'm not a pin cushion, you know. Please, whoever does it better do the job.'

Her face pinched with resentment, the phlebotomist untied her rubber tourniquet. Her eyes coolly appraised Emily. 'Be my guest.'

Strapping on her own tourniquet where the phlebotomist had positioned hers, she went down on one knee and gently tapped the back of the man's hand and waited till she could feel the fatness of a vein plump up with blood.

'That's getting too tight,' Mr Patel complained.

Emily smiled at him kindly, before lowering her eyes back to the job. 'I'm sorry. Just another few seconds and it will be over. Then no more needles.'

'Just get on with it, girly, I want to have some feeling back in my hand.'

'It's already done, Mr Patel,' she answered, snapping off the tourniquet.

'Good job. I didn't feel a bloody thing.'

He smiled at her closed-mouthed, curving his black moustache. His bald head, small ears and dark-shadowed nut-brown eyes reminded her of a meerkat. He patted his round stomach. 'I'm fat because I'm a diabetic and I'm a diabetic because I'm fat.'

Handing the tubes of blood to the phlebotomist, she mumbled a quiet apology, aware that the technician was peeved at being shown up. Square-jawed and with an overbite, her hair saved her from being plain with its salon-smooth brown bob.

The woman smiled at last. 'Don't be. I rushed it. Thanks for your help. I've heard that you're good.' She gave a mock-stern look as she placed the tubes in a clear plastic bag. 'Just don't do me out of a job.'

Emily finished off admitting the patient. He had come in the night before surgery as he lived alone and they wanted to ensure he omitted his morning insulin and also stayed nil by mouth. He had arrived on the ward while she was in the middle of getting a handover of the other patients and now she was behind on their care. At eleven o'clock she had nearly finished dishing out the medicines and was grateful that she'd been given Shelly to work with, who'd gone around taking patients' observations, settling them into bed, giving out fresh water jugs, hot drinks and generally making Emily's workload lighter.

'Coffee or tea?' Shelly called down the corridor in a loud whisper.

'Tea, please.' Emily made a T with her two forefingers.

After last night the atmosphere on the ward felt calmer. She had heard nothing about Jim Lanning from Barrows and apart from the new nurse, a stunning Spanish woman named Zita, who was also an agency member, the team was as it was the night before.

Shelly was checking her face in a small compact mirror when Emily joined her at the nurses' workstation, an area carved out in the corridor of private rooms. The area was open-plan, providing work space, a monitor displaying the current data of all the patients on the ward, telephones and stationery. The station had a counter and on the nurses' side where they sat, night lights had been fitted to shine down on the desk and not in their faces.

'This lipstick is so good I'm going to get it again. I have to scrub it off most of the time. You'd suit this colour with your black hair and blue eyes. You know, you have a really interesting face. You remind me of someone.'

Emily stiffened, holding her breath as she waited for Shelly to realise her gaff and recollect again who she was.

She clicked her fingers. 'The girl with the green tattoo.'

Emily released her breath, annoyed with herself for being foolish. Shelly was just having a normal conversation with her. She smiled noncommittally and hoped the level of conversation was going to be a little more stimulating. This was the first time she had been alone with Shelly since being a patient here. It was her first chance to ask her some questions.

'The girl with the *dragon* tattoo, you mean. The book's good.'

Shelly put away her mirror and scrunched up her nose. 'Nah, I'd rather see it on the telly. Yeah, you look like her. The foreign film, not the one with Daniel Craig. Though you look a bit like her too.'

An image of multiple face piercings came to mind and Emily wondered who she would prefer to look like: her mother's choice, Anne Hathaway, with her cut-off hair and pulled-out teeth; or Shelly's, the Swedish actress with her fierce face. 'Shelly,' she said casually, trying to steer the conversation away from makeup and movies. 'You know the day I was a patient here?'

Shelly fluttered her eyelashes dramatically. 'How could I not, when it was me who doled out all that TLC on you?'

'You remember the next day when I woke up and you gave me tea? Do you remember me asking you about what happened to the patient in the bed beside me and telling me that you guessed she'd been moved during the night?'

'Nurse Jacobs?'

Emily jumped and hot tea splashed her hand. She quickly put down her mug and wiped the liquid away with her other hand. She had not heard the ward sister approaching and wondered how much she'd heard.

'Is everything alright down this end?' Barrows asked.

'Yes, Sister. Shelly and I have just sat down. The patients are all settled.'

'Well if that's the case, I'll borrow you if I may, Shelly, to give me a hand with some of my patients. I'm a little behind.'

Shelly stood up. 'Of course.'

'Bring your tea with you, dear, you can drink it down my end. I'll follow you shortly. I just want a quick word with Nurse Jacobs.'

Emily felt tense as Shelly departed, and hoped the 'quick word' was going to be about the patients.

Barrows didn't keep her in suspense. 'I'm afraid I overheard some of your conversation, Nurse Jacobs, and I think perhaps we should discuss this … concern of yours. This patient you believe you saw?'

Emily felt her face turn scarlet and was glad the main lights were dimmed, offering some coverage. 'I … I just wanted to check if perhaps Shelly might have seen her too.'

Barrows stood perfectly still, her next words spoken softly, almost to herself. 'Dear oh dear.'

Emily spoke before thinking. 'You must surely understand that if you think you've seen someone, you would want to check. I'm not saying she was definitely there. I just wanted to be completely sure in my mind that she wasn't.'

'Nurse Jacobs, am I right in thinking this isn't the first time you've imagined seeing someone?'

Emily stared at her, bewildered. How could she know that? Surely she didn't have access to her counsellor's notes?

'Hospital gossip is deplorable, my dear, but nonetheless these things have been said about you, and while I have sympathy with what you've gone through, I simply cannot have you working here if such behaviours are still happening.'

Emily's face must have shown her shock and she so regretted bringing up the subject with Shelly. She could not lose her job and go back to the endless days of alone time ruminating about Zoe. She wanted this structure in her life; she wanted to keep going forward, to have a different focus each day, people to talk to about normal things. She was surprised when Barrows passed her a tissue. 'Don't cry, my dear. Would it surprise you to know that I once thought I saw a ghost in my old hospital when I was a student nurse?'

Emily dabbed her eyes and stared at the woman in disbelief.

'It's true, my dear. Old tales told by others fuelled my imagination into believing it was true. The ghost was reputedly a patient who haunted the ward at night, having died there many years ago as an old man. It was said he came and sat with the nurses at night or was found by bedsides talking to the patients. For weeks

I was terrified of walking into that ward at night for fear of seeing him. The night I thought I saw him standing at the end of the ward rooted me with fear. I had no intention of going up to him. Then a patient rang their call bell and I was forced to go and check on them. I kept my eyes fixed to the floor as I made my way down the ward and when I eventually looked up he was gone. It was a good job I did go and answer that call bell. The patient who called was in urgent need of help. She was having a post-operative bleed following a tonsillectomy.'

Emily felt calmer after hearing the story. Perhaps Barrows wasn't so bad after all. Maybe she was just old school and went by the book.

'I'm sorry for my behaviour, Sister Barrows. I really will pull myself together.'

Barrows nodded. 'Good. I hope you can. And I don't think The Windsor Bridge Hospital is old enough yet to warrant ghosts,' she said with a wry smile. 'You really were the only patient in that room that night, so I hope that puts your mind at rest.'

After she'd gone, Emily felt embarrassed and yet relieved. She also felt more settled. She was grateful Barrows had shared something so personal. Even if it was completely different to her own 'ghost', it at least showed a different side to her. And Eric could be right too, of course. She may well have seen that young woman before; maybe as a past patient? Or she may even have been a visitor that day who had wandered into Emily's room for a short time, felt tired or unwell and had lain on the bed briefly. This wouldn't have been normal behaviour, but who knew how people behaved? She could also have been a patient that day, newly arrived like her, but in the wrong room, like she herself had been, and then lost her bracelet as she was hurried out of it. It was just the wrong room. *The wrong room*. Emily suddenly cringed as the thought took hold. The woman had simply been in the wrong room!

She felt stupid for not thinking sooner about this logical reason for her being there. She could have saved herself this stress, and she hoped Barrows wasn't thinking of getting rid of her. She was almost tempted to go and speak to her again, to put forth this realisation, but that would give the ward sister reason to think her mind wasn't on her job. She was now glad she had told no one other than Eric about the bracelet she found.

Perhaps she could find the patient to give it back to her. She could look in the property book and see if her name was in there. A duplicate carbon copy would be there if the girl handed over her bracelet for minding or had any other valuables recorded. It would be dated and countersigned by the patient.

The log book was kept in a drawer at the nurses' workstation. Emily flicked back to the date of her operation and saw several entries. Four of them were female names, including her own: Emily Jacobs, next to which it said, 'White metal belly-button ring with stone'. She had forgotten to remove it before coming into hospital and only put it in for safekeeping because it was a real diamond, real white gold. In the property book jewellery was described as yellow metal or white metal to save the risk of being wrong – a gold bracelet could turn out to be brass, a diamond ring merely a crystal. The three other names sounded English, not that that was anything to go by. For all she knew, given that she hadn't spoken, the young woman could well have been English and called Linda Parker or Julie Donald. She would search their names, check back through records, get their dates of birth to at least show if they were of a similar age. For now, though, she would keep her mind on her job. She could relax. She had worked out the reason the girl had been there and she could accept that what she had seen in the night was in fact just a nightmare. How foolish she had been to have become so worked up by something so easily explained. She smiled to herself, relieved that it all finally made sense.

Chapter Eleven

'Slow down, Nurse Jacobs. Anyone would think there was a fire!'
Barrows said as Emily rushed past her, head down, carrying an
injection tray.

'Sorry, Sister Barrows, can't stop. A patient in room three has
been waiting for a commode for the last ten minutes,' Emily
cried, gritting her teeth. She was sick of hearing herself addressed
as Nurse Jacobs. The overuse of titles made her feel as if she was
playing a part in a drama from the 1980s. Nurse this, Doctor that.
Only the healthcare assistants were addressed by their first name,
as if their rank didn't qualify them for surname use. Even their
name badges only gave their first names, which she thought was
an insult. Emily sorely missed her old department where everything was familiar, less starchy – filled with real people. Nurses
who burped and farted and sweated. Doctors who scratched
their armpits and ate rubbish food and moaned about ordinary
things. They ran, even if there wasn't a fire, because speed was of
the essence. She'd revised her opinion that A&E was the busiest
place on earth to work. All areas of nursing were probably equally
busy, including The Windsor Bridge Hospital. Today, though,
everything was getting on her nerves, especially this over the top

correctness. The hospital felt like a place built for *The Stepford Wives* – everything had to be perfect and proper.

She dumped the used injection tray on the counter in the treatment room and rushed back out, heading for the sluice to fetch a commode. This was her first shift back on days, with only one day off after finishing nights, and she was tired and felt as if she were doing all the work. Why weren't the other nurses answering the call bells? She had enough to do with prepping patients for theatre, giving out morning medicines, sorting out discharges. Ricky was on a shift and so was Shelly. They should be making sure the patients' other needs were met.

Setting the commode by the patient's bed, she juggled drip lines and drainage bags before helping the overweight woman onto it. The woman peed as soon as her bottom hit the seat.

'Would you like me to leave you for a minute?' Emily asked.

The woman shook her head. 'I'll only be a second. If you leave me I'll be stuck here for ten minutes. I'm not meant to strain, the doctor says. But all the tablets you keep giving me bung me up.'

Emily nodded sympathetically. 'I'll get the doctors to look at your medicines. See if they can give you something.'

'My Cora goes to one of them clinics and has her bowels washed out.' She chuckled. 'Treats it like she were having her nails done. It's a bit like having a jet wash, I should imagine. Fancy paying good money for that. Surely it can't do your insides any good.'

Emily smiled patiently, willing the woman to hurry. Her first patient was due to go to theatre in five minutes.

As she scooted back along to the sluice, she spied Dalloway stepping into one of the patients' rooms – the first patient on the list of people to be seen to. Dalloway would be checking to see that he was ready for theatre. She quickly emptied the commode, washed her hands and headed after him. He was in the middle of pulling the patient's theatre gown back in place, the brief examination over. The patient's wife stood next to him.

'So we'll see you shortly then,' said Dalloway. 'Do you have any questions?'

The man's eyes looked bleak. He shook his head. 'There's no turning back now, is there?'

Dalloway shook his head.

'I'm going to have to live with a bag for the rest of my days.'

The man's wife stepped forward and squeezed her husband's hand. 'Neil, don't think about that, think about the fact that you won't be in pain anymore.'

Tears glazed his eyes and he rubbed them hard. He had every right to be upset. Having his large bowel removed would change his life. The fact that it would also save his life was of little comfort to him right now.

'Can't he have something to calm him before he goes down to surgery?' asked his wife. She was dressed immaculately for such an early hour of the day. Her hair was styled, her face made up, her clothes picked carefully. There were no leggings and loose tops for a long day visiting, which was what Emily usually saw.

Dalloway nodded, a frown between his eyes. 'Of course. He should already have had a pre-med tablet.' He spotted Emily behind him. 'Nurse Jacobs?'

Emily quickly picked up the prescription chart at the end of the man's bed. She had already given out the medicines. His was the last room she had been to. She could remember putting the yellow tablet in a medicine pot. Her eyes scanned the columns left to right and up and down, ending with today's date. Her finger swept across the row of the 'once only medication' prescribed, before moving back to the tiny box where her initials should be. Only they weren't. The box was blank.

'Nurse Jacobs, has the patient had his pre-med?'

Emily looked at the man in the bed for an answer. 'Did I not give it to you?'

'Surely you'd know whether you had?' his wife answered tersely.

'I don't know, nurse. One day goes into the next here. I have seen you today, but to be honest, love, you could have given me anything, for all the notice I take.'

'Well, that's disappointing,' the wife said bluntly, her eyes fixed on Emily. 'Surely you would know if you had given my husband a tablet? Surely you sign for the drugs you give?'

Emily felt her face flame. Her mouth was dry. She could remember the tablet. She was sure she had given it to him, so why hadn't she signed for it? Why were her initials absent?

'I'm sorry Mrs . . .'

'Jeffries, for Christ sakes. You can't even remember his bloody name. What sort of place are you people running here?'

'Anna, calm down. If you were here long enough you'd see that they don't have time to stand still. They're rushed off their feet every second. And I don't need anything to calm me. It's not as if it's the first time I've been to theatre.' Neil Jeffries looked at Mr Dalloway. 'I'm ready when you are.'

Dalloway looked back at his patient, but not before casting a disparaging look at Emily. He smiled at the man. 'I'll see you shortly, then.'

Back in the corridor he turned on her swiftly. '*That* was highly embarrassing. Did you give him his pre-med or not, Nurse Jacobs?'

She shook her head. 'I'm sure I did. I remember seeing it in the medicine pot. I—'

'Nurse Jacobs, you are beginning to worry me.'

His words rooted her to the spot. Her mouth fell open.

'Mr Patel's operation had to be cancelled yesterday morning. It seems that he was not kept nil by mouth and had eaten. My understanding is that he was your patient. He came in the night before for the very reason of keeping him nil by mouth.'

Emily felt her stomach clench and she trembled as she tried to recollect yesterday morning, but her mind was a blur. She remembered admitting him, inserting a cannula into his fat arm. She remembered her conversation with Sister Barrows. The rest of the night had passed without incident. She handed out the morning medications, helped with the early-morning tea round, handed over the patients to the day staff. For the life of her she could not remember giving any fluids or food to Mr Patel.

'I don't understand. He *was* nil by mouth. I would never have given him anything to eat. I'm positive that I didn't.'

'The same way that you're sure you gave Mr Jeffries his pre-med? Are you unwell, Nurse Jacobs? Sister Barrows has some concerns.'

She shook her head vigorously. 'No, Mr Dalloway. I'm perfectly fine. Just tired and a little confused by this morning's events.'

He looked at her sternly. 'May I then suggest you take the rest of the day off and go home?'

'Go home?' Her voice was shrill with alarm.

'Yes. I can't afford to put this hospital's reputation at risk. I'm giving you the easy way out here. Simply go home sick. See your GP even; to see if you're fit to work.'

In the end she feigned a migraine, though it was only a partial untruth as a hammering inside her skull tapped hard with every push of the pedals she made as she cycled home. She was distraught at having to finish her shift so abruptly. She rode through the park and her eyes met her sister's eyes as they stared out at her from one of the posters she'd put up. She had never felt more alone.

'Are you pleased now, Zoe?' she whispered bitterly. 'Have I not been punished enough?'

Chapter Twelve

With a mug of mint tea cradled in her palms, Emily gazed around her sitting room in a daze. The room was silent and bathed in morning sunlight. She had been home for ten minutes and had made herself tea, shrugged off her uniform and was still trying to come to terms with the fact that at only nine o'clock in the morning she had already been to work and was now back home – in disgrace. Dalloway was worried about her and that was enough to set her nerves on edge. Her job could be on the line. She had seen how easily they had got rid of Jim Lanning when he had cocked up. She was still new in her job, in the probationary period; her employment could be terminated if they thought her unsuitable.

She remembered shaking the tablet into a medicine pot, remembered checking Mr Jeffries' prescription chart and was then interrupted to take a call from a relative wanting an update on her mother's condition. She had locked the medicine trolley and gone to speak to the woman. The tablet would still be inside the medicine trolley, sitting innocently in the medicine pot, never having been given, which is why she hadn't signed for it. It was a simple error, and could happen to any nurse. Interruptions during medicine rounds had caused many a drug error. It was the reason for trying to introduce the wearing of red tabards during drug rounds with the words DRUG ROUND IN PROGRESS. PLEASE DO NOT DISTURB emblazoned on the back. Emily had never worn one and was aware that some patients and relatives had viewed the message negatively. They seemed to think it was the only good time to ask a nurse a question.

Emily picked up her mobile and dialled the ward number. She was in luck when Ricky answered. 'Sorry for disturbing you, Ricky. I wonder if you can just check something for me?'

'Hey you, how are you? Barrows said you went home sick.'

'I'm OK, just a stinking headache. Sorry to bail out on you guys.'

'It's OK. We're doing fine. What's up?'

'Ricky, do you think you could open the medicine trolley and just check to see if there's a medicine pot sitting there with a yellow tablet in it?'

'Hang on a sec.'

Emily could hear the background noise of the ward as she waited. There was another phone ringing, a call bell ringing and voices close to the desk talking. Ricky's voice was back in her ear. 'Yep, yellow tablet in medicine pot. What do you want me to do with it?'

She sighed with relief. 'Ditch it, please.'

'I will do and hey, don't worry about Mr Patel, he's going down to theatre later. So everything is OK.'

When the call ended she felt calmer. At least one mystery had been solved. Though she was embarrassed that others thought it her fault that Mr Patel didn't go to theatre yesterday. She had no recollection of even checking on him prior to finishing her shift, which was a worry. She must have, even if it was just a quick peek at him. It was the stress of the last two weeks that had done this; it had exhausted her and to boot, she'd been sleepwalking during the night, something she hadn't done in a very long time. She found the evidence this morning: a cold mug of tea, still full, sitting where she'd placed it on the draining board. By the look of the darker colour, settled in the bottom of the mug, she'd used cold water from the tap and not boiled water from a kettle. It was ridiculous and unfair to have only one day off between finishing nights and starting back on days. No wonder she was sleepwalking and couldn't think straight. She felt punch-drunk. To add to the stress, Dalloway thought her unfit for work. With her mobile still in her hand she made a call to her GP surgery. She'd try and get an appointment for today and beg Monica, her doctor, to declare her fit for work, if necessary.

The receptionist found her a cancelled appointment for two o'clock. She had no idea how she would fill the hours until then. Her flat was immaculate, her laundry basket empty of both washing and ironing. She could watch television or read a book, but neither inspired her. She could just rest, as Dalloway suggested, and maybe sleep. 'What do you think I should do?' Her eyes swung to where Zoe's photo was, in pride of place on the second shelf on her bookcase. It was the perfect position because at night she could switch on a battery candle to cast a glow on Zoe's face. Except the photograph wasn't there. Emily gazed around the room. The last time she had touched it was after her session with Eric, when she'd come back to the flat and cried, picking up the photo and saying cruel things to Zoe. She was sure she had placed it back down, that she hadn't wandered around and put it somewhere else. Walking from corner to corner, she checked down by the sides of her sofa and underneath it. She looked behind cushions, under a newspaper. She went into her bedroom, which was as uncluttered as her sitting room, but it wasn't there. The kitchen and bathroom proved the same. For good measure she looked in the fridge, freezer, microwave and oven.

She opened the door to the spare bedroom, seeing Zoe's wall and her stuff in bin liners and cardboard boxes on the bed opposite. On top of one of the bin liners, lying face down, was the photo frame. Had she put it there during the night? There was no other explanation for it. She must have. She picked it up and turned it over and felt her breath catch in her throat. A white envelope had been sellotaped to the glass. The envelope was unsealed. Emily lifted the flap and slid out a sheet of paper. Her eyes stretched wide, her body shook as she read the message:

I'm not coming home Sis. Please stop looking for me. X

*

The new police enquiry office for Bath opened a couple of years ago opposite the old police station, on the same street, and was known as the One Stop Shop. The old police station on Manvers Street, closed after nearly fifty years, was now the property of the University of Bath. It felt strange that it was no longer the building for the police, the forecourt now empty of police vehicles. The visible presence of authority used to reassure Emily – perhaps because she always kept on the right side of the law and had no fear of seeing them. It was a shame to see it gone.

She made her way to the reception desk. Pale blue and low, the countertop had a silky finish and shone clean and new. She could see clearly into the small office space, which made the whole experience of being inside the police station feel more friendly. On the back wall behind the desk was a map of the city centre, stamped with the Avon and Somerset Constabulary crest. A young female officer looked up at Emily, her black and white cravat loose, a small fan beside her teasing strands of her pale hair.

'How may I help?'

Emily didn't recognise her and suspected that she was new. She knew most of the officers by name or face, having visited this place regularly last year. At one time she was so familiar with the layout, she could tell when the posters up on the walls had been changed or updated. She had not been here for a while, though, not since the six-month review of Zoe's case in January of this year. She'd met up with Geraldine a handful of times since then, but their meetings hadn't amounted to much more than a social chat about how Emily was doing.

'I have an appointment with Detective Inspector Sutton.'

The officer smiled politely. 'Yes, she telephoned. She'll be here shortly. Do take a seat.'

Emily nodded and moved away from the desk. In her handbag, inside a clear polythene sandwich bag, was the envelope and note. She'd had the presence of mind to keep them protected only after she'd handled them, gripped them and breathed on them as she tried to inhale any scent left by Zoe. The shock was wearing off and questions were buzzing through her mind. Had Zoe come to her flat? Where was she? Why didn't she come home? Did this mean she was alive? And how could she do this to her? Put her through a year of misery and fear and not knowing. Was Zoe that cruel?

Being at the police station brought back the memories of those initial fear-filled days. Geraldine Sutton arriving at her parents' home to meet the family of the missing girl. Police traipsing through at all times of the day to ask more questions or to keep them updated with what was going on. A policewoman named Ruth appeared most days at her parents' home to act as family liaison officer and keep reporters away from the front door. In those first weeks they were hungry for a story that might suddenly get bigger. A body found. A murder investigation. Emily had moved back home temporarily for a couple of weeks to offer support and be around to help answer any questions, and she'd been grateful of the policewoman's company. On the news channels Zoe's image constantly stared back at them from the screen and Emily knew that if Zoe saw the photo their parents had picked to give to the police, she'd hate it, as it was one of her with a small blemish of an acne spot, on her forehead. Those first weeks of waiting and hoping that the police would find Zoe had been the most intense moments of Emily's life. Then slowly, steadily, all the activity seemed to stop. The reporters disappeared. Ruth stopped coming. The police had no leads. Zoe had vanished into thin air.

Swallowing hard, she tried to calm herself. She had phoned Geraldine Sutton immediately and had asked to see her, telling her that she had found something. The detective had agreed to see her in the next hour. She had walked to the station on auto-pilot; blindly and numbed.

Geraldine Sutton had several shopping bags in her hands when she arrived; shiny plastic and paper carrier bags advertising the shops she'd visited: Next, H&M, Karen Millen and House of Fraser. She nodded at Emily and walked over to the desk. 'Can you put these in the office for me, please? I'll collect them later.' The officer took the bags and DI Sutton turned to greet Emily properly. 'Sorry about that. I'm going to a wedding and nothing fits. You'd never believe when I started this job that I was a size ten.'

Emily smiled. She thought Geraldine Sutton a very attractive woman. She was curvy, with skin that always looked slightly tanned and glowing, thick dark brown hair and a face that needed little makeup to enhance her big hazel eyes and full lips. The fact that she was overweight by a couple of stone didn't detract from her attractiveness. Emily knew she was in her early forties and had two children under the age of four. She had been part of her life since Zoe went missing, and Emily had cried on this woman's shoulders more than a few times.

'So, you want to grab a cup of coffee somewhere?' asked Geraldine. There was no interview room available at this enquiry office, so they would have to go to another station if an interview needed to be recorded, but for now a coffee shop would be fine. They had met a few times in such places when Emily wanted an update.

They headed down Manvers Street, with the railway station in front of them, and crossed Brunel Square to a place called Graze, a large modern restaurant – bar that was built around the arches of the railway. It was a popular place for train spotters to hang out as the outdoor seating area fenced off by railings butted up against platform two at Bath Railway Station.

A high-speed train pulled in, visible through a window. The carriage doors opened and a stream of passengers poured out. Past peak time in the morning, many of the crowd would be tourists coming to visit the famous city.

The two women walked to the far end of the restaurant, to a table that had a half-circular leather couch where they could sit comfortably. Emily asked for mint tea, hoping the beverage would ease the tightness in her throat. Geraldine ordered a caramel latte and a round of toast. 'I'm starving. I missed breakfast in the hope that I could squeeze into a size fourteen dress.'

'You don't need to lose weight,' Emily said.

'It's alright for you to say that when you're as slim as a reed.' Geraldine looked at her properly. 'Though I'm glad to say you no longer look like a puff of wind would blow you over. You look well, Emily.'

She gave a self-deprecating look. 'I'm getting there. Thanks for the flowers, by the way.'

Geraldine had sent her flowers a month ago to mark the first anniversary, a small offering to lessen the sadness of her day, and Emily had been surprised, the gesture striking her as unusual that a police officer would do this, and she hoped it was not done out of guilt for not finding Zoe. The blame was not on her shoulders.

'You're welcome.'

A waiter arrived and placed down their drinks and the toast and they stayed quiet until he left them alone again.

'So,' Geraldine said. 'What have you found?'

Emily placed the polythene sandwich bag on the table. She had inserted the sheet of paper so that the message could be read through the clear cover.

'Jesus. When did this arrive?' Geraldine was staring at Emily in total surprise.

'I found it at just gone nine this morning. I came back from work because I had a headache. I found it attached to a photo frame, with a photo of Zoe, which had been moved from its usual place in my flat.' Emily didn't mention it may have been she who had moved it. She didn't want to confuse things.

Geraldine's mouth dropped open, her eyebrows rose high. 'Your flat? Someone was in your flat? You mean, this wasn't just posted through your door?'

Emily took a shaky breath. 'No.'

Geraldine's eyes fixed on the note in her hands. 'I am totally surprised, I have to say. That's not what I was expecting at all. Do you recognise her writing?'

She shrugged. 'It's all in capitals, so I don't know. Maybe? She calls me Sis in it. It's what she calls me. I'd have to find an old birthday card or something with her writing, to check it by. You'd think I'd know my own sister's handwriting, but we only ever texted or Facebook-messaged. Everything we send today is done by typing something. I'd have to go through her stuff to see what I can find.'

'Do you think it's genuine?'

Emily's eyes shot open and her face stretched wide to stop the threat of tears. She knew Geraldine was just doing her job, but her words caused her chest to ache. For the first time in a year she was hoping that her sister was not lying in some grave, her body still waiting to be found. This was the only evidence that indicated she could still be living.

'Don't you?'

Geraldine pressed her lips together, concern on her face. 'I don't know. How would she have got into your flat? Does anyone else have access to it? Are you dating?'

'She has my spare key. I presume she got in that way. She and the landlord are the only ones to have keys to my flat. I gave her the spare key to feed my fish if I was ever away. Not that she ever did. She always forgot.' She pulled a guilty face. 'After she disappeared I forgot about the fish altogether. The poor little things floated to the top one morning. But she used to go there to study as well. There were fewer distractions.'

Geraldine sipped her coffee and left a film of foam across her upper lip. She wiped it clean. 'Here's what we're going to do. You're going to find something with Zoe's writing on so that we can compare it against this note. I will check to see if any CCTV cameras are located around your road and if so, hopefully spot her on one. If she visited your flat this morning it should be an easy search. I don't suppose you've tried calling her?'

Emily shook her head. 'I didn't think of it. It's been so long since I called her mobile. Though I still search for her on Face-book. I post photos of her, asking if anyone has seen her.' She pulled out her mobile and a second later she was calling Zoe's number. Both women heard the recorded message: 'Please hang up and try again.'

Geraldine gave a small tut. 'Well, that's to be expected. As you know, there's been no activity from her mobile, social media or banking since she disappeared. She's been missing for thirteen months and this note may be the first contact she has made. But why now?'

'Maybe because she just turned twenty?' said Emily, hopefully. 'I don't know. Maybe she's been out of the country and has come back and spotted one of the posters. Or, like the note says, she wants me to stop looking.'

Geraldine sighed again. 'This is going to be hard for you. Please don't get your hopes up. We will do everything we can to check out if this is genuine. Another thought that crosses my mind: could one of her flatmates have done this? Maybe as an act of kindness? Perhaps they found your key and thought about what you're going through. We'll ask them, of course. Ask if any of them have had any contact with her. I'm thinking that we should check the photo frame for prints and have the note and envelope sent to the lab. We have Zoe's fingerprints on file. Her DNA. Though not a sample of her handwriting, if memory serves me right.'

Emily sipped her tea while Geraldine munched on the toast. Everything was happening so fast. In a short time she might know if her sister was still alive.

Geraldine eyed her with concern. 'So, you came home from work unwell. Are you OK?'

'It was just a headache. It's gone now.' She decided she wouldn't mention the last two weeks, the lead-up to the real reason she was sent home – her preoccupation with finding a so-called missing patient. She was just glad she had an answer to that particular problem, now that she needed to concentrate on Zoe right now and not have her mind elsewhere. Finding that girl to give back a bracelet was the last thing on her mind. It was probably of little value anyway. She could no longer afford to think about someone who had briefly stepped into her life when Zoe was out there to find. That's where she needed to focus. Her year of searching may finally be coming to an end.

Chapter Thirteen

Geraldine stopped at the traffic lights as she waited to cross the road. Everywhere she looked she could see tourists. Hear them. Their excited voices pitched loudly, speaking in other languages as they pointed at the buildings around them. She shamefully took for granted this beautiful city and bemoaned its hilly streets, especially after shopping.

The lights finally changed and she continued her walk back to the One Stop Shop to collect her bags. The note and envelope in the sandwich bag were now in her possession. She would send them to be chemically treated and ask for it to be done as a high priority. Then she would wait for Emily to find something with Zoe's handwriting on before setting in motion the need for analysis. She wished she felt more excited by this message. While she was prepared to keep an open mind – lots of people disappeared every day and were found – the disappearance of Zoe had always struck her as sinister. She believed the young nurse had met with someone that day, someone who had caused her harm, and that it was only a matter of time before the body of Zoe Jacobs was found. She didn't fit the profile of a runaway. Being in debt or failing exams had caused many people to commit suicide or run away from their troubles, but in all the interviews with friends, family, colleagues, her GP, her tutors, Zoe was considered a lover of life. Her character suggested she could weather such pressure and disappointments, ride them out. Nothing in her character suggested that she would abandon her family, especially her sister, and go into hiding. It was this collective opinion, and the lack of an indicator of a serious problem in Zoe's life, which decided for Geraldine to believe that Zoe was missing unintentionally.

If that was the case, and Zoe was in fact already dead, who had placed the note in Emily's flat? Clearly someone who had access. The landlord? A friend? Someone more sinister?

Geraldine had worked her fair share of missing persons cases, and seen the hope slowly diminish as each day passed until a light extinguished in the eyes of the family waiting for news. In Emily's eyes the light never went out. She suffered long and hard to keep it burning brightly, and guilt played a large part in keeping it alive. If only. The cry of the guilty meant that they punished themselves, tortured themselves because they believed they could have done something to prevent that person disappearing. They thought that they should have done *this* or they could have done *that,* usually citing all the things that they didn't do. Emily had punished herself to the point of making herself ill. Her search for her sister had almost walked the flesh off her bones. She had taken things to the extreme by crawling into a mortuary fridge, and Geraldine truly believed that if Emily could have dug up freshly covered graves in the days following Zoe's disappearance, she would have.

If things had gone better from the outset of the investigation, maybe things would be different now. Maybe the mystery of Zoe's disappearance would have been uncovered. The best thing she could do for Emily was to find Zoe, though Geraldine didn't hold out much hope of that happening anytime soon. Her large team at the beginning of the investigation had been reduced to just her, and support officers as and when new evidence came to light. Geraldine was just a point of contact for the family. Zoe's case was assessed as high-risk three days after she went missing. The golden hour had well and truly gone by then. And so too had the hospital CCTV footage showing her heading to the short road used by delivery vehicles. Unfortunately, they hadn't been able to view the footage again due to a power surge at the hospital the following day and the digital data was not backed up and stored on a server. The fact that the police officer in charge of the footage had had the chance to record it when he first looked at it, using either his goddamn phone or getting someone at the hospital to download the CCTV onto a USB stick, had seriously annoyed Geraldine. He'd discovered the problem with the footage when Geraldine asked for it, coming back from the hospital sheepishly, saying that there was nothing they could do to help. It was vital evidence that would have shown the vehicles on the road that Sunday morning at around the same time that Zoe would have been there, but now it was gone for ever. CCTV was not in place along the main road where she would have come out. But Geraldine's best guess had always been that she was picked up before she ever got there. And whoever took her still had her or had disposed of her body somewhere.

Geraldine carried the guilt of that cockup as if it were her own. The team had done everything else they could; a full-scale search had been put in place, along with force helicopters, dogs, divers and search teams. All enquiries made. Press statements released. TV appeals made. At the first review, twenty-eight days later, they had nothing to show for the long hours put in and the costs incurred. They had absolutely nothing except for their own failed fuckup. A plod who failed to secure evidence, which then got destroyed – and it only got worse from there. The gormless git then couldn't bring to mind anything he had seen on the tape. Geraldine remembered that Emily had tried so hard to remember any cars she might have seen on the footage, but all she could recall seeing was her sister.

She wished she had more faith in this note being genuine. She would certainly treat it as such. Yet fast-forwarding a few days, she simply couldn't see herself making a statement to the press with the news that Zoe Jacobs had been found.

Monica Summers hugged the patient who came into her office, then stepped back as if fully appraising her. 'Well, you don't look ill, so I hope this is a social visit.'

Emily sat down and surveyed her GP and friend, a friend she had given little thought to for some months now. The two had become friends when Monica had worked one day a week in the emergency department to better her clinical skills. Though a highly trained general practitioner who spent her days diagnosing, treating and referring, she had felt her hands-on skills with life-threatening emergencies were out of practice. She had shadowed Emily and taken every opportunity to improve herself, and not just with the emergencies. She inserted cannulas, catheters, set up drip lines, sutured wounds, stapled wounds, put dislocated shoulders back in place, set broken limbs in casts. She had arrived nervous, with clammy hands, a fish out of water, and Emily had looked at the tiny woman with her small features and mousy hair – who she later learned could pack a mean verbal punch when she needed to and had an intellect Emily could only envy – and taken her under her wing. Their relationship had worked on all levels, and until Zoe's disappearance they'd had regular contact. Emily had been invited into the doctor's home, met her husband, her son and had enjoyed being part of a stable, loving family for a while. The only time she saw her old friend now was as a patient.

'Well, I'm here because I meant to get you to declare me fit for work.'

Monica made an 'o' shape with her mouth, a small frown bringing her thin eyebrows together.

'I think I lost the plot for a little while, Monica. Well, no, that's not true, I got fixated on a situation, a missing patient, but I'm fine now. In fact, I'm better than fine.'

Monica was blinking fast, clearly not having a clue what her patient was trying to tell her.

Emily drew a breath and started at the beginning, and a good ten minutes later Monica was still wearing the same expression, only now her brows were almost touching her hairline.

'Oh my goodness, you poor thing. What a terrible ordeal you've been through, and now you have all the hope and worry of this letter you have found. Are you sure you want to work while all that is going on? I can sign you off sick, you know. It's not a problem. It would be entirely understandable following today's discovery.'

Emily shook her head. 'If I need time off, I'd rather take unpaid or compassionate leave. No, I need to work, Monica. I can do both – assist the police and carry on with my job. Being busy is the best remedy for me.'

'You certainly look well. Have you discussed all this with Eric Hudson?'

Emily's thumb instinctively went to her mouth. 'Of course,' she mumbled as she chewed a corner of her nail.

'And he's OK with everything you've told him?'

Emily shrugged. 'I haven't yet had a chance to tell him that I've found a reason for seeing this missing patient in my room.'

Monica wrapped her arms around herself, as if trying to get warm. 'It's so good to see you. I've been so worried about you. Are you sure you're doing OK?'

Emily nodded vigorously, feeling unnerved by Monica's concern. 'I'm fine, Monica. Just get me back to work. I can do the rest.'

With a sick note signed by her GP declaring her fit and well, Emily slowly walked out of the surgery. The excitement upon discovering that Zoe might be alive was starting to fizzle out. She hated the attention of people worrying about her.

Geraldine stood up to let PC Ruth Moore take her seat in front of the bank of screens. At Geraldine's request, she'd been dispatched to take over the search for a sighting of Zoe Jacobs' face, because she was more familiar with Zoe's image. Ruth had been the family liaison officer assigned to the Jacobses, though it had been a long time since any of them had contacted her. They went straight to Geraldine instead if they wanted information. The CCTV control room was only a short stroll from the One Stop Shop, and Geraldine had wandered up to start the search herself. So far she hadn't found any sighting of Zoe Jacobs. She had viewed footage from four street cameras covering that area and had seen only Emily leaving her flat and returning to it this morning. Geraldine now wanted Ruth to concentrate on Emily's road again, but for the day before. If that proved unhelpful, she'd ask her to go back another day. As the constable got comfortable in the chair, Geraldine peered over her shoulder. Although they had a clear view of the street, the doorway to Emily's flat was out of shot. She would ask Emily when exactly she had last seen the photo before it was moved, to help pinpoint more accurately when the note might have been put there. Emily had found the note this morning, but it could have been there for a few days.

She tapped the officer's shoulder. 'I'm going now. Call me if you spot anything.'

Ruth nodded. 'How's Emily holding up? This must have really shaken her. Last time I saw her, the poor thing looked like a basket case.'

Geraldine pulled a face. 'Best not use that description. At least not in anyone's presence.'

Ruth wrinkled her brow, then caught on. 'No, of course not.'

'She's doing well by the sounds of things. Back at work.'

'Gosh,' the surprise in Ruth's voice was evident. 'She is doing well. I liked her counsellor, mind. I'd recommend him anytime.

You remember when Emily used to almost camp out at the station? He'd come and talk to her after we gave her the same old, same old. He had a lovely way about him.'

As Geraldine exited the Guildhall, she glanced at a couple kissing on the entrance steps. The magnificent building, which housed, among other things, the twenty-four-hour CCTV control room, was also home to the Mayor's Parlour, city archives and the Registry Office. It was this last purpose which she suspected was the reason for their being there, seeing the small bunch of white roses clutched in the woman's hand. Switching her gaze away she scrolled through her mobile contacts and tapped Eric Hudson's number.

'Hello, DI Sutton,' she heard him say.

Geraldine smiled. She loved the sound of his voice. It was measured, warm and with a hint of humour in the tone. If she could fancy a man for his voice alone Eric would win hands down. Her husband's voice was pure Bristolian. She had become used to his, 'Where you tos?' and 'Don't do that, minds.' Though she was trying to ensure that the kids didn't copy him. Her oldest, Tommy, had asked the ice cream man for a 'gert' big one only yesterday.

'Hello Eric, I'm just calling regarding Emily Jacobs. How do you think she's doing? I'm not expecting you to break any patient confidentiality or anything, I just want your take, really, on this latest find.'

The psychologist remained silent and for a second Geraldine wondered if they were still connected.

'What latest find?'

Geraldine was glad he couldn't see her face, feeling suddenly foolish. Why should Eric know about something that had only happened this morning? 'Oh, it was just a thought that if she had told you, you might have an opinion. It was only discovered this morning, so no doubt she'll tell you sometime. Emily found something. I can't really say what at the moment, Eric, as it's now part of an ongoing enquiry. The information would need to come to you directly from her. Do you understand?'

'Sure,' he replied, his tone of voice more serious. 'I'll let Emily tell me. Is it a good find?'

She sighed. 'I don't know yet. It's certainly something we need to check out.'

As they said their goodbyes, Geraldine saw she'd received a text from Emily:

Thanks for the tea. Both scared and excited for the next few hours. Praying you spot her soon.

Geraldine sighed. She hoped Emily would find a sample of Zoe's writing and lay to rest her concern that this letter was not quite kosher.

Chapter Fourteen

Emily was sure the bin liners in her spare bedroom had been touched since she last went through them. She hadn't noticed it that morning when she found the note. She had walked out of the room with the note in her hand and hadn't gone back in. She now wondered whether she had touched them while on her little walkabout. Geraldine had replied to her text, reminding her to look for the handwriting sample and warning her not to handle the photograph frame again as she wanted it dusted for fingerprints. Emily wondered if they'd also check her flat for other places Zoe may have touched: the front door, this bedroom door and possibly these bin liners. The bin liners sat on top of cardboard boxes covering the length of the single bed, set against the wall. On the opposite wall were Emily's investigations – her notes, photographs, maps, newspaper cuttings curling at the edges; her year of searching for Zoe at a standstill. The narrow space between the bed and 'Zoe's Wall' was the space where Emily did her thinking, as if by being among Zoe's things she would find her sister more easily.

She had last looked through the bags and boxes in the days after they'd arrived. The police had already been through them and taken what they wanted. They still had items such as Zoe's laptop, and a hairbrush and toothbrush from which they'd obtained DNA, in evidence. The rest had been left in Zoe's bedroom until it arrived at Emily's flat. She had folded the clothes neatly and washed the ones that had been delivered straight from a laundry basket. She threw away the half-used bottles and tubes of toiletries and boxed the more valuable and personal items such as makeup, jewellery, CDs, photographs, text books. From memory there were no diaries. Zoe had never been the type to keep one. Growing up with technology, she had used it to her advantage. With mild dyslexia she had used a laptop through most of her secondary schooling, and for her studies and assignments as a student nurse Emily was fairly sure she had done the same.

The twisted necks of a couple of bin liners looked loosened, the shoulders of the bags less full. Had Zoe taken some stuff? Clothes she perhaps wanted? In the top of one of these bags was Emily's leather jacket. She was sure of that because when she had found it among Zoe's clothing she had recalled that it was Zoe who last wore it at the music festival because she was cold. One whiff of the collar and she had instantly smelled her sister's perfume, and for that reason had kept it bagged tightly to preserve her essence.

There were ten bin liners to look through. She started with the ones that looked fuller and undisturbed, ending with the two that she suspected had been opened recently. Her leather jacket was not in any of them. She could empty them all out properly, but felt sure it wouldn't be there. It had definitely been placed right at the top of one of them. And now it was missing. She didn't know whether to laugh or cry. Zoe could be wearing her jacket right this minute, waiting for Emily to come and find her.

'Oh Zoe, why are you doing this to me?' she whispered. 'Why don't you just come home?'

A memory of her little sister saying her prayers sprang to mind – though this had never been taught or encouraged by their parents. Wearing her favourite nightie, a pink one printed with Cinderella, she had peeked through her hands to see if Emily was watching and listening and giggled when she saw that she was, before changing the words to the prayer Emily had taught her. 'Now I lay me down to sleep. I pray the lord to have some sweets.'

She had been a sweet child. But spoiled. At twelve she was borrowing Emily's makeup and clothes as if she were a teenager, trying to grow up too fast. Emily had come down hard on her a few times, which then resulted in sulks. When she decided she wanted to be a nurse, Emily hadn't leapt with joy, as her sister had never liked hard work and was therefore choosing the wrong profession. Her grades had only just been good enough to get her into nursing, and she'd passed them with a lot of tutoring from Emily.

Emily knew that she would have to tell her parents about the note and suspected she was more likely to find something like an old birthday card at their home. While she only ever received a text saying 'Happy Birthday' or 'Happy Christmas', their parents would have received cards.

She would go over there tomorrow and find something with her sister's writing on. She was on an early shift and wanted to go into work to see Dalloway and reassure him that she was fit for the job. There was no more need for him to be worried.

Emily finished her shift the following day feeling satisfied. It had been a good day and nothing dramatic or untoward had happened. Patients had gone to theatre, had their operations and were recovering nicely. Dalloway was happy. She could see in his eyes that he was no longer perturbed by her behaviour and after his ward round had even complimented her on a job well done. She had a lightness in her step, despite the fact that she had just done an eight-hour shift with barely a break.

She was on her way to her parents' house, intent on getting what she needed. Geraldine was wasting no time and nor would she. The detective inspector had arranged for a crime scene investigator to visit Emily's home at six-thirty that morning to collect the photograph frame, which had been placed in a large evidence bag. Geraldine had texted her the night before to forewarn her of the early time, and Emily had reassured her that it suited her as she was on early shift and would be awake. Emily texted Geraldine in the afternoon to tell her her plans and also to ask if her parents could not be informed just yet about the letter she had found. She didn't want them taking up Geraldine's time needlessly and looking for another five minutes of fame. She would clean their house as she normally did and while doing so, would search for a birthday or Christmas card. When they had proof that the note was from Zoe they could then be told. No doubt her mother would phone some reporter, maybe hoping for a pay-out for her story. Though Emily would be surprised if she had any takers for a story of a missing adult who'd written a letter saying she wasn't coming home. What her parents seemed to forget was that it was not illegal for an adult to go missing. They were lucky the police had looked so long and hard for Zoe already and were now prepared to act on this new find.

Her head down, she checked her mobile for any replies from Geraldine. There were two. One simply read, 'OK'. The second caused Emily to sigh:

Will need to discuss further. Your parents are next of kin.

Emily bumped into someone walking the other way. It was her fault for not looking where she was going. 'Sorry,' she said, and then stared in concern at the small woman. Panicked eyes were trying to focus. Dressed in a short-sleeved white blouse and dark skirt, her legs bare and feet puffy, encased in white-laced plimsolls, she looked frazzled. Her upper lip was perspiring and tendrils of hair clung to her damp forehead.

'Hey, are you OK? Can I help?'

She stared at Emily frantically. 'I need to find my niece. She come here and now she no go home.'

'OK, OK, we'll find her. What's her name? What does she look like?' Emily asked, staring at the faces passing them.

The woman waved her hand in agitation. 'She small. She has dark hair like me. She very pretty and she young woman.'

Emily placed an arm around her shoulder and steered her towards the entrance. 'OK, that's good. Let's go to reception and see if they can help to find her.' She pressed the call button for the lift. 'What day did she come in? Today? Yesterday?'

The woman pulled away and Emily was alarmed at her panicked state. Her upper body was shaking, hands pressing hard against her mouth. 'You no understand. Katka no go home. My sister tell me she not get off plane. Dr Dalloway say he don't know where she gone. But she come here first. She then must take plane home, but she not return and my sister blame me. Katka is only daughter.'

Emily wanted to take her somewhere more private and was relieved when the lift door opened. She bundled the woman into it and tried to calm her. 'Don't upset yourself. I'm sure everything will be alright. When did Katka come here?'

'Thirty June,' she cried, her voice muffled by her hands.

Emily stared at the bowed head. She felt a ringing in her ears, a sickness in the pit of her stomach. She must have misheard her. Thirtieth of June. The day she had her operation. The day she saw a young woman in a bed beside her. She sucked back the cry, clamped her hand to her mouth and saw the woman raise her head.

Her eyes fixed on Emily. 'You know something?' she said excitedly.

Emily shook her head fast.

'You know something. I see in your face.'

She shook her head again, inching away from the woman. When the lift pinged and released the doors, Emily stepped back fast, straight into Dalloway.

He put a steadying hand on her shoulder and would have spoken but for the wail of the woman behind her. 'Oh Dr Dalloway. They still no find her.'

He immediately went to the woman's aid and, in the privacy of the lift, enfolded her in his arms. 'Shush now, Maria. Katka will return home. You must not despair. She will return.'

Wanting to leave them before the woman questioned her again, Emily quickly slipped away, dashing for the stairs. Her heart was pounding. The good feeling she'd had all day had evaporated. The problem she thought gone had come back. Was it possible that the young woman she had seen had been this woman's niece? Who was now missing? She wanted to run from the situation. Deny she had seen the woman. She had Zoe to consider.

Keeping her head down, she hurried to the car park. She would not think about it now. The woman's niece was probably safe and sound. She would drive to her parents' house. Do the job she was given. She could not get entangled in someone else's misery. Yet as she drove away from the hospital, all she could think about was that she had not imagined the girl in the bed beside her, her small arm hanging limply over the side of the bed, her hand jerking each time they pressed her chest. All she could think was that she now knew her name.

Emily could tell her parents had not yet been told about the note. Geraldine had either not found time to speak to them or was delaying telling them. They were sat in their usual places in the smoke-filled sitting room with the television on, her father snoring and her mother already looking to pick a fight.

'Found time to see us, then? From your new job?'

'Sorry, Mum, it's been another busy week. But I'm here now, so I'm going to give the house a tidy. You want me to get you anything while I'm here?'

Her mother turned her head away and resumed watching *Escape to the Country*. Emily slipped out of the room, making her way upstairs. There were three bedrooms: one that belonged to her parents, one that had been her own and one that had belonged to Zoe. Hers and Zoe's were now empty shells. There was just a bed and wardrobe in each, though the last time she was in there dusting, she had noticed her sister's bed had been made. She didn't think this had been done in the hope of Zoe returning. It was more likely that her father slept there on account of his snoring.

After half an hour of rummaging through her parents' bedroom drawers Emily found what she was looking for: an old birthday card for their father, a pint of beer on the front. She knew it wasn't from her as she would never pick a card advertising any form of alcohol, jokingly or not, for either parent. She opened it and was instantly disappointed. Zoe hadn't written a single proper word. Instead she'd put a row of kisses, and written luvya followed by the letter Z in blue ink.

She continued to search for others, but that was her only find. Evidently her parents were not sentimental enough to keep mementos from their daughters. She sat on her parents' bed in frustration, her mind only half on the job. Bumping into Maria had completely thrown her. Just when she thought she had answers for why that young woman had been in her room, she'd now heard Maria's niece was missing. She found it difficult to concentrate, and wished that her life was simple. Why couldn't it be easy to find a goddamn piece of paper with her sister's handwriting? It was ridiculous. There had to be something her sister had written on. She could not have reached adulthood without a sample of her writing being left somewhere. There would be patient notes, for a start. She would have to write in them. But finding a sample of her sister's handwriting from a patient's notes would be a mammoth task. She would have to track down tutors to find out which wards her sister was placed on, which patients she had been allocated. She would let Geraldine know of her concerns and hope that she could come up with an answer. In the meantime, she would keep searching and pray that her sister's fingerprints would be found on the note or that she was seen on CCTV.

She could not lose hope. Zoe was out there. As she thought about this she was haunted by another memory, of another young woman, who was also missing.

Chapter Fifteen

Geraldine put aside the plastic bowl of salad remains, trying to convince herself that the Subway salad had filled her. She would have liked it more if it had come with one of their warm baked breads so that she could make a sandwich out of it. The report on her screen had been a shock. She hadn't expected to receive it so quickly. She felt a sense of relief that she had held off from speaking to the Jacobs parents, because what could she tell them now? Their daughter had received a message from their other, missing daughter and the only prints found on it were Emily's. The only prints found on the photograph frame were Emily's as well. So, either someone had worn gloves, or else . . .

She had yet to reply to Emily's text about being unable to find a sample of Zoe's writing. She had yet to reply because she knew how much manpower and how many hours such a task would take. It could be done, of course, but she would rather find an easier way, a less costly way. The search through CCTV had drawn a blank. A sighting fitting a description of Zoe Jacobs was seen, but it was of her sister, Emily, the two so alike it was hard to tell them apart. Geraldine had sent two further officers up to Margaret's Buildings to check with shop, business and café owners in the hope that they had their own security cameras that might have captured an image of the missing woman. Two of the businesses did have them, but on both recordings she was not seen.

She hoped this wasn't a desperate ploy of Emily's, a kick to get the investigation going again. Such things had happened before, usually from desperate parents suddenly coming across an item of clothing that their child was wearing, found two streets away, because they heard that someone 'funny' lived there. They used desperate measures to keep the police looking – and ensure they didn't give up.

She would visit Emily and tell her the outcome of their findings and see what reaction she received. Her gut instinct was telling her there was something off about this letter business. Had Emily made herself believe it was genuine before coming to the police with her find? Did she believe in something of her own making? Was it a convenience that a sample of Zoe's handwriting could not be found?

Dipping two fingers into the salad bowl, she swiped the strands of lettuce though the residual dressing. Starving herself was not going to make her slimmer. She had a week to go before the wedding and wondered if she could sweat off a stone by then by wrapping herself in clingfilm.

Emily parked two streets away from her road in a residents' permit spot. It was the only space she could legally find. Unless you had off-street parking, owning a car in a city like Bath was more hassle than it was worth, especially if you were able to walk or cycle to work. She rarely used it, unless she was visiting her parents, and as it drew nearer to having it serviced she thought of getting rid of her car altogether. It would be cheaper to get a taxi for the short journeys she made, but it was the thought of that sudden imagined call from Zoe, always in the middle of the night asking her to come and rescue her, that made her keep it.

At eight o'clock it was still daylight, but there was a nip in the evening air and she shrugged her cardigan on as she made the five-minute walk to her flat. She'd heard nothing back from Geraldine since her last text and was hoping to have heard some news from her by now.

Turning right onto Catharine Place, she walked along the pavement and suddenly went rigid, her feet stuck to the ground, her body unable to move, her eyes wide and staring at the image ahead. Some thirty metres ahead of her she saw the back of a woman, as tall as herself, of a similar build, with short-cropped black hair. She wore a short tan leather jacket nipped in at the waist, her long legs in dark jeans. Emily's breath hitched in her throat and she had to make an effort to get her voice to work. 'Zoe!'

The woman carried on walking and Emily broke into a trot. 'Zoe!' she hollered. For a brief second the woman paused and turned her head a fraction and Emily's trot sped up to an all-out run. 'Zoe, stop right there!'

The woman turned the corner and went out of view and Emily ran faster, her eyes fixed on the corner where Zoe had disappeared. Her legs were pumping hard and her breathing was ragged. She looked for a gap between the vehicles to cross the road, then made a dash between two parked cars. She heard the screech of brakes before she felt the blow to her hip sweeping her off her feet and landing her hard down on the bonnet of a car on the opposite side of the road.

She lay there, winded, and groaned with pain, the breath knocked out of her.

An elderly man leaned over her, visibly shaken, his hands waving all over the place. 'You just ran out! I couldn't stop,' he yelled in her face.

'Did you see her?' she asked him.

'I'm calling an ambulance. You need to be checked over.'

She made to sit up and he pressed her gently back. 'Please, just stay still.' Emily could hear him on the phone requesting an ambulance and wanted to stop him.

'Did you see her?' she asked again in a stronger voice, agitated and unwilling to lie still.

'See who?'

'My sister,' she cried. 'I was running after her.'

The man shook his head, bewildered. 'I didn't see anyone, not even you.'

'I've got to get after her. I can't let her disappear again.' She struggled up and slid off the bonnet onto her feet. Her face white, the colour leached away. Then slowly and without murmur she slid all the way to the ground.

Her injuries were minor; soft-tissue bruising to her left hip, which would leave her sore and stiff for a few days, but no bone injuries. They put her collapse down to a simple faint, her blood pressure falling as she stood up too quickly. A senior nurse practitioner had examined her and was happy for her to be discharged if her next set of observations stayed stable.

Emily lay back on the trolley, the curtains pulled round the cubicle to give her privacy. They had opened three times so far as ex-colleagues heard of her admission and popped in to say hello. She'd smiled and reassured each of them, waving away their concern, and now lay listening to the familiar sounds of what was once her world. The muted conversations between doctor and patient, nurse and patient, told her exactly what was happening. She didn't need to be in the cubicles with them to see their expressions or their actions to know exactly what was going on.

The woman beside her had a fractured hip, the right one, and the nurse with her was trying to insert a catheter. 'Betty, keep still, I'm just going to bend your left leg. You'll feel a little warm water between your legs. Then I'm going to pop a tube in and you won't have to worry about that anymore.'

The child opposite her had broken a bone in his arm. She could hear his cry which sounded older than that of a toddler but still quite young. Mum was trying to comfort him and the doctor was attempting to give him intranasal diamorphine. 'Can you make a big sniff for me? A really big sniff?' The doctor made a snorting noise through his own nose and the child cried harder. 'Can you just tilt his head back a little? Well done, Toby. What a good boy you are. Now, a big sniff for me.' With the intrusion of a syringe up his small nose, the boy wailed, took a breath and sniffed mucus and tears back up his nose. 'Good boy. All over. You have a cuddle with Mummy now.'

The same sounds, the same injuries, the same treatments. Emily wished she'd come back to work here. A year ago she couldn't set foot inside the place, but lying here now she realised she was ready again. She could be doing a job she loved and not one she was only doing for the sake of having a job.

The curtain opened and Jerry Jarvis, one of her favourite doctors, stepped in. His hair was as black as hers and his blue eyes were almost navy. He grinned mischievously. 'Well, well, well, if it isn't Emily Tomb Raider. Been fighting with cars, I hear.'

Emily screwed up her face in mock annoyance. He had called her this after hearing about her episode in the morgue. He'd hugged her after she was brought in with mild hypothermia. 'Only you could do that,' he'd said. 'Gutsy,' he labelled her, before giving her a new name: Emily Tomb Raider.

'Shut up, Jerry.'

'I hear you're slumming it in the private sector, dealing with one whole patient at a time.'

'It has its moments—'

'Please don't tell me you're rushed off your feet.'

She tried to act offended, but her lips twitched.

'There she is. Knew she was in there somewhere. So now you've had yourself a little holiday, when are you coming back here?'

She gave what she hoped was a mysterious look. 'You never know.'

He patted the top of her foot. 'Good. I'll be seeing you soon, then. In the meantime, you have a visitor.'

She gazed, confused.

'A DI Sutton, I believe.'

Geraldine pulled a chair close to the trolley. When she sat down she was looking up at Emily. 'How do you put this thing lower?'

Emily leaned over and pointed out the correct foot pedal. 'That one. Just press it with your foot.'

The bed lowered, Geraldine sat down again. 'You certainly get yourself into some scrapes. What on earth possessed you to run out in front of a car like that?'

Emily looked at Geraldine, finding it hard to say what she saw for fear of not being believed. The fact that she had not heard from her since early afternoon worried her. What was Geraldine not telling her?

'I thought I saw Zoe,' she blurted out.

'Thought?' Geraldine didn't look overexcited by the possibility and Emily felt a worry in her gut.

She needed this woman on her side if she were to find Zoe. She was just being oversensitive. It was not surprising given all that had happened in the last forty-eight hours. 'I'm sure I saw her. My leather jacket has gone missing and I'm sure Zoe has taken it, was wearing it. I saw the back of her and was chasing her and then I ran out into the road and I lost her.'

Geraldine gave a brief nod. 'Well, we'll check that out, of course. In the meantime I do have an update for you. Nothing positive, I'm afraid. The only fingerprints found on the envelope, note and photo frame are yours. Also we've checked CCTV footage and we have you captured a few times, but no sighting of Zoe.'

Emily stared at her, waiting for more, but Geraldine sat silent. The feeling of discord seemed to grow. Then she noticed the tiredness in Geraldine's face. The woman had probably been at work all day and was still working now by being here with her. Hers was a busy job and Emily was not the only one who needed her time. She felt easier. She couldn't bear it if Geraldine thought this was all in her mind. A fabricated note? Her leather jacket missing? Emily wasn't stupid, and knew that finding the letter must have caused Geraldine to wonder who put it there other than Zoe. All that mattered was that she didn't think it was she who had put it there.

'Her writing will be somewhere. On patients' notes—'

Geraldine cut her off. 'I think the best thing to do is wait and see if there is any other way you can retrieve a writing sample.'

Emily flinched, embarrassed, hurt by the abrupt tone.

A moment later she heard the detective pull back the curtain. 'Give me a call, Emily, if you get anything else.'

Emily nodded, then felt her throat tighten as she saw Geraldine try to smile. She heard the softened tone: 'Sorry for being offish,' she said. 'It's been a long day.'

Emily stared fixedly at the gap in the curtain, made by Geraldine's departure, lecturing herself for being so sensitive, for taking it so personally, and almost, but not quite, convincing herself that Geraldine had not been cross with her.

Chapter Sixteen

Emily had ignored the texts she'd received from Eric, but now he'd contacted her formally, by email, and she was fuming. He wanted to see her weekly again. If she hadn't met Maria she would be happy to see him, happy to dance into his office and shout, 'Zip-a-dee-doo! I found the reason for that woman in my room. She was simply in the wrong room!' But as that was now in question, she wanted to avoid him, having the bigger problem of perhaps knowing who she lay beside. Knowing her name. Until she decided what she was going to do, if anything, she didn't want him picking at her brains. She'd send him a text shortly and plead tiredness for not replying sooner, mention she'd had a minor accident and would see him as soon as she was able. She wasn't exactly up and running yet, so it wasn't a lie.

She had been on a day off following her accident and was grateful she didn't have to call in sick, and then spent the day taking painkillers and putting cold compresses on her hip. She'd gone to work the next day as normal and had tried to walk off the stiffness. Today she was moving easier, her mind focused solely on her job and everybody else's as well. She was aware that she was beginning to get on people's nerves. They'd declined her offer of help, they'd told her to slow down, take a breather, find a patient to talk to or maybe sort out the linen cupboard, which was where she was now, replacing sheets and pillowcases on the correct shelves and unpacking more linen to add to the pile. There was so much other stuff dumped in there: equipment not put back in the right places, boxed Christmas decorations and a spiky fake Christmas tree poking out from a shelf at calf-level. She'd cluttered the floor with all the stuff she was intending to remove from the small room, including a large cardboard box marked 'Lost Property'. She'd find out what the hospital did with its lost property other than dump it in a box.

A half hour later, the room was how it should be: a storage place for linen. The only thing to remove now was the lost property box. She eyed it curiously and budged it with her foot, feeling its heaviness as it barely moved. It was too heavy to carry. She'd need a sack trolley, or else to lighten its load. She knelt down and raised the flaps. A navy towelling dressing gown was folded on top of other stuff. She took it out and placed it to one side. A flowery toiletry bag zipped closed lay next, then an electric shaver with adaptor plug still attached to it, more clothing, grey jogging bottoms, a black Superdry hoody, a pale pink satin pyjama top, a tangle of mobile phone chargers, then the cause of the real weight: books, both paperback and hardback. She took them all out and immediately saw bright yellow fabric underneath. She pulled it free and held it up and saw details she had forgotten: short sleeves and pink piping around the neckline; an embroidered pink flower on the right breast. The top was made for a small person and she realised now that it was more of a cropped top. Emily's chin trembled and fear prickled her chest; it was further proof that she had not imagined the woman she had shared a room with. This top, the bracelet and the other contents still in the box – a folded pair of jeans and worn leather flip-flops – proved she existed. Barrows was wrong when she said no one else had been in that room with her. Was she just mistaken, or had she deliberately lied?

In the changing room she showered quickly and flung open the cubicle door when she barrelled straight into Meredith. Meredith grabbed hold of her to keep her upright. 'Jesus, Emily, you nearly took my legs from under me! What's your rush?'

Pulling away, she didn't realise Meredith had a hold of her towel until she was left naked. For modesty's sake Emily half turned and Meredith gasped. 'Oh my god, what have you done?'

Emily looked down at her hip. The bruise had spread to the size of a dinner plate, deep navy at its centre and purpling at the edges. 'I fell over,' she simply said.

'Off what? A building?' Meredith asked sceptically, then handed back the towel.

She covered herself. 'Didn't put my arms out to stop my fall.'

Meredith puffed out her cheeks, her eyes round with surprise. 'I'd get that checked out if you bruise that badly. And go a bit slower.'

She carried on drying herself, hoping the anaesthetist would leave. She liked Meredith, but now was not the time to talk to her. Unless the conversation was work-related, she didn't want to talk at all. Her throat felt like it was stuffed with a hard ball that would not dislodge. Her emotions were so tightly wound, any act of human kindness was likely to set off a flood of tears. She could not stop thinking about the clothes she'd found in the lost property. Where did she go from here? Should she see Geraldine and report it? Speak to Dalloway? Tell Eric? Emily didn't know who to turn to. Eric had replied to her text asking her to make an appointment at her earliest convenience. What was that about? Was he that concerned about her mental state that their next appointment had to be as soon as possible? Would he have men in white coats holding straitjackets at the ready, just in case? He had been counselling her for a year. She trusted him, or she thought she did, until now. Right at this moment she didn't know who to trust.

'Earth to Emily?'

She looked up and realised Meredith was talking to her.

'I said, have you found a date yet to go for that drink?'

She stared at Meredith and wondered why this exciting, quirky, intelligent woman was even bothering with her. What on earth did she have to offer her? They were poles apart. Meredith probably lived in a large swanky house back in the States, and drove a flash car and had a successful, handsome husband. She rented a poky two-bedroom flat with ageing hand-me-down furniture, a car that wouldn't pass its next MOT and a fractured past. Maybe Meredith had heard of her missing sister, her claim to fame, and wanted a bit of light entertainment, to hear from an insider's point of view what it was like to live under that media spotlight.

On the brink of fobbing her off with some excuse, she stopped herself. Why not go out and have some fun? It would take her mind off everything. It's what normal people did every day. She couldn't remember the last time she had even sat in a pub. The only outings she had gone on in the past year, if she could consider them that, were the meet-ups with Geraldine. During those meet-ups, she had got to see the insides of coffee shops during daytime hours. If the worst came and she bored her companion, she could always get a taxi home.

'Yes, I have. I'm free tomorrow, Saturday or Sunday, then I'm back on nights.'

'Great, let's make it Saturday then.'

They exchanged mobile numbers, and then Emily was free to get dressed in peace.

Outside the hospital she hunted in her rucksack for the key to her bicycle lock. She needed to put it on a chain around her neck, as she wasted more time looking for it than anything else in her bag. Impatiently she emptied out the contents and watched in frustration as loose change rolled away. Her eyes followed the money until a pair of white plimsolls stepped into her vision. She raised her face and saw Maria.

Emily stood rooted. 'Hello Maria,' she said cautiously, 'are you here to see Mr Dalloway?'

Maria shook her head quickly, her eyes darting over Emily's shoulder. 'No, I come to see you.'

Emily's eyes opened in alarm. 'Me?'

'Yes. I speak only to you.' Her eyes were restless, flitting back and forth, tension in her entire being. Emily looked at the ground at her scattered belongings. She hunched down, throwing the contents back in the rucksack, her hands trembling, feeling flustered by the woman's presence.

'You know something. I think you see Katka?'

Emily saw a mixture of hope and fear in Maria's face. Her hands were clasped together as if in prayer. Emily wanted to deny it. She had no idea who that young woman was yet, and had no proof that she was this woman's niece.

With the last of her things retrieved, Emily stood back up. 'Why don't you ask Mr Dalloway for help?'

The woman spread her hands in despair, her mouth trembling. 'Dr Dalloway a good man. I work for him long time as nanny to his daughter, but he not believe Katka go missing. He believe she come home soon. I need you to talk to him. Tell him you see Katka.'

Emily's heart tapped hard against her ribs. 'But I didn't! I really didn't.'

'You lie. I know you lie.' Emily saw the conviction in the woman's eyes as she spoke.

Emily shivered, despite the warm day. Maria was so certain. And what if what she had said was true, that Katka was in that bed beside her? If this woman was right, and it was her niece, then she had no choice but to help. She knew all too well the fear of not finding someone you loved. She knew what this woman was going through. Someone may have made her niece disappear and hidden her clothes in lost property, maybe thinking no one would ever find them. Only they hadn't banked on Emily being a witness. Of her seeing who had worn those clothes. She had seen what she was not meant to have seen by simply being put in the wrong room.

Maria reached into her skirt pocket and pulled out a folded piece of paper. 'Dr Dalloway's home. You go see him. You tell him truth of what you see. You make him believe Katka missing.'

With the piece of paper now in her hand, Emily was left standing there long after Maria disappeared from view. She shivered again, this time more violently. She could not walk away from this. Something had happened inside that hospital. A patient had disappeared and only she would admit to having seen her.

Chapter Seventeen

Emily could hardly believe she was turning up at his home uninvited. His house, built on top of a hill, only came into view once she passed a wall of tall trees. Her stomach knotted at the thought of speaking to him. He may consider this an imposition and simply close the door on her.

Her car turned into a private road taking her up to the house, and she knew there was no turning back now. She parked and stepped out into the heat. The air was still, not a leaf moving on the trees, and the silence was so complete she could hear bees buzzing in the flower beds. The hot July day was holding onto its heat even approaching evening.

The eighteenth-century converted barn was stunning. A feature wall of tinted grey glass stood in place of what might have once been the main opening to the barn. Two large porthole windows built into the stonework either side of the sheet of glass gave an impression that the house had a face: two round eyes and a long Nordic nose was watching. She eyed the house up and down and decided he must have old money or earn a great deal from his private practice. The front of the property, an open courtyard compacted with grey gravel, allowed for parking and turning space for several vehicles. A pale gold Alfa Romeo was parked. Raised lawns and low shrubs surrounded the courtyard. A drystone wall and a line of trees followed the slope of land for several acres, before giving way to a view of patchwork greens that spread far and wide. A small paddock to the right of the building had separate access through a five-bar gate, which was presently closed, with a stone-walled stable beside it. In the distance Emily could hear clip-clopping and a woman's voice calling, 'Good girl, good girl.'

Sat atop a dark brown horse, the woman came into view and Emily stood still as she waited to be seen, but the woman didn't notice her as she steered the horse to another gate with access to wide open fields. Emily wondered if she was the wife. Dressed in jodhpurs, riding boots and navy polo shirt, there was something striking about her bearing, her graceful poise and red hair flowing down her back. Emily watched the horse pick up its stride and the red hair begin to bounce rhythmically with the motion, a brief halo of orange, as the sun picked out its striking colour. It was a beautiful sight, and one that she could have watched for a while if she wasn't so conscious of where she stood.

Emily pressed the doorbell and bit her thumbnail as she waited. A child opened the door, a dusting of flour on her bright pink T-shirt and goo on her fingertips. Her hair was a similar colour to the woman on the horse. She stared at Emily open-eyed and open-mouthed, showing two new top teeth. Emily was about to say hello when the door opened fully. Dalloway was suddenly standing there, an expression of welcome falling from his face as he saw his visitor. He stared at her, amazed.

'Isobel, please return to the kitchen,' he quietly instructed, his voice mild.

The child hid her face in his side. He patted her hair. 'Be a good girl and go back to the kitchen. We'll finish the cakes soon.'

Emily watched her walk away and was then left to face Dalloway alone. 'What brings you to my home, Nurse Jacobs?' he asked bluntly, not disguising his surprise.

Through dry lips Emily managed to speak. 'I'm sorry for turning up like this, but I really need to talk to you.'

'Well, you'd better come in then,' he said stiffly.

Emily followed him into the hallway then through an archway to an enormous space, the original size of the barn still obvious. The flagstone floor seemed to go on for ever. Stone walls rose to a height that would be impossible to reach unless you were a wall climber or had a very long ladder. A tapestry, the likes of which you would expect to see in a museum, hung on one of the walls. It was big enough to cover a modest sitting room floor. A wood burning stove was at the far end of the room, its flue rising up the wall, again drawing the eye to the height of the room. Down the end of the room where she stood, a gallery was approached by an oak staircase, the wood shiny and spotless. She held her breath and waited. It felt strange to see the surgeon in his own surroundings. He appraised her and she could see that he too was waiting.

'I'm sorry to disturb you at home, but I thought it better to talk to you here than at the hospital.'

'Would you mind telling me how you know where I live?' His tone was clipped, and she felt heat rise in her face.

'I . . . umm . . . Your nanny gave me your address. She wanted me to speak to you,' she finished lamely.

'Maria? Maria gave you my address?'

She nodded.

He looked shocked. 'You'd better sit down.'

He stepped towards three massive settees, artfully arranged to face the floor-to-ceiling window which gave an unobstructed view of the land beyond.

Emily was wondering if she could ask for the loo; nerves were making her want to pee.

'Would you like a drink?' he asked.

'A glass of water, please. And—'

'Up the stairs, first door you come to,' he said, pointing up at the gallery, clearly guessing her need. 'The downstairs loo presently has a plumbing problem.'

After using the loo, she splashed her face with cold water and used his fluffy brown towel to dry herself. She felt sick with nerves. In the mirror, her face looked ashen, her blue eyes staring wide. The armpits of her white cotton shirt were damp with sweat and she wished she'd worn darker clothing. The day had built to sticky heat with a storm in the air and she hoped rain would come soon. On the landing she could hear the sound of drilling coming from the floor below and guessed it was the plumber at work.

Dalloway was placing a tray on a low table as she came down the stairs. A glass of water set beside teacups, a teapot, small jug and bowl of sugar. With her attention fixed on him, Emily nearly slipped in her leather-soled sandals and grabbed hold of the banister.

Dalloway looked up. 'Those stairs are slippery in the wrong footwear. You're better off in bare feet.'

Emily walked over to him and sat down, and Dalloway placed the glass in front of her. Emily picked it up and took a long swallow and said, 'Thank you.'

He poured tea for them both and placed a cup and saucer near her. He then sat down on the opposite couch and waited for her to speak. She was reminded of Eric and wished for a moment that he was there to support her.

'So why did Maria give you my home address?'

She took a deep breath. 'I think something irregular has happened at the hospital.'

He blinked and pulled his head back sharply. 'Really?'

'I think that something has happened to a patient that you may not know about. A young woman. The woman who was in the bed beside me when I was a patient. I think it's possible that she may have been Maria's niece, Katka.'

He made a harsh sound and pulled out of his seat, half rising. 'Good grief!'

'Please! Wait!' Emily rose as well. 'Please, just hear me out.'

He teetered for a moment, then flopped back, his hands raised in resignation.

She pushed on before she lost courage. 'I saw a woman in the bed beside me. She was small, dark-haired, maybe foreign. I talked to her before I went down to theatre. In the night I was disturbed by noise. There were people, or certainly at least one person, around her bed trying to resuscitate her. One of them gave me something to put me back to sleep, and despite what

Sister Barrows said, it wasn't Diazepam. It doesn't work that fast. I was asleep in seconds. The next day, as you know, I was told I had been the only patient in that room and even though I knew it to be untrue, I was willing to think nothing more about it until I found this.'

From her bag she took out the tissue-wrapped bracelet and unfolded it for him to see. 'I found this on the floor on my first shift back, the night Mr Davies' patient Mrs Harris had to go back to theatre and we were putting the room back in order afterwards.'

Dalloway looked at the bracelet without touching it. 'Carry on.'

'When we had shared the room, I had seen this bracelet on her wrist, so I picked it up, put it in my pocket and took it home with me. The next night I intended to show someone, perhaps Sister Barrows, but then we had a chat and she reassured me that I was the only patient in that room. And then a more logical reason came to me as to why I had seen another patient; I should never have been in that room in the first place. I was put there by mistake. So the woman I saw there could also have been put there by mistake. Two patients briefly meeting in the same room because of a mix-up of rooms. I was prepared to believe this is what happened until I met Maria.'

'So what you're saying is you now think the patient you saw beside you was Maria's niece?'

Emily swallowed hard and nodded. 'Something has happened to her.'

Dalloway leaned back and covered the lower half of his face for a moment. He sighed heavily into his cupped hands, his eyes fixed on her in despair. 'Please don't tell me you've told Maria this? That this is the reason Maria has been avoiding me the last few days? My god, that poor woman . . .' He stared at Emily in disbelief. 'She's been with us since Isobel was a baby! And now she's thinking that I've had something to do with her niece going missing?'

Emily shook her head in denial. 'No! Not at all. She just wanted me to talk to you. To tell you what I had seen.'

'And you did, perfectly well, and now Maria has flown home today to support her family, no doubt telling them that Katka has gone missing from the hospital.'

'But I didn't say that. I didn't tell her that's what happened.'

'But she now thinks it, doesn't she? So you must have given her reason to believe it.'

Emily was trembling. This was not the way she was hoping this meeting would go. 'She said Katka went missing on the thirtieth. The same day I was a patient there. Surely there must be a connection?'

'Other than the one you've already given yourself? The brief meeting of two women. You have no proof it was Katka even if it might be true. Katka may well have come into the hospital, looking for me, and wandered into your room and you saw her. It doesn't have to mean any more than that.'

'But she's missing, Mr Dalloway. How do you account for that? I believe something has happened, other than this simple explanation.'

'So why bother coming to me?' he snapped back. 'Why not just go straight to the police? Because surely you must think that I am also involved? I think we need to pause on this.' He stood up, rubbing the back of his neck, his shoulders tense with agitation. She realised it was the first time she had seen him out of scrubs or a suit. The casual clothes, jeans and pale blue shirt looked tailored and expensive. She was in the house of someone who was used to the finer things, someone successful and prominent, and he was now walking around thinking about what she had just told him – probably wondering whether to call the police.

Eventually, he turned. 'I think I'm going to have to speak to my lawyer. I can't have you thinking something so outrageous has happened at the hospital. Allegations like this will ruin the reputation of the hospital.'

She stared at him stunned, her lips tremulous. 'Can't you just check it out?'

'Check out what, exactly?' he all but shouted.

She shrugged, agitated. 'Ask the staff what they know. I'm sure Sister Barrows knows something.'

'Ask them what, Nurse Jacobs? Has a patient gone missing from our hospital? Oh, and by the way, not just any patient, but my daughter's nanny's niece? Because that happens all the time, doesn't it? A patient you personally know disappearing.' He saw her eyes shoot open, saw her pain and winced. 'Sorry, I didn't mean to remind you of your sister.'

An ache pressed her eyes and she closed her lids to ease them. 'She's never out of my mind,' she said with a teary smile. 'Look, I'll go. I should never have come here. I'm sorry I did.'

'You're a good nurse, Nurse Jacobs.' He tutted mildly. 'I can't keep calling you that while you're in my home. You're a good nurse, Emily, and I can see that you're upset.' He slowly shook his head. 'I really don't know what to say to you. You do know how far-fetched this all sounds? How very disturbing?' He saw her discomfort. 'What I'm saying, and without trying to offend you, is simply that I cannot believe something "irregular" like this has happened, or that it is in any way connected to Katka going missing. I don't know what you saw, Emily, but I'm not happy that Maria is now involved in this. I have no doubt that her niece will turn up and this will have caused her a great upset for no good reason. What I do think, and I'm sorry if this sounds harsh, is that your sister's disappearance has left you susceptible to getting caught up in other mysteries such as this.'

She gave a hesitant nod.

He waited for her to look at him. 'And I have known Sister Barrows a good number of years, and I cannot stress enough that this woman will not have been involved in anything underhand, let alone something as serious as what you're suggesting. I will not be questioning her. Understand that.'

She nodded more firmly this time, relieved that they were nearing the end of their conversation. She was exhausted, and just wanted to be out of his home as soon as possible. Seconds trickled by, the silence deafening. Then he spoke.

'What's she like, this sister of yours?' His tone was gentle.

Emily swallowed hard, her hand seeking the comfort of the chain around her neck. People so often avoided the subject. They hated mentioning Zoe's name for fear of reminding her of her disappearance.

'Wilful, up to all sorts, wants to save the planet and every animal and child with it. Loving, spiteful at times. Selfish when she wants her own way. She has a bit of everything in her.'

He sat down on the arm of the couch. 'You're close.'

She nodded. 'Very. More than most sisters.'

'Emily, I'm not playing psychologist here. I can only imagine what you've been through, which is a great deal. It would not be any wonder that your mind plays cruel tricks on you. It doesn't make you any less capable as a nurse or as a person. It just makes you more vulnerable. Susceptible.'

Emily stared at him, knowing the direction his thinking was taking, knowing Eric already thought something similar. She pulled on the chain around her neck, her fingers twisting it tighter in agitation.

'What's that you're fiddling with?' he asked kindly.

She reached into the neck of her blouse and pulled out the silver chain which held a silver pendant shaped like an inverted comma. 'Yin Yang necklaces that fit together. Zoe had them inscribed with the word "Sisters". Hers has the last letter missing, though. The inscriber didn't leave enough room.'

He nodded as if he knew something. 'A special piece of jewellery, then? Like I said, Emily, I'm not a psychologist. I'm just playing devil's advocate, helping you consider this from all angles.'

She nodded some more, feeling the weight of her head as tiredness took over.

'Rupert! Why is Isobel making cakes alone? Have you seen the mess she's—' The red-haired woman interrupting them abruptly stopped speaking as she saw Emily sitting there. 'Sorry, I didn't know we had visitors.'

'Jemma, this is Emily Jacobs. She works at the hospital and is visiting about a work-related situation. Emily, this is my wife, Jemma.'

Emily stood up to shake the woman's hand. 'Hello, I'm just about to leave.'

Jemma Dalloway looked at her quizzically. Up close the woman was rather beautiful, her skin unblemished and flushed from her ride. She was considerably younger than her husband, their child young enough to be his granddaughter. Maybe he had deliberately waited before starting a family, until his career was well and truly established. Another decade and Dalloway would be nearing the end of his career and his young family would want for nothing. The woman's deep brown eyes were probing Emily's. 'Gosh, it must be important to come and see Rupert at home?'

Emily was saved from answering as Dalloway spoke: 'Emily has been most helpful in bringing a problem to my attention.' He looked at Emily. 'Let me show you out. We'll catch up again in a few days.' In the hallway, he stopped at a slim side table and opened a drawer. He handed her a business card. 'My number, should you need to get in touch.'

As Emily walked back to her car she was no less reassured, and worried that Dalloway would phone his lawyer. Maria had come to her asking for help and she could now be in trouble for slander. Maria had gone back home to support her family, but her niece was still missing and despite what Dalloway had said,

Emily believed her niece would never return. How could she if it was her in that bed, her they were trying to resuscitate? Her bed empty next morning? Emily didn't believe she was missing. She believed she was dead.

Geraldine had no idea what this interview would bring and was almost tempted, for reasons that were beginning to unsettle her, to ask another colleague to sit in her place. It was four days since she had last seen Emily and she felt bad for the way she'd acted. She was not insensitive but she knew she'd hurt Emily with her sharpness, and Emily was beginning to concern her. She had checked out CCTV footage, got an officer to search for the woman Emily chased, but she hadn't told her the outcome. That the woman in the leather jacket she had run after had some resemblance in height and colouring but was ten years older than her sister. A full-face image of the woman proved beyond doubt that she was not Zoe Jacobs. Geraldine had thought of ringing Emily and she would have to in the next day or so, but she wanted to let the dust settle first; give Emily time to think things through. She'd tell her when this meeting was over. This unexpected request for an interview had come as a surprise, and for once Geraldine hadn't suggested they meet up at a coffee shop. She'd requested Emily come to the station. Geraldine had made the trip to Keynsham police station and had been told that Emily was now in one of the witness interview rooms. She had picked the location not for Emily's benefit, but her own, as she could walk it from her home just around the corner. Her own base, Concorde House in Emersons Green, was several miles down the road. She slipped on her jacket, pondering what was to come.

There was no sign of resentment in Emily's manner, but she looked nervous and Geraldine spotted the slight tremors in her fingers as she placed her hands on the desk. She said hello and joined her. The interview desk had been set next to a wall, with a recording device and monitor on it, which was linked to a data storage programme called Evidence Works. The equipment was positioned at the end of the desk so as not to obstruct the view of interviewer or interviewee.

'This will be a digital audio and video recording. I take it you wish this interview to be recorded?'

Emily gave a hesitant nod.

Geraldine pressed the relevant buttons and made sure everything was in order. She then gave the date, time, her name and rank. She asked Emily to state her name; then settled back and asked Emily why she wished to speak to the police.

'I wish to report a missing patient,' she said.

An hour later, in the quiet of the office she was using, Geraldine shrugged off her jacket and rolled her stiff neck. Her mind was whirring with everything she had just heard, trying to decide what to do and what to believe. In a million years, she hadn't expected to hear a story like that. But was it a story? At the very least she had to speak with this nanny person, drive to some high-up consultant's house and check out exactly who the nanny was. She would get her details and contact number from her employer, though she didn't relish turning up out of the blue with Emily's theory that someone in the hospital was involved with the disappearance of this nanny's niece, and it was most likely that she was dead.

Emily had given her the name Nina Barrows, the senior ward sister, as she had felt sure that Sister Barrows must know something. She had also told Geraldine that she had just come from the doctor's house, leaving Geraldine no option but to act sooner rather than later.

At ten o'clock at night, though, she was making no house calls. Tommy was unwell and she needed to get home, buy more Calpol on the way and relieve her husband for a few hours. He'd had a temperature and had thrown up and now wanted his mummy. Tomorrow morning would be soon enough. Emily had let three whole weeks go by before reporting it and this concerned Geraldine. Why had she waited so long? Waiting until tomorrow wasn't going to change anything and would give her time to form a plan. She would play back the recording and listen to Emily's story again, looking for any holes in it.

The other thing she had to consider was that there had been no reporting of a missing patient from The Windsor Bridge Hospital. Which could possibly lend weight to Emily's suspicion of some sort of cover-up. This was problematic for Geraldine. Was this missing person a figment of Emily's imagination? She was under enormous pressure. She'd gone back to work – much to Geraldine's surprise – had an operation only weeks ago, been knocked down by a car chasing a woman she believed to be Zoe, found a note from her missing sister and was convinced she was witness to a patient disappearing, whom no one else would admit to seeing. A police constable had been sent to question

Zoe's flatmates about having her key to Emily's flat but they'd denied having anything belonging to their missing friend, bar her mug in a kitchen cupboard and a top that one of them had borrowed. Geraldine would dearly love to have a chat with Eric Hudson and press him for an opinion. She would really like to ask him if she *should* be concerned about Emily.

She liked Emily, and she sympathised over this terrible ordeal that she was going through. But the best-case scenario was that Emily had fabricated this whole story, and if she *had*, Geraldine would come down hard on her, mental health issues or not. It was an offence to waste police time.

Chapter Eighteen

The woman who opened the door looked Geraldine up and down, inspecting her thoroughly. 'Oh,' she said.

She looked harassed, her movements jerky. Her red hair was scraped up in a loose bun, revealing her fine-boned features. She had one shoe on.

'Is everything alright?' Geraldine asked.

The woman waved her into the hallway. 'No, no, everything is fine. I was just expecting someone younger. The agency called you a girl.'

The woman opened a shoe box and hunted through it. 'For god's sake, I can't find anything. The house is a mess. I've had to cancel a dental appointment. Isobel hasn't even had her breakfast yet. I'm sorry, but she's really playing up this morning.'

'And you're . . . ?' Geraldine prompted.

The woman looked confused. 'Jemma Dalloway. Did they not tell you my name? God, this is such a mess. Please tell me they told you this wasn't just a day job. I don't see any cases with you. If so, I'll ring them now.'

Geraldine realised Jemma Dalloway had mistaken her for someone else. She would hang fire a little longer before she revealed who she was. 'No, they didn't tell me that.'

Jemma stood straight and planted her hands on her hips. 'Well, that just takes the biscuit. What am I supposed to do when you go home? I've got the horses to mind. This house. Isobel. And, of course . . .'

She stopped speaking and hung her head.

'I'm sorry, I can't stay,' Geraldine answered truthfully.

'It's not your fault,' Jemma replied. She closed her eyes briefly and sighed in frustration. 'Maria going home couldn't have come at a worse time.'

'Maria?'

'Isobel's nanny. My lifeline. My saviour.' She bit her lip and tried to smile. 'God, I'm selfish. The poor woman has gone home desperate.'

Geraldine opened her eyes wider to encourage her to keep talking.

Jemma suddenly seemed to realise she was telling some complete stranger her personal business. She tilted her head and her eyes swept over Geraldine again, taking in the business suit, the pale lilac shirt, her confidence, her direct eye contact.

'You didn't give your name?'

'Detective Inspector Geraldine Sutton from Avon and Somerset Police.' Geraldine pulled out her warrant card to show Jemma.

Her mouth opened. The penny dropped.

'Oh my god, I've been rattling on and you're not here from the agency at all. You've come to see Maria, haven't you?'

Geraldine gave a sound of disappointment.

'She's gone home. She said she was going to call the police. I didn't realise she had. Rupert feels so damned guilty. He should have driven her to the airport and put her on the plane. We both feel guilty.'

'Maria didn't tell us anything.' Again, Geraldine decided to stick with the truth.

'Oh dear, her English gets worse when she's stressed. And she's worse again on the phone. Her niece Katka didn't get on her flight. Rupert was going to take her to the airport. He was going to finish work early. Katka went shopping in Bath and then met him at the hospital, but then he had an emergency to deal with. He's a surgeon. He called her a taxi instead and left her to make her own way. We feel so bad because her English is non-existent. And she's so young. We should have let Maria take her. We're waiting to hear from Maria to see that *she* got home alright. She should have called by now.'

Geraldine was becoming more interested by the minute. Maybe there was something to Emily's story after all. It seemed that there was indeed a missing young woman.

'What was Katka doing here?' she asked.

Jemma dragged her fingers through her hair. 'She was mainly here to visit her aunt. But probably to see if she liked it here. We told Maria she should learn to speak English.'

Geraldine was now thinking she would have to speak to Rupert Dalloway. Get him to give his account of the situation.

The phone on the hall table suddenly let out a piercing ring. A young girl came running into the hallway, her hair tangled and loose, wearing her pyjamas.

Jemma stopped the girl just in time before she picked up the handset. She admonished her silently by pressing a firm finger to her own lips.

'Hello, Jemma Dalloway speaking.'

From where she stood Geraldine could hear the excited voice of a woman speaking rapidly.

'Slow down,' Jemma said. 'Speak slowly.'

The voice became softer, the dialogue slowed down. A serious expression covered Jemma's face. 'Oh dear, I'm sorry to hear that, Maria. The police are here now asking about Katka.' Jemma looked over at Geraldine and raised a finger. 'Katka's still missing. Would you like to talk to Maria?'

Geraldine shook her head. 'No, that's fine. You talk to her.'

Jemma carried on talking, nodding a few times as if her caller could see her. 'I understand. Well, we'll just have to make do until you can come back.'

The child was jumping up and down, agitated, clearly understanding the gist of the conversation. She was older than Tommy by at least two years; Tommy had just turned four but the girl's behaviour reminded Geraldine of his when he was unhappy. In fact, her behaviour was not so different to Danny, her two-year-old, though he behaved better than his older brother.

'Calm down, Isobel,' Jemma said, as the call ended. 'Maria will be back soon.'

The doorbell rang and as Geraldine was nearer to the door, she opened it. A young, pretty woman stood there; smiling. She wore a fawn dress with a white collar, brown laced shoes, white gloves and a brown hat on her head, Mary Poppins-style, with the letter N crested on a hat badge. A Norland Nanny. She had a suitcase at her side. 'Hello, I believe you're expecting me. I'm Felicity.'

Geraldine waved goodbye to Jemma Dalloway, perturbed that the matter now had to be dealt with seriously. It had not been a wild goose chase, and now she had to consider if there was more truth to Emily's story. She fervently hoped not and that this niece was merely missing. She hoped Emily had taken this nanny's concern over her missing niece and had fitted it to something she only thought she had witnessed. The only way to prove what had happened was to find the niece. And find her fast. Otherwise Geraldine was going to have an investigation on her hands that was the stuff of nightmares. 'For fuck's sake,' she said under her breath as she made her way to her car. Emily certainly kept her busy.

Chapter Nineteen

Emily slept poorly. All night her mind had been going over the interview with Geraldine. She had walked out of the police station feeling fragile, exposed, out on a limb. Geraldine had offered no reassurance that she had done the right thing by speaking to the police. She had acted officially, giving no hint of what she thought of the situation. Emily felt sick with nerves.

At work she felt worse. At every corner she turned she had expected to see Dalloway or Barrows. Having spoken about the two of them to Geraldine last night, she felt sure the secret was stamped on her face. But she made herself go to work for one reason – she had to find proof that Katka had been a patient there. Maria's testimony that she'd come to the hospital, and Emily having seen her, was not going to be enough evidence that something had happened to her. Proof had to be found.

She had come in earlier hoping to look at the operating lists for the day she herself was a patient, hoping to find Katka recorded as one, but there were too many staff around, even at that hour, to risk looking. She wondered why Katka had been a patient in the first place. Had she become ill while waiting to go to the airport? Had she been brought into the hospital, even though it was private, because it was the nearest one? And if so, why hadn't anyone informed Dalloway? Had a different doctor attended to her? She had no answers to these questions. She felt wrung out. Her shift was nearly ending and she was yet to come up with an idea about where she would find this proof.

The emergency call bell sounded and she froze momentarily before pelting out of the treatment room, her eyes scanning the corridor. The light outside Neil Jeffries' room was flashing. Mrs Jeffries was standing in the doorway, frantic. 'What's happened? He was asleep when I left him.' She grabbed Emily's arm to get an answer.

'Move out of the way, Mrs Jeffries. I need to get to your husband.'

'I had only been gone for five minutes,' she screeched.

Shelly was already in the room, moving locker and visitor's chair away from the bed. Neil Jeffries' lips were swollen and his tongue protruded from his mouth. He was wheezing as he tried to draw in air.

'Shelly, Grab the crash trolley, he needs adrenaline *now*, and put out an arrest call,' said Emily.

While she waited she placed an oxygen mask over his face and turned the flow up high. She pressed the start button on the monitor to get his vital signs. His lips were blue and she worried they wouldn't get an airway in with so much swelling. The skin of his eyelids had ballooned. A rash had spread across his face and chest. Behind her she could hear Mrs Jeffries yelling for Mr Dalloway. 'Mr Dalloway. Anyone? I want someone here who knows what they're doing!'

As Shelly wheeled in the trolley, Emily gave orders. 'Put defib pads on his chest, Shelly. Do you know how?'

Shelly nodded.

Emily had already looked at the man's bare chest. He needed some of the hair gone to allow the skin to make contact with the pads. 'Shave his hair, you've seen it done. No messing. Just do it quick.'

Shelly got on with the tasks efficiently. There was no sign of the crash team and he was about to stop breathing. Emily prepared to insert an airway. She switched on the overhead lamp and shone it directly into the man's face. Pulling his lower jaw open, she immediately saw the back of his throat was occluded. She was not going to get an airway in. She heard the sound of running feet and looked up gratefully. Dalloway and Meredith rushed into the room.

'Anaphylaxis. His airway is occluded. I'm not sure whether inserting a tube is going to be possible.' She said this last thing to Meredith as it would be her who would be managing his airway.

'What's happening to him?' Mrs Jeffries wailed.

'Something has caused him to have a severe reaction.' Dalloway answered. 'We're going to treat him now.'

'What did you give him?' Her tone was accusing and Emily didn't need to look at the woman to know the question was directed at her.

Instead she spoke to Shelly. 'Shelly, take Mrs Jeffries to the waiting room. Make her some tea and stay with her, please.'

'I'm not leaving. I don't trust you,' the woman protested.

Shelly intervened and cajoled the woman away. Meredith had already inspected the airway. Dalloway had just given intravenous adrenaline. 'I'm going to have to do a tracheotomy,' Meredith said. Dalloway and Emily immediately prepared a station. After removing items from the top of the bedside locker and placing them on the floor, they used the surface to open a sterile dressing pack. Emily opened size six sterile gloves. Dalloway opened a sterile scalpel, sterile forceps and a narrow airway. In the bottom drawer a small bottle of iodine was found and he trickled brown liquid directly onto the patient's skin. Speed was of the essence. There was no time for correct procedure. Meredith doused her hand with alcohol rub before pulling on the gloves. She tutted. 'Could have picked a bigger size.'

Dalloway donned a pair also. He placed a finger on the man's throat, feeling for the place where he would cut. 'Emily, can you change that suction tube to a Yankauer and get ready to apply suction.' Emily pulled one from the crash trolley and went to the wall behind the bed and changed the flexible catheter for a more rigid, wider tube that would suck fluid faster.

'You want me to cut and you insert the airway?' he asked Meredith.

'Good plan. Ready when you are.'

The three stood together as close as they could get without hindering each other's part in the procedure.

Dalloway picked up the scalpel and sliced the blade an inch down the man's throat. He took the forceps and spread the first layers of skin. He drew the blade back though the bloody line, making a hole in the man's throat and said, 'Suction.'

Emily cleared the blood fast and Meredith inserted the narrow tube. Cut, suction, insert. It was done.

Emily breathed a sigh of relief. Neil Jeffries' eyes flickered open and she spoke to him. 'You're doing fine. You have a small tube in your throat temporarily to help you breathe. Don't speak. Just rest now.'

He blinked and tears trickled down his temples. He had been afraid. Emily gave a small nod to let him know she understood.

Over the next hour his condition stabilised. He was given more drugs: hydrocortisone, chlorpheniramine, salbutamol, which would open up his airway, reduce the swelling and relieve the symptoms and he improved considerably. He would go to theatre to have the opening in his neck sutured closed, but not today.

Mrs Jeffries had not yet come back to the room. Dalloway and Meredith were with her letting her know how her husband was.

Meredith now came back into the room, her expression serious.

'What's up?' Emily asked, thinking she was going to have to speak to Mrs Jeffries. She had no idea why her patient had had a reaction. It was nothing she had given. He had received only his prescribed medications, which he'd been on the last few days and would have reacted to by now if he was allergic to any of them.

'The police are here.'

Emily stiffened. She didn't wait to ask Meredith who or what they were there for. She just wanted to hide.

Her heart was pounding as she made her way along the corridor. Geraldine was standing at the end. The door of the waiting room opened and Mrs Jeffries stepped out and immediately saw her. 'I don't want you anywhere near my husband. You're a god-damn liability! First you can't remember if you gave him his tab-lets, and then you give him something that almost killed him. I've just told Mr Dalloway that you should be struck off. If I see you go near my husband again, I shall remove him from this hospital.'

With her voice and words ringing in her ears, Emily made the last few steps as if walking through mud. Her legs felt leaden after the verbal attack. She was almost hyperventilating by the time she reached Geraldine.

'You need to sit down,' Geraldine said, and from nowhere she produced a plastic chair, right there in the corridor. Emily almost fell onto it.

'Why have you come here to see me?' she gasped frantically.

Geraldine shook her head. 'I haven't, Emily. I'm here to see Mr Dalloway.'

When her breathing steadied, Emily got up off the chair and excused herself. Slowly she made her way to the waiting room, relieved to see that it was now empty. From the water cooler she took a paper cup, filled it to the brim and drank it back in one go. Her eyes stretched wide, and her mouth opened and closed as she gulped in air. She felt cold and clammy and her stomach was doing somersaults. She only just made it to the plastic waste-paper bin before she threw up. Dalloway was being interviewed and she was terrified he would say that she had made it all up.

Chapter Twenty

The office was blessedly cool and Geraldine felt instant relief at not being clammy. As the surgeon settled behind his desk. Geraldine remarked on the situation she'd witnessed. 'Looks like you had an unhappy customer on your hands.'

He grimaced. 'Indeed. Mrs Jeffries can be a tad volatile when she's displeased. But in fairness she has just witnessed her husband gasping for his life.'

'She seemed to be blaming the nurse.'

He shrugged. 'I have no idea what caused it, to be honest. We've only just got him out of the woods and I haven't yet had a chance to investigate the situation.'

Geraldine gave a guilty look. 'And now I'm taking up your time.'

'The receptionist said you'd like to speak to me quite urgently.'

'Well,' she shrugged, 'urgent as in quite quickly. I don't know whether what I want to speak to you about is an urgent matter or not. That's why I'm here.'

He settled his elbows on the arms of his chair and clasped his hands, his attention focused.

'I've been out to your home this morning, Mr Dalloway.'

'My home?' He looked shocked.

She raised a hand. 'Yes, nothing to be alarmed about. Your wife and daughter are both fine and Mrs Dalloway was very helpful.'

'Dr Dalloway,' he said.

'Sorry?'

'My wife, she's a doctor too.'

Geraldine thought this irrelevant right now, but if he wished to correct her that was fine by her. She wondered if his wife was a GP seeing as he addressed her as Dr Dalloway. She knew that only surgeons, especially senior ones and consultants, were addressed as Mr/Miss/Ms/Mrs. It was because of some centuries-old tradition in the medical world. Until her own obstetrician explained it to her she'd previously wondered why Jac Naylor in *Holby City* was always addressed as Miss Naylor. 'Right, well in that case, Dr Dalloway was most helpful in explaining about your nanny's missing niece.'

He leaned forward, sitting up straight. 'Sorry, you've lost me. You went to my home because of Maria's niece? Has she been found?'

Geraldine shook her head. 'Not that I'm aware of. I believe Maria has arrived safely home, but that her niece has still failed to return.'

Dalloway was frowning. 'That is a worry. So what's happened, did Maria contact you, or the police from her country?'

Geraldine kept her eyes on his face. 'No. Maria didn't inform us. A statement was given yesterday evening from a member of your staff saying that a patient went missing from this hospital three weeks ago, and the belief is that this missing woman is the niece of your nanny.'

He looked stunned. 'Good grief. So after she left me she went to see you? I'm afraid I know exactly who made such a statement. Nurse Jacobs. And now she's well and truly muddied the waters. Poor Maria. She must be going out of her mind with worry. First let me tell you – sorry, who did you say you were?'

'Detective Inspector Geraldine Sutton with Avon and Somerset Police.'

He nodded. 'Thank you. Well let me tell you, Detective Inspector Sutton, that on both accounts neither is true. We most definitely have not had a patient go missing, and Katka was never a patient here.'

'Is there any way you can prove that?'

He nodded again. 'I sincerely hope so. You can talk to everyone who worked here that day, that week even. I can show you the entire operation lists for that week. I can have every member of staff who looked after Nurse Jacobs on the day of her operation brought in here so that you can question them. In particular, I can bring in the anaesthetist who looked after Nurse Jacobs and the senior ward sister, Sister Barrow. Sister Barrow has been having some concerns about Nurse Jacobs since she had her operation. To be honest with you, we really wish we'd known who she was when she started here.'

Geraldine was surprised. 'So you didn't know her sister is Zoe Jacobs?'

'No,' he said quietly. He palmed his hands together to make his point. 'Look, I can't tell you where Katka has gone. And I feel entirely responsible that she hasn't yet returned home, as it should have been me who drove her to the airport and made sure she got her plane, but an emergency came up and I couldn't leave the hospital. I called a taxi to take her instead. I can prove this, too. And surely the airport can prove if she checked in and got on a flight or was even at the airport that day?' There was a note of hope in his voice.

'Why haven't you reported Katka missing?'

His expression was frank, as if he were expecting the question. 'Because I don't believe she is. I'm sorry if that sounds blasé, but in the four weeks she spent with us she proved to be a bit of a free spirit. Maria was constantly checking to see where she was when she didn't return at the time she had said she would. One thing I know is that she wasn't looking forward to going home. I wish I could tell you more, but I can't think of anything else that will help. I do want this matter cleared, though. The Windsor Bridge Hospital is still in its infancy, and its reputation is at stake. I'm sorry if that sounds pompous, but something like this hitting a newspaper will be ruination. So please, ask your questions, check anywhere you want to in this hospital. I only ask that you do so discreetly.'

'If it's OK, I will speak to other members of staff. Is Sister Barrows on duty?'

'She isn't,' he said. 'But she's here at the moment for a meeting. I'll go and find her. You can use this office.' He stood up and was at the door before speaking again. 'Emily Jacobs is an excellent nurse. Highly trained and competent, despite the misgivings of that patient's wife. In the short while she's been here she's proved that. I cannot imagine what she has gone through, and is still going through, but I do believe in all sincerity that she is unwell, and that worries me if she's to continue working here.'

While Geraldine waited for the senior nurse to arrive she was having similar thoughts. The Windsor Bridge Hospital was a far cry from the sinister description Emily had given in her statement.

First, it didn't feel like a hospital, but rather a luxury hotel, and was a vast improvement on other hospitals that she'd visited. She'd be happy to come here as a patient, if she could afford it. Before she left she'd ask Dalloway to email her his nanny's details. She would have to contact the woman to get her niece's details. The surgeon said Maria was constantly checking the whereabouts of her niece. She would therefore have a mobile number, which would be a good starting place at tracking her down.

Eric was alarmed by the state of Emily when he saw her. Her face was chalk white and she had not stopped trembling since she sat down. He was not a medical doctor, but he recognised shock when he saw it.

He placed the glass of water in her hands and encouraged her to drink. He let her sit there, quietly, and waited.

Several minutes passed before she seemed to become aware of her surroundings, her eyes looking around his office in surprise as if wondering how she got there.

'I called you, didn't I?'

'Yes. You called from work and came here by taxi.'

She shook her head. 'I don't even remember getting into a taxi.' She looked down at her uniform. 'I didn't even change.' She stared at the floor around her chair. 'Did I bring my bag with me?'

'No.'

'Well, how did I pay for the taxi?'

'I did, Emily. I came and helped you out of it.'

She shook her head slowly, her voice bitter. 'This is like the beginning all over again. Forgetting how I got to places and suddenly finding myself there. I once stood in a queue in Sainsbury's with a trolley full of food that I would never normally buy and I put everything on the conveyor belt, watching each item roll along being priced and beeped. Beep, beep. When it came to the end the assistant asked me how I would like to pay as I just stood there. I said, I don't know. I haven't got any money.'

Eric remembered the episode. Zoe had only been missing for a matter of weeks and when not out searching the streets for her sister, Emily had ended up in places she could never recall going to. She had taken train journeys to desolate stations and on one occasion had sat there all day until a passenger, an off-duty policeman, noticed her and put her on a train back to Bath. She had gone to nightclubs, and as a single, attractive woman she was naturally noticed. She was noticed more when she wore pyjamas and slippers, and a call was put out to the police. She was vulnerable and should not be out alone. Eventually such behaviours ceased and she carried on as normally as possible. Mainly by keeping busy, looking after her parents and searching for Zoe. In recent months she had made great strides, and Eric had begun to get to know the real Emily Jacobs, the one he had become fond of, who had a sharp wit and a warmth and inner strength that had been stripped from her in the early days. She had risen out of the depths of depression and come back fighting, her sole intention to return to the job she loved. Looking at her now he was transported back to those early days and felt what she felt. It was like the beginning all over again.

'I went to see Geraldine Sutton last night. I gave a statement to the police. I reported that missing patient. And now she's at the hospital questioning Mr Dalloway, but they're not going to find any proof, Eric. And then she'll think I made it up. I think she thinks I've made it all up. She thinks I wrote the letter from Zoe. Only my prints are on the letter. But I saw Zoe. I chased her along the road and would have caught her if that car hadn't hit me. Everyone is conspiring, Eric. I went to Mr Dalloway's home and their nanny is no longer there. They're trying to make me think this is all in my head. You don't think that, do you?'

Eric was alarmed by what she was saying; particularly in her belief that she had seen Zoe. He was unable to give her the answer she wanted and wondered if he would have to refer her to a psychiatrist. Clearly things had escalated since their last appointment and a lot had happened. She was floored, by the look of her. She had clearly not heeded his advice. She had gone a step further and brought the matter to the police.

While he was qualified to treat her for mental and emotional suffering and offer psychotherapy, a psychiatrist was a medical doctor who could prescribe medication and who may unearth a physical cause. Emily had been doing very well until recently, but Eric could not ignore his concerns. If she was having psychotic episodes and hallucinations, then he had to consider the possibility of schizophrenia.

'Emily, I want you to see one of my colleagues.'

She looked at him and then seemed to stare through him. When her voice came it sounded hollowed out, empty of emotion. Slowly the shock of finding herself here was wearing off, and she was now alert to what he was saying. 'Very well, Eric. If that's what you want.'

He nodded. 'It's for the best, Emily. I'll get you an appointment as soon as possible. In the meantime, I'd like you to rest. Eat well and sleep well. Are you still taking Zopiclone to help you sleep?'

'Yes, unless I'm working early. They make me too sleepy otherwise.'

'Would you like me to call your parents, maybe have your mother stay with you tonight?'

She shook her head, glancing away. 'I'm staying at theirs tonight. It's already arranged.'

He was relieved. Her senses and emotions were not so impaired that she needed hospitalisation, but nonetheless he was reassured that she would not be alone.

As he put her into a taxi he felt a rare wave of frustration. She was his patient and she had been doing so well. He had imagined these sessions eventually ending and Emily resuming a normal life. He could not envision that any more. She was his patient and he had failed to make her well.

Nina Barrows was left feeling disturbed after being interviewed by the police. She had never been interviewed by them before, and though it was more of an informal chat, she felt as if she'd been picked over, put under a microscope. Geraldine Sutton had asked her several questions in relation to Emily Jacobs' admission and Nina had answered as best she could without breaking patient confidentiality. She confirmed that as a patient Emily Jacobs had a nightmare post-operatively and was given something to settle her during the night, and woke the next day believing there had been another patient in the bed beside her. Nina Barrows was disturbed, though, because she really couldn't be sure of exactly what Emily had seen. She needed to speak to Mr Dalloway, have him reassure her that there was nothing to worry about. Except that she *had* seen a young woman that day fitting the description Emily had given, standing with a suitcase outside the hospital. And she had seen her come in.

Emily swallowed the half-glass of vodka neat. She then stepped into the shower and stood under the cold running water, shivering as every inch of her skin was drenched. She had been floored by every shock she had received today; punch-drunk to the point where she thought her head would explode. When she walked into her flat she had two choices: lie down and accept that she'd lost her mind, or convince the police, Eric and her colleagues that she hadn't. She didn't know whether it had been Katka in that bed beside her; now she only wanted to prove that she had seen *someone* in it. She no longer cared whether that someone was a visitor or a worker in the hospital that day, or whether the person's reason for being in Emily's room was because she was tired, unwell, in the wrong room or had simply got fucking lost on her way to the bathroom. Emily just wanted this whole business to go away. She would hunt this woman down if it was the last thing she did, and when she found her she would march her in front of everyone who had ever doubted her.

Stepping out of the shower she felt cold, and she welcomed the discomfort. She squeezed the bruise on her hip until she gritted her teeth. She was alive, more awake than she had been in a long time – and she was angry. In the space of a week people she counted on were showing other sides to their characters, like Geraldine, who had alarmed her when she had turned up on the ward like that. Why hadn't she at least given her warning that she was coming to speak to Dalloway? Given her the chance to make sure she wasn't there? She must surely realise the difficult situation she was in. And Eric, with his oh-so-quick decision to refer her to one of his 'colleagues'. Yeah, right. Why didn't he just come out and say psychiatrist? She had played along with his suggestion, slipped out the lie that she was staying at her parents' house. As if she would. Just like she had no intention of seeing a psychiatrist. She would not be labelled something she was not. She would fight this alone, and when she was done she would walk away – maybe to California, once she found Zoe – and start again.

Slicking back her wet hair, her blue eyes stared back, determined, from the mirror. She had a plan, the only one she could think of, as a last-ditch attempt to prove that this woman existed.

Chapter Twenty-One

She stepped into the lift and held the door as Shelly called out. 'They called you in tonight as well? I'm only working a twilight shift. Eight till midnight, on account of working this morning.' She scrutinised Emily as the lift rose to the next level. 'You look gorgeous. I knew red lipstick would suit you.'

Emily smiled. She had worn makeup for a good reason. 'No. I'm off tonight, like you should be. I only came in to collect my bag. I left without it after I finished work.'

'Poor you, having to come back. I imagine you forgot it after the upset of dealing with that cow, Mrs Jeffries.'

'Hey-ho, these things happen.'

In the changing room she quickly collected her bag, nodding at Shelly sympathetically as she as quickly departed. 'Have a good shift, won't you?' she called as she left.

Walking back down the corridor, she pushed open the door to the stairs, making her way down to the floor below. The hospital had a security guard at night and she wanted to track him down. She knocked on the closed door and it was opened by a tall, dark-haired man in his late thirties. The muscles in his arms caused the sleeves of his shirt to stretch taut. He smiled. 'What brings you to my door?'

Emily sauntered into the small office space. She had seen him looking at her and before tonight had ignored him. His name was Gary.

'Hello, Gary, I have a teeny favour to ask you.' She pulled a hopeful face.

'Is that so?' he asked, perching on the edge of his desk, his legs splayed, arms crossed in the manner of a man confident of his own attractiveness.

'Uh, huh. I need to check something. You see, I was a patient here three weeks back. On June the thirtieth. Do we keep CCTV for that long?'

He nodded. 'We do.'

'Oh, good. You see, I think a patient stole something from me and I can't accuse anyone without proof. My job would be on the line if I did that.'

He made a sound of disgust. 'That takes the P. You look after them, then they do that to you. It's usually us lot accused of things like that.'

She murmured agreement. 'I know. You see why I need your help.'

'Leave it with me. I'll soon find your thief.' He stood up and reached for his uniform jacket. He took out a hip flask, untwisted the lid and poured a measure. 'Here, you're off duty, aren't you? You look like you need a drink. Get that in you.'

She took the lid cautiously and sniffed.

'It's only vodka. For medicinal purposes, of course. You never know when you're going to come across someone in distress.'

She cringed inwardly at this display of machismo. The confident look in his eyes made her uncomfortable. He must have thought he was well in with her to reveal this behaviour.

She sipped and then slugged it back.

He put on his jacket and she realised he was not staying. 'Are you not going to look now?'

He shook his head. 'I can't just yet. I have my rounds to do.'

'I could look if you put it on for me. I'm good with technology. Then I could wait here till you come back and show you if I find the person. I've got nowhere to rush off to.'

He smiled to himself and rubbed the side of his face, weighing up the options. Turning around to the desk, she moved to his side and saw the screen on his monitor. It was split into sixteen squares to show multiple live feeds, images of various parts of the hospital in each square. She could see the corridors on the first and second floors, the corridors of the four wards, the entrance foyer and the car park. 'We keep video footage on here. It's easier to check back, not that we ever do. I've been here for two years and I've only ever been asked to look back on something once. That was a theft as well. One of the cleaners pilfering cleaning products. They carted stuff out every night till management cottoned on. He could have opened a shop with the amount of stuff he had taken. Maybe he did.' He laughed.

Emily continued to smile as she waited impatiently, while he tapped away at the keyboard, for him to find the file for the date she needed. She relaxed when the screen flickered with video footage of the corridor to Allen Ward and she saw the time and date in the upper right corner. 'Thank you, Gary. I'm so grateful.'

He paused the footage. 'It's not the clearest image but you can tell who's who. There's no sound, though. Just images.' He squeezed her shoulder. 'Well, keep my seat warm and I'll be back,' he called, doing a corny imitation of Arnold Schwarzenegger.

She sighed with relief as he left and then sat down in his seat, her eyes fixed on the screen. She pressed play and soon she was transported back to the day of her operation. Images of Shelly, Barrows, Dalloway and Meredith appeared every so often as they walked along a corridor at various times, sometimes carrying things or pushing trolleys. She noticed Shelly hoick up her bra strap occassionally as it slipped down her arm. She saw the cleaner vacuuming with a cordless Henry. And then she saw herself coming back from the bathroom. She had just put on her theatre gown and was holding her toiletry bag close to her chest, probably to hide the fact that she was braless. She stared at her own image and thought she looked like a waif, vulnerable, and different to the person who'd looked back at her in the mirror earlier. She watched herself disappear into the side room. This was the moment she would have first seen the other patient in the room. It would only be another minute and the girl would walk right out of the room. Emily jolted and hit pause. There she was. Her face looking right up at the camera, with her yellow top

with pink piping, her slight form and cloud of dark hair. There
was a glint of silver on her wrist. Emily had finally found her.

Her eyes fixed on the face and she touched a finger to the
screen, feeling a connection to this young woman. She looked so
young. What had she been doing there? Then a memory caused
her to close her eyes as she heard the sounds again. Sounds that
were like a captive bolt cattle stunner. Thunk, thunk. Two abrupt
muffled sounds hitting that small chest – not once but twice.
Her bed was empty the next morning. The linen fresh and new.

Her vision blurred. She had not imagined this woman. She
had not imagined what happened to her in the night. They had
told her that she was the only one in that room. They had told
her she had imagined it. Someone had lied, for one purpose only
– to cover up a death. Something had gone wrong and she was
sure that this young woman had died. Was it her? Was it Katka?
Either Dalloway or Barrows had to have known that she was
there. There was no way they couldn't. They had tried and failed
to make this disappear. Either they had colluded, or only one of
them was guilty.

It was time to let them know that she had not given up.
Dalloway had given her his mobile number and for the first
time, she called him.

His voice was clipped when he answered. 'Rupert Dalloway
speaking.'

'I can prove she existed,' she said.

She heard his intake of breath. 'Emily?'

'What happened to her, Mr Dalloway? Did she die and you
covered it up?'

'Emily, are you at the hospital?'

'Yes, and I've called the police,' she added, intending to do so the second the call ended.

'Emily, I think you need help.'

Emily held back tears. Why wouldn't he admit what was going on? Was he as innocent and genuine as he sounded? Someone was covering something up. 'I've seen her. The patient who was in the bed beside me. Maria's niece.'

'Where are you in the hospital, Emily?'

Emily had no intention of telling him. She didn't trust him. She wanted this video recording kept safe for the police to see.

'You're not well, Emily, you realise that.'

She laughed harshly. 'So you would have me believe. You're very clever, Mr Dalloway, and I'm sorry if you're not the guilty party in all of this, but someone is.'

'You're making mistakes, Emily. Look at today.'

With a shaking hand she moved the phone away from her ear and ended the call. Scrolling through her contacts, she stabbed Geraldine's name. The phone rang and rang and then she heard Geraldine speaking and quickly spoke over her, till she realised it was a recorded message. Desperate for it to finish, she hurriedly told her where she was and what she had found. 'Hurry, Geraldine. I've seen the missing patient. I found Katka. Dalloway already knows I'm here at the hospital.' She then hung up. Dalloway's words rang in her ears. Why had he said she was making mistakes? Because she had gone to the police and reported a missing patient? Because she was wrong to think it was Katka? Or did he mean something more pertinent to today? Did he think she had done something to Neil Jeffries, that she had in some way caused that reaction, that she was to blame?

She minimised the file on the screen. She moved the cursor down the list of channels in the grey bar to the file named Allen Ward, dated for today. The incident happened as she was due to finish her shift. She tapped the backward arrow of the recording, her finger ready to press play. The images changed fast. A few minutes later, she clicked. Mrs Jeffries was coming out of her husband's room. She turned left, heading for the visitor's bathroom, the dining room or perhaps the exit. She had said she was gone for five minutes, so unless she smoked, the first two options were more likely. On her heels, Shelly also exited the room, a cardboard urinal in her hands. Emily looked at the time of the recording. There were still a few minutes to go until the emergency call bell was pulled. The corridor stayed empty. Emily waited and less than a minute later, Mrs Jeffries came hurrying back along the corridor, checking over her shoulder twice. She reached the door and looked back again before quickly disappearing into the room. A moment later she peered out the door, her head inching slowly forward, before making a sudden dash, almost a run, back the way she had come. Halfway along the corridor, she stopped. She fiddled with the strap of her bag, opened it to check the contents, then zipped it closed and held it firmly to her side. She smoothed her hair and seemed to come to a decision. With her shoulders pulled back, she took a slow walk back to the room. At the doorway she looked in. Then, raising an arm in the air, she waved it over her head, opened her mouth and made screams that Emily couldn't hear.

Emily paused the video, her eyes fixed on the screen, her mind assembling everything she had just seen. It was Mrs Jeffries who had caused this problem. Her behaviour indicated that she'd been up to something very suspicious. She had done something to her husband and that made her a very dangerous woman. She clicked the file closed, her mind whirring. She needed to report this as soon as possible. Geraldine was her best bet. She'd show it to her at the same time as showing the one of Katka. Despite everything else she had to worry about, Emily could not let this woman get away with what she'd done. For now, though, she wanted out of this room before Gary came back. She wanted somewhere to hide.

Chapter Twenty-Two

Geraldine listened to the recorded message again on her mobile and stared at the far wall in her office in disbelief. Emily had just stated that she had found Katka. She had seen the missing patient. Which was a miracle, considering Katka was well over a thousand miles away, in her own home, her own country, Romania. Only minutes ago, with the help of Katka's surname, Geraldine had looked at Katka Vasile's Facebook photos. Ten minutes ago she had been speaking to the young woman on the phone. Geraldine had spoken to both her and her aunt for several complicated minutes, with much of the conversation being a repeat of the same apology, formed of few words: 'I sorry. I sorry for much worry. I home now. I safe. She sorry. She home now. She safe.' Katka Vasile could not be in two places at once. So whoever Emily had seen, it was not her, which led Geraldine to rise from her chair with a decision to make. She needed to bring Emily in for a stern chat. Or else get her the help she needed. This behaviour had to stop. She scrolled through her contacts until she found Eric Hudson's name. She was sure he would want to know that the police were concerned about his patient. She hoped so anyway, because she was becoming just a little weary of dealing with her.

The corridor was quiet. There was no sign of Gary or anyone else. Offices were locked for the night, doors were closed, all was quiet. Should she wait outside the hospital until Geraldine arrived? She needed to pee and at this time of night the changing room would be empty, the staff out on the wards. She could wait there. She made her way back up the stairs and realised her legs were shaking. Reaction had set in because of what she had found and set in motion. The enormity of what she was involved in struck home. Dalloway and Barrows' worlds were about to be rocked. She was being reckless. She shouldn't chance meeting them while alone. She should wait outside. Turning back down the stairs she saw the top of Gary's head moving upwards towards her. 'Fuck,' she said under her breath. She would have to take the lift instead.

Easing the door open, she peered into the corridor, looking both ways. There was no one in sight, so she made a run for the lift. Then a voice cracked the air like a whip. 'Stop right there, Nurse Jacobs.'

She staggered as if poleaxed, trying to stay on her feet and turning to face Barrows, her eyes startled and scared. Barrows looked at her accusingly.

'What are you doing here at this time of night?'

She turned a shoulder, showing her rucksack. 'Collecting this. I left it here after work.'

Barrows was not fooled. 'Shelly said you were here over an hour ago. She thought you were on duty. What have you been doing since then?'

Her thoughts scattered. 'I umm . . . I.'

'What are you up to, Nurse Jacobs, skulking around the hospital at night? Do I need to call security?'

Emily felt cornered. Was this a trick? Was Barrows in on it with Dalloway? Was she intending to imprison her until he arrived? She still had no idea which one she could trust, if either. She could outrun her, though.

'I asked you a question!'

'She's here because of me. It's my fault, Sister Barrows. I asked her to help with a patient.'

Emily swung her head round, her eyes latching onto Shelly.

Barrows was aghast. 'Wearing her civvies, you let her help you with a patient?'

Shelly gave a dismissive shrug. 'It's no big deal. The patient didn't care. He wanted out of a wet bed, it was as simple as that.'

Barrows was red in the face, her lips pressed tight. 'See yourself out, Nurse Jacobs,' she said coldly, before marching away.

Emily slumped forward and breathed in hard. 'Jesus Christ, this place is doing my head in. I'm not sure I can stick it much longer, Shelly.'

'Me neither,' Shelly replied.

She gazed at Shelly. She could trust no one. Not even her. Geraldine would arrive soon. Dalloway might arrive even sooner. She needed to get out of the place and keep watch for who arrived first. She shook her head and made towards the lift. Shelly stopped her in her tracks. 'You found her, didn't you?'

She turned in surprise.

'The patient. You've found her, haven't you?'

Emily advanced towards her. 'What do you know about it?'

Shelly shook her head. 'We can't talk here. Barrows will be back. I need a coffee and a vape. Let me grab some and I'll meet you in the changing room.'

Emily sank down on the floor and leaned back against her locker. She wondered if this was the last time she would be in this room. After tonight she could not imagine she would be welcomed back. Dalloway and Barrows were sure to be taken in for questioning. The best thing she could do was hand in her notice and make a clean break from the place. She could be back working in her old department as soon as next week. They were always desperate for staff.

She heard the door push open. Shelly came around the corner carrying two mugs. She handed one to Emily and pulled a red vaporiser from her pocket. Sucking hard, she blew a plume of smoke that a steam train would be proud of. Emily giggled.

'They'd see you coming a mile away smoking that thing.'

'At least it doesn't set off the fire alarms.'

She took another drag and blew up at the smoke detector defiantly.

'What do you know about this missing patient? What happened to her?'

'I don't know anything,' she said, staring Emily straight in the eye. 'God's honest truth, I don't.'

'But you said to me the next morning that you thought she'd been moved during the night.'

Shelly shook her head. 'I said something, but I'm not sure I said exactly that. My shift finished in the afternoon the day before. Another patient could have been admitted and discharged before I even came back on duty the next morning.'

'So what made you think I'd found her tonight?'

Shelly stared at her. 'You. I knew you were up to something. You've been here well over an hour. And Barrows got me suspicious as well. She asked me if you'd said any more about being in that room. About seeing that patient. She seemed ... worried. I guessed something was amiss when you asked about her before. I never actually saw her, but I had no reason to believe you didn't. Dalloway and Barrows were discussing you after you were discharged. She was trying to make out that you'd hallucinated, imagined a patient beside you.'

'She was there,' Emily said wearily. 'I just saw her on CCTV.'

'God, Emily, I wouldn't like to be in your shoes.'

She stood up. Geraldine must surely be here by now. Her legs felt like jelly. Her eyes were heavy. Reaction had certainly set in. She could sleep for a month. 'Don't worry about me, Shelly. The police are on their way.'

With Shelly behind her, she stepped out of the changing room. The atmosphere was quiet and still. The corridor suddenly seemed so much longer. She placed a hand against the wall to steady herself. She could hardly think straight. She looked back at Shelly – the care assistant was edging back into the room – and saw something in her eyes. 'Did you put something in my coffee?'

Shelly shook her head. 'You're imagining it,' she said. Emily made a grab for her, but the door closed in her face. Her eyes focused on the keypad, the numbers blurring. She needed to get out of there, to find Geraldine and get some fresh air. She slowly turned her head and saw them at the end of the corridor. Lined up, side by side, standing there – waiting. Geraldine, Dalloway and Barrows. Behind Geraldine were two uniformed police. She saw the confident manner in Dalloway and knew that they weren't there for him. They were there for her. She slumped to the ground and through the fogginess she saw them reaching for her, lifting her, felt a solidness beneath her as they lay her back down. The ceiling above was moving, each dimmed square of light passed over her. Voices reassured her. She closed her eyes. They had nothing to say that she wanted to hear.

'It's for the best,' she heard someone say. Best for who, she wanted to ask. For the first time in her life she wanted to die; to be taken away from the life she was living.

She let Zoe's image fill her mind and she reached out and touched her sister's face. 'Stay with me,' she whispered.

Chapter Twenty-Three

Geraldine felt sick. It had all happened so quickly, so efficiently. One minute Emily lay there collapsed on the corridor floor, the next she was being carted away on a trolley. The decision to take her away had come from this psychiatrist now stepping forward to speak to her. He was impressive, both in his physical appearance – very short-cut grey hair following the shape of his head, well-tailored suit fitting his tall frame – and in his intellectual air.

'We'll keep her in overnight. Dr Hudson is an AMHP, and an application to detain her has now been made. Approved Mental Health Professional,' the psychiatrist explained, misreading the query in her eyes.

'I know what it is,' Geraldine said. She was confused. She'd spoken with Eric Hudson less than an hour ago. He surely couldn't have decided on this without first seeing Emily? 'How come a decision was made so quickly? Did Eric Hudson make this happen?' She felt crass as she saw his stiff smile.

'It wasn't a quick decision. Dr Hudson had already referred Emily Jacobs to me this afternoon. She presented with symptoms that justified his decision to refer her. His understanding was that she was to stay with her parents tonight, but her mother has no knowledge of this arrangement. The important thing is that she's now in a place of safety. He's on his way here now, as I believe he received a call from the police to say she was here at the hospital acting irrationally. Are you intending to arrest her, or charge her with something?'

Geraldine frowned. 'That's true, I did call him. Though we only intended to question her. Or worst case, to detain her. I forgot you had a psychiatric wing here. Being private, I don't tend to think of it. But I suppose it's the best place for her to be right now.'

'The presence of the police can sometimes have a somewhat alarming effect.'

She prickled. Was he suggesting Emily had collapsed at the sight of the police? She had howled when they had lifted her off the floor, her arms feebly pushing them away. 'It was a precaution. Solely to keep her safe. We had no idea what condition we would find her in. She's going through some serious stuff, I hear?'

He gave a confirming nod. 'Dr Hudson has briefed me. Though I would prefer to form my own opinion for the meantime,' he added, as if she were about to launch into gossip.

Geraldine felt her chest flush with warmth. 'Of course,' she replied, rattled. 'As do I. As the officer in charge of the investigation of her missing sister, I've formed a close relationship with Emily.' Geraldine wanted to let him know that she was not a frumpy woman in her forties without a brain on the back end of a career. She had a brain too. She chased murderers, criminals, the undesirables.

He took her barb for concern. 'She will have a full assessment. You can rest assured. And now, if that's all, I'd like to check on my patient, see that she's settled.'

Geraldine watched him go. She couldn't get out of her mind the image of Emily standing there as she realised they were waiting for her and she felt . . . guilty. The look in Emily's eyes as she realised she was cornered was haunting.

In the corridor she saw Sister Barrows.

The woman looked formidable. Tall, straight and angular, with a face set rigid. Her eyes, though, showed something different: an inner turmoil.

'Very unpleasant business,' Geraldine commented. 'The psychiatrist seems a bit scary.'

The ward sister blinked hard as if to clear her vision. 'Dr Green is a remarkable man.'

Geraldine was glad she now knew his name. She would avoid him if she ever had a mental health problem. 'Why do you think Emily's so convinced she saw this woman?'

Barrows folded her arms, her face mute. She had worn the same expression when Geraldine questioned her before.

'You're a nurse. You must have an opinion?'

The woman shuddered. 'The whole thing is preposterous.'

Geraldine waited and, when nothing was forthcoming, said: 'That's it? Simple as that?'

'What would you have me say?' she asked coolly. 'She was clearly not ready to resume duties. Perhaps the anaesthetic caused a reaction, but you would have to ask the anaesthetist about that.'

Geraldine felt sorry for Emily that she had worked in such a seemingly uncaring place. No wonder she unravelled. Her work was what she lived for.

Her parents were first-class failures, but she would let them know their daughter was in hospital. It was the least she could do for Emily. If by some miracle they stepped up to their role it would be something. Despondent at all she had seen and heard, she turned to leave. She had a report to write up and her children to get home to. Her bed. Her safe world. She hoped Emily was feeling safe.

Emily couldn't tell if it was night or day. She was in a bed and had been undressed. Beneath the cotton gown she was wearing her underwear and was relieved she'd not been stripped naked. The bed was tucked against a wall with a bedside table to her right. The dimmed ceiling light cast a warm glow over the room, which was a comfortable size for a single room, twelve foot square at a guess. The far wall opposite was fitted with the type of furniture found in a hotel bedroom. A single wardrobe attached to a desk, a leather tub chair, a lamp on the desk and, surprisingly, carpet on the floor. A picture hung on the wall above the desk and the blinds on the window behind her were fully closed. On the same side wall as her bed was a door, a slim light wood affair, but it was the second door facing her that her eyes fixed on.

Behind it were the people who put her in here.

She would stay calm. It was her best defence. No more tears. She would play this right, because right now her only chance of getting out of here was to give the right answers. Make the right noises. She knew enough about mental health care to get by. She would admit to depression, anxiety, seeing people who she knew weren't really there – and blame it all on Zoe. Zoe was her trump card. The reason and cause of this setback. She had just passed a first anniversary. She had the right to fall apart a little bit. Geraldine would be relieved if she told her she had made it all up. She would of course apologise for wasting police time. She hadn't intentionally set out to do so, but while Zoe remained missing, her mind created a set of characters that she could focus on, people that she thought needed rescuing. A transference used as a coping mechanism to take her mind off thinking solely of Zoe. This is the picture she would paint and when they saw it and judged her sane, she would walk right out of here.

Wriggling out of the bed she found the light switch and turned the bulb brighter. She opened the door near the end of her bed and saw a small en suite bathroom containing a shower, toilet and sink, two white towels, a mini-sized toothpaste, a deodorant and soap, a comb and toothbrush and a pair of paper disposable knickers. She stepped into the room, looking for a lock, and had to make do with just shutting the door.

She used the loo and showered quickly and then dressed in her own clothes which were hanging in the wardrobe. The hangers were plastic and attached to the clothes rail. She put on her sandals and combed her hair. So far no one had disturbed her. She crossed over to the blinds and found a switch on the wall and pressed it. They made a soft whirring sound as they opened and dull daylight came into the room. The walls were painted a soft blue with white patches deliberately added to resemble clouds. The picture was of a beach; sunny sky, a stretch of sea and sand dotted with small waves breaking the surface of the green sea. The window was one sheet of glass with no opening. She now knew exactly where she was: the top floor of The Windsor Bridge Hospital. It was the modern psychiatric wing, which she had avoided visiting when invited on her tour of the hospital. Now she was there without a choice.

She was a patient. A psychiatric patient. A strike two had been added.

Chapter Twenty-Four

Geraldine banged the front door with the flat of her hand. How loud did these people have their telly? She could hear Holly Willoughby talking from outside. She banged again and stood still on the only clean spot she could find on the short path, which consisted of two square slabs of concrete, half covered by bin bags which seagulls or foxes had attacked. Buttered bread and cans leaking baked bean juices smeared the ground.

Finally she heard someone behind the door. 'You better not be a fucking salesman.'

Doreen Jacobs opened the door. With barely a change in her expression, she greeted Geraldine. 'Oh, it's you. I should have known it was Old Bill by the knock. What brings you here, DI Sutton?' She said Old Bill as if she were an old con, but as far as Geraldine was aware she'd never come under the radar of the police before Zoe went missing. Maybe she just didn't like the police or blamed them for failing to find her daughter.

The woman had changed little over the last year. With her short fair hair, she reminded Geraldine of a lot of women she'd met in her career. They were hardened and mean-faced, with features pinched of any warmth or charity. She was short and fat with big beefy arms that could probably crush you in an embrace. Her daughters got their height and dark hair from their father. She made no attempt to invite her visitor in. Geraldine was tempted to toy with her, to tell her they had new information on the whereabouts of their missing daughter, just to see if she got a reaction, but she was a professional and would not lower herself to such behaviour. She found Doreen Jacobs a hard and callous woman, a conniver, whose character and manner of speaking bore little resemblance to her older daughter. It was a wonder that she had produced someone like Emily.

'I'm here with news about Emily—'

'We know,' she interrupted. 'The doctor rang last night and told us. She was meant to have been staying here by all accounts.'

Geraldine sighed inwardly. She should have anticipated that would happen. She'd had a wasted journey. 'Oh, right. Well, it's good that you know. I'll leave you to it then.'

She turned to leave. The woman's words stopped her. 'I'm not surprised they locked her up. She was never right as a kid.'

Geraldine stared. 'I beg your pardon?'

'I said she was never right. She was never like a normal kid. She was born grown up and not in a good way. She was constantly watching you. Always lurking in doorways. Her eyes on everything you did. When Zoe were born, if she'd had her way, she'd have disappeared with her sister. I used to have to watch her and make sure she didn't run off with her. She tried taking charge like she was the mother. Organising baby feeds and nappies and leaving me lists of when I should feed her sister, change her, as if we were simple-minded. She was nine! A clever little mare who thought she could do it all.' She smirked and her washed-out blue eyes gleamed knowingly. 'And she could. It wasn't anything she couldn't tackle, she could mind a baby as if born to it. In the end we let her. Why not? She thought she was better than us, so now it was up to her to prove it. I'd like to know who she thinks changed *her* nappies. Fed *her* her bottle. The fucking fairy godmother? Before Zoe was born we used to listen to her talking to herself. To her imaginary friend! She had a whole fucking room of them. Lined up teddies and dolls who she believed talked to her. I never heard a word they said, mind. It was all in her bleedin' head. And Zoe was just one more to add to her collection.'

Geraldine felt her stomach knot in anger. What the woman described sounded like the very lonely life of a child who took comfort from toys and then later from a baby sister in the absence of feeling it from her parents. She had coped the only way she knew how.

'Do you not like your daughter, Mrs Jacobs?' she asked bluntly.

The woman looked at her, appearing not in the least offended. She pulled out a packet of cigarettes from her tracksuit pocket and used a Bic lighter to light one, then she inhaled deeply and blew the smoke out of the side of her mouth, avoiding Geraldine's face. 'What's to like? We don't know her. She lived here until two years ago, but we didn't have a clue what she thought. She mostly kept to her room. The only one let inside her room was Zoe so she could fill Zoe's head with grand ideas.' She inhaled again and looked away. 'I hate to say it, it's a wicked thing, I know . . . but I wish it had been her who had gone missing, and not my Zo.'

Geraldine got back in her car. She was shaking. Little shocked her in her job, but the brutal words she had just heard were some of the worst she had encountered. To wish one child gone in favour of another was an affront to nature.

Doreen Jacobs had revealed a great deal in this conversation. She had abused Emily unremorsefully, using her to bring up her own sister. The picture painted couldn't have been clearer, and Geraldine imagined nine-year-old Emily carrying a baby, changing nappies, giving feeds and walking the long, lonely nights soothing a crying baby. Taking comfort from someone who was real. Before Zoe went missing Emily must have been incredibly resilient to have borne such an upbringing. She wished she'd got better under the care of Eric and did not need this more serious intervention of hospitalisation.

She started the car, wondering if the hospital would let her visit. Was there a cooling-off period before visits were allowed? Emily would surely need things brought in, and somehow Geraldine couldn't see Doreen Jacobs ferrying her stuff. She needed to be careful, though, for Emily's sake. She was not her friend. She was a police officer.

Their relationship was strained now. She felt as if she had deserted a sinking ship and left Emily drowning.

She sat up straight, took a steady breath and looked in her wing mirror before pulling away from the Jacobs' house. She was a police officer. She could only do what was right. She could not rewrite the bad things that had happened, nor find everyone who went missing. She would be there for Emily when she needed her and that was the best she could do.

Chapter Twenty-Five

Classical music was playing through speakers at low volume. A dozen or more people were in various stages of activity. Some were sitting at tables eating or pouring cereal into a bowl; some were pouring brown liquid from a flask, or buttering bread. They looked like ordinary people making themselves at home. She wondered if those more easily identified as having mental problems were locked away elsewhere.

She was spotted as a new arrival by a woman with brown curly hair who was smiling and walking her way. She wore furry toy slippers on her feet, pink bunnies with floppy ears. 'Help yourself, love. There's coffee and tea over there. Or breakfast if you want?' Emily murmured her thanks and walked over to the trolley. She was not yet ready to eat, but she was thirsty. She made her way to an empty table and sat alone, checking out her surroundings as she sipped lukewarm coffee from a plastic mug.

The open-plan living area was large and rectangular with plenty of room to move around. Armchairs, beanbags, low round coffee tables and round dining tables had been set out on three sides of the room, to offer a choice. A large TV, out of reach on a wall in one area, was presently switched off. Book cases were dotted in various places. Paintings of landscapes hung on the walls. The whole place looked comfortable, a place where you could relax and forget your troubles, until you spotted the four cameras high up in each corner of the room and realised you were being watched.

A wiry young man sat down at a table next to her. His back was taut; well-defined muscles were clear under his T-shirt. The blond quiff on his head was a good four inches high and she wondered how long it took to style. He took a paper napkin and spread it out neatly on the table. He took a knife and carefully centred a slice of bread in the middle, before cutting off the crusts and removing them from the napkin to place on the tray. He now cut the single slice of bread in half. Emily watched, fascinated. But he was not done yet. He cut each half-slice in half again and then each quarter-slice in half. He finally cut each of those in half. The bread was now cut so small that it resembled scrabble pieces without letters.

The woman with the brown curly hair approached him. 'Be a good lad, Gems. Eat your bread and butter.'

He gripped the blunt, plastic knife, his knuckles white, and stared at her. She saw something in his eyes and she backed away. She came over to Emily's table instead of returning to her own. 'He'll be alright once he's had his meds. Won't you, Gems?' she called out.

Gems ignored her. He was eating one cube of bread at a time, Chewing each tiny morsel slowly.

'He's not really called Gems, but we call him that on account of his hair,' she said, touching the top of her head. 'You know, like the biscuits.'

Emily smiled.

'I'm Molly, or Mol, if you prefer.'

'Emily.'

'You looked a bit shell-shocked when you walked in here. First time?'

She nodded.

'You get used to it after a day or so. Give it a week and you'll feel at home.'

She looked at Molly in alarm. 'How long have you been here?'

'I'm on a twenty-eight-dayer.'

Emily's eyes questioned her.

'Under section two they can keep me here twenty-eight days. On day twenty now and counting down. They're trying to sort out my meds to stop me going cuckoo.' She grinned. 'But it's a fat lot of good, I've always been a nutcase. Having bipolar drives me round the bend.' She roared with laughter, realising what she'd said. Then leaned in close and lowered her voice. 'Give Gems a wide berth. You don't need to worry about the others, but he's unpredictable.'

She left her then and Emily finished her coffee. She stilled as she saw a member of staff heading her way. It was a male psychiatric nurse wearing a plain white tunic top and navy trousers. 'Good morning, Miss Jacobs, my name's Ben. Dr Green has arranged for you to have a medical examination. If you've finished breakfast, would you be happy to have that now?'

She stood up. 'Sure.'

'If you'd like to follow me.'

Emily's legs trembled as she followed the psychiatric nurse across the room to a pair of closed doors she had not previously noticed. He pulled out a retractable ID card connected to a belt loop on his trousers and she watched him swipe it through a panel on the wall. The doors buzzed and made a clicking sound as they unlocked and he pushed them open, leading them to another corridor. No bunch of keys jangled as he walked. No echo of his footsteps rang out on hard corridor floors. His access and exit were made by using a simple piece of plastic and soft carpet muffled his shoes. They passed closed doors until they came to one with a silver nameplate inscribed in black: Treatment Room.

A short, slim man rose from behind the desk. He wore glasses and a brown suit with a shirt and tie. He looked younger than her, and a little geeky with his floppy fringe. 'Good morning. Please sit down. Dr Green has requested you have a medical examination, and with your permission I'd also like to take some blood?'

Emily willed herself to relax. This is where it began. From now on they would be watching her and listening to her every response. 'Good morning. That's fine. Always good to get an MOT,' she said lightly.

He smiled a little awkwardly, and she imagined him more suited to working in a laboratory. 'You slept well?' he asked.

'Very, thank you. The bed is very comfortable.'

'That's good. I understand you recently had surgery and were also hit by a car earlier this week. So, Ben is going to step out and swap places with a female nurse so that I can examine you. Is that alright?'

'Of course. Would you like me to get undressed?'

'Please. You can go behind the curtain. There's a gown you can put on and a couch to lie on. Get yourself comfortable and we'll pop back in.'

She started shaking behind the curtain. She was giving them free rein to carry out this exam. If she'd refused, she wondered how they would have reacted. Would they hold her down? Somehow she didn't think so. But it would be a black mark against her.

She settled on the couch and breathed steadily.

A female nurse accompanied the doctor; she smiled a greeting and stood by Emily's side. The doctor took a stethoscope and listened to Emily's chest. He shone an ophthalmoscope into her eyes. He instructed her to follow his finger. Then asked her to close her eyes and place her own finger on her nose, pull it away and retouch the spot at a steady pace. He took a tendon hammer and tapped behind and in front of each elbow, each forearm, below each knee and the back of her ankles to test her tendon reflexes. He scraped the pointy plastic end of the hammer along the soles of her feet and her toes curled downward.

At the sight of her injury, he gently palpated it. 'Some blow you got there.'

She murmured a yes. 'I was stupid not to look before crossing. I hope I didn't give the driver too much of a shock.'

He looked at her and pulled a face. 'Yes, we tend to forget that sometimes.'

Pulling aside her gown, he examined the small scar from her operation. It was pink and healing. He had checked her fully, head to toe, giving her the most thorough examination she'd ever had. There had been no expense spared, and she wondered who was paying for it all. This was a private psychiatric ward. You could not come here without money. She wondered if a similar arrangement was in place as with the surgical unit, and the NHS was footing the bill. Or was she entitled to free treatment because she worked there? She had not fully looked at the perks of her contract. This could be one of them.

When she was dressed she found him sitting at the desk, his eyes on his screen, typing. 'I'm arranging for you to have a CT scan. This should be done later today. In the meantime, is there anything concerning you that you'd like to ask?'

'Apart from the fact that I'm here, you mean?'

He heard her wry humour and acknowledged it with a small smile. 'Indeed.'

'No, I have no other concerns. Thank you for asking.' She stood ready to leave. 'There is one thing. Am I able to make a call? I don't seem to have my bag with me and I'm not sure what your rules are in any case.'

'I'm sorry, you will have your personal items returned to you, but we don't advise the use of mobile phones. We encourage a peaceful environment and try to avoid the possibility of taking unauthorised photographs or videos. It's protection for us all, you understand. You'll be meeting with the ward manager, who'll be best able to explain about your stay here and telephone access.'

She hesitated. 'Believe it or not it's only to call Allen Ward, about a patient I nursed yesterday. I wish to pass on something I forgot to mention in his notes.'

The request took him by surprise. Clearly not many patients had asked to use a phone for this purpose.

'In that case,' he said, and stood up and came around the desk, 'press zero for the operator and then the extension number. I'll leave you for a moment.'

As soon as the door shut, Emily dialled the extension number to Allen Ward that she already knew off by heart. She sighed with relief when she recognised the voice, and remembered the name of the receptionist. 'Paula. I haven't got long. I need to speak to Meredith.'

Hearing the urgency in her voice, Paula quickly replied, 'Hang on a sec; she's just wheeling a patient back from theatre. I'll grab her.'

She heard footsteps, then, 'Hey, you bailout, thought we were out on the town tonight? Talk about finding an excuse to ditch me.'

Emily smiled, feeling less alone. 'We will when I get out of here.'

'So, what's up?'

'Meredith, just listen and don't interrupt. Last night I viewed the CCTV footage of the ward. I was looking for something else but came across something that is quite shocking. The anaphylaxis yesterday was caused by his wife.'

'What?'

She heard the shock in Meredith's voice. 'Meredith, trust me. I saw her come out of the room. She was clearly up to something. She has to have given him something. No one else did.

You need to see it for yourself and then do something. She may try it again.'

Meredith was silent and Emily had to prompt her. 'Meredith, you'll watch it, won't you? You don't have to take my word for it. You can see it for yourself if you ask Gary the security guard if you can view it.'

She heard a deep intake of breath and then, 'Yes, alright. I will. God, Emily, there's never a dull moment with you, is there?'

She smiled again. 'There is. Only not right now. Take care Meredith, I've got to go.'

She pulled her shoulders back, relatively unscathed and reassured that she had done what she could to protect Neil Jeffries, then she left the office, before realising too late that she should have asked Meredith to look at the recording of Katka. She should have gone to her from the beginning. The onus was not on her to protect the place. She was a locum, there only temporarily, and seemed like the type of person who was una-fraid to ask questions.

Hiding her disappointment for the lost opportunity, she raised her chin higher for the benefit of the two men standing waiting for her in the corridor. It was still point one to her. She had come across as a polite and considerate human being who still cared for her fellow man while she was locked up. Let them watch her. They would find nothing unbalanced about her.

Chapter Twenty-Six

Dalloway and Barrows sat in front of the monitor and Meredith stood behind them looking over their shoulders, pulling a face at Nina Barrows' back as the woman moaned again at how awful it was to have the police in the hospital last night. The ward sister looked exhausted and cranky. Her night shift had ended two hours ago and she should have gone home by now, but insisted on staying to see what Nurse Jacobs had found. Gary Burge looked none too chirpy either as he stood leaning against a wall. He had been called in as he was best qualified to take them through the CCTV recordings. He'd grumbled a couple of times, telling them that he'd be starting his shift that night later than normal because of coming in now. He'd need a bit of shut-eye to make up for the lost hours.

They ignored him, other than to ask him to bring up the file for yesterday. The room was uncomfortably warm with all four of them in it, and the scent of Burge's aftershave was cloying. The first images of Mrs Jeffries and then Shelly coming out of the patient's room were now playing on the screen. All three of them watched in silence. The only sound was a small gasp, a few minutes later, from Barrows.

Dalloway paused it on the shot where Emily disappeared inside the room and Mrs Jeffries was standing out in the corridor. He cleared his throat. 'So what do you both think?'

Emily was spot on, thought Meredith. 'Emily's right. She saw what we're looking at and was convinced that Mrs Jeffries was up to something.'

'She wasn't looking at this last night,' Gary interrupted from behind. 'She was looking at the thirtieth of June.'

Meredith threw him an impatient glance. 'She was looking at this. How else do you think we know about it?'

Barrows waved her hand at the screen. 'It's hard to say. You can't actually see anything. We don't know what happened inside the room.'

Dalloway gave a nod of agreement. 'Her behaviour looks suspicious, but it could be suggested that Shelly had been the one giving him something. She was attending him.'

'Shelly?' Barrows' face curdled. 'The girl's a menace, but I hardly think she'd do that.'

'Why do you call her a menace?' Meredith asked. 'And I don't think Mr Dalloway was suggesting something deliberate.'

Barrows threw a look at Dalloway before she answered. 'She can't take simple instructions, for one. Considering she's new and only here on a bank basis, she's far too sure of herself. She's impertinent as well. I want her gone from here.'

Dalloway inhaled noisily, glancing at her with an irritable look on his face. 'Can we keep to the issue at hand? What are we going to do? Call the police or monitor the situation ourselves?

We don't know yet what caused the reaction. It could be something quite innocent.'

'I doubt it.' Meredith said, surprised. 'Mrs Jeffries' behaviour looked extremely odd. But you're right, and he has no record of being allergic to anything.'

'He may be allergic to something we're unaware of,' said Barrows, helpfully. 'They don't always tell us. Often they just name the medicines or things like nuts or latex allergies.'

'My mum's allergic to celery,' Gary piped up.

Barrows' head swivelled as if on a stick. Her eyes pinned him to the wall. 'Do you mind? You're only in here because we needed you to set this up.'

He raised his hands in mock surrender. 'Sorry. Don't mind me. I'm only the man you dragged out of bed to come and help you.'

'What was Miss Jacobs doing in this office anyway?' Barrows asked, clearly irked.

He folded his arms sullenly. 'She wanted me to help her find a patient who had stolen something from her. She said she had been a patient herself and needed proof before she could do anything about it.'

'And did you find this proof?'

'I left her to it. I had my rounds to do.'

'This is getting us nowhere,' Dalloway said. 'I think we should resume this discussion in my office.' He looked at Gary. 'I expect to hear nothing of what was said in this room, Mr Burge.'

'Value my job too much for that, Mr Dalloway. Nothing will pass my lips about it, be assured of that.'

The three visitors to the office prepared to leave. Gary opened the door for them. 'You know the easiest solution would be for me to rig up a camera inside the room. I could monitor it from here. You wouldn't know it was there.'

Dalloway gave the man a long and hard look. Barrows and Meredith kept quiet. Then Dalloway said, 'Would you mind stepping out of the room for a minute and close the door?'

Gary shrugged. 'Sure.'

Almost ten minutes later he was invited back inside. Barrows and Meredith passed him to leave. Dalloway shut the door behind them. He then turned to Gary. 'How easy would it be?'

Gary's smile was smug. 'Like I said, you won't know it's there.'

Emily lay on a narrow table. It moved in and out of the large doughnut-shaped scanner as X-rays were taken of her head. She could hear clicking and buzzing and whirring as the machine rotated around her. She reached up and touched her neck and immediately heard a voice talking over the loudspeaker.

'Place your hand back down, Miss Jacobs. Stay nice and still please. Not too much longer now.'

She mumbled an apology and lay still again. Her neck felt bare without her necklace. She had only removed it once before, on the day of her operation, and she felt lost without it. She wondered if Zoe was still wearing hers and squeezed her eyes, fretting as dark thoughts filled her mind. Would it still be around Zoe's neck when they found her? Could it have slipped somewhere as her flesh putrefied? Emily wished such images would not come to her. She had to hold on to the belief that Zoe was still alive, still warm flesh and blood. She had to find a way to get out of this place so that she could carry on searching for her.

Others may have given up on the hope of her being alive. Geraldine perhaps, and maybe even Eric had doubted her ever being found. But she couldn't. She owed it to her sister to find her. It hadn't been Zoe in that street. Geraldine made a point of telling her this after she made her statement. She'd also suggested Emily look a little harder for her missing jacket. The way this had been said had implied that Emily had only half looked in the first place. Her missing jacket was probably still in one of those bin bags. She hadn't emptied them completely. It could well be in the bottom of one of them, which now made her actions feel foolish. Yet in her heightened state, after finding that letter, it was not unreasonable that she would be on high alert for any sighting of her sister. She was wrong to think she had seen her, and wrong about the jacket, but she was not delusional about finding the letter. She didn't write it and she didn't stick it on Zoe's photo. She didn't dream that up, and nor did she dream of seeing this missing woman, Katka. Her image was large as life up on that screen, and her only regret was that she'd shared finding her with Shelly.

Seeing Shelly edge back into the changing room and close the door on her while she collapsed suggested a betrayal. She denied that she had given Emily anything, but Emily knew someone had given her something to make her collapse like that. She'd been given two drinks: coffee from Shelly and vodka from Gary. Either could have been doctored. But Gary had no involvement in any of this other than being the security guard who worked there. Shelly had been there from day one. Unless her betrayal was simply an order from Barrows or Dalloway? They could have ordered her to put something in that coffee. Yet if that was the case, why hadn't Barrows tried to detain her? She'd almost demanded Emily leave the premises. If that was genuine and she had wanted Emily gone, Barrows' words suggested that she was innocent of any wrongdoing and wasn't involved in any of it. Emily needed to find a way to talk to her. Get *her* to look at the footage and see for herself that this woman, Katka, was real, before someone else got to it and had it wiped. If that happened and she lost the chance to prove her existence, she stood to lose her own freedom. Proving what she had seen was proof of her sanity. Without it she could be kept locked up for a long time. Emily's fear of that happening was all too real. Shelly knew about the video. And soon, too, could others.

Geraldine was not really surprised when she wasn't let in to see Emily. The doctors were still examining her. She sat in her car, feeling unsettled, and was aware that it stemmed from her being partly responsible for Emily being admitted to the place, even if reason said it probably was for the best. At least Emily was now being looked after. Right from the moment she had first met Emily she had known she was dealing with a highly intelligent young woman, who had, at best, a fragile mind plagued with hope and fear at not knowing why her sister had gone missing. At worst, if closure was never given, she would never know what had happened, and, tormented by images of a horrible death, her mind would fracture as a result. The arrival of the letter out of the blue like that didn't make sense. Did Emily write it herself? Geraldine had no way yet of knowing. But if Zoe was alive, why hadn't she just phoned or texted her sister to tell Emily to stop looking? Especially given that she had never been one to communicate by letter. Had Emily made herself believe her sister had written it?

Geraldine knew one thing. She had seen similar behaviour from Emily before. Two months into the investigation Emily had called the police to get a woman to open her front door because she was positive Zoe was inside the house. She had heard a baby crying and thought this was the reason her sister had gone missing – to hide a pregnancy. The anxious woman, who finally opened the door hugging her baby, cried fearfully that she'd seen Emily following her in the street several times and when she saw her outside her house banging the door, she had called the police. Under the circumstances, and at the time, Geraldine accepted Emily's behaviour; someone going out of their mind with worry, and clinging on to hope, was likely to do such things.

The story of the missing patient believed to be related to the Dalloway's nanny, though, was a whole other level. Why had she not called the police the day it happened if she thought a patient was missing? Why wait until after she met with the Dalloway's nanny? Had her mind grasped hold of this nanny's tale and made it a part of her own imaginings? Fitted it with this missing niece like the last piece of a jigsaw? Then handed it over to Geraldine as proof of a crime? Geraldine was only glad she hadn't made it a formal interview to question the surgeon and ward sister. She had saved herself the embarrassment of explaining to her DCI why she was pursuing this line of enquiry. Glancing at the entrance to the hospital, she watched as the doors slid open and she saw Eric Hudson emerge. She took relief that it wasn't really her doing that Emily had been locked away. Even before what happened last night, Eric Hudson had already set plans in motion by referring her to a psychiatrist. She looked up at the top floor of the building and imagined Emily in there feeling betrayed and alone.

Eric was now walking through the small hospital car park to his car which sat alongside Geraldine's. They clearly had the same intention – to visit Emily. She wound down her window as he drew near. 'They're not letting me in. They said she's still being assessed. How is she?'

He shrugged. 'I didn't get to see her either.'

He held up a bunch of keys. 'She let them give me these, though. I'm going to her flat to get her some clothes.'

Geraldine thought Eric kind and was glad that Emily had someone doing this for her. Her mother certainly wouldn't.

'Are you going there now?' she asked.

He nodded.

'You want some company?'

He looked hesitant. 'Er, I'm not too sure on that. Do you think she'd want you in her home?'

She shrugged. 'I don't see why not. I've been there plenty of times before, and I bet Emily would rather I went through her smalls than you.'

He smiled. 'You may be right. And I've never been there before, so your help would be good. Do you want to leave your car here? I'll drop you back afterwards.'

Geraldine got out of her car by way of answer. She was pleased to be going with him. He could reassure her that Emily was in the right place.

Chapter Twenty-Seven

From the doorway Emily saw Gems sat perfectly still on the chair at his desk, his hands placed on his knees. They were red and scaly from too much washing. He hadn't moved in over a minute and was staring at a spot on the wall in front of him. She could tell at a glance that he had obsessive compulsive disorder; she recognised his behaviour from past patients she had nursed. There wasn't a dent or crease in the covers or pillows on his bed. Not a stray thread or speck of dirt marring the floor. The wardrobe and bathroom doors were closed fully. Three toy cars were lined up on the windowsill, a red, a blue and a yellow, spaced equally apart, bonnets facing forward, in perfect alignment. Four books stood in order of height, a few centimetres apart to prevent them touching. A pair of leather slippers and black slip-on shoes were placed in precise neatness against a wall, toes touching the skirting. On his bedside drawers a bottle of hand gel had been centred as if needing to be seen at all times. She wondered if the staff knew about the hand gel, whether he hid it from sight normally, and had forgotten to hide it now. Perhaps the liquid was alcohol-free and he was allowed it?

His hand suddenly shot out and with one finger he touched the spot he was looking at. 'I see you,' he said loud and clear, and for a moment she thought he was talking to the wall. She jolted and he turned his head and stared at her.

'Get away,' he growled and jumped up from his chair.

Emily backed away fast. She didn't like what she saw in his eyes. He was looking at her as if memorising her face. She hurried back to the lounge to find Ben waiting for her.

'There you are. Dr Green has asked to see you, if that's convenient?'

Emily wanted to say she'd be busy, could he come back another day, but this next step was the most important one she would take. This psychiatrist was going to analyse her mind, to decide if she needed to stay there. Her fate was in his hands and she had to convince him that she was safe to be let go.

Geraldine and Eric stood in the middle of Emily's living room, silently looking around. Eric looked a little awkward and Geraldine could understand why. It felt like an intrusion of Emily's personal space. The walls, she noticed, had been painted since she was last there. The pale grey brightened the room, but it still lacked a homely touch, as if Emily had no time for such frippery. Geraldine suspected she gave little thought to her own comfort, her mind no doubt always on her sister. More photographs of Zoe had been dotted around the place since her last visit. The one she said she kept on the bookcase, still in police evidence, was the best one, though. These others were merely of her sister posing for the camera. The one Emily prided herself on had captured something more private. Her face was in repose, Geraldine recalled, and there was a gentleness in her eyes.

She turned to Eric. 'I'll get her stuff. Are you OK with that?'

'Sure, I'll just check around, make sure everything's alright.'

In Emily's bedroom Geraldine found a small wheelie case. She took some T-shirts from a drawer, a smart-looking pale grey tracksuit from the wardrobe, a pair of dark blue jeans and a light blue hoody. From another drawer she took a selection of underwear. She spotted a pair of trainers in the bottom of the wardrobe and added these to the collection. On the bedside drawers she found a smaller-sized photo of the one the police had, and added that.

From the bathroom she collected what she could see. Once the few bottles and tubes had been removed, the bathroom looked bare. On a pine shelf she spied a small makeup bag and added it to her bundle.

She ensured bottle tops were on tight and placed everything neatly inside the case before zipping it closed.

She placed it in the small hallway and saw Eric standing at an open doorway, peering into a room. She joined him and her eyes instantly went to a wall covered in Post-it notes. Dozens of yellow and green squares of paper made a frame for a map stuck with numerous pins. Newspaper cuttings with bold headlines jumped out at her:

MISSING. STUDENT NURSE. HOSPITAL PATIENT.
FEAR GROWING.

She felt her throat tighten. 'I feel we have let her down.'

Eric heaved a sigh beside her. 'I'm sure you did everything you could to find her.'

'I'm talking about Emily, Eric. Look at this room. She did this because we failed her.'

'She never told me about this room,' he said quietly.

Geraldine moved in to get a closer look at the Post-it notes. 'Every one of these has details on. Names. Numbers. She was running her own investigation by the looks of things. I could really cry for her, you know. We did everything we could. And still we didn't find her.'

'I don't think she ever blamed you,' Eric said.

Geraldine rubbed her face. She felt tired. 'Well, she should have. At the three-month and six-month reviews, when we were no further on and were just managing expectations, she should have raised merry hell and brought the roof down on our useless heads.' She looked at him bitterly. 'The yearly review was last month and I sent her a bunch of flowers to mark the anniversary. Tell me what sodding use that did. Apart from assuage my guilt.'

Eric didn't say anything. No doubt, he knew her frustration mirrored his own.

She turned away from the wall and gazed at the bin bags and boxes covering the single bed. Geraldine realised that this was where Emily had said she'd found her sister's photograph and the letter, and that all of the stuff on the bed must be Zoe's. 'Do you mind hanging on for another few minutes?' she asked.

'Sure. I'm in no rush.'

Geraldine pulled one of the bin bags off the bed and plonked it on the floor. She upended it, easing the bag off slowly to keep the contents piled. She got down on her knees and examined the folded clothing, before carefully pulling the bag back over it all. Eric watched her do this to a second bag before he spoke.

'I thought you needed a search warrant to do something like this?'

'Why would I?' she asked, suspecting he thought this an invasion of Emily's privacy, knowing in some way that he was right. 'She gave you permission to be in her home and look for clothes. I'm looking for clothes.'

'You empty them and I'll re-bag,' he offered.

It was in the seventh bag, in a separate plastic carrier, that Geraldine found the leather jacket. A light flowery perfume scented the room as she unfolded it. She held it up for inspection. It was the same colour and nearly the same style as the one the woman Emily chased was wearing. But it was not missing and it had not been taken by Zoe, as Emily would have them believe. She folded it back into the carrier, pressing air out of the bag. 'I knew it had to be here. She said it was missing. You know she chased a woman wearing a similar one, believing it was Zoe?'

He looked surprised and Geraldine saw that this was news to him.

'She said something about chasing Zoe, but I don't know the full story.'

'Is her mind that sick, Eric, that she goes chasing after strangers in similar clothing?'

She got up off her knees and stared at him. 'I think Doreen Jacobs has a lot to answer for. Did you know about the type of upbringing Emily had?'

He stayed silent and she shoved past him, irritably. 'Surely you can confirm what the bloody woman already told me herself?'

'Yes, I knew,' he said. 'Her upbringing isn't so unusual, though. In large families particularly, the older children help bring up the younger ones.' He paused as if marshalling his thoughts. 'In Emily's case I believe she was an unloved child and that would have left her feeling disconnected. When her sister was born she internalised this emotion. She would have loved Zoe almost obsessively.'

'Blimey, that almost sounds like a bad thing.'

He nodded. 'It can be. She had disconnected from her parents and discounted them as being capable and, in all bar name, had taken on the role of a mother. She would have been under enormous pressure, especially when Zoe wasn't in her care. Leaving lists was a way of maintaining control. Emily told me she used to sniff her sister when she got in from school to check if her mother had been smoking over her.'

'Christ, that is extreme.' She heaved a sigh. 'I don't know how you do it. Listening to all that stuff would depress the hell out of me.'

They walked back out of the room, away from Emily's wall, both silent and contemplative.

Maybe Emily really was in the best place to get better, thought Geraldine. She felt uncomfortable with Eric's theory that Emily would have loved Zoe almost obsessively. She loved her sister. Geraldine was sure of that. Yet . . . as a police officer she had come across men who had stabbed the women they loved because they left them. Women who stabbed the men they loved because they cheated on them, and one thing she learned from all of them was that love was no barrier to being killed. Not when it became obsessive. The thought now clung to her mind like an unwanted visitor. Obsessive love can turn to hate.

Chapter Twenty-Eight

Emily was beginning to wonder how many corridors were in this place, and how many doors you had to go through to get to the exit. Ben, the psychiatric nurse, kept her company. His and Dr Green's were the only names she'd kept hold of. Ben's, mainly because he was the only psychiatric nurse who'd dealt with her so far; she'd seen a handful of others, flitting in and out, but usually just to take a patient away with them. And Dr Green's because he was the psychiatrist she was about to meet. They made small talk along the way. So far they had discussed the weather, the hot summer and global warming.

He stopped outside a room and knocked on the door. There was no sign indicating the purpose or occupant of the room. It was a door she feared opening. Behind it lay the unknown. She felt powerless, defenceless as her mind jumped to endless possibilities that could befall her this day . . . She calmed her giddy thoughts as a voice beckoned. Ben nodded at her to open the door.

The room was an unexpected delight. The walls were a pale gold, the floor was dark oak. Plantation-style pale cream shutters framed the window. Racing-green velvet armchairs begged to be sat on.

The man who invited her in smiled. 'Good afternoon, Miss Jacobs.'

He was standing by a fish tank built into the wall. Its size was extraordinary. It was like an aquarium at a zoo, bringing ocean life straight to you. 'Come and take a look.'

She moved closer and stared at the rainbow of colours gliding in water. The coral bed swayed in slow motion. Her eyes fixed on the seahorses with delight. She laughed.

'They're beautiful, aren't they? They change colour very quickly. They're masters of disguise. Truly unique. They are among the only species on earth where the male gives birth. They take fathering to a whole new level and they stay with Mum for ever.'

She gazed at the seahorses, transfixed. She didn't want to look away from their beautiful world. She felt her eyes fill.

'They make me cry, too,' he said, and handed her a white linen handkerchief.

She smiled at him, dabbed her eyes and handed it back. 'Thank you for telling me about them.'

'Come and sit down,' he said.

Dr Green waited until she had sat down. He wore an aura of calmness. His suit was well fitting, the colour matching the silver of his hair. The plain dark grey of his tie neatly knotted at the collar of his pristine white shirt. His black shoes were shiny and new. Emily had imagined him to be dressed in a brown suit and brogues, not this picture of elegance. She tugged at her less than clean summer top. She'd worn it last night and was now wearing it again. Eric would be bringing some clean clothes soon. She'd been surprised when the ward manager told her that he was happy to get her some things, and she hadn't refused the offer.

'So what would you prefer to be called? Miss Jacobs or Emily?'

Her mouth was already dry. 'Emily's fine.'

'Well, Emily it will be then.'

The table between them held a jug of water and two tumblers. He poured water in both glasses and set one close to her.

'Talking is thirsty work.'

She smiled again. She was liking this man. She just prayed that he liked her too.

'So Emily, I'm going to tell you a little about why you're here and why we want you here. You can stop me any time you like. And please, try not to be alarmed.'

She took a shaky breath and nodded like a fool. It was happening right now. He was going to mention a word she was terrified of hearing and there was nothing she could do to stop him saying it. She swallowed hard and dug her nails into the palms of her hands.

'Eric has become a little concerned about you. He tells me that you have been doing very well up until recently. He's apprised me of the last twelve months and it does indeed seem as if you have made great progress. Something, though, in the last few weeks appears to have knocked you out of kilter and it is this that concerns us. Your physical examination shows that you are fit and well and your scan shows a remarkably normal brain. So that's all good news. It's what's going on inside that brain that we have to get to the bottom of and see if it's a little unwell or maybe, Emily, very unwell. All good so far?'

'Yes,' she managed to say. 'All good.'

'So here's the thing, Emily. You can help us to help you by staying here so that we can find out what's put you out of sync. Today is about helping us find out what may be causing you a problem. I want to discover what challenges your well-being and see if there is a way to support you better and make life easier for you.'

Emily nodded, though no words had yet formed in her head. She was scared about saying the wrong thing. Her shaky breath sounded loud to her own ears. She was finding it hard to hide how nervous she was. 'Yes, I think I do know why I've become a little unwell, to put it that way, if you like. The last year has been painful for me, to say the least. When my sister went missing it was as if my whole life had been turned upside down. So far, my sister has yet to be found and this uncertainty, this lack of knowing what has happened to her, has felt like a black hole that I've fallen through and can't get out of. There had been no light at the end of the tunnel to guide me until recently, when I went back to work. Working has been my salvation; helping others and focusing on their needs has given me back a life. In view of everything I've gone through, I feel I've coped well.'

Dr Green nodded encouragingly. 'Eric would agree with you,' he said. 'He believes that going back to work was the right step forward. I'm a little concerned, though, that one step forward has now taken you two back, as it appears that things then started to go wrong and you stopped coping as well as you had been.'

She sat forward, her expression earnest. 'Look, I know that everything I said I saw, and tried to prove was real, was just a way of coping. I completely accept that I had a post-op night-mare, probably caused by the anaesthetic, and in my need to take me out of my own painful reality I stepped into a world where I was no longer just looking for Zoe, I was looking for someone else too. Recently I had to pass the second birthday of Zoe's without her there, and Eric said particular dates are harder to cope with. Accepting that she may never come back is something that I am struggling to come to terms with. I can't believe that I may never see her again . . .'

The psychiatrist sat silent and Emily didn't know that there were tears on her face until he reached forward and handed her his handkerchief a second time. For a moment she looked at it and wondered what to do with it.

'You must have a big supply of these handkerchiefs,' she said with a watery smile, 'if you have to hand them out to all your patients.'

'I do,' he said. His eyes were amber, like a silverback, she thought. Restful and watchful and unobtrusive. 'It's hard to imagine never seeing someone you love again.'

'I've imagined finding her for so long that to even consider it not happening is a betrayal. As if I've given up on her. Looking for her is all that has kept me going. To be honest with you, last night felt like it was the final straw. I felt like I wanted to die.'

Concern showed in his eyes when she raised her head, and she immediately wished she could retract this last statement. 'I don't feel that way now. It was only a passing thought. I'm being truthful with you. I've told you I fully accept that my behaviour has been at odds with what is seen as normal, but I'm completely well now. I'm not seeing imaginary people or hearing voices that are not there. I imagined these things only as a coping strategy, and the fact that I know this surely tells you that I am in control of my mind now?'

'Eric tells me that last night you believed you had found this missing patient. Had you seen her?'

Emily looked away, not knowing how to answer. To admit she had seen the patient could go against her. To deny seeing her would mean that she would have to come up with a different reason for why she was at the hospital, at that time of night, in the first place.

She shook her head. 'No, I hadn't seen her. I made that up because I was there for another reason. I wanted to check the hospital CCTV recordings and discover who had stolen something from me. When I was a patient here I had a piece of jewellery taken from me and I wanted to see who had taken it.'

'So it wasn't a missing patient you were looking for?' he asked, sounding interested.

'Yes. I mean no,' she said, desperately trying to hang on to her train of thought. 'I was looking for another patient, the one who took it. I'd found it, but I still wanted to find out who took it in the first place. You see, I mean . . .' Emily could no longer think straight. She had a hard job even remembering what she'd just said. 'She was wearing it. I could see the glint of it on her tiny wrist.'

'Take your time, Emily,' he suggested calmly. 'Who did you see?'

She stared at him, desperate. His voice was hypnotic, his manner calm, eyes kind. She needed to tell him the truth.

'Her!' she cried at last. 'It was her! I found her and now she's dead.'

Dr Green leaned forward, his eyes not leaving hers.

'Are you talking about Zoe, Emily?' he asked gently.

'Zoe?' she cried in disbelief. 'I'm talking about the patient who's gone missing. The one they're all denying. They're covering it up, which is the *only* reason I'm in here. They have to shut me up!'

The silence was deafening following her outburst. The air stilled. Emily sat perfectly still, desperate to be out of the silence and hear something that would put her back together. Her heart rate slowed when she heard the sounds of the aquarium reach her ears; the soothing hum of the water pump, aerating the water to keep the beautiful creatures inside the tank alive. Her eyes sought out the bright colours of the seahorses and she envied them their perfect world.

'Am I here voluntarily?' she asked, hoping it was the case, so she could walk out of here.

He tilted his head, his eyes meeting hers. 'Being here must come as a shock to you. For the moment, Emily, we'd like to keep you here. Dr Hudson and I discussed your care late last night. He's concerned that your health and safety could be at risk. Therefore an application has been made to detain you for seventy-two hours. During this time we'd like to monitor you, give you time to talk through any worries and basically let you rest while we carry out further assessments. You have the right to refuse treatment, and I'm glad that so far you haven't, but you don't have the right to leave here just yet.'

Emily only remained seated in the chair through sheer will-power. She wanted to hurl herself from it and demand he let her go right this instant.

She sat, pale and shaken, as she stared back at him. The word SECTIONED screamed in her head. A strike three! Eric had put her here. She reached for the glass of water and gulped, feeling its wetness dribble down her chin and soak through the thin material covering her chest.

'It's always a shock to hear this,' he said, reading her mind. 'It can make you feel very scared, but you have nothing to fear.'

'There really isn't anything wrong with me,' she said as calmly as she could.

He smiled encouragingly. 'Perhaps tomorrow, when you're rested, we can talk some more then.'

She let herself out of his office, on legs that would barely hold her, and saw Ben waiting for her. On the journey back to her room there was no small talk, no exchange of pleasantries. She moved one foot in front of the other all the way back to her room. He departed silently and after she closed the door she made the last few steps to her bed. She picked up a pillow, pressed it hard against her face and stuffed it into her mouth to muffle her screams.

Her life, her freedom, had just been taken away. Everything that she had experienced in the last year had led to this day. The voice in her head taunted her loud and clear. Tell them what you did, Emily. Tell them and this can all stop.

Chapter Twenty-Nine

Meredith was pleased she was on duty this morning. Realising her night out with Emily would no longer be happening she'd offered to work, and was now able to keep an eye on Mr Jeffries. She pressed the dressing back in place, satisfied the wound in the man's throat was closing naturally and wouldn't need to be sutured. She'd removed the tracheotomy tube from his throat an hour ago and he was maintaining good oxygen saturation levels. The swelling had completely subsided and the rash had diminished to a scattering of pale pink spots. But he still looked shattered, which was to be expected considering what he'd gone through. He was recovering from major surgery and yesterday's emergency had set him back.

The nurses told her that he had yet to look at his abdominal stoma and averted his eyes when they changed his bag. It was still early days, she'd told them. Give him time. His eyes were dull and Meredith could clearly see that he was depressed. The fear of nearly dying had done him no favours.

'You've been in the wars, haven't you, Mr Jeffries?' she said. 'It's bad enough having one operation without us lot scaring the hell out of you by putting a tube in your throat.'

He didn't comment.

'We have no idea what caused that reaction in you. It says in your notes that you're not allergic to anything.'

He gazed at her bleakly. 'I'm not, apart from shellfish. I had a reaction once to shellfish in the Seychelles. I've never touched the stuff since. It ruined the honeymoon.'

'And you never thought to mention this before? Have it listed as an allergy?'

'What's the point? I'm not going to be served it here, am I? That happened five years ago. And like I say, I have never touched the stuff since.'

'Was it a bad reaction?'

He nodded. 'Bad enough. I was covered in hives. My lips blew out like a Mick Jagger cartoon. My nose doubled in size. The doctor had to give me a shot. I spent the week in bed while poor Anna had to make do on her own. I looked like something from a horror show.'

Meredith stared at him, pretending to look stern. 'It sounds as if you had a very serious reaction. You should really have mentioned it and have it recorded in your medical notes.'

He shrugged glumly. 'Well, you can do that now, can't you?'

'Didn't the doctor tell you to see your GP when you got home, and that you may need to carry an Epipen?'

She could see him becoming distressed by all the questions. His hands were fidgeting with the blanket, and his eyes were beginning to well. She felt guilty for badgering him. She placed a steadying hand on his shoulder. 'Sorry. I don't mean to upset you,' she said, her voice gentler. 'And as you say, we're not likely to give you shellfish here.'

'Soup,' he said. 'That's all I want at the moment. And Anna brings it in fresh.'

Meredith kept her expression even. 'You had some yesterday, I hope, before all that happened? I don't suppose you felt like eating afterwards.'

'Yes, she fetched me some and fed it to me like I was a baby. She'll be in soon.'

An image of the immaculately dressed woman came to mind. 'She's a smart-looking woman, your wife.'

A smile cracked his face. 'That she is. I'm lucky to have her. My first wife died while I was building up my business, and after that all I had was my work until Anna came along. I had been lonely as hell. All the money in the world doesn't make you happy unless you have someone to share it with. And now she's stuck with an old codger like me.'

Meredith smiled. 'I'm sure she doesn't think that.'

He looked sceptical. 'My problems with my bowel started not long after we were back from the Seychelles and since then it's been one hospital appointment after the other, one operation after the other. It's no fun for her. She should have married some-one younger, in good health.'

'I'm sure she wouldn't swap you,' Meredith teased.

'Maybe not,' he sighed.

Meredith straightened his top cover. She moved over to the sink and washed her hands. While drying them she stared around the room, her eyes discreetly searching for the camera. It had been installed while Mr Jeffries was having an X-ray. She searched hard and was reassured that she couldn't spot it.

Mrs Jeffries arrived at that moment and Meredith appraised her. She looked much younger than her husband. She wasn't quite a trophy wife, but she was still a good fifteen years younger than him. Though to be fair, Neil Jeffries looked much older than his fifty-one years. His medical condition had clearly taken its toll.

Mrs Jeffries moved over to her husband's bed. Her scent was fresh, her hair was glossy and straightened and she was wearing designer clothes. The navy summer trousers topped with a plain white T-shirt and silver accessories were worn by someone who considered their image carefully. She leaned over her husband and kissed him. 'Hello, darling.'

Meredith acknowledged her with a polite smile.

Mrs Jeffries' green eyes swept over the anaesthetist, clearly dismissing her as unimportant. 'I meant what I said yesterday,' she said crisply. 'I don't want that nurse near my husband.'

Meredith made no comment, addressing her patient instead. 'I'll check on you again later. Try and rest now.'

'She's very keen to make us believe that Emily caused this,' Meredith said to Dalloway, in the privacy of his office.

Barrows was already in the office when Meredith tracked Dalloway down. Back on day shifts, the woman looked rested after some sleep. Meredith was happy to share her opinion with both of them. They needed to know what was going on.

Dalloway nodded. 'I agree. The woman witnessed a drug discrepancy caused by Nurse Jacobs and is using it to fuel blame.'

Meredith sat down. 'Her husband may have just given me the real cause. Soup.'

Barrows frowned. 'You mean food poisoning?'

'Not exactly,' Meredith replied. 'You were right. He does have an allergy not listed. Shellfish. He had a severe reaction five years ago. He tells me the only thing he's eating is homemade soup, which his wife brings in for him.'

'But she wouldn't have had time,' Barrows protested. 'She was in that room in less than a minute. She couldn't have given it to him that quickly, surely.'

'Well, it may only have taken a spoonful to cause a reaction. Or she may not have gone back to his room to give it at that time. She may have gone back to take the evidence away.'

Dalloway gazed at Meredith, looking appreciative. 'So, she would have fed him while in the presence of Shelly. Shelly would have witnessed it.'

'Witnessed what?' Meredith said back. 'A wife feeding her husband?'

'But if he'd reacted sooner, she would have been caught out,' Barrows pointed out.

'And all she would have to say is she forgot about his allergy,' Meredith said in a persistent tone. 'Five years ago she had known he had an allergy, but it was a long time ago. She made him a fish soup and completely forgot about it.'

'She also has an opportunity to blame someone else,' Dalloway remarked. 'I spoke to Shelly. She said she'd just given him a bladder washout via his catheter, hence the urinal in her hand. Mrs Jeffries could say Shelly used the wrong solution to irrigate his bladder.'

'Ridiculous,' Barrows argued. 'The connector on those irrigation bags will only connect to a catheter. And they're stored in the sluice, not in the treatment room.'

'It still doesn't stop her suggesting it,' he countered.

Barrows stood up. 'I'm regretting letting that man install a camera. We could all be in serious trouble. A camera hidden in his room without his permission is an invasion of his privacy. While he expects to be exposed to our eyes while in his presence, he doesn't expect us to be watching him through a camera while he uses a commode.'

'We can always remove it, if you're that concerned,' Dalloway replied.

She stared at them both frankly. 'I just don't like the fact that Mr Burge has something on us.'

Dalloway stood up. He came around his desk and placed a hand on Barrows' shoulder. 'Leave Gary Burge to me, Nina. You get on with what you do best. Keep looking after our patients the way you always do. If she's going to try anything again, we have a duty to stop her. Calling in the police at this stage is going to create all sorts of problems. We have nothing really to give them yet. And I don't want their presence alarming everyone. All we need is a headline citing us in a scandal and the award we're up for will be snatched from our hands. Funding and interested parties for future developments will be turned to dust.'

She sighed wearily. 'I no longer care, to be honest with you, Rupert. This whole recent business has fairly worn me down.

Emily Jacobs did us a good turn bringing this to our attention, if it's true. She certainly didn't imagine this.'

He squeezed her shoulder. 'I know that, Nina.'

'I'm very spooked by all of this. You know that, don't you?'

'Maybe you could do with some time away.'

Her eyes closed briefly. Then she seemed to pull herself together. She moved from under his hand and put a little distance between them. She straightened her uniform, her manner unapproachable. 'That won't be necessary. I'm sure we won't have any further visits from the police.'

She closed the door behind her as she left the office. The silence was loaded. Then Meredith broke it. 'Christ, she's repressed or depressed. Take your pick. I can't wait to get back to California and a happy life again.'

'We shall miss you, Meredith,' said Dalloway.

Chapter Thirty

Emily's entire body felt tender. She had lain curled in a tight ball throughout the night, trying to block out the fear that she wouldn't be freed. Nurses had checked on her throughout the night making it impossible for her to forget where she was. Supposing Dr Green decided to keep her longer? Or decided that she needed long-term care? The patients around her looked no worse than she did, but like her, they were all being kept here. She could shout all she liked that she was different, that she was not mentally ill, but Dr Green needed to make up his own mind about her and she didn't have a clue what he thought. In the meantime, she was trapped. After breakfast she would go back to her room to be away from all these strangers. She couldn't stand to be thought the same as them.

She looked up as she heard a shriek. Molly was holding her arm as if in pain and Gems was on his feet looming over her.

'I only wanted to help you,' she cried. 'You hurt me.'

'Don't touch my things,' he roared.

Emily jumped up. Molly needed to back off. Gems pulled back an arm, then swiftly, straight-armed, fist clenched, shot it forward and punched her face.

Molly toppled backward, howling and clutching her face, blood streaming through her fingers.

Gems followed her, his body language suggesting his intention to attack again.

A siren sounded and Ben was suddenly running to the rescue along with another male nurse. Two security personnel followed them. All four men gathered around Gems, blocking his escape. Molly lay on the floor crying as she was comforted by another female patient.

Gems slumped, his shoulders dropped, his arms hanging loose. 'She made me,' he cried. 'She touched my things.'

He was led away quietly, without resistance, by the second male nurse and the guards, and Ben was left to deal with Molly. His voice was kind and reassuring. 'Come on, Mol, let's get you cleaned up and assess the damage.'

'He shouldn't be here, Ben,' she wailed. 'He'll kill someone one of these days.'

Holding napkins to her nose with one hand, she held onto Ben's arm with the other. Emily could hear him soothing her each step of the way, and heard the buzz and click as locked doors released their locks and they were able to walk through them and out of sight, leaving a silence behind them. Emily and some of the other patients stood looking at each other in the aftermath or stared at Molly's blood on the linoleum floor. If Gems had hit Molly any harder, he could have knocked her out and done some serious damage. She wouldn't be having a check-over in any treatment room then; it would be a blue-light job to A&E.

Breaking away from the group, Emily went and found some paper napkins. She came back and placed them over the small pool of blood, watching snowy-white tissue turn to red. The staff had come running so quickly, she thought, staring up at the blue covered cameras. They were watching them all the time.

Chapter Thirty-One

Nina Barrows knocked on the security office door and was relieved when it didn't open. Gary Burge was taking a break from his new spying duties. He had been switched from night shifts to day shifts to suit visiting times. Mrs Jeffries had left the building a half hour ago after visiting, and it was assumed that she'd be gone a while and would come back at teatime. Gary was at the end of a mobile should he be required to come back immediately if she did reappear. Nina had a key to the office and wanted to move in and out of it without being caught. She wanted to check something that she was beginning to question.

She let herself in and shut the door behind her. Gary had made himself comfortable. On the desk he had a kettle, some mugs, coffee and powdered milk. Two pot noodle tubs sat side by side with an open bag of marshmallows and a tube of Pringles. A dirty pillow was on the chair, and she shoved it to the floor. She must remember to put it back afterwards.

She sat down and pulled the wheeled chair close to the desk. There were now two monitor screens, the one that was there before and the second one that Gary was using to watch Mr Jeffries' room. The patient was asleep by the looks of it, his eyes closed and hands resting on top of the blanket.

She glanced away. She hadn't come in to take over from Gary. It was the hospital computer she was there for. She hoped the file she was looking for was easy to find. She clicked the 'start' button and then 'documents' and was relieved to see in the video library the files were named and dated right back to when the hospital first opened. She scrolled slowly, hesitantly, and then faster as she realised she was still only in January of last year. Concentrating and watching the months of this year moving up the screen, passing May she slowed right down as she neared the date she was looking for. Four videos were named on that date: Nash, Austen, Allen, Sulis. She clicked on Allen Ward.

Ten minutes later Nina sat back in a daze. She had replayed what she had seen twice to be doubly sure that anxiety wasn't making her eyes deceive her, and now there was no doubt. Cameras that everyone had forgotten were there, had recorded events that in most eyes would seem unimportant, normal happenings. Unless you knew what shouldn't be there. In her long career in nursing she had never been faced with a situation like this, and the burden of knowing the seriousness of her find was like a giant weight bearing down on her narrow shoulders. All their futures would change if this video was discovered. The hospital's reputation would be in tatters. Her simple, ordinary life, as she knew it, would be over.

She had come prepared to find answers to worries that were beginning to niggle. She had come to reassure herself that there was nothing to fear. She had everything to worry about now. If Emily Jacobs had already discovered this file – or Gary Burge for that matter – it was only a matter of time before two and two would be put together. Nina had to make a choice about where she stood when the ship went down.

She clicked the file closed. She picked up the pillow and put it back on the chair. She stared at the computer, aware of all that it held. She could simply break the damn thing or even steal it. She could walk out of here and pretend everything would be alright. But Emily Jacobs had a determination in her and Nina didn't think that would ever go away. She was like the detonator of a time bomb set to go off and cause unlimited damage. And the clock was counting down.

The sun had almost gone down and the sky was red outside her bedroom window. Emily was surprised at how long she'd slept. She had crawled into her bed after breakfast and lain there ever since. Dr Green had requested no further session with her, today and that troubled her. He'd said they were going to chat some more. But maybe he was in no hurry to see her. She'd given him much to think about. The seventy-two hours would be up by tomorrow, but somehow she couldn't see her stay ending there. He would look to label her with some disorder, possibly even suicidal in light of her telling him that she'd wanted to die. She had given him plenty of reasons to consider keeping her longer.

An ache in her breast made her get out of bed, and in the bathroom mirror she saw a redness and swelling around the scar. She touched it and felt heat. Taking the towel she wet it with cold water and held it against her. She was run-down, that was the problem, and suspected she would need some antibiotics.

She also needed to eat. She had barely touched food since being there, any appetite gone. Taking the towel away, she settled her jumper back down. She needed to think her way out of this situation and find a way to prove what she had seen. She could not stay locked up. That was not an option.

Only Gems was sitting at a table when she made her way to the dayroom. He had more scrabble pieces of bread in front of him. She quietly took a knife and buttered some of her own. The metal trays that would have earlier held food for supper were empty and clean and the warming lamp over them was switched off. Snacks of fruit and bread were all that was on offer. She wondered what his mood was like and how often he reacted the way he had this morning. Molly's words hinted that he was dangerous and had lost control before, and she was reminded of Molly's conviction that one day he would kill someone.

Emily picked up her buttered slice and palmed the hard, plastic knife in her hand, feeling its smooth and rounded contours. She wondered if she could turn this into a weapon. She walked over to his table and waited till he looked up. 'I like the red car on your windowsill,' she said.

Without waiting for a response, she turned and walked back in the direction of the rooms.

A full five minutes passed before he came to his doorway. Emily was sitting on his bed, broken pieces of bread scattered around her, butter smeared on his hand gel from where she had touched the plastic container. Without looking, she knew the books were a heaped pile, his footwear spread across other parts of the room. The yellow and blue cars were on the floor beneath the windowsill, and in her hand she held his red car. She played with the wheels of the small toy to tantalise him. At the foot of the bed she had placed the knife and now waited to see how he would react.

A low guttural sound came slowly from his throat, like an animal's warning. His nostrils flared and he seemed to sniff her presence as much as see her. His body shape changed, his shoulders becoming wider, his arms bulking with muscle and face contorting. His mouth was wide, his teeth bared, and he growled and charged.

Instinctively Emily tried to run, but he was on top of her already, his fists landing blows on her head, her jaw, her ear. She tried to roll over and felt the breath knocked out of her as he punched her full in the belly. She gagged and vomit rose up her throat. He now straddled her hips, pinning her flat on her back and her arms could only protect her face as he rained down blows on her chest and shoulders. She could taste blood in her mouth and spat it out. She gasped for breath and readied herself to scream when a searing pain entered the side of her left breast. Unable to turn from it she went rigid with shock. Her eyes shot open and she stared into his eyes. He was going to kill her. She was going to be that 'someone' one day. Then his face pulled back fast and his weight was gone.

She heard voices, all male, all loud, all talking fast. Then Ben spoke. 'Jesus, he stabbed her. Get an ambulance, fast.'

Through bloodied lips, she smiled.

Chapter Thirty-Two

Jerry Jarvis's expression had just about returned to normal. The initial fear at seeing her battered body had now gone from his eyes. She was still on one of the beds in the resuscitation area, but no longer surrounded by an emergency team. Only he stood next to her. 'You are one lucky bunny,' he said. 'The knife was plastic, but the struggle has opened up your breast scar, which by the looks of it was ripe with a haematoma. You're going to be the death of me, Emily Tomb Raider, if you keep coming in like this.'

She reached out and grabbed his wrist. 'I can see that you're going to discharge me, aren't you?'

He looked her in the eye, his expression regretful. 'They're telling me they can nurse you there.' He took hold of her hand. 'Shit, Emily. I'm so sorry you're there. What's going on with you?'

She pointed at the pulled curtain around them and whispered, 'Are they behind them?'

He shook his head. 'Out sitting on the chairs. They've not moved from them. They're waiting for me to tell them how bad you are. And you are pretty battered, but nothing that rest and painkillers won't cure. The scar has gone back together with a couple of Steristrips and I'll give you antibiotics for any infection. I can't see how I can keep you here.'

'You could say that I am in a bad way, I've got a wound infection. You need to admit me for intravenous antibiotics?'

Jerry stared at her, shaking his head in bemusement.

Her eyes locked on his, her voice serious. 'Please, tell them you're keeping me in. I haven't got time to explain everything now, but I'm only in that place because I have uncovered something very bad that happened at The Windsor Bridge Hospital. So bad that people are going to go to jail for it. If they take me back I will never be able to prove what I know happened. They will keep me locked up for ever to keep me quiet.'

He leaned close as he too now whispered. 'And what are you hoping another day here will give you?'

'A chance to prove I'm sane, for one. A chance to show the police everything I've discovered.'

His eyes shot open in disbelief. 'You mean, you think you're just going to walk out of here?'

'You mean you won't let me?' she asked in a wounded voice.

'Let you?' he blustered. 'You'll barely be able to get up off this couch.'

Her voice was determined. 'Jerry, I can and I have to. And I won't drop you in it. I'll be gone in seconds if you can distract them.'

He closed his eyes in despair. She waited. Without looking at her he said, 'Give me a minute.'

After a long minute, he stepped back through the curtains carrying a patient's property bag. 'My jumper. Your top is covered in blood. My trainers, as you have no shoes with you. Fifty pounds, that's all I've got, but I don't advise you get a taxi unless you can disguise yourself. My hat is in there too, along with painkillers, antibiotics and dressings, and the keys to my flat. I won't be back till the morning. I'm on the night shift.'

Her eyes glazed with tears. 'You believe me without even knowing what's going on?'

He leaned over and gently knuckled her forehead in a spot without bruises. 'Of course I do. Someone has to.'

Nina switched on the second lamp in her small sitting room, chasing away the shadows. Her visitor was late. She had gone to evening mass after work in the hope of divine intervention, but God wasn't talking to her. She was on her own with this. She had already drunk a large sherry and now poured herself a second one. Waiting for her visitor was stretching her nerves. She had rehearsed what she would say, which would be short and to the point, just to get it over with. There was no way of dressing it up or undoing what she knew. She was at least giving them warning.

She stared around her small sitting room, the two high-backed armchairs she'd inherited from her parents, the old-fashioned sideboard bearing scratches on the doors, which she never sanded as a reminder of their beloved Labrador. The silver tray, crystal decanter and sherry glasses were one of her parents' wedding gifts, passed down to her like most of the furnishings and objects filling this two-bedroom house which had once also been theirs. She was born in this house, had lived in it all her life, and if at one time she had hoped to share it and see a child sleeping in the second bedroom where she used to sleep, that notion left her a long time ago. Minding elderly parents had taken that time almost sneakily, until she realised she was alone and it was all too late.

Her doorbell rang. Placing the sherry glass down, she took a calming breath and went to open her door.

'Oh,' she said, stepping back in surprise. 'What are you doing here? You're not who I was expecting. What do you want?'

'Only to give you this,' her visitor said, while moving into the hallway and closing the door.

'Give me what?' she asked, startled by the invasion of her home.

The hand that held the knife didn't hesitate and she gasped as she felt it enter her flesh, through her ribs, all the way to unresisting softness. She stared down at the handle sticking out of her. She looked into the eyes of her killer and saw they were smiling and thought, how rude to smile. *How rude . . . when you know I'm dying.*

Chapter Thirty-Three

Geraldine had a decision to make concerning the two separate incidents that had occurred the night before: a woman found murdered in her home this morning and an escaped psychiatric patient from A&E. Ideally, she would like to focus only on finding the missing patient and leave the murder case to Detective Chief Inspector George Crawley, the SIO in charge, if she wasn't so concerned that there may be a connection between the two incidents.

Emily had absconded from A&E, and no sighting of her had been reported. Nina Barrows was one of the people that Emily thought was involved in this missing patient fabrication. Geraldine now had to consider if Emily had any involvement in Nina Barrows' death. From all accounts Emily was in a bad way, badly beaten, and would struggle to even walk. Was she even physically able to carry out such an act? Was the timing just a coincidence? And was Emily innocent of any wrongdoing? The woman had been found by her neighbour, a railway worker leaving his home at five this morning, after seeing her front door ajar. Emily was at large.

Before she decided on a course of action she would have to speak to Crawley, to put him in the picture with the various possibilities. She would give him a possible motive and suspect. And in doing so, relinquish responsibility for Emily Jacobs, as much as she was loath to. She was not looking forward to this day at all, and had to remind herself that Emily was an ill young woman. Had she heard voices telling her to do this? Had she gone to the woman's home to maybe question her and something had gone badly wrong? There was no way of knowing what she had got up to. She was a psychiatric patient. Anything was possible. She needed finding as much for her own safety as for the safety of others. Geraldine had to consider all of this because Emily had once more put herself in the firing line.

The water in the shower tray was running clear, the last of the pink washed down the drain. Most of the blood was dried, spilled blood from her breast scar where it had burst open. She managed to keep the Steristrips from getting wet by covering them with a waterproof plaster. Her chest and stomach were marbled with fresh bruising, adding to her collection of older ones on her hip and thigh. The fresh scab on her lower lip worked free, and she'd tasted the slight saltiness of fresh blood before rinsing her face. Her body was moving easier under the hot spray and she had taken the full quota of painkilling drugs before the hour they were next due. She needed to be dressed and out of here before Jerry got home. He'd put his career at risk by helping her. The least she could do was to be out of his flat when he got home.

Twenty minutes later she was ready. Jerry's clothes made her look like a teenage boy, especially his rugby cap. As a bonus it hid her bruised forehead and covered her short dark hair. She had no idea what her plan of action would be, but getting out of here had to be the priority.

DCI George Crawley was a bear of a man, with a broad back, sloping shoulders and thick arms, and a large head taking the lead whenever he moved forward. His office was based at headquarters in Portishead, but the incident room for this murder enquiry had been set up at Kenneth Steele House, the base of the Major Crime Investigation Team, in Bristol. Its location suited both cities, Bath and Bristol, as well as the surrounding towns and villages. It was kitted out to solve major crimes and its air of seriousness never failed to impress Geraldine.

The freshly assembled team of officers were giving the SIO their full attention, as they would be well advised to do if they didn't want to end up with Crawley's heavy paw landing on their shoulder. He was an impatient sod at times, particularly with those who asked questions for the sake of asking. Geraldine could hear the bite in his voice as he answered a newly recruited DC. 'Now, let me think about that one. Are we going to be visiting her hospital? She worked there. She went there most days. People there might know her, might even know something. It may have even been one of her colleagues who had killed her. I can't think of any reason why we'd go there. Can you?' The blond DC's ears turned red to match the patches on his cheeks, and Geraldine bit her lip in amusement. Crawley had earned his rank through a solid career of hard police work and had solved more cases than most other police officers, and not just because of his length of service. He'd passed that benchmark while still in his forties. The job was, then as now, as much a part of his DNA as the blood and bones of his body. If at times he was irascible, Geraldine put it down to his approaching retirement. She could not see him ambling off to join the rest of the retirees without a roar or two of protest.

She stood at the back while he listed the tasks he wanted actioned, picking out individuals to take charge of them. His priorities were focused on gathering information, finding eye witnesses, working out Nina Barrows' last movements, possible motives and – most wished for – finding the murder weapon with prints on its handle.

As his briefing came to an end and officers shuffled off to do his bidding, she came up to the front to speak to him. She knew he liked her and had put in a good word on her last promotion. She had started off as a DC under his supervision and regretted none of her time as part of his team, learning from someone who had seen it all.

'Hello Geraldine, you look like you have something on your mind you wish to discuss?'

She took a photograph of Emily from behind her back and handed it to him.

He stared at it briefly. 'Emily Jacobs,' he stated. His eyes went to whiteboards behind him, to the only photograph presently pinned up, a head and shoulders shot of Nina Barrows in uniform. 'The connection?' he asked.

Geraldine shrugged reluctantly. 'She's missing, as you know, and something she told me, something very off-the-wall I might add, has Nina Barrows' name mentioned in it.'

He eyed her for longer than was comfortable. 'You look worried, Geraldine.'

'I'm not,' she said confidently. 'I'm sure she didn't do it. I just think you should know Nina Barrows' name has come up recently.'

'Sure is not the same as know. Sure is an opinion. Let's you and I have a little chat and see how sure I am after that, shall we?'

Feeling as if she'd just been transported back in time, Geraldine felt a familiar quake in her shoes and followed in his wake to the office he used when he was here.

Chapter Thirty-Four

An hour later Geraldine was back at her own office, with Eric for company, watching the local Monday-morning news on the wall-mounted television. The main topic was the murder of Nina Barrows. A blue tarpaulin tent had been erected over the front door of the victim's house and two female police officers, wearing yellow hi-vis vests, stood guarding it. Geraldine was grateful for Eric's presence, feeling that he alone understood the turmoil she was going through. He'd turned up to offer help finding Emily as soon as he heard that she was at large, and Geraldine was prepared to hear any insight he might have that would lead them to her whereabouts. Along with a police helicopter with infrared camera, police dogs and handlers, beat bobbies and PCSOs, the search had gone on till late last night and there was still no sighting of her. The hospital was sandwiched between Locksbrook Canal and Penn Hill, giving someone plenty of opportunities to either hide or get injured.

Geraldine took a sip of the takeaway coffee Eric had brought her, needing the hit of caffeine. 'Where is she?'

He shrugged. 'She could be anywhere. The thing is, she has few friends, unless she's met up with one from her past. I take it you've already checked with known associates?'

'Yeah, we have. Her GP sounds like a good friend. She said she'd call us if she hears from her. Her parents have heard nothing, but that's no surprise. We've got officers at her hospital now, killing two birds with one stone, questioning everyone about Nina Barrows and the possibility that one of them might have seen Emily or have had contact with her.'

'You've tried calling her or tracking her phone?'

Geraldine gave a pained look. 'She's not got one with her. She got taken in as an emergency patient, remember. They didn't pack a bag for her or anything, or put in a handy mobile for her to use.'

Eric leaned against the office windowsill. 'What about if we put out an appeal to her? Simply saying we need to talk to her and let her know we're worried about her.'

'You think she'd trust us?' Geraldine's face showed what she thought of that suggestion. 'I think that door's long closed.'

'She might. We've been there with her since the beginning. Who else has she got to go to?'

'Well, that entirely depends on the reason she's out there in the first place. Was it simply to get free, or did she have something she wanted to do?'

Geraldine's eyes went back to the television as she heard the name Jacobs being spoken. Her mouth fell open as she stared at the images now appearing on the screen. She raised the volume.

Doreen Jacobs was preparing to talk to a reporter; the backdrop was the woman's house. John Jacobs had a dress shirt on over baggy jeans and needed a shave.

'Mrs Jacobs, you must be greatly concerned for your daughter's safety. Is there anything you'd like to say to her to bring her home?'

Doreen folded her arms and gave a hard stare into the camera. 'If you can hear this, Emily, get yourself back to that hospital.'

The news reporter kept the microphone a fraction too long in front of Doreen, clearly expecting to hear more. Doreen simply stared. The reporter tried another tactic to get the woman to open up. 'This must be a very difficult time for you both. Your younger daughter, Zoe, went missing over a year ago, and now Emily is missing. This must bring back terrible memories of that time.'

Doreen shook her head stubbornly. 'I've got nothing to say on that.'

Geraldine sighed. 'Thank god for that.'

But Doreen wasn't done yet. 'It's got me thinking, though, whether she had anything to do with her sister's disappearance.'

Geraldine shot out of her chair. 'For fuck's sake!' she shouted at the television screen. 'What the fuck is she doing?' She stared at Eric in disbelief, stabbing a finger at the television. 'She's out to hang her own daughter. Can you believe it? What an utter cow.'

Eric shook his head in disgust. 'Whether she truly believes that or not, she should never have said it on live TV.'

'What do you mean, whether she believes it or not? Of course she doesn't believe it. She's just looking for attention.'

'She may do, Geraldine,' he said quietly. 'In the absence of another suspect, she may think it was Emily who took Zoe.'

Geraldine gaped at him. 'And would you mind telling me how long you think she's been harbouring that little thought? Please don't tell me you think it too?'

He put a hand up to calm the sudden tension between them. His voice was warm and soothing. 'I've never thought she had anything to do with the disappearance of her sister, but I have thought that guilt is holding her back. Guilt for perhaps not loving Zoe as much as we think she did. It would stand to reason that she would have some resentment towards a younger sibling, taking all the love of both parents while Emily put in the hard graft of bringing her up. Then when Zoe is an adult she's still clawing at Emily for support, both financially and emotionally. Emily would feel the burden of guilt if she, at any time, wished Zoe gone so that she could live her own life. That's all I'm saying, Geraldine. Her mother may think her involved for another reason, the one I already gave you, or it could be as simple as disliking her older daughter. I feel guilty for even thinking this of Emily, so please don't think I'm the enemy here. I just want to help.'

The tension eased and she gave him a sorry look. 'Where the bloody hell is she, Eric? That's what I want to know. Dr Green has given me no confidence that she is safe.'

She had spoken to him an hour ago and his concern was that Emily may be having thoughts of taking her own life. He'd filled her in about why Emily was taken to A&E in the first place. The psychiatrist was of the firm opinion that she had deliberately put herself in harm's way by goading another patient to attack her. That she elicited the reaction intentionally. Eric hadn't offered an opinion when she relayed this to him. She pressed him nor one now. 'What was she hoping for, Eric? Letting herself get beaten up like that? To feel more pain, as if she hasn't suffered enough?'

Eric lowered his head, slowly shaking it as if he had no answer. His voice, though, when he did reply, was leaden. 'Maybe to be punished,' he said.

Chapter Thirty-Five

Gary shoved a marshmallow in his mouth, wishing he'd never bought the damned things. He prided himself on keeping fit, but eating all this junk food while sitting down all day was bound to be adding chunk to his sides. The main reason he liked night shifts was so he could go to the gym during the day. It wasn't the same when finishing a day shift; by then he was knackered and just wanted to sit in front of the box.

At least this morning and this afternoon had been interesting, watching the police come and go. Seeing nurses and doctors go into an office with a closed door for questioning. The news of the murdered ward sister had been aired on the radio and telly. She'd been a misery guts as far as he was concerned. Not that he voiced that opinion when questioned. They'd talked to him for five minutes. It had been straightforward. In and out. Job done. Imagine if he'd told them he was on a surveillance job waiting for another crime to take place. They'd have looked at him with a bit more interest then, he reckoned, and not just seen him as a security guard. He'd tried to get on to the force a few years back but hadn't got past first base. There was no reason given. He stretched his arms above his head, trying to loosen his back. He should have brought in his weights; he could have given himself a proper workout while he watched the screen.

He shoved another marshmallow in and chewed it quickly as he saw Mrs Jeffries coming along the corridor. He watched her on the hospital camera until she disappeared into the room, then he switched his gaze to his own monitor.

In her husband's room, he saw her lean over to peck her husband on the cheek. *No proper kiss then*, he thought. On the two other occasions he'd seen her visit he'd seen no sign of this soup. She mostly sat looking at her mobile. A smile appeared on her face every so often at something she was looking at. She opened her large bag and brought out a newspaper and handed it to Mr Jeffries. She pulled out a bottle of juice and placed it on his locker. Then she sat down and crossed shapely legs. It was a hot day and she was wearing above-the-knee culottes.

A nurse popped her head in the room. On the other screen Gary could see the food trolley out in the corridor. Mr Jeffries shook his head at the nurse. The nurse carried on pushing the trolley to the next room and Mrs Jeffries stood up. Gary watched her reach in her bag again and saw a blue flask emerge in her hand. He grabbed his phone and speed-dialled Dalloway.

Emily swallowed some water to wash away the aftertaste of the tablets. The bottle was nearly empty and she would have no chance to buy more. She had bussed it out to the village, not risking using her car, and was reassured when the driver said, 'Good lad,' for giving him the right money. She'd bought two bottles of water from the local shop and a whole cooked chicken, and under a tree at the edge of a field, out of sight, she'd sat and eaten and watched the house. The hours dragged by and twice she'd fallen asleep, the pain in her body made less by lying still, and she'd missed any comings or goings to the house. Two cars were now parked beside the Alfa Romeo, so she worked out that while she slept, the Dalloways had received visitors.

She gazed up the hill, following the grey stone wall. It was lined with trees and she saw one that was leafless and dying, its bigger neighbours denying it sunshine and room to grow. It was the way of the world. The stronger always survive. She was getting weaker lying there, and she still hadn't made a decision on whether to just go up and knock on the door or bide her time and keep watching.

What was she hoping for by being here? If she was seen, Dalloway would call the police. Was she hoping to catch sight of Maria? According to Dalloway, the woman had gone back home. Was she hoping to prove this a lie? She would have gone to see Barrows if she knew where the woman lived. She daren't camp outside the hospital just waiting for her to materialise in case she was caught. Which is why she'd come to Dalloway first. She had nowhere else to go to get answers. If he was innocent, and it was a big if, she could appeal to him to hear her out and see for himself the video of this missing patient standing in the corridor of his hospital. He would realise for himself that she hadn't imagined her. If it was Maria's niece and if he was innocent, he would want to know. But until she knew for sure which, Dalloway or Barrows, was involved, she could trust neither and was on her own. She needed proof of innocence or guilt before she made her next move. All she could do in the meantime was watch and wait in the hope she would see something that would lead her to the truth.

Emily ducked quickly, even though it would be impossible to spot her where she lay. Jemma Dalloway had come out of her home wearing a long turquoise evening gown, her red hair curled loose over one bare shoulder. In her hand she carried a black suit bag, held high to prevent it trailing the ground, and placed it in the boot of the Alfa Romeo. She waved at the house and Emily wondered if Isobel was at a window. She climbed in the car and a short while later drove past close to where Emily hid, close enough for Emily to see her immaculate makeup, and then she was gone. Somewhere dressy, clearly.

She checked the little alarm clock she'd borrowed from Jerry's and saw that it was twenty to seven in the evening. Without it she would have been unable to tell the time, having neither wristwatch nor mobile with her. She could imagine, having spent a day without technology, in a village far from the hustle and bustle of city life, under different circumstances, it to be calming. If she ever got out of this mess she vowed to be uncontactable and at one with nature more often.

She thought of Jemma, dressed up in her finery and now possibly heading for the city. It gave her pause for thought. Was Dalloway joining her for the evening? Were his clothes in the suit bag that Jemma had been carrying? If so, it meant that

Isobel was at home with a minder, possibly a temporary nanny. This was an opportunity to have a proper look inside the house, to determine for sure that Maria wasn't there. Maybe Isobel might know something. Isobel had already met her, so Emily wasn't a complete stranger. She could say she'd come to see Maria and go from there. It was a long shot, but one worth taking. She popped a third tablet from the blister pack and swallowed it dry. She would wait just a little longer to give these pain killers a chance to work. Otherwise they'd be calling her an ambulance when they saw the pain she was in.

Dalloway sprinted along the corridor with a mobile pressed to his ear and two preloaded syringes in his hospital jacket pocket. If he was too late it might be necessary to treat the man.

'What's going on, Gary?' he asked for the umpteenth time, his mind preparing for what he would face.

'She's putting a towel across his chest. He seems reluctant as he's making no effort to sit up. She's stroking his cheek and talking to him. Oh shit, he's just nodded and she's turning to the flask. She's got the lid off. You need to hurry because she's poured some in the cup and she's got a spoon in her hand.'

Dalloway sped past the lift, almost crashing into a nurse pushing a treatments trolley, and nearly knocked himself down as he bounced his shoulder off a wall. He righted himself and took off down the corridor, his eyes fixed on the room ahead. He took the open doorway at a speed near impossible to break, and fairly flew across the room just in time to knock the full spoon of soup flying out of Mrs Jeffries' hand. Panting and barely able to get his words out, he pointed at her. 'Not again, Mrs Jeffries. There's no second chance, I'm afraid.'

He could see in her eyes that Meredith was right. She was panicking, but not to the point where she was ready to give up and admit what she'd done. She was pouring the liquid back into the flask, screwing the lid on it and trying to jam it in her bag. She glanced towards the doorway.

'Not so fast,' he said as she tried to brush past him. 'The police will want that flask.'

She stared at him mutinously and he'd already decided that if she tried to run, he'd let her. So long as he kept the flask, the police could deal with the rest.

Neil Jeffries was in shock. He seemed unable to read what was happening, his eyes darting from Dalloway to his wife, back and forth like a tennis umpire, trying to join all the dots.

His wife glanced at him desperately. 'Neil, tell this man to get out of my way. I'm taking you out of here. This place is a disgrace!'

Something shifted in the man's eyes. His gaze went from the flask in the surgeon's hands to his wife's face. He stared at each for several seconds. 'But it's just soup,' he said, looking to his surgeon for an answer. 'Tomato soup.'

Dalloway held the man's eyes. 'We think it has seafood in it.'

An anguished cry came from Neil Jeffries, and Dalloway saw a different person to the patient he cared for; the businessman he'd first met who built a multimillion-pound empire and had faced his illness head-on. The man looked stricken.

'You did this to me,' he cried wretchedly, looking at his wife in disbelief. 'How could you? How could you?' he asked.

Anna Jeffries stared at her husband with bitterness in her eyes. She patted the air once, twice, as if swatting away a fly. 'It's not what I signed up for,' she said simply.

Chapter Thirty-Six

Geraldine was perturbed that another name linked to Emily's was now under investigation. It seemed preposterous that another incident connected to The Windsor Bridge Hospital had happened. Tony Martin, the sergeant on duty for the evening, had gone there to arrest a patient's wife, Mrs Jeffries, on suspicion of attempted murder. The weapon, a flask of soup, was now police evidence and was sitting in an ordinary fridge downstairs in his office waiting to be collected and taken to a laboratory for testing. Geraldine had seen this woman on Friday shouting at Emily in the ward corridor, accusing her of giving something to her husband that had almost killed him. Yet it now seemed that it was she who had done something to her husband. Geraldine was unsettled by this revelation, the fact that Emily had been accused outright of doing some harm to this man and was at large when this further incident had occurred didn't sit well with her. She would ask Sergeant Martin what evidence he had against Mrs Jeffries, and if she was honest, was hoping it was concrete enough to cast suspicion away from Emily. She was in enough trouble. The investigation into the death of Nina Barrows was going slowly, according to Crawley. He'd been irritable on the phone when he'd called earlier. The woman, he said, was unmarried and had a career in nursing. She had lived alone, and never had visitors, based on the fingerprint evidence found in her home. So far they had found nothing in her history to suggest a motive for her murder, and without other evidence or even the weapon to lead him a different route, Crawley was now pinning his hopes on the murderer being either a random stranger or Emily Jacobs. Geraldine's 'sure' that Emily didn't do it was a far cry from his opinion. A full search party had been out all day, a watch had been put on her parents' home, Emily's home and the hospital. Her photograph was stuck up all over the city for the public to see, and there were still no clues as to her whereabouts.

Geraldine mused on how sad it was that Emily's face was now pinned up in the same places as her sister's – both missing, but for entirely different reasons. She yawned and stretched. It was nearly nine o'clock and she had been there since just gone six this morning. She should go home and see her family and try and get rid of the bags from under her eyes with slices of cucumber. She was going to look a sight at her friend's wedding tomorrow. All the things she intended to have done beforehand: hair coloured and cut, a manicure and pedicure, had all gone out the window. And even tomorrow's booked annual leave could go south if George Crawley had his way. His manner had become a tad prickly for her liking. He seemed to think that she was more likely than anyone else to know Emily's whereabouts. As if she had a fucking crystal ball to tell her these things. She was being harsh, she knew; he would be under enormous pressure to get results and was just taking out his frustration on anyone connected to the case. She would of course come in to work, if she had to, and already planned to drink only orange juice at the wedding, but it would be nice to have a day off from work and not have to think about Emily for once.

To not have to worry about how much trouble she could be in.

Emily woke up, startled. The light under the trees had changed colour, and while still plentiful, it had taken on a dusky hue as night began to fall. She had no idea of the time and reached for Jerry's clock. She was shocked to see that it was ten past nine at night. She had a raging thirst and felt the heat against her hands as she touched her face. Her breast was pulsating and felt heavy; an infection had set in. She had foolishly forgotten to take the antibiotics and now scrabbled in the plastic carrier bag for some. Groaning inwardly when she couldn't see them, she guessed she'd left them at Jerry's. She sucked the last drop of water from her bottle instead and placed it in the carrier. She would ask for more when she got to the house and could only pray that Isobel was not now in bed.

Standing up, she settled Jerry's cap on her head, picked up the carrier bag and began the arduous walk up the hill. The two other cars were still parked, so at least she could guarantee someone was at home. Her eyes scanned the windows as she got to the top, but she saw no one looking out at her. At the front door she listened for sounds coming from inside, and was cheered at hearing Isobel's laugh. The child was not in bed so she could still go with Plan A.

She rang the bell and waited. Isobel opened the door as before and stared out at her curiously, not recognising her until Emily removed her cap. 'You've got a sore head,' she said. 'Did you fall over?'

Emily smiled. 'Hello, Isobel. Yes, I have a sore head and I did fall over.'

'I've got a sore knee,' she announced, pointing to a tiny dry scab.

'Poor you. Can I come in and see Maria?' Emily asked.

The child shook her head. 'You can't. She's not here. She—'

'Jesus, Isobel, how many times have I gotta tell you not to open that door?' The voice was so unexpected and so recognisable, Emily had to grab hold of the door frame. What was *she* doing here? What was going on? Was her mind playing tricks? Had she imagined hearing that voice?

The door went to shut in her face and she quickly put her foot out to stop it.

'What the—' Emily heard, before the door swung back and she saw Shelly standing there, large as life.

'What are you doing here?' Shelly asked, astounded. There was no friendliness in her face. Her hand fell on Isobel's shoulder protectively.

'I could ask you the same,' Emily said back.

Isobel pushed off the weight of the hand and dashed back inside the house, leaving the two of them alone.

'Do you realise that with one phone call the police will be here? They're searching for you, Emily, and have been since last night.'

'You didn't answer my question, Shelly. What are you doing here?'

Shelly folded her arms. 'What do you think I'm doing here? The Dalloways have gone out for the evening and I'm babysitting.'

Emily pulled back in surprise. Her answer made sense. Sort of. Without Maria, the Dalloways were without a babysitter. Dalloway must have asked Shelly at the hospital if she'd mind his child.

'Oh, I see.'

'You don't look well, Emily. You need to go back to hospital.' Her voice was marginally less hostile, but no more welcoming.

Emily leaned against the door frame and reached into the carrier bag for the empty water bottle. 'Would you mind if I fill this? I ran out of water.'

Shelly eyed her cautiously. 'I'll do it. But I don't think I should let you in. Stay there and don't move.' She took the bottle from Emily's hand and rushed away.

When she returned with it, Emily would leave. She could see she would get no help from Shelly and wouldn't be surprised if she wasn't already calling the police.

Emily would chance her luck, and find a pay phone, if the village had one, and call a taxi. She would get away from here, maybe to Bristol where she could find a room that cost a lot less than thirty-six pounds a night, the sum total left from the money Jerry gave her. Shelly returned quicker than expected and gave her the filled bottle. Perhaps she hadn't called the police after all.

'Thank you,' she said before gulping half of it down. 'I'm sorry to have troubled you.'

Shelly pulled the door more closed. 'You need to run, Emily. They're not just coming after you to take you back to that hospital. They think you killed her.'

'Who?' she asked, shocked at what Shelly had said.

'Sister Barrows.'

Emily nearly tripped over her feet as she stepped back stunned. 'Barrows is dead?' she uttered in disbelief.

'Murdered,' said Shelly.

Emily lurched side to side as if drunk, her hands reaching out to hold onto something. The shock was making her giddy. 'It wasn't me. I didn't kill her,' she said desperately, wondering why someone had killed the woman. Was it connected to what Emily had uncovered? Had she discovered that Emily was telling the truth about a patient being in the room? Was she wrong in thinking Barrows had been involved? She had to get Shelly to believe she wasn't the murderer.

'Shelly, it wasn't me. Maybe Sister Barrows found out that I didn't imagine that patient beside me. Maybe she found out something that got her killed. I'm not the killer, Shelly. You have to believe me.'

A terrified scream suddenly pierced the air and Isobel came running to them, fear stamped on her pale face. 'You have to come, Shelly. There's blood!'

Shelly turned on her heel, shouting over her shoulder to Emily to leave. Emily made to follow and Shelly swiftly turned and shoved her back. 'Where do you think you're going? Get out of here or I will call the police.'

Isobel was grabbing Shelly's clothes trying to drag her forward, using her small body to push her. 'You have to hurry, Shelly. Please,' she pleaded.

Isobel managed to move Shelly into the hallway, and with the child in the way Emily pushed past and moved though the archway into the living room. There was no sign of blood anywhere, no one standing there, injured. The living room looked the same as when she'd visited before.

Shelly was furious. 'Who do you think you are? Get out of here now,' she said.

Emily looked at the desperate child crying. She looked frightened by Shelly's anger. Emily took a step back. She put a hand up and backed away. 'It's OK. I'll go.'

'No, you won't. I need you,' a voice said.

Emily raised her head. She stared up at the gallery, stupefied, her heart thumping, her mind unable to assimilate what she was seeing. Her eyes fixed on Meredith as if she were an apparition. Everything she thought she knew clouded with confusion. The friendship formed, the kindness given; it was all play-acting, trickery with intent to take her mind off what she'd discovered – they had all tried to get her to believe it was all in her mind.

'Snap out of it, Emily,' Meredith shouted, making her focus. 'We've got an emergency. We need to act fast.'

Emily took the first tread of the staircase, all aches and pains in her body now forgotten. Meredith needed her help. Emily acted instinctively. Meredith said it was an emergency, and Emily was good in emergencies.

Chapter Thirty-Seven

Geraldine wondered how much longer she would have to wait for her chicken chow mein. The Chinese takeaway was not particularly busy, which is why she'd pulled up outside in the first place, but it seemed to be taking them an age to get her order ready. She flicked through the car magazine at hand, seeing flashy cars on every page, and wished there was something more interesting to look at. Her mobile buzzed in her pocket and she discarded the magazine gratefully. She recognised the number and groaned inwardly.

'Hi Tony,' she said quickly, in the hope that the call would be equally quick. 'What's up?'

'Sorry Geraldine,' the duty sergeant said. 'I know you've only just left the place, but we've had a call from a doctor asking to speak to you. He wouldn't make do with one of us. Wouldn't tell us what it was about.'

'You get a name?'

'Yes, a Jerry Jarvis. I'll text you his number.'

'OK. Cheers, Tony. Have a good night.'

When she finished the call, she saw the tiny Chinese woman, barely able to see over the countertop, smiling at her widely.

'I put prawn crackers in to say sorry for your wait.'

Geraldine took the white paper bag and thanked her. She heard her phone buzz again and knew it would be Tony's text.

In her car she phoned the number. A confident voice answered. 'Jerry Jarvis speaking.'

'Hello, this is Detective Inspector Geraldine Sutton. I believe you wish to speak to me.'

She heard the intake of breath. 'I do. Only I'm just in the middle of something. Any chance I can call you back?'

Geraldine could hear background noises and made a guess. 'I take it you're at work?'

'Yes, A&E.'

'Which one? Bath? Bristol?'

'Sorry, didn't think. I'm at Bath.'

Smelling the aroma of her late dinner, her mouth watered. 'Is it urgent?'

He sighed. 'I really don't know. I think it is. I—'

She cut in. 'I'm on my way. I'll be there in fifteen minutes, give or take.'

Before pulling away, she made one more call to let her husband know she would be home even later.

Emily stared around the room in disbelief. While on automatic pilot she tapped glass ampoules of drugs, snapped nibs off the top of them and drew up the liquids into separate syringes to have ready to hand to Meredith on her command. She was not familiar with the names of some of them, only the steroid and diuretics, so had little idea what they were for. The lofty space, big enough for three good-sized double bedrooms with room to spare, was presently sectioned off into two areas divided by hospital screens on wheels. Through a gap she could see an operating table and anaesthetic machine and shivered at the thought of surgery taking place there. She had yet to look properly at the patient in the bed, knowing only that he was young and small, and that there was a pool of yellow bile and a patch of fresh blood on the sheet. She gazed at him now and was shocked to see he was a boy of maybe five or six, it was hard to tell. His eyes were closed, his small face half covered by an oxygen mask and tubes invading several parts of his body: his arms, his neck, up his nose and from his penis. The catheter bag held a few thimbles full of dark orange urine. He was hooked up to monitors and machines, and wires trailed across his narrow chest attached to him by sticky pads.

'Who is he, Meredith?'

Meredith had yet to say what the emergency was but looking at his colour Emily was guessing that the problem was with either his kidneys or his liver. His skin was yellow, his face puffy and his abdomen swollen. A large dressing covered the right side of his abdomen, looking freshly leaked with blood. She suspected this was the blood Isobel had seen. She placed her hand on his skin and it was hot to the touch.

'What's wrong with him, Meredith?'

Meredith ignored her and carried on injecting the next drug, her eyes on the monitor as it beeped his heart rate, blood pressure, respirations and oxygen levels. He'd barely passed any urine, was running a fever and wasn't responding. If these readings were calculated on an early-warning score chart and Emily was at a hospital, she would be pulling the bell right now to have the whole emergency team attend with every available expert at hand.

'Who is he, Meredith?' she asked again.

Meredith raised her head, anxiety stamped on her face. 'He's Rupert Dalloway's son. My nephew. Shelly's nephew. And he needs our help.'

Chapter Thirty-Eight

Jerry Jarvis made tea for them both. He put sugar in hers and carried the mugs to a treatment room so they could talk. He shut the door. Geraldine thought him incredibly attractive. His very dark hair and blue eyes would certainly cause a flutter to the heart. She wondered what he wanted to speak to her about, and was feeling strangely bemused after following him from room to room, patiently waiting for him to tell her the reason. She suspected it was his ease with dealing with people that was leading her by the nose so willingly.

She took back the lead. 'So, Dr Jarvis, what do you wish to speak to me about?'

'Jerry,' he said. 'Call me Jerry. I'm concerned about Emily Jacobs.'

Geraldine abruptly rose from the chair she had just sat down in. 'Jesus, you should have said immediately that this was about her. Have you heard from her?'

'No, no, please sit back down. I have no news to give you. I'm aware you're all out looking for her. It's been on the news all day. I haven't heard from her, but I am extremely worried about her.'

Geraldine sat back in her chair, immediately firing questions. 'How do you know her? What's your connection?'

He leaned against the examination couch, looking very much the doctor in his uniform of dark green tunic and trousers, his expression concerned. Geraldine imagined he would show a similar demeanour if he was about to impart bad news to a relative he'd made to sit down.

'I treated Emily last night. I saw the condition she was in. She's battered and bruised and has an infection in a recent operation site. I'm worried that she's out there alone and possibly ill.'

'How ill are we talking?'

He shrugged. 'Anything from a bad infection to sepsis.'

Geraldine could tell he was keeping something back, but for now she'd press lightly. 'And what's your personal connection?'

He shook his head as if he didn't know the answer. 'Friends, I hope. I've worked with her a long time. Eight years, I think. I was teasing her after the car accident that she should get herself back here to work. We miss her.'

Geraldine had forgotten about Emily being hit by a car. So much seemed to have happened to her in the last week, it was hard to keep track of it all. 'So you saw her then as well?'

'Yes. She seems to be having one accident after the other. She's going through a pretty tough time, I would say.'

Geraldine's thoughts turned inward for a moment. The mention of having more than one accident jarred something in her. His words described someone who was accident prone or just unfortunate. Or, she realised, worryingly, someone suicidal.

Maybe, like the attack she'd orchestrated, she'd also caused that car to hit her by deliberately walking out in front of it. She gazed at the young doctor and was done with going lightly. As much as his manners and handsome face pleased her, she had a job to do.

'What aren't you telling me, Jerry?'

He stayed silent, his eyes averted.

'You helped her escape, didn't you?'

Geraldine felt sorry for him as he told of his involvement in helping Emily flee, of the supplies he'd given her to help her on her way. She was sorry for him, because if it proved that Emily was involved in the death of Nina Barrows, then his career was over and he could be facing jail time.

'Did she hint at what she might do or where she might go?'

He hung his head in despair. 'She said she was going to prove that she was sane, and also something that she uncovered at The Windsor Bridge Hospital.'

His answer eased Geraldine's concern somewhat. If she was really intent on doing that then she was not intending to take her own life. If she was looking to prove something had happened at her hospital then it stood to reason that she would start with the people she thought were involved, which put Emily right back in the frame for Nina Barrows' murder. Had she murdered the woman because she wasn't taken seriously? If so, then who else might she feel hadn't taken her seriously, or was, in Emily's eyes, to blame for her being put in a psychiatric ward? Dalloway? They had a watch on the hospital, a watch on her parents' home and on Emily's home. Where they didn't have a watch was at the Dalloways' home. Emily knew where Rupert Dalloway lived. She had visited him once before.

Her heart beat faster as a rush of images filled her mind. Emily with a knife in her hands, a manic look on her face. Jemma Dalloway talking too much, her husband trying to calm things down. Their child running from parent to parent for comfort, not knowing how dangerous their visitor was and getting in the way. She stood up fast, already making for the door.

'I've got to go, Jerry,' was all she could say.

Chapter Thirty-Nine

He had a son. A second child. Dalloway had only spoken of Isobel. He also had a son, and the child was clearly very ill. Meredith said the boy was her nephew, Shelly's nephew. They were family, all related to Dalloway somehow, and she hadn't had a single clue as she'd worked alongside them. They had kept it completely hidden from her. Never once mentioning the fact that they were family. They were caring for this child in his home when he should clearly be in a hospital. Meredith was trying to save him. This was not a hospice setup. Not with all this equipment surrounding him. They therefore had a reason for wanting no one to know how ill he was.

The hospital bed was raised high and it was surrounded by the same tools and machines, in the same arrangement, as in a high-dependency unit. There was room to get to the head of the bed if airway management was needed, and oxygen and suction were within easy reach. The boy should be in a hospital was the constant thought on her mind. Surely Meredith must see that?

She could sense the character of the boy from this room. He was a lover of cricket, that was for sure, unless it was his father's choice of décor. Posters of a dozen players adorned the walls. On a bookcase were a pair of off-white cricket pads, two bats, a bundle of wicket stumps, gloves, cricket helmet and brown leather cricket balls. Some shiny and new, others worn and dulled. She wondered how long ago he had last played and how long he'd been ill.

'Why isn't he in hospital, Meredith?'

Meredith stopped pacing the floor. She had started pacing just a few minutes ago, but it seemed like for ever. She stared at the monitor as it bleeped a fresh set of vital signs. She wrung her hands, clearly agitated. He was not improving and Emily was growing alarmed. Surely he would die here if they didn't get him urgent treatment?

'Meredith, you need to get him to hospital. He needs scans, maybe surgery. You're a good doctor, but he needs a team of good doctors to get him out of this crisis. What's wrong with him?'

Meredith moved closer to the bed. She stroked the boy's brow. 'I told you I was here for family, because he is part of my family. I didn't lie to you. His name is Walter and he already has the best doctor, his father, looking after him.'

There was a flicker of movement at the bedroom door. Shelly stood inside the doorway. She carried three bottles of Coke in her hands. 'I thought you could do with a hit of sugar,' she said to Meredith. 'She's asleep. I had to read her a dozen stories before she'd go off.'

Emily realised she was wearing her uniform, the same one she wore at the hospital. It hadn't really registered before, having never seen her out of uniform. But it made sense that she would wear it here too. She was nursing, after all.

'How's he doing?'

'He needs to be in a hospital,' Emily answered.

Shelly glared at her. 'I wasn't asking you.'

'Your nephew needs to be in a hospital,' she repeated. 'Or are you both blind? You're covering up something and I am certain that it has something to do with Maria's niece. You both know I didn't imagine her.'

Shelly laughed. 'You're so wrong. Maria's niece is back home. You saw nothing!'

Meredith began pacing again and Emily was enraged. 'Stop fucking pacing, Meredith, and do something. Make the call. He needs an ambulance.'

'I can't,' she said. 'I simply can't. I have a life to get back to. A child of my own. I can't.'

'You think you'll be going back to that if he dies? You think you can hide your involvement in all this for ever? Who do you think they'll blame?'

Meredith stopped still, her eyes finally showing some sense, a desire to do something. Emily nodded at her encouragingly. Meredith stared at the boy, then slowly she reached in her pocket and pulled out a mobile.

Shelly stilled her hand. 'You,' she said calmly, leaving Meredith's side, walking slowly towards Emily. 'You'll be blamed. You forced your way in here, an insane woman on the run, having already committed one murder. They'll blame you.'

Emily stared at her as if she were mad, and maybe she was. There was more madness in this room than anything she'd seen in that psychiatric wing.

'You'd let him die to save yourself?' Her eyes swung to Meredith, now seeing no sign of the mobile in her hand. 'You'd both let an innocent child die? You despicable people. You call yourself a doctor, Meredith. You have no right to be one.'

Shelly held out one of the bottles. 'Shut up and drink your Coke, Emily. You look like you could do with it.'

Geraldine munched on prawn crackers, washing away the saltiness with slugs of Coke. She wished she had another officer to keep her company, but this was an impulse decision. She recalled the 'subtle' rebuke she got from Dr Green for bringing uniformed officers to catch Emily the last time. It was all very well for him to think that, but if he did her job he'd think in terms of safety at all times. She'd considered her options, one of which was whether to alert Crawley. He should really be the first to know now that Emily was marked as a possible suspect. But Geraldine was not yet ready to involve him. She'd rather find Emily quietly, without all guns blazing to frighten her away. She mashed another handful of crackers into her mouth, keeping her eyes on the road, her mind on the visit ahead.

It was a long shot. She knew that. But one she had to take.

Dalloway was going to be surprised to see her turning up at his house at this time of night. That's if he was there and not at work. She'd already decided what she'd say. She was there on the basis of making him aware that Emily was still at large and could turn up, if she hadn't already.

Yet she couldn't see Emily as a murderer. Despite the earlier image she'd painted in her mind. She was gentle. Ill. But a killer? Geraldine shivered in the semi-darkness. She needed to keep thinking positively and not be sucked into that shite that came out of Emily's mother's mouth. How could she think Emily had anything to do with Zoe going missing? Was she just a malicious woman? Geraldine hoped Crawley hadn't taken the woman's words seriously. He'd be tearing his hair out if he didn't get a firm lead soon. Crawley by name and crawly by nature, he didn't let up until he unearthed something. She just hoped it was soon, to take the heat off Emily.

She chewed her bottom lip. Supposing she was wrong, though, and she *was* responsible for her sister's disappearance? Eric said that Emily would have loved Zoe almost obsessively. Did love turn to hate between the sisters? Had she been reading Emily wrong all along? Did Emily know what had really happened to Zoe? Was she perhaps responsible in some way? And had she made herself ill as a result of keeping quiet about it? If she was there at the Dalloways' home, Geraldine had no idea what mental state she would find her in. Maybe she should have taken someone else with her. For all she knew, Emily could be dangerous. The fucking maybes were driving her crazy.

Chapter Forty

Emily wondered how many hours she'd been at the house. It seemed like for ever, and the sky through the porthole windows was pitch-black. She'd come to realise that Shelly was no ordinary healthcare assistant. The conversations between her and Meredith as they discussed the child's condition highlighted a firm medical knowledge. She spoke with confidence of trying different drugs and increasing dosages of the ones already used. She knew more than Emily, that was for sure. Emily wondered if she should make a run for it. They couldn't both chase after her. Meredith would have to stay with the child. Shelly didn't look built for running, though there was power in those shoulders; she had felt their strength in that push downstairs. Of the two of them, Shelly concerned her more. There was a meanness in that red slash of a mouth, and while Meredith was clearly the more educated and the doctor minding this child, Shelly showed she was in charge. There was a shrewdness in those blue eyes. She was planning ahead all the time. The chair she had positioned in the doorway, the one she sat on now, was a tactical move to keep Emily in the room. The scalpel blade she held in her hand, which she tapped against her knee, was a warning. Emily would not get past her without a struggle.

'I can prove it was Maria's niece in the room with me,' she said abruptly. 'I saw her on hospital CCTV footage. Neither of you will get away with what you did to her. You were both by her bed when she was dying.'

Shelly eyed her scornfully. 'So explain how a dead woman is alive in her own country, then?'

'Come over here, Emily,' Meredith interrupted. She was using a portable ultrasound machine and moving the wand over the child's abdomen. A surgery site was uncovered, the scar clean, but the area distended. 'I'm going to put a drain in. He has fluid collection.'

Emily stayed still. 'He's not getting any better, Meredith. I'm not going to help you any more.'

'I need your help,' she uttered between clenched teeth.

'And he needs to be in a hospital.'

Shelly stood up. She pointed the scalpel at Emily. 'Get over there and do your job.'

'Are you going to use that on me if I don't?'

'Just fucking test me, why don't you?' she snarled.

'Who was that patient, Shelly? If she wasn't Maria's niece, then who was she? Because someone was beside me in that bed and she died.'

'And so too will this boy if you don't get over here and help,' Meredith hissed.

Emily moved over to the bed, her legs feeling like lead. She could feel the heat of her own body coming through her clothes. So much for running, she thought. She was struggling to just walk. She leaned on the bed for support and pulled back fast as she heard the boy groaning.

She smoothed his brow and made soothing sounds. His eyes were opening and as he saw her, she smiled. 'Hello, Walter.'

A small hand came up and pulled the mask from his face. 'Your face looks strange,' he said weakly, his young voice rasping. 'Smudgy.'

Emily's eyes darted to the monitor to see his blood pressure and saw it was nearer to normal than before.

Meredith moved up the side of the bed so that he could see her face. 'Hello, Champ. You've been asleep a long time.'

He smiled with effort. 'Hello, Merry.'

She kissed his forehead and put the mask back on his face. 'I need to pop a little tube in your belly, Champ, but you won't feel anything, I promise you.'

Emily moved back from the bed. She refused to stand there and just watch Meredith do her thing. She would run for it, even if she had to crawl to get help. She could not let this carry on. She calculated the distance between the bed and the doorway and looked for a weapon she could use against Shelly. She took her first step and went no further. She had just heard the unmistakable sound of a car engine, the wheels crunching on the gravel. Peering out the porthole window, she saw bright headlamps, and then the colour of the car as outside lights came on. The Dalloways were home.

Geraldine slammed the brake and pulled hard in against the hedgerow as the car in front of her, coming from the opposite direction, shot across the lane making a sharp right into the private road. Geraldine followed at a slow pace, letting it get ahead. Through the windscreen she'd picked out the shapes of Mr and Mrs Dalloway.

Rupert Dalloway was climbing out of his car as Geraldine pulled alongside him. He looked immaculate in a dinner suit and bow tie. She tried not to question whether he'd been drinking and driving. For a start, she didn't have a breathalyser kit with her, but instinct told her he wouldn't break this type of law. Mrs Dalloway stayed in the car, letting her husband deal with the visitor.

'Good evening, Detective Inspector,' he said, looking unperturbed by her arrival. 'What brings you out here at this time of night?'

'A friendly warning, Mr Dalloway. Emily Jacobs is still missing and we just wanted to alert you to that fact, on the chance that she could turn up at your home.'

'That's very civic-minded of you, coming all this way when a phone call would suffice.'

'It's my job, sir. And you can't see over a phone call. I wanted to be sure that you're safe.'

He smiled. 'Well, as you can see, I am.'

'And those inside?' Her eyes went to his house.

He nodded once. 'Those inside also. I spoke with our childminder only minutes ago to let her know she can get along to bed, that we're almost home. She would have told me of any visitors or concerns then. She can't hide it when she's anxious.'

Geraldine smiled politely. 'Well, that will be all then. I'll wish you goodnight.' She moved to get back in her car, then turned around again. 'It's good news about Maria's niece.'

'Katka?' he asked, puzzled.

'Yes, I spoke to her. The mobile number you emailed me, I got hold of Maria. I spoke to them both. It's good news that's she safe.'

The confusion cleared from his eyes. 'Yes, it is. And I'm glad I was proved right. Maria told Jemma that she'd met up with a boy she didn't want to leave.'

'Ah, that explains it. So a good night, then?' she said, wishing her mouth would shut and stop with the prattling.

'I beg your pardon?'

'Dinner suit. I take it you've been somewhere nice?'

'Ah, the giveaway,' he nodded. 'Yes, we have. The hospital was up for an award.' He paused to give her a chance to say something else. Then smiled politely. 'If that's all, I now intend to have a well-deserved drink, so I'll bid you goodnight and a safe drive.'

Geraldine got back in her car. In the rear-view mirror she saw him standing there, unmoving and watching, as she drove away.

He was aloof, maybe even a little cool, but what else should she expect? She was not above being a bit aloof herself at times, especially if someone turned up unannounced at her front door.

She eyed the road ahead, irritably. She had a wedding to go to tomorrow for which she would have liked to have had an early night. Instead, she was going home late, hungry and having wasted an entire evening.

Emily held her breath as she heard footsteps coming up the wooden staircase. If she had a chair she would sit down before she fell down. Fever and fear were making her legs terribly weak.

Dalloway stood at the doorway, taking everything in. Emily's presence, Shelly standing with a scalpel in her hand, Meredith's anxious face, the tension in the room. His gaze then fixed on the boy in the bed and Emily saw anguish fill his eyes.

'I've done everything I can, Rupert,' Meredith said tremulously. 'He's more stable now. He's just spoken to us.'

'You should have called me,' he said in a voice suppressed with emotion.

'I was going to, Rupert, but I was busy sorting him out,' she replied defensively. 'I'm just about to put in a drain.'

He gave a sound of utter despair. 'A drain! Will you look at him, Meredith. Just look at him! He's rejecting it, you stupid woman.'

Emily could hold her tongue no longer. 'I told her to call an ambulance hours ago. They were both prepared to let him die.'

'You shouldn't have come here, Emily,' he said. 'The police are looking for you.'

'Well call them, then. I'll go quietly with them.'

He shook his head regretfully. 'Now is not the best time to have them in my home. You'll have to stay here a little while longer, I'm afraid. Walter needs me.'

'They said he's your son.'

'He is, Emily,' he said in a voice leaden with sorrow, as he glanced slowly her way, and Emily found it hard to dislike him. He looked beaten.

'He needs to go to hospital. You can't keep him here.'

With slow movements he pulled the bow tie from his neck and unbuttoned the collar of his shirt. He took off his jacket and laid it across the foot of the bed, and then he moved up to his son and leaned down and cradled the small head in one hand and stroked the sallow cheek with the other. 'My beautiful boy,' he whispered.

'Call an ambulance, Mr Dalloway, it's not too late,' Emily urged.

He straightened up and smoothed the red-gold hair. 'My son has had enough of hospitals. He spent the first year of his life in hospital. He has been through such a lot. His kidneys eventually failed and he has spent most of his life on dialysis. The real kick in the teeth is that one organ's disease leads to the failure of another. When the liver is affected, there is no machine that will help that. And I thought we had beaten that bastard. All I wanted to do was make him better.'

'Don't give up, Rupert.' Jemma Dalloway cried from the doorway, startling them. She had silently come up to the room, and now stood there with tears slowly falling down her face. 'Don't you dare do that.'

Dalloway said nothing. His face said it all and she searched it long and hard, desperate for him to agree with her, to witness anything but this hopelessness and finality, before she suddenly clutched her breast, gave a cry of agony, her eyes widening in horror as she saw what he had already seen. Dalloway crossed the room and held his wife. Emily saw them now, as they were. Despite their wealth and success, despite Dalloway's gift of healing the sick, they were simply parents facing a terrible ordeal.

'You told me he would live,' she cried bitterly. 'You told me this would save him.'

Dalloway rested his head on top of hers. 'I was wrong, Jemma.'

Emily's eyes were glazing, whether from the emotional trauma she was witnessing or the raging infection taking a hold of her. She only knew that if she didn't lie down soon, she would fall down. She watched as Shelly went over and wrapped her arms around the couple. The image seemed incongruous, and she wanted to tell her to get away from them and leave them to their privacy. Dalloway's arm moved from his wife's shoulder and encompassed Shelly in the gathering. Emily stared at the bizarre huddle. She needed to get away from here. She needed to be gone from this house.

Trying to focus, she looked for the door. Then Shelly's sharp voice broke her concentration. 'You can try again, Rupert. It's not too late. You have another donor right here.'

Emily raised her head in shock. They were all staring at her. Shelly, Dalloway and Meredith were all probing her with considering eyes. Jemma was looking at her as if she was the next great hope. Fear made her find her voice. 'You would kill me to take my liver?'

Shelly flung out her arms expansively. 'You're such a drama queen, Emily. We only need a slice. Not the whole thing. And it will regenerate in a few weeks.'

Emily's legs buckled and her knees went hard to the ground. She struggled to get up, but her limbs refused to obey. She slumped sideways, knowing it was futile to even try to get back up. Her head felt heavy and she let it fall back and the softness of the carpet cradle her. The images of the cricketers stared down at her and she imagined hearing the satisfying crack as ball hit bat, seeing a sunny day, green grass, blue skies. Then in her mind she heard a similar sound, of ribs cracking, as if surgically snapped. She whimpered and tried not to imagine her broken bones, her opened body, trying to bring her mind back to the sunny day, green grass, blue sky – anything to stop the sound of breaking bones.

Chapter Forty-One

Through a gap in the screen she watched the boy's eyes flutter open. He was alone and she wondered where everyone else was. They had put her on the operating table behind the screens and put the side rails up to keep her from rolling off, and initially she feared that they had already operated on her, until she saw she was still wearing her clothes. She felt desperately ill and had a raging thirst. The sky was still dark and she wondered how many hours were left until morning. It would surely be daylight soon? She felt as if she'd been sleeping for hours. She called to him, 'Hello, Walter.'

He gazed in the direction of her voice and she reached out an arm and grabbed hold of the screen, wheeling it aside to see him better.

He gave a weak smile. 'Are you sick too?'

She nodded. 'A little.'

'Daddy's trying to make me better, but I don't think he can. I think I'm a little bit too ill.'

Emily swallowed the lump in her throat. 'Your daddy's a very clever doctor.'

'I know, but it would be better if Daddy was just Daddy now. Then he can just talk to me and not be busy. He could take me in the garden and play cricket with me. Isobel could run for the ball, though she's not very good at catching.'

'And Mummy?'

'Mummy could go back to being a doctor. She had to stop working when I got ill.'

Emily felt tears form. He had it all worked out. He had planned how he would like things to be. His entire family consisted of medical experts, and between them they were battling to save his life and he wanted them all to stop and just be with him. She didn't want him to give up hope.

'They'll get you better, Walter. They love you very much.'

He sighed tiredly and closed his eyes. 'I know, but I don't want to be sick anymore. I just want to play in the garden.'

When she next woke, Dalloway was sitting on the edge of her bed, her wrist in his hand as he injected fluid into a pink cannula. She was in a bedroom in a single bed, sunlight bathing the walls a pale lemon, no longer lying on an operating table. He was unaware that she was awake, his head lowered. She saw that he was still in the same shirt as the night before and wondered if he had sat up all night with his son. A sheet covered her body, leaving her shoulders bare, its lightness a blessing against the throbbing of her left breast. She watched him replace the first syringe with a second smaller one and guessed it was saline to flush residue from the cannula.

'You moved me.'

He didn't jolt at the sound of her voice and kept a steady hand on what he was doing. She was not surprised. He was a surgeon and could not afford to be easily unnerved. 'Yes,' he answered.

'To a room next door. We needed you out of there. And lying in a bed's more comfortable.'

'The woman I saw wasn't Katka, was she?' The mystery of the woman was starting to make sense now. Katka had returned to her own country. She hadn't been Katka at all, but some other woman who looked like her.

'Her name was Sophia,' he said without looking at her. 'She had been a friend of Katka's. They came over together. Katka stayed here and Sophia stayed in the city, looking to find work. She spoke good English and had been over here before.'

Sophia. She said the name aloud in her head. Her name was Sophia.

She clocked the last thing he said. She had assumed the girl couldn't speak English. She now wondered if it was the fear of what she faced that had kept her silent.

'Only she had a small problem,' he continued. 'She was pregnant. She had it aborted over here, not by me and not at The Windsor Bridge Hospital, let me add. She had come prepared with money to pay for it and the name of a clinic already. I would never have known about it but for the fact that she came to our house one day with a fever. Jemma put her to bed and asked me to examine her when I got home from work. It was nothing too serious, she just hadn't given herself enough time to recuperate. I gave her antibiotics, much the same way as I'm doing with you now, and took bloods just to be sure, and she went on her way and I forgot about her. I had more pressing things to think about. Walter had just become seriously ill. I went into work to clear my desk, so to speak, when I got her results back. It was like looking at a lottery win. She had blood group B – the same as Walter. Only ten per cent of the population in the UK have this blood type.'

'Surely you or your wife could have been a donor, donated a slice of your liver as Shelly so crudely put it?'

'We couldn't. Trust me, we had already tried all family members. None of us was a match. You don't understand. It was like a sign—'

'You mean an opportunity,' she said with scorn.

'It was the answer. Waiting for a dead organ donor when we had a healthy live one, with blood group and HLA matching, with little risk to the donor, was like a dream come true. I don't know how much you know about transplants. Rhesus negative/positive does not matter with liver donation as the Rh antigen is only present on red blood cells. Really it is only the blood group and human leukocyte antigens matching that is important. We had a perfect match.'

'One thing I do know,' she said scathingly, 'is that you had to have tested for that. And you did, because you were on the lookout for a donor.'

'Time was of the essence, Emily,' he said earnestly. 'And we were running out of it. His life could be saved. Sophia was desperate for money; she understood completely what I was asking of her, and she was going to be paid very handsomely for this gift.'

'Instead she lost her life, though, didn't she?' Emily reminded him. 'You let that happen.'

He looked askance, his eyes wounded. 'I have never let someone die deliberately. She died because . . . she simply died, they said.' His voice was heavy with regret, his hand forming a hood to hide his expression. 'I wasn't there.'

She lay still, suddenly comprehending that night. 'You weren't even there?' she said. 'While her life ended, her heart stopped, you'd already abandoned her. You were here with your son, saving his life while she died. And you don't even know why, because she wouldn't have had a post mortem, would she? They would have discovered what was missing from her body, otherwise. So what did you do with her?'

He stood up and turned so that he didn't have to face her. 'You don't need to know those things, Emily.'

'And now you're going to do the same to me,' she uttered bleakly.

He turned back to face her. 'I'm going to get you well, Emily. You're septic. I had to resuscitate you.'

She stared at him, surprised, and looked up. A bag of IV fluids and a smaller bag with IV antibiotics fluids were dripping into her arm.

He made to leave, and she found she didn't want to be alone. 'So where was Katka when all this was going on? Her going missing was the reason I thought it was her in that bed.'

'That's what they do when they're seventeen, isn't it?' he said with a weary smile. 'Go off and have a good time and forget that people will be worried about them. Maria told Jemma that Katka missed her flight by going to the wrong gate. Instead of waiting to catch the next one, she returned to Bath and met up with her boyfriend.'

'Did she not go looking for Sophia? Was she not worried that her friend had disappeared?'

He shook his head. 'She had her own agenda, I suspect. She possibly thought Sophia had found work. She may have been too wrapped up with her boyfriend to even think about her friend.'

Emily's eyes misted with sadness. 'Zoe was like that. She'd go off, without a word where to, and leave me to worry. It's true, that's what they do when they're seventeen. Is that how old she was?'

He knew she was asking about Sophia. 'She was nineteen.'

This time he got as far as the door. He looked back once more. 'Thank you for everything you did for my son last night, Emily.'

'Is he any better?' she asked, hopeful.

He slowly shook his head. 'He's dying, Emily.'

He closed the door quietly behind him, leaving her in more fear with those words. Shelly seemed to know she could be a donor. She must therefore already know Emily's blood group.

If he was dying, they would need her to save him.

Chapter Forty-Two

Geraldine balled up the new pair of tights she'd just laddered and threw them across the bedroom in frustration. That was the problem with trying to go with seven deniers. You couldn't afford to have fingers, let alone fucking fingernails – they were meant to magic their way up your legs or be put on with a pair of cotton gloves. She stomped across to her drawers and hoped she'd find another light-coloured pair among the black ones. She didn't know why the wedding had to be so goddamn early. Most people didn't get married until at least one o'clock. An eleven o'clock wedding was too early, in her estimation. And a Tuesday was just an odd day to get married, full stop; it put everything else out of sync. Her parents were minding her children and keeping them overnight which would make it a long day for them too, seeing as they'd picked them up at nine o'clock this morning. Still, the bonus was that she would have a lovely day out with her husband, where for a change they could sit without hearing the perpetual cries of 'I want' from their children.

Her hands suddenly went still as she thought of the Dalloways returning from their night out last night. Echoes of the previous night's conversation came back to her; Rupert Dalloway telling her he'd just spoken to their childminder. The way he spoke about her implied that he was familiar with her. He was so confident that she was alright. 'She can't hide it when she's anxious,' he'd said. These words were about someone he knew well. And yet their new nanny had only just started with them. She had been a young woman called Felicity, who hadn't seemed at all anxious to Geraldine's mind. Jemma had sat in the car while they were talking; if she hadn't, she may have clarified better what her husband meant by that remark. She now felt uncertain about the outcome of that visit. A simple remark that could mean something or nothing was making her feel twitchy, and she knew she wouldn't settle until she checked it out. Geraldine closed the drawer. She went to the top of the stairs and called to her husband. Standing in her knickers and bra she put on her best apologetic face. 'You're going to have to go ahead without me.'

Sensing someone in the room, Emily opened her eyes. Isobel was standing on one foot, practising balancing, her arms outstretched, concentration showing on her young face. Emily wondered how long she had been there. She had drifted in and out of sleep since Dalloway's visit and now desperately wanted the loo.

'Hello, Isobel,' she called to the girl.

The child grinned. 'How long can you stand on one foot?'

She chuckled, thinking that given her present condition, maybe no time at all. 'Isobel, can you tell me where the loo is?'

The girl pointed at the wall straight ahead of her and Emily turned her head and saw a second door in the room. Gathering the sheet around her, securing the wheelie drip stand with the other hand, she managed to get out of bed. 'Won't be long,' she said.

'Walter said your face looked strange.'

Emily smiled. 'He said the same thing to me.'

'I don't think you look strange.' She fidgeted with her pigtails, staring at Emily long and hard. 'Daddy said you were sleeping, but I didn't believe him.'

Emily's legs turned to jelly from the effort of standing. She planted each foot forward like a toddler learning to walk. 'I was, but I'm not now.'

'Good,' she said in a serious tone, as if a very important matter had been settled. 'I didn't like it when you were asleep.'

Emily was smiling to herself as she let herself into the en suite bathroom. She was a funny little girl, maybe a tiny bit precocious, but it was understandable that she would want attention, having a younger sick brother taking up the larger portion of their parents' time. She just wanted to be noticed.

After washing her hands, she let the sheet fall from her and went over to the full-length mirror. She inhaled sharply as she took in the state of her body. The only places free of bruising were from mid-thigh to her feet. The rest of her was a myriad of colours: red, purple, green, yellow and blue and almost black, she was startled to see, across the side of her left breast.

She looked as battered as she felt. No wonder her body was septic. She realised it was probably the reason that she was still in possession of all her organs. They would want the infection to clear from her body first. She bit down hard on her lip to stop the cry escaping. She didn't wish to distress the child in the room next door. She would get well soon enough with Dalloway looking after her. It was only a matter of time before she would be fit for surgery. Fixing a smile on her face, she went back into the bedroom to find that Isobel had gone. The brief entertainment, wrestling her mind from the darkness and throwing her some light, had disappeared, leaving her only with thoughts of what lay ahead . . .

Chapter Forty-Three

Someone had been in the office. Gary stared down at his chair and saw the pillow turned over on it. He hadn't noticed it yesterday during all the excitement with the police being in the hospital to investigate the murder of Sister Barrows, and then that patient's wife being caught in the act had been a real adrenaline rush. After today he was going back on his preferred night shifts. He'd only come in to dismantle his own equipment, though he was surprised he'd been asked to by Dalloway, seeing as it was evidence, and the police may want to see it. Perhaps Dalloway was nervy about the camera being put in place, though he ought not to be as it had saved a man's life. Gary would have liked to have been recognised for his part in all of that. It may give him a second chance at joining the police force. At forty-two he didn't reckon he was too old to join. He was fitter than most blokes who were a decade younger. And he was observant.

He had flipped that pillow after spilling half a pot of yogurt on it. The pink stickiness had gone on his trousers as well as mostly between his legs. He'd damp-cleaned his trousers, but he had just turned the pillow over. Someone had moved it, but he couldn't be sure if this had been before yesterday or since. He stared around the room, curious to see if anything else had been touched. Finding nothing out of place, he settled his eyes on the computer screen. Other than that patient's wife with her soup thing, something more was happening here, something not quite right. A ward sister had been murdered for a starter. Emily Jacobs had come to his office all sweetness and light in search of a thief, which he didn't really buy, considering that prior to that night she'd always given him the frigid stare. She'd been on the search for something alright, but had it really been for something as simple as a thief?

He remembered the date she was interested in and turned the pillow back over, sitting down. He could be in for several hours of viewing, but nothing else more urgent was calling him. He would look for her in her normal clothes or a patient's gown, as she'd said she had been a patient here and go from there. Getting more comfortable, he set about finding the file, feeling a frisson of excitement at the prospect of unearthing something. He'd look good in a policeman's uniform and could see himself with his ID number in a silvery white on his epaulettes. Perhaps he could fast-track to detective, given his age and experience. He decided that if he found something suspicious on any recordings he was not going to go to Dalloway with it and miss out on the opportunity of being named as the finder. He'd give it straight to the police, so that his name was already known to them when he next applied.

'Officer Burge,' he said aloud, already imagining his role. 'I am the police, so step aside.'

He chuckled and reached for the marshmallow bag, stuffing the last two blobs of pink and white into his grinning mouth.

Geraldine packed the boot of her car with her brand-new outfit, hoping she would still get to attend the wedding at some point today. She had on her work skirt, blouse and jacket and bare legs, deciding in the end that it was too warm for tights. The flowered slide holding back her hair was not what she'd normally wear for work, nor were the diamond earrings, or the application of a full face of makeup. She'd been planning on looking gorgeous for her day out, rather than chasing up on something that would probably prove to be an innocent remark. Dalloway was going to be annoyed if she turned up with the same excuse a second time. 'Well, tough titty,' she said under her breath. It was her job to worry about incidentals, or anything else that concerned her for that matter. She would be failing at her job otherwise.

She pulled out her mobile, calling Sergeant Martin's mobile instead of the landline, to get an update from last night. Hopefully there would have been a sighting of Emily.

Tony Martin picked up on the first ring and she could tell he was driving because of the echo of the car indicator.

'Hi Geraldine, what are you up to, calling me on your day off? I thought you had a wedding to go to?'

'I do. I'm just checking in before I go, to see how everything is going.'

He barked a laugh. 'It's quiet. There's still no sighting of your missing patient. I'm on the way to The Windsor Bridge

Hospital to see if I can get any more on this Mrs Jeffries who tried to murder her husband. I don't just want to go to the Crown Prosecution Service with a flask of soup in my hand.'

She laughed. 'You got it off to the lab safely, I hope.'

'Of course. But I'm only expecting it to be tomato soup with some sort of fish base. From what I gather she knew he was allergic to it.'

'So you definitely think she did this?' asked Geraldine, hoping it wasn't Emily who was involved instead.

'She was caught red-handed, which is why I'm heading there now. To get more proof.'

'So nothing new otherwise?'

'Nope.'

'OK, Tony, you have a good day then,' she said and rang off.

She tapped her fingers impatiently on the steering wheel, noticing her nail varnish had already chipped, and wished she could let go of this disquieting feeling and just go back in her house and carry on getting ready, the matter put from her mind, so that she could enjoy her friend's wedding. She hunted around in the passenger footwell in search of something to drink and spied the half-full bottle of Coke she'd bought to go with her Chinese, and an open packet of wine gums. Was Emily safe and sound, or half dying from some serious infection? In a few hours she would have been missing for two whole days. Anything could have happened to her in that time. Including her death, Geraldine feared. There were too many outcomes to consider and she sighed with resignation as a decision was made for her. She'd drive over to Dalloway's house and ask him outright what he had meant. She would try and work out if he had been talking about Felicity. She would be gone for an hour at most, and then could get on with enjoying the rest of her day.

Emily's eyes shot open as she felt someone grip her hand. Something was being pressed into her palm, and her knuckles and fingers were being forced to curl around a hard object. Her heart was hammering at being so abruptly woken, and she stared at Shelly with startled eyes.

'You done it?' Shelly asked.

Emily shook her head in confusion.

'Not you, dummy,' Shelly replied impatiently. 'Her.'

Emily turned her head and saw Meredith on the other side of the bed, a syringe in her hand, a relieved look on her face. 'It's done.'

They both stepped back and Emily instinctively made to get up, but her limbs were unbearably heavy, her head weighted like a boulder, her tongue thick in her mouth as she tried talking. 'Wov yer gin me?'

'Shut up,' Shelly answered, and then handed a long-bladed knife to Meredith, holding it gingerly by the blade with finger and thumb gloved in blue rubber. 'Now cut me,' she said.

Emily barely registered what she was seeing. But she heard Shelly cry out and saw bright red blood streaking down her arm.

'Mad,' she said slowly through numbed lips. ''Uckin' mad,' she mumbled, before her eyelids unwillingly closed, and she could see and hear them no more.

Chapter Forty-Four

Dalloway opened his front door with a bloodied cloth in his hand and Geraldine stepped back in alarm.

'She's not here,' he said bluntly.

Geraldine's eyes opened wide. 'I'd better come in. I take it you're talking about Emily?'

'Look, she's gone. You need to find her out there. I can't talk, I'm dealing with an injury.'

'I really need to come in, Mr Dalloway, if that's the case.'

He marched away, leaving his front door open as an invitation for her to follow. Geraldine closed the door, walking towards the sound of snuffles coming from a room. She was led into a kitchen that looked like it had come straight out of a glossy magazine. Rich wood countertops and sage-green units surrounded a table that could happily seat a dozen. It was a work table as well as a place to eat, judging by the dents and knife scores marring it, but she bet they were the original markings of this table and not a new job, made to look fashionably distressed.

A blonde, curly-haired woman was sitting on one of the chairs, her face flushed with pain, mascara smudged beneath her eyes.

She was pressing some gauze against her arm. Dalloway had a batch of fresh gauze set out in front of him, a small plastic pot of clear orange fluid and a packet of Steristrips.

He dabbed gauze into the liquid and said, 'OK, take your hand away.'

Geraldine saw a two-inch slit above the woman's elbow. It wasn't quite a needle and thread job, but it certainly needed more than a plaster. She stayed silent while Dalloway brought the skin edges together and bandaged it with a clean dressing. 'Go and take some paracetamol and have a lie-down,' he instructed the woman.

Geraldine stepped forward and directed her question at the woman. 'Before you do that, if you could spare a moment to answer some questions, that would be helpful.'

Dalloway made the introductions. 'This is my niece, Shelly. She's been helping us while our nanny is away. Shelly, this is Detective Inspector Sutton.'

Geraldine smiled, damning her stupidity for not thinking this the reason why Dalloway had known his childminder's behaviour so intimately, especially as he was related to her. 'Hello, Shelly, would you like to tell me if you have any experience of seeing Emily Jacobs?'

Shelly glanced at Dalloway and reached out with her uninjured arm to hold his hand. 'I heard banging at the front door and went to open it at the same time as Rupert. When I opened it, Emily was there, looking crazed. She tried to get past me when she saw Rupert, and I put up an arm to block her. I didn't see she had a knife in her hand until she cut me.'

Her face looked like it was about to crumple. Geraldine warded off the tears. 'You're doing well. What happened next?'

'I slammed the door. I think I caught her arm, because she dropped the knife and then Rupert took charge.'

Dalloway pointed to the draining board where a long-bladed knife sat. 'I gave it a minute or so before opening the door again and by that time she was gone. I've searched the grounds and could find no sign of her, and even though I've kept windows and doors locked since your visit last night, I searched the house to be sure. She didn't get in here, so she's out there somewhere.'

Shelly was nodding. 'Yes, a minute or so later I heard a car. It wasn't parked outside, because I couldn't see one through the window, so it must have been down the drive, because I definitely heard one.'

Geraldine pulled out a kitchen chair and sat down. 'Do you mind if I sit down? It's awfully hot in here.'

Dalloway moved across the room to open a window. 'It's the Aga, and I've kept the windows shut just in case.'

Geraldine returned her attention to Shelly. 'You said Emily's name as if you know her.'

'I do,' she replied, sounding surprised. 'I'm a healthcare assistant at the hospital. I've worked with her. Yesterday I was questioned at work about her, and about Sister Barrows as well.' Her mouth trembled. 'I thought she liked me.'

Dalloway put a reassuring hand on her shoulder. 'This isn't about you, Shelly, it's about me. Isn't that right, Detective?'

Geraldine gave a noncommittal look. 'Well, that's what we'll find out. Was anyone else injured?'

Dalloway shook his head. 'No, my wife is out with our daughter. It's the school holidays. Isobel has a playdate today.'

Geraldine was not fond of words like playdate, the modern term for saying your child was at a friend's. Recently Tommy had been invited for a playdate by a mother from the nursery. She'd have felt more comfortable if the mother had just said would he like to come over and play. Maybe she was an inverted snob, she realised, associating the word with wealth and status. She hoped not, and that it was more a case of hanging on to a language used by her own mother.

'So, what happens now?' Dalloway asked.

'Well, I'll report this back,' Geraldine replied. 'We'll need to take statements from you both. The search for Emily will be widened to take in this area, though I'm not sure how much that will help, if she has a car. What were you doing here, Shelly?'

She shrugged. 'Like Rupert said, I'm helping out. I babysat last night.'

'I thought you had a replacement for Maria?' Geraldine directed this at Dalloway. 'The lady I met.'

'Yes, well, she only stayed a day,' he answered. 'Isobel didn't really take to her. She only wants Maria.'

'I see,' she said, thinking how nice it must be to have a nanny to ease the load while you worked. She had to make do with a husband as they passed like ships in the night, juggling shift patterns, taking over from each other to mind the kids. 'I'll take the knife back with me. We can put a watch on your home.'

'Do you really think that's the best idea?' Dalloway asked. She probably won't come back here, but if she does and sees a police presence, she may scarper again. I have a man at the hospital who can rig me up with a camera so that we can watch for anyone approaching the house. At least that way we'll have warning, and I can call 999 immediately if she turns up.'

His suggestion may be worth considering, thought Geraldine, but it was not her decision to make. She would have to report back to Crawley and let him know what this fishing expedition had landed them. He was going to be mad as hell with her for not coming to him in the first place. If she'd told him of her concerns last night, he would already have had a watch on the Dalloways' house and Emily may have been caught by now, keeping safe the public at large.

The chance of getting to the wedding was moving further away. An unpleasant feeling that she was going to be blamed for the incident here was creeping up her spine. If the worst should occur, like another death, she could kiss goodbye to stepping one day into Crawley's shoes.

Gary had just found Emily dressed in a hospital gown in a video recording when he heard a knock on his door. Clicking pause, the screen held the image of her standing in a corridor on Allen Ward. He was slightly thrilled when he opened the office door and saw a police officer, his rank evident by the three stripes on his shoulder. Gary made an awkward movement with his hand and elbow as he almost saluted.

The tall, angular man took off his cap and tucked it under his arm. His hair was sandy grey, his complexion a similar tint. 'Good afternoon. I've been pointed in this direction to see a Mr Burge, who I'm told will be able to assist me. I take it that's you? There seems to be a lack of anyone else in charge upstairs. Everyone I've spoken to so far says he or she is new and only here for the day to help out.'

Gary stepped aside so that the man could move into the small room. 'Yes,' he agreed. 'There's a lot of agency staff on today. The whole place has been bedlam since the death of Sister Barrows. I'm beginning to think that she used to run the whole place.'

Gary unfolded a chair which he kept at hand for the occasional visitor. He set it right so that the man could sit down. 'Would you care for some tea or coffee?' he asked.

'No, thank you. I'll just get to the point of why I'm here, if it's all the same to you.'

Gary swivelled his desk chair so that he too could sit down, and at the same time took in the mess of the desk behind him, wishing someone had at least called to forewarn him of the visit.

'Of course.'

'My name is Sergeant Tony Martin. I was the arresting officer for Mrs Jeffries. The purpose of my visit now is to see if you have any CCTV footage that will show her prior to the incident happening. I had hoped to speak with the doctors who attended Mr Jeffries, but it's my understanding that they're both off duty today. Though I already have a statement from Mr Dalloway, the consultant.'

'Yes, a lot of the more senior staff will have booked annual leave today. They are probably nursing hangovers, hence the reason for agency staff today. The hospital was up for an award last night. The minions weren't invited,' he said with a conspiratorial wink.

Sergeant Martin made a movement with his lips which might have passed for a smile. 'So, down to business. I see behind you two monitors, so I'm hoping one of these will give me what I want.'

Gary shuffled his chair further along the desk to make room for Sergeant Martin to move closer and saw the man's gaze fix on the still image on the screen.

'Emily Jacobs,' he said. He looked at Gary curiously 'Remind me when we're done looking for images of Mrs Jeffries to come back to this.'

Gary felt his face warm and hoped the sergeant didn't think he was spying on female staff. He'd explain why he'd been looking at her image afterwards, when this other business was dealt with. Clearing his throat, he knew he was about to make Sergeant Martin's day by handing him irrefutable evidence.

'I have the whole crime on tape, Sergeant Martin. You'll be able to see exactly what she did.'

Tony Martin raised an eyebrow.

'Show me what you have,' he simply said.

Gary started eagerly tapping away at the keyboard, his heart beating in excitement. He would ask this man to put in a good word for him and would give him one of his printed cards with his details on so that his name would not be forgotten. This

could be him one day, coming into an office and seeing someone like himself with all this crap of sweets and crisps across the
desk, knowing the man had less important things to do. He sat
up straight and then saw a hand reach for a tube of Pringles.

'Do you mind?' Sergeant Martin asked. 'It makes the time go
quicker.'

Gary grinned. So they were human after all. 'Help yourself,'
he invited, flipping off the cap of the smarties. 'If it helps us concentrate, it's what we gotta do.' He missed the resigned look on
the man's face beside him, or the intake of a long-drawn breath.
His eyes were straight ahead as he sucked on a sweet.

Chapter Forty-Five

Geraldine could hear Crawley's teeth grinding and hoped he didn't snap a tooth in anger. She'd decided this conversation was best had face to face, and not over the phone from the safety of her own office. She'd driven to the Major Crime Investigation Team base to let him bawl at her, if he saw fit to.

He had listened without interrupting, but his face had become redder and she was now waiting for the explosion.

Instead, he inhaled deeply through his nose and seemed to calm down with his eyes closed for a moment.

'Dalloway's suggestion is out of the question. The man can still keep a watch without a camera. I want officers at every entrance to his property, keeping a proper surveillance on the place.'

'There is only one entrance. He has a long private drive.'

'I thought you said the house was on a hill? If that's so it can be reached up a hill.'

Geraldine grimaced, feeling foolish. She'd described the property and layout only minutes ago. A house out in the middle of the countryside up on a hill. She had been thinking that there was only the one route Emily could have taken if she had a car. Only one driveway.

Crawley looked at his wristwatch. 'Time is ticking on. I want a team out there to find a good spot before evening. I take it the knife has already gone for analysis?'

'Yes,' she confirmed.

'You asked for a rush job, I hope?'

She nodded.

'Well, that's one good thing,' he said. 'Let's hope it has blood from Nina Barrows and prints from Emily Jacobs on it, and then we've got her.'

Geraldine nodded reluctantly, feeling almost tearful at the turn of events. This morning she would have bet her life on Emily being innocent, and now she was at a loss to come up with any reason to still think that. She'd left Dalloway's home completely disturbed, telling herself as she drove the journey back that there must be another explanation for Emily's behaviour, to not give up hope of Emily being innocent. It wasn't hope she needed. It was a miracle. Emily had slashed a woman's arm trying to get at Dalloway. She'd committed a crime! Was it her first or second one, though?

Geraldine felt utterly miserable. Her husband was at her friend's wedding eating lovely food and drinking champagne, her new outfit was in her car, and she would not get to wear it or taste any of the fine food or drink on offer.

'Go and get yourself a cup of tea or something, Geraldine. You look shattered,' Crawley said, not unkindly. She was lucky it was him in charge of this case, otherwise it might have been a 'go and clear out your desk, Geraldine'. She smiled her thanks and closed his office door quietly behind her. She'd grab a sandwich as well as a cup of tea and then phone her husband and have a five-minute moan to him, tell him she was sorry she still wasn't there and that she'd do her best to get away. But she wasn't banking on it.

Her mobile buzzed in her pocket and she pulled it out wearily. Tony had texted her. 'Ring me urgently!' it said.

Feeling as if she were going to be slapped in the face with more bad news, she rang him.

Night had fallen when Emily came to. A lamp had been turned on by her bed and the lemon walls had more of an orange glow in the soft light. She was still being given fluids. The bag of normal saline attached to an infusion line was three quarters full and she watched the slow droplets of clear fluid hypnotically enter the chamber. They were keeping her hydrated, which was possibly why she felt little effect from whatever they had injected her with. They were either being kind or they wanted her healthy for selfish reasons. The pain in her breast had considerably lessened, leaving only a vague tenderness, and her body felt only a memory of achiness as the infection cleared. She imagined they had given her the maximum dose of antibiotics and then doubled the strength in their haste to get her well again, and she had no doubt she was receiving the best medical treatment on offer in this house. She wondered where they all were. She could hear no sounds coming through the walls. Perhaps, like her, they were resting, reserving their energy for what was about to come. The bottle of water had gone from on top of the bedside drawers and had not been replaced, so she had to think it was deliberately taken to keep her nil by mouth. If that was so, then they were planning for surgery soon.

She spotted the plaster in the crook of her arm and guessed blood had been taken from her. But where were the blood tests taking place? There was no way Dalloway would have a path lab facility setup in his home. Maybe a pathologist was in on this sick set up, or Meredith was ferrying the blood into The Windsor Bridge and putting them under another patient's name. Was that the real reason she was put in that room, as backup in case their first attempt failed? Sister Barrows had said she was put in that room in error. Was that the truth? That Shelly made a mistake? She wished she could believe that, but it just didn't ring true. At the time, had Shelly been aware that Emily was blood type B? When she was put to sleep, after Sophia had died, was she tested as a match for Walter? Her blood work checked to see if she was a suitable candidate? Was she picked out as a future donor? Emily wished she knew more about transplants, but it was such a specialised area of medicine. She did know blood type O, the universal donor, was the only other blood group that was a match for a type B recipient? Why hadn't they been able to find a match in this blood group for Walter? Had chances come along and he was too ill at the time to face surgery? He was ill now, and they were going to take a chance. Had he not been high enough up on the waiting list for a transplant? Or had Dalloway simply decided he was going to pay for it and find the perfect match himself?

Nothing would surprise her, after knowing Dalloway had operated on his own son, in his own home. He most likely had every machine and device available for major surgery on hand, in case it would be needed, while Shelly collected spare donors.

The night of his son's operation would have required careful planning and timing, and she had difficulty envisioning him doing it all alone. There had been more than one carer at Sophia's bedside that night when she was fighting for her life – she was sure of that now, because she had only stopped watching the action at Sophia's bed because someone had startled her and shone a torch in her eyes. Therefore at least two people had been present, possibly Meredith and Shelly. So, who had helped Dalloway? Or had he simply kept Sophia's liver on ice until the rest of his team could join him? She would ask him when she saw him next. If she was going to die she deserved to know the answers to all of it before her life ended.

And her life would end, she believed. Dalloway had said he was going to get her well. Shelly said that her liver would regenerate in a few weeks. But now that she knew what they'd done, and what they now intended, how could they let her live?

She trembled at the thought. Her parents would not miss her, she knew. It saddened her greatly to have been born their daughter and know they had no love for her. The truth was that her absence would make little difference to other people's lives. Unlike the difference Zoe had made to hers. She mourned the loss of her sister, thinking how sad, how cruelly fate had set the score even, to think she might see her again, only for it to never happen. It would be she who would become missing. She they would look for. The chance to see each other again would be gone for ever. This was her punishment.

The burden of guilt had all but crippled her. The weight of it was more punishing than anything she'd had to bear so far. She had tried so hard to believe that the version of events she had given the police were true; thinking with time it would get easier, that the lie she had told would make the pain go away. What she hadn't banked on was hearing Zoe's accusatory voice in her head all the time. For what she had never revealed to anyone was that she had seen Zoe that day, walking to that road, a skip in her step as she dangled her shoes, her face lifted in the morning sunshine without a care in the world. She had watched her and had been so angry. She had never felt anger like it before. Never felt hatred like she had in that moment for her baby sister.

She closed her eyes to erase the images and then tensed as she heard the door open. Someone stood silhouetted in the door-way, their shape difficult to make out, hidden by the long flowing surgical gown. Whoever it was had come for her.

Geraldine ignored the security guard who stood like an excited puppy hopping from one foot to the other, eager to do their bid-ding or in need of a pee. His voice was too loud as he invited her into the office, offering her tea, coffee and even a chair with a grubby pillow to sit on. She discarded the pillow to a corner and pulled the swivel chair to the desk to sit beside Tony.

'I'm too nervous to look,' she said.

A paused image of Emily in a hospital gown was on the screen.

'You'll kick yourself when you do,' Tony replied dryly. 'I've already looked.'

She breathed in, readying herself. 'Hit me with it.'

It was less than a minute of footage, and Geraldine had held her breath for most of it. The image now paused was of a small dark-haired young woman. She had walked out of the same room that only a minute before Emily had entered.

Geraldine felt her stomach tie in knots. Everything that Emily went through to prove this woman's existence had been ignored. Her medical history and past behaviours had been held against her in the most appalling way. They may as well have turned her mad by doing that to her. If they had broken her mind it would come as no surprise. She remembered the light going out in Emily's eyes the last time she saw her, remembered the coolness she'd displayed towards her in the hospital after her accident. She must have felt utterly abandoned. No wonder she let herself get beaten, if it was her only means of escape. She would have been desperate to get out of the place to prove to them she hadn't imagined or made up this woman. Geraldine felt guilty for giving up on her. Emily had not mentioned seeing the woman on CCTV in the recorded message she had left for Geraldine. Only that she had seen the missing patient, *seen* Katka, and Geraldine had jumped to the conclusion that she was hallucinating and had focused only on that.

This footage proved that she had been telling the truth. What it was unable to prove was whether Emily was a murderer. Had she been turned mad or turned bad? Had she become a killer, created by them?

'How did you find this?' Sergeant Martin asked the man leaning against the wall.

He shrugged. 'I dunno. I just looked for it.'

'Yes,' he said impatiently, 'but what made you look for it?'

He looked less sure. 'Nurse Jacobs coming here the other night, I suppose. She had said she was looking for a patient who had stolen something from her. Then we had all that business with the woman giving her husband something she shouldn't. I just—'

'And how did you know about that?' Tony interrupted. 'What brought it to your attention?'

His mouth twisted, his brow furrowed in concentration. 'Well, it was her, I suppose. Nurse Jacobs. She told them. Mr Dalloway, Sister Barrows and the doctor from America all came here and looked at the footage. The American doctor told me Nurse Jacobs had found it, and told them about it.' He paused, before adding, 'I suppose it's down to her that his wife got caught.'

Sergeant Martin gave a confirming nod. 'That's right, DI Sutton. Though the recording Mr Burge has just shown me was not the hospital recording Emily Jacobs viewed. This recording is of a patient's bedroom. It shows the patient's wife in the act of preparing to give her husband soup.'

Geraldine raised her eyebrows. 'When did the doctors and the ward sister come to view this footage?'

'Saturday. Mid-morning,' Burge replied.

Geraldine could not have been more surprised. Emily was locked up then. She was admitted to hospital Friday night. She escaped A&E on Sunday night. How had she managed to pass on this information? Why had she even cared enough to do so?

She reached for her mobile just as it rang. Crawley's name came up on the screen. She answered with trepidation.

'We've got one result back,' he said without the preamble of a hello. 'They're still analysing it for the blood of Nina Barrows, and need a sample from the woman who was cut with it today. But it has Emily Jacobs' prints on the handle. A warrant for her arrest has been issued.'

Geraldine swallowed hard. 'I have some things to tell you that may change your mind about an arrest warrant.'

'Well it can wait,' he barked. 'You can tell me everything you know about this young woman when we catch her. And if you're not going to that wedding you were meant to have gone to hours ago, you can help out. Take a team with you and get out to this doctor's place, though I don't see her returning there to try a second attack. It's more likely she's on the run. If she does turn up, however, you call me first,' he added.

When the call ended Geraldine rubbed her face to relieve the tension. Her entire body felt taut.

'I have some paracetamol if you have a headache,' she heard the security guard offer.

She swivelled slowly around in the chair, her intention to take her frustration out on him, but she couldn't do it. She was not a bully, and the man, without realising it yet, was in enough trouble. 'Yes, please,' she said instead.

Chapter Forty-Six

At the doorway, Emily stood on trembling legs. The bedroom had been rearranged; Walter's bed was no longer there. Instead he lay on one of the operating tables. A second one had been positioned close by, waiting for her to climb on. She'd briefly thought of trying to escape as Shelly walked behind her along the landing leading to this room, but gave up the intention before a plan was formed. She was tired of running, hiding and feeling alone. Maybe her life could save this boy's; there were far worse ways to die, she imagined. Or maybe, despite everything she knew about them, they would let her wake up.

Apart from the pictures up on the wall, the entire area now resembled an operating theatre. It held the same equipment, gave off the same sounds and even smelled like a theatre. The taint of disinfectant products hung in the air. They would have sterilised the place thoroughly before they could begin.

Shelly pointed at a curtained screen. 'There's a gown behind it that you can put on.'

Emily shuffled over to the screen, trailing her bed sheet behind her. The bag of IV fluids had been removed from her arm. The cannula had been capped to avoid bringing the saline drip. She was hydrated enough and she could only hope they'd put up more saline to replace the body fluids she would now lose. That they would take what they needed and not leave her to die. She dropped the sheet to the floor and pulled on the gown, its small printed pattern advertising The Windsor Bridge Hospital. Through a gap she could see Meredith and Dalloway gowned up and busy with equipment.

'How did you manage with just a team of three of you?' she asked.

'There were four of us,' Dalloway answered mildly. 'My wife, Jemma, like her sister Meredith, is also an anaesthetist. Jemma helped me here. It was hard going, particularly for me, going straight from performing one operation to another. But we managed, didn't we, dear?'

Emily peered through the gap and saw a fourth person, gowned up and hair covered in a theatre cap. She looked unrecognisable as Jemma Dalloway. Emily would never have guessed she was Meredith's sister either, with her red hair. 'We did, dear, and we shall do so again,' she said crisply.

Emily stepped out from behind the screen.

'You have to take that off,' Shelly said, pointing to Emily's neck.

Emily reached up and protected her necklace. 'I'm not taking it off. It's all I have left of my sister.'

'Well we'll just remove it when you're asleep then,' Shelly said with a spiteful smile.

'Is this despicable creature related to you, too?' she asked Dalloway.

Dalloway raised his head and stopped what he was doing, his expression regretful. 'I'm sorry if my niece has offended you, but she's fiercely protective of those she loves. Shelly has sacrificed much to support us through all of this.'

'She's not a healthcare assistant, is she?'

He slowly shook his head. 'No, she's not. That role was only temporary. We needed people on the inside, the situation being what it is. She's a qualified nurse. A scrub nurse in theatres, in fact, a senior sister in London,' he said with a hint of pride. 'We have much to be grateful for.'

Emily wondered how he could be proud of such a person and thought that blood is indeed thicker than water. She thought back over the last few weeks and saw clearly now that Shelly had been playing not just the part of a healthcare assistant, but also a different person. In the background mostly, and being nice when they needed her to be. She must have been laughing the whole time, smirking when Emily instructed her on how to do things. She realised Shelly must have been watching her constantly, and had an enlightening thought. 'It was you who gave Mr Patel something to eat.'

Shelly sighed. 'Well, you were just too brilliant, Emily. And I needed a way to get you out of there. You were never going to stop looking for her. I had to keep working there just to keep an eye on who you were talking to. I was hoping you'd take the fall for Mrs Harris. I told Jim Lanning you'd done a HemoCue test when he popped along to the loo, and was hoping Barrows would believe you had and not told Lanning the result, which would have resulted in your being sacked. He should have checked with you, of course, that you had. He was a crap nurse, who should have been able to tell how poorly she was without the test being done.'

'She could have died!' Emily exclaimed.

'She didn't, though, did she? And Rupert has already told me off, so enough of your sniping.'

Emily eyed her with contempt. 'You should be ashamed of her, not proud,' she said to Dalloway.

'We cannot all be the same, Emily,' he offered quietly. 'Shelly takes things to the extreme sometimes, but she had Walter's interests at heart. For that, I have to forgive her.'

Talk of Walter brought her back to the present. 'Will you please put my necklace back on afterwards?' she asked him.

He nodded. 'Of course I will. I understand how much it means to you.' He patted the empty operating table. 'Hop up, then. We're ready for you.'

'Are you even qualified to carry out such an operation?' she asked, desperate to stall him. She could refuse to have it done. Fight them off. Try to make Dalloway see reason and end this madness.

Shelly barked a laugh. 'You don't know anything about him, do you?' she jeered. 'You don't know anything about his early career. Rupert was a pioneer in transplant surgery working in London and around the world at specialist centres. His life involved more than just removing gall bladders. Patients worshipped him for saving their lives with a transplant,' she said in awe.

'Thank you for that, Shelly,' Dalloway said. 'Though you make it sound like my life now is dull. The excitement of landing in a helicopter with the transplant team wasn't always fun. I got hellishly sick at times on the damn thing. And my family has more than made up for the excitement of those days. You're in safe hands, Emily. I won't let you die.'

Emily wanted to believe him. She undid her necklace, preparing to give it to him, noticing his hands were without gloves. He had not yet scrubbed up. Tears flooded her eyes as she walked the final few steps, her body shaking hard with fear. Would theirs be the last faces she would see? She lay down and turned her head to the side so that she could see the boy's face. He was so young, she thought, too young to die. As the clear mask came down over her face, she whispered to him, 'Good luck, Walter.'

Geraldine was pleased Ruth Moore could accompany her. Pleased she'd not been busy elsewhere. When not acting as a family liaison officer, Ruth carried out her regular duties as a police officer. The bonus was she knew Emily's background and didn't need the long story, only the short version as to why they were there. She was also happy to be the driver and parked tidily in a layby up one of the lanes, which gave them a clear view of the entrance to the private drive. Geraldine had two uniformed officers, who'd also come with them, positioned under some trees and had asked them to remove their hi-vis vests and put their radios on covert mode, as she didn't want the fluorescent markings or the display screens on their radios highlighting their presence for passing vehicles when nightfall came. So far, in the short while they'd been there, no traffic had come this way. All officers involved in the operation were on a designated radio channel, and Geraldine had turned hers down low to cut out the noise in the car. She didn't want to hear Crawley every five minutes asking for an update. It had just gone nine o'clock in the evening and the sky was dark with rain clouds. It had stayed fine all day, and she was glad of that for her friend's sake. The bride and groom had had a wonderful day, according to her husband. She hoped the rain would stay off another few hours for the planned firework display.

'This could be a long night,' Geraldine murmured.

'I'm on nights so I don't mind,' Ruth said. 'I've been asleep all day.'

'I'm wide awake, but it's not down to sleep,' she replied. 'My nerves are on edge since finding out Emily really had seen a woman in her room. She never imagined her. We may have unhinged her by not believing her. Pushed her into killing someone.'

'I pray to god she didn't do it,' Ruth remarked. 'I like Emily.'

'Well someone did, that's for sure. And her prints are on the handle.' A moment later she turned in her seat so that she could face Ruth. 'Why didn't others see the girl then?'

'Because maybe they didn't see her? In Emily's room, that is.' Ruth mused. 'Maybe to them she was just another patient, wandering in and out of rooms. Have we found out who she is yet?'

Geraldine shook her head. 'No, not yet. Mr Dalloway and Nina Barrows denied she was ever there when I questioned them. Emily was convinced that it was Katka Vasile, but I know for a fact that it was not. While small with dark hair, the girl on the CCTV footage was not her. She could, like you say, have simply been another patient. Dalloway was going to go through the operating lists with me, but we didn't get any further than that. I didn't feel the need after speaking with him and Nina Barrows.'

'But why did she think she'd died?' Ruth asked.

Geraldine sighed with frustration. 'Maybe, as Nina Barrows said, she had a nightmare and dreamed it.'

Ruth shrugged. 'Maybe she was a patient and she simply died?'

Geraldine gazed at her quizzically. 'You mean she was in the bed beside her, even in the night?'

'It's possible.'

'But why deny this happened? So as not to upset her?' Geraldine's eyes were sceptical. 'I don't buy that. Emily's a nurse. She's used to death.'

'Maybe it was because she was young? Or maybe,' Ruth added, 'she shouldn't have died. They gave her the wrong drugs? Put up the wrong drip? Did the wrong operation?'

Wrong drugs? Wrong drip? Wrong operation? Geraldine didn't like the sound of any of those suggestions. Had they lied to Emily to avoid an inquest? To hide the cause of death? Lied because of the very fact that she was a nurse, and would know what she had seen and what she was talking about if questioned? Had they really let a patient die in a British hospital and not reported it? Emily said she didn't think the patient was English. But that didn't mean she didn't live in this country. Relatives may not have known she'd gone into hospital. Perhaps there was no one to question why she had died.

Maybe she shouldn't have died. The sentence beat a firm path through Geraldine's mind. A death that shouldn't have happened. A patient who nobody had known about. And worse, whose death hospital staff had tried to cover up. 'Shit,' she said aloud, her mind going ten to the dozen. She died! That's what this was about. Emily witnessed her death. She heard them in the night trying to save her. Then they had to make out that she had never been there. This had been made easier because there had been no relatives knocking on their door. 'Jesus Christ,' Geraldine cried. 'Emily, the poor girl, has been made to look mad because she witnessed it.'

She flung open her car door. 'Jesus Christ, Ruth, we shouldn't be sitting here. Emily's been missing two whole days. She's not been seen since Sunday and it's now Tuesday. She hasn't gone back to her flat. She hasn't been to her parents' home. She hasn't got in touch with anyone asking for help, as far as we know. She hasn't been seen by anyone. Therefore it's highly likely she's up in that house being kept by Dalloway and goodness knows who else. Until now Dalloway's home is the only place we haven't been keeping tabs on. If they've covered up a death, they'll do everything they can to shut Emily up.' She was half out of the car. 'Where the fuck is my brain? Sometimes I wonder.'

'Whoa,' Ruth cried, busy scrambling out of the car to answer, 'we don't know that the girl is dead.'

'Yes we do,' Geraldine said with conviction, staring at the house up on the hill. 'Get the other two. We need backup.'

Ruth reached for her radio.

Chapter Forty-Seven

Dalloway placed the necklace in a bathroom drawer. His surgical gloves lay ready beside the sink. A nailbrush and scrub soap were set out for his use. He turned on the mixer tap and began the well-practised art of proper handwashing, gliding the soap up to his elbows and following through with the brush. Meredith had been involved in the preparation of the patient: drugs, fluids, numerous infusions to set up, and monitoring machines that would be needed in an operation such as this. Her part of the procedure should be done by now. Her role played a significant part in the two operations he was about to perform. His was merely the cutting and removal of the smaller left lobe of a liver, which would regenerate in a few weeks as Shelly had said. There would be the same rate of growth when implanted inside his son.

As he donned his gloves, he caught sight of his face in the mirror and saw that behind the steady stare of a surgeon there was a man who knew he was about to do wrong. He would go to prison for this, probably for the rest of his life, but it was a freedom he was prepared to give up for the life he could give back to his son.

Ready, he made his way back to a room that had been turned into an operating theatre for a second time.

Geraldine was struggling to keep up with Ruth's pace and stopped to draw breath. She had instructed the two PCs to navigate their way up the hill and circle the place on the lookout for an unlocked entrance. Under no circumstances could they enter the premises unless they had her say-so.

Ruth held out an arm for her to grab hold of, and half pulled her up the sloping drive. They were of a similar age, but unlike her, Ruth was trim and in great shape. After this job was over she would get fit, lose weight and not eat crap food anymore. As they approached the gravel drive she eyed it with frustration. They would have to quietly edge their way around through the flower beds to reach the house. Following Ruth's lead, she put one foot in the dirt after her, remembering the property had a motion sensor outdoor light. There were two more cars now parked, besides Dalloway's Alfa Romeo – one that she suspected belonged to Jemma Dalloway. There were lights on downstairs, but she could hear no sounds of a television or music or even the sounds of cooking. She wished they lived more like the Jacobs. The army could invade their home and they'd only realise it after the television was turned off. She concentrated on following in Ruth's footprints. If she was wrong and Emily was not inside the house, she would deny that they had done this damage and blame it on a badger instead.

She stiffened as she heard the voice of one of the PCs. 'The back door is open.' Not because she could hear him in her earpiece, but for the fact that he may as well have not bothered using his radio, for all the good it was doing at keeping their presence undetected, when she could hear him without it. He could have just stepped out and called to her.

'Shut up,' she hissed back, wishing she'd told him not to use his radio so close to the house. Or better still, not use it at all. She let a full minute pass before she tapped Ruth to proceed. They would advance towards the back door, as she certainly wasn't going to chance a knock at the front door.

Dalloway stared at the patient on the operating table in confusion. She was exactly as he had left her nearly an hour ago. Anaesthetised, and apart from the addition of a tube down her throat to ventilate her, she lay with nothing more done to her. No drip lines had been set up, no infusions had commenced, no arterial line had been inserted for measuring her blood pressure. There were no wide-bore cannulas in the crooks of her arms. She had the same pink cannula which he had inserted last night. It wasn't robust enough for the kind of fluid intake she would need. The blood, for starters, wouldn't push through that narrow lumen.

He looked at Meredith for an answer. 'What's going on? Why isn't she ready?'

'Ask your wife,' Meredith replied.

'She can't survive this, Rupert,' Jemma stated. The tone in her voice was firm. Cold, even.

He stared at his wife, to be sure he understood her meaning. 'I can't just let her die, Jemma.'

'You have to, Rupert,' she said firmly. 'You know you do.'

'What are you hoping for, Jemma? That I'll cut part of her liver away and just let her bleed to death?'

'You could take it all,' she said, quietly.

'I'm not a murderer!' he shouted.

'You have no choice, Rupert. Otherwise we will all go to prison.'

'I am prepared to go to prison for this, Jemma, you must surely realise that! I'm prepared to go to prison for what I've already done. I'm not going to let her die – she's saving our son's life!'

'And what about the rest of us?' she asked coldly. 'What about Isobel and Walter? I would also go to prison. Who would look after them? Meredith will go to prison. Her son needs his mother. Shelly will face prison for longer than the rest of us,' she hissed.

Dalloway's eyes went to Shelly. She avoided looking at him. 'Why for longer, Shelly?'

She clasped her gloved hands together, her manner unfazed. 'You don't need to know why, Rupert. You just need to do what's best for your son. You're the only one who can save him. And he will need you when this is done.'

She moved over to the table and pulled up Emily's gown and then deftly half turned her onto her left side. Meredith switched on the operating lights. Jemma came forward with a kidney dish which held a metal-handled scalpel with a razor-sharp blade. 'Take it, Rupert. Save our son.'

He stared back at his patient and saw that the area from the side of her belly to up and over her lower ribs was painted a wet orangey brown. Shelly had prepared the site.

He picked up the scalpel with a steady hand and made the first cut.

Geraldine eased into the kitchen, her finger indicating for the two young police constables to stay where they were. She beckoned Ruth to follow. They had their radios to call them if necessary. If they all trooped through the house, the chances of making a noise increased. She trusted Ruth, more than herself, to walk through silently. She was far nimbler for a start. They came out of the kitchen and made their way along a flagstone corridor coming to a stone archway that brought them into an astonishingly large living area. The ceiling above was all dark beams, and the shape of it reminded her of a church, as the place was big enough to hold a fair-sized congregation. The Dalloways were not present. Ruth pointed to the stairs and Geraldine frowned at all the wooden steps they would have to climb, imagining the creaks and squeaks giving away their presence. Ruth took off her shoes and nodded at Geraldine to do the same.

In bare feet Geraldine led the way, each tread beneath her solid and unmoving. At the top she stood and listened and made out sounds coming from a room at the end of the landing. The door was closed, making their journey to get to it undetected easier. If it opened, however, they would be spotted immediately.

She edged slowly along the landing, the noises inside becoming clearer. She could hear a sucking noise. The sound was not unlike that of a vacuum when a sock is sucked up the tube.

She placed her hand on the doorknob, turned it easily and gave the door a gentle push. The sight in front of her didn't match what she was expecting to see. Her wildest imagination wouldn't have produced what lay before her. It was like she had opened the door on a film, the room the screen, the scene unfolding in 3D. Then she heard Dalloway's voice. 'Suction, please.'

The four people standing around the operating table hadn't noticed them and Geraldine inched even closer. Through a gap between Dalloway and the person beside him, she saw a body on the table. A wide slit in the skin stretched open by surgical instruments revealed a shiny deep red glistening mass. She moved her gaze up the table and saw the side of a pale face with short black hair tucked behind an ear. Emily.

'Step away from the table, Mr Dalloway,' she said loud and clear.

Only the briefest reflex of a shoulder gave away his disturbance. 'I can't do that, Detective. I've just nicked her liver.'

Geraldine felt her insides revolt, the earlier ingested sandwich threatening to make an appearance. She took sips of air to keep it at bay, feeling herself shiver with her reaction. She was too fucking late.

'You've killed her,' she uttered.

'Hardly,' he stated calmly. 'It just needs some diathermy. More suction, please.'

'Step away from the table!' she barked the order. Ruth came up beside her and Geraldine heard the sharp, swift click-clack as her baton fully extended. She raised it ready to attack.

On weak legs Geraldine moved a little closer to the table, feeling sick that she had mistaken the word 'nicked' for taken, and watched as Dalloway used a long instrument to burn the area that was bleeding. It made a loud buzzing noise each time he used it and she could smell the burning of human flesh. It wasn't dissimilar to the smell of barbecued meat. She heard the same sound she'd heard from outside on the landing and saw a tube probing at the organ, sucking up a pool of blood that was not getting any smaller. Dalloway mopped the bleed with white gauze, stared at the area for a moment more and then stepped back from the table.

'What are you doing, Rupert? You need to carry on. Ignore her!'

Geraldine instantly recognised the woman's voice behind the surgical facemask. Jemma Dalloway.

'You need to get a surgical team here now,' Dalloway instructed.

'Rupert, please! Please, don't stop!' his wife begged.

'And my son will need an ambulance immediately,' he said.

Geraldine gaped at him. 'Your son?'

He pointed at something ahead of him and the two people on the opposite side of the operating table moved aside to let Geraldine see.

A small boy lay on a second operating table. He was wearing an oxygen mask on his pale face, and his body was wired up and connected to numerous machines.

'My son is dying, so please be quick,' he urged in a voice heavy with emotion.

The cry that came was so raw, so desolate, Geraldine felt an internal stirring as she recognised the cry of a mother who had lost hope. She had heard this sound before, at death scenes, when a mother cradles her child for the last time. She pulled out her phone.

She saw Dalloway move back to the operating table. 'What are you doing?' she asked suspiciously.

'Closing her,' he answered firmly. He turned and she saw in his eyes that he knew it was over, his offer genuine. 'It will be quicker, less risk. We'll bring her round in time for an ambulance to take her in.'

She nodded slowly and saw his look of gratitude. 'Two ambulances, then, as fast as you can, and DI Sutton, one more thing: Emily has a necklace in a drawer in my bathroom. Please ensure it's returned to her. It's important to her.'

Geraldine moved back to make the call and two of Dalloway's team closed in to help him. She took in the sights surrounding her and knew that no matter what the future held for her in her career as a police officer, this was something she was never likely to come across again. A doctor she was about to arrest saving the life of his victim.

Chapter Forty-Eight

In the intensive care unit in Bath, Eric sat opposite Geraldine and looked remarkably alert, given the time was approaching three o'clock in the morning. Geraldine had texted him to let him know Emily was found, and she was surprised that he was here. He was a kind man, but this level of care went beyond the call of duty. She wondered if he felt guilty for playing a part in having Emily sectioned.

Emily was sleeping deeply and Geraldine gazed at her face, hating the fact that she still had to consider her a suspect in the death of Nina Barrows, that she had positioned a police officer outside the unit doors. Until the four involved in her unlawful operation were questioned she would still have to be guarded. And all Geraldine could do was hope Emily was innocent and that one of that four were guilty of the crime.

Emily had been checked over by a surgeon on her arrival at the hospital, and while her badly bruised body had caused some alarm, little needed to be done to ensure her recovery other than fluid replenishment, pain control and observations. The surgeon had said that, apart from the small nick to her liver, which they'd scanned and said was fine, her operation had been a simple

open-and-close case, which was aborted before any serious cutting took place. Dalloway had done a good job closing her up
and she would make a full recovery, albeit with a curved scar
above her liver to remind her of the ordeal.

Geraldine stood up. She beckoned Ruth, who was standing near the exit, to come over and take her place. As senior
officer, Geraldine was needed elsewhere. Before that, though,
she had one last thing to do for Emily. She reached in her jacket
pocket and pulled out the chain and pendant she had found in
a drawer in Dalloway's bathroom. Leaning over the bed, she
carefully fastened it around Emily's neck so it would be there
when she awoke.

Two police officers were stationed outside the entrance to the
paediatric intensive care unit, in Bristol. Permission to let the
parents sit at the bedside of their dying son had been granted
by Crawley. The curtains were only partially pulled around the
five-year-old boy and Geraldine could see both parents from
where she stood at the nurses' station. Dalloway and his wife
were sitting on blue plastic chairs as close as they could get to
him. Dalloway was smoothing the child's brow, his wife holding
his hand.

Shelly Dalloway and Dr Meredith Moretti had been denied this
privilege. They were arrested at the scene of the crime and were
already in custody and waiting to be questioned. The Dalloways'
daughter was in the care of the social services team. Geraldine
stood completely still, her eyes and ears noticing everything. The
lump in her throat grew heavier at the sight of all the ill children

on the ward. All the teddies and toys, the bright blue and yellow floor and colourful bed covers could not hide the complex medical equipment surrounding them saving their lives. There was a constant beeping of machines; a reminder that these little ones were not simply sleeping, but in need of care. She could never be a nurse, especially a paediatric nurse seeing children this unwell. Her heart wouldn't take it. She was tough, she knew, and maybe if she didn't have children she could do it but seeing the small shapes in the beds around her, all she could think of was her own two and how desperate she would be if anything ever brought them to this place.

A wail suddenly came from across the open unit, and two nurses made their way to Walter Dalloway's bed. Dalloway was standing, his wife half lying across the bed sobbing inconsolably as he stroked her shoulder. The curtain was fully drawn to enclose them in privacy. Their son had died.

Emily saw Eric sitting beside her bed when her eyes opened. He was sleeping with his arms folded, his head lolled to one side. Daylight showed her where she was – the intensive care unit, where she used to bring patients from the emergency department. She had a simple drip line up and was attached by leads to a cardiac monitor, but other than this, nothing too serious seemed to be going on with her. A nurse walked over to the bed, her manner calming. 'Don't try and get up just yet. I need to check your dressing.'

Emily peered under the sheet and saw a large dressing covering the right side of her abdomen.

'The policewoman is just in the loo, she'll be here in a minute to talk to you, but in the meantime please be assured that the dressing is only covering sutures. You have not had any further surgery.'

Emily stared at her. 'What about Walter Dalloway?' she asked.

The nurse shook her head, her expression regretful. 'The policewoman said he died, I'm afraid. He was in the Bristol Children's Hospital, in the paediatric intensive care unit, and his parents were with him.'

Emily closed her eyes as they welled, and felt her hand being taken hold of. 'It should have been me,' she said. 'He was too young to die.'

'And he was too ill to live, Emily,' she heard Eric say. She opened her eyes and saw that it was him holding her hand, a comfort given in the absence of family or friend.

'It's all my fault she died,' she whispered to him.

Eric sat silent, his eyes not leaving her face, his own showing only kindness.

'I saw her, Eric. I saw her walking to that road and instead of calling out to her to say I was there and taking her home with me, I watched her and let her walk in her bare feet hoping they'd be sore by the time she got home. I was so angry with her for once again needing me. I went back to my car and just sat there, punishing her. Then I went into the hospital to fetch her, knowing all the while she wasn't there, she had already gone, and I pretended I didn't know. I apologised for her behaviour and then went looking for her. I thought that by that time she'd be back at her flat. And all the while she was alone, really needing me to stop whoever took her, because that's what I believe now happened. I let it happen, Eric, because for once I forgot.' The tears in her eyes couldn't hide her desolation. 'I forgot that I loved her,' she whispered brokenly.

Eric let her cry. She had much to cry for, and his silence and presence was all she needed for now. Later he would help her heal. He would begin at the beginning, getting it right this time. She no longer had to carry this burden of guilt alone. She was his patient for however long it took.

Rupert Dalloway signed a written statement detailing his full involvement in the death of Sophia Trendafilova. The statement said that she was a nineteen-year-old from Romania, who had given her verbal consent to being operated on after the entice-ment of payment but died as a result of Dalloway performing an illegal operation on her. He also confessed to a second illegal operation carried out on Emily Jacobs, though the statement outlined that this had not been successfully completed as it was interrupted by the arrival of the police. He had yet to admit to where he had disposed of Sophia Trendafilova's body, and Geraldine was hoping he would do so now in this second inter-view with her and Crawley.

Crawley had yet to say anything other than to give his name and rank for the benefit of the recording, and so far was letting her take the lead. It was not the norm to have a DCI and a DI carry out these interviews; there were officers highly trained to do this job. Geraldine knew this was one last hurrah for Crawley to interview a suspect, and as both were previous specialist inter-viewers in their careers, the custody sergeant had kicked up little fuss. She pulled out a chair to sit down. The chair beside Dalloway was empty. He had declined the offer of a solicitor. Dalloway was the first to speak. 'How is Emily?'

'She's doing well, Mr Dalloway,' Geraldine replied. 'They've moved her to a surgical ward.'

'Please convey my sincere wishes that she has a speedy recovery. My behaviour is unforgivable, so any apology would merely add insult to injury, but I want her to know all the same that I am deeply sorry for what I've done to her.'

'I'll do that. And you can show you mean that by helping us now. Did you have any involvement in the death of Nina Barrows?'

Dalloway shook his head. 'I had no involvement in her death whatsoever.' His face was grey and drawn and he looked aged.

Crawley placed a photograph on the table. It was of the knife that Shelly said Emily had dropped. Crawley let it sit there for several seconds before he spoke. 'I cannot imagine what you are going through. To lose your son after battling to save him with such extreme measures has come as a mighty blow, no doubt, and for that you have my sympathy. Emily Jacobs, too, has gone through immeasurable suffering this last year, even more so if she turns out to be an innocent party in all of this. She is presently being considered as a suspect in the killing of Nina Barrows. It would seem to me almost indecent to let an injustice continue, given all that she has already gone through, wouldn't you agree?'

Dalloway nodded fiercely.

'So while you say you have no involvement in Nina Barrows' death, do you know of anyone who *might* have had some involvement?'

Dalloway looked away.

'You strike me as a man who has integrity, Mr Dalloway. In spite of the unlawful pathway you have taken in order to save your son's life, I do believe you to be a principled man. So, with respect, I ask you to consider a fair answer to the question I put to you.'

'Emily didn't have a knife with her as far as I am aware. Nor did she come to my home brandishing one. At the time it was claimed she had done so, she was in one of our bedrooms recovering from a serious wound infection.'

'So would it be true to say that Shelly Dalloway was mistaken in seeing her carry one?'

'Yes, it would be true,' he said.

'The arm wound inflicted upon your niece – do you have any idea how she came by that injury?'

'No.'

'Would it be fair to say that it was unlikely to have been caused by Emily?'

'I don't know. I wasn't there when it happened. She materialised with the cut at about the same time as the knock on the door from DI Sutton.'

Crawley glanced at him thoughtfully. 'My understanding, and correct me if I'm wrong, is that you and your niece together gave a detailed account of what happened. Your niece stated that Emily came to your door, tried to reach you, but was obstructed by Shelly, whereupon she was cut with a knife that was then dropped by Emily as her arm caught in the closing door. Your niece then stated that she heard a car, leading us to believe that Emily had left the house, which of course we now know to be untrue as she was in bed in your house at the time.'

Dalloway leaned back in his chair. 'I followed her lead. I knew it was untrue, but I followed it nonetheless.'

'You more than followed it, Mr Dalloway. Your own account was full of lies,' Crawley said bluntly. 'Your niece must have seen the arrival of Detective Inspector Sutton and staged the whole thing.' He paused, then said, 'You still haven't answered the question as to whether you are aware of any involvement in the death of Nina Barrows from anyone else you know.'

'I can't answer that question,' Dalloway replied, sounding tired.

Crawley sighed. 'Oh dear, I was truly hoping that you would help.'

He stood up, and Geraldine was surprised. They had not yet asked the whereabouts of Sophia Trendafilova's body.

Dalloway sat forward and tapped the photograph. 'You haven't asked me about the knife.'

Crawley sat back down and waited.

Dalloway seemed to be having some inner battle in his mind as fleeting expressions crossed his face before finally settling to show the bleakness he was feeling. 'It belongs to Shelly. It's part of a set I gave her. You'll find the others in her home. My niece is the person you need to be questioning about Nina Barrows' death. Not Emily. Emily has been through enough already.'

'And what role did Nina Barrows play in all of this?' Crawley asked.

Dalloway shook his head. 'She didn't have one. She would never have known we were using that room for Sophia until Shelly put Emily in there by mistake.'

Crawley gazed at him sceptically. 'By mistake? A planned illegal operation which your niece was involved in, and you're telling me she put Emily Jacobs in there by mistake? It doesn't ring true, Mr Dalloway.'

'You'll have to ask her why she did it then. I have no other explanation to give. All I can tell you is that Nina Barrows was not involved until she got herself involved. She phoned me on Sunday afternoon to tell me she had found CCTV footage showing a young woman coming out of the same room where Emily Jacobs was a patient. She wanted answers, because she now believed Emily was telling the truth about what she'd witnessed.'

'And you told no one about this call, I take it?'

'I told my niece,' he said quietly.

Crawley stared at him in surprise and then slowly shook his head in disappointment. 'You're either a fool, Mr Dalloway, or you're not as principled as I first thought. And I'm beginning to think it's the latter. You told your niece because you knew she would sort the problem. It's as simple as that. And that makes you culpable.'

Dalloway stared back defiantly. 'I had no idea she would kill her. I was going to see her at her home, but Shelly said it would be better coming from her. She said she would go and talk to her. I would never let someone be killed to save my skin.'

'And yet people have died, Mr Dalloway. Maybe not to save your skin, but they have died because of what you set in motion. Sophia Trendafilova, Nina Barrows, who you must surely have realised, when you heard of her death, was killed by your niece.'

Dalloway looked away.

'And your son, Mr Dalloway, he too has died.'

Dalloway shook his head and his eyes filled with unshed tears. 'I did not kill my son. I tried to save him.'

'By taking the life of someone else. We've already interviewed your wife and your sister-in-law. They both say the same thing. That your intention was to let Emily Jacobs die. Is that true?'

Dalloway sat perfectly still. The tears were finally falling, and his face was bathed with their wetness. He seemed too calm, as if a weight had lifted from his shoulders. 'Yes, it's true. They had no idea that that was my intention until I started operating.'

Geraldine wondered if he'd just told a lie to take blame away from his wife and sister-in-law, to make their guilt less. She remembered how Jemma Dalloway begged him to not stop the operation and ignore the presence of the police. As far as Geraldine was concerned Jemma Dalloway was just as guilty as her husband of this crime. Her intention had been solely to save her son, and if Geraldine hadn't got there in time then Emily would most definitely be dead.

Chapter Forty-Nine

Later that day, Shelly Dalloway sat sullenly across the interview table, having just confessed to the murder of Nina Barrows. Geraldine saw no remorse in her face and felt the woman was more piqued by the knowledge that her uncle had outed her. She was the last of the four to be interviewed, and Geraldine would be glad when it was over. Crawley looked every inch the senior detective and she was proud of the way he had conducted himself. She wished he had another ten years to go before his retirement. He still had so much to offer. She felt grubby from her time with each of the suspects and couldn't wait to breathe air that was not contaminated by their presence.

'Did Nina Barrows know of your relationship to Rupert Dalloway?' she asked the woman opposite her.

'No,' Shelly replied in a droll tone. 'She had no idea. The place is so up itself they only give healthcare assistants a first name on their badge. I got the job while she was on holiday for the sole purpose of being there at the right time to do my bit.'

'Your bit being to take care of Sophia Trendafilova after her surgery?'

'That, but also to assist with the surgery. I'm a qualified theatre nurse.'

'I'm interested to know how you all thought you could get away with performing an illegal operation without anyone being the wiser. Surely you knew you ran the risk of being caught?'

She shrugged. 'You'd have to work in a hospital to realise that patients come and go all the time, and once they're in a room sometimes no one else sees them other than the doctor or the nurse.'

'Or other patients,' Geraldine said. 'Did you put Emily in that room by mistake, or deliberately?'

'Well, that's the thing about hospitals.' Amusement glinted in her eyes. 'As soon as you become a member of staff you get given all these privileges. You get to see confidential medical notes. You see prior medical conditions. What blood group they are, etcetera etcetera. You see interesting things that may become useful. Emily being in that room may have become useful.'

Geraldine stared at her coldly. 'You put her in that room for the purpose of using her if things went wrong with your first victim? Isn't that right? That's why you put her there?'

Shelly laughed. 'You should see your face. You really believe that? It would have been OK if Sophia had stayed out of sight until her surgery was due. Rupert brought her in far too early, put her in his office. It was sheer bad luck that Emily saw her. She wasn't going down to theatre till that evening, after all the other lists were done and the interfering theatre coordinator had gone home. But she wandered out of the office to the room we had picked out for her and Emily saw her. Which was a bit of a nuisance really, because otherwise, when things went wrong, Emily could have been convinced that she'd only dreamed her.'

'She still became useful, though, didn't she?' Geraldine goaded.

'She was in the right place at the right time,' said Shelly.

Geraldine moved on to the next set of questions she had to ask. 'Why did you kill Nina Barrows, Shelly?'

Shelly smirked. 'She called me a menace.'

'You killed her because of that?' Geraldine asked in a voice filled with derision.

Shelly tutted, and then answered, 'No. Because she was becoming a problem. She couldn't keep her beak out of it. She had Rupert all hot and bothered. She had to go.'

'So you went to her home and simply killed her?'

'Well we didn't have tea first, if that's what you're asking.'

Geraldine stayed silent.

Shelly leaned back and stretched her arms wide. 'Yes. It was no big drama. In and out before she knew anything about it. She died gracefully, let me tell you.'

Geraldine eyed her disdainfully. 'And yet you carelessly left her front door open?'

Shelly smirked again. 'Who said it was careless? She needed to be found while Emily was on the run.'

'So you deliberately set Emily Jacobs up as a suspect?'

Shelly nodded, beginning to look bored. 'You lot sometimes need leading by the bloody nose. Her escaping hospital was too good an opportunity to let pass. She had a knack of being in the right place at the right time. From my point of view, that is. Barrows said Emily had passed out with fear when you lot came to capture her. She didn't. She just couldn't stand up after what I gave her.'

Geraldine felt her blood boil and wanted to reach across the desk and slap Shelly's face at the cruelty she'd inflicted on Emily. She had watched her collapse in that corridor, and hadn't questioned the cause of it, instead taking Dr Green's assumption that it was fear of a uniformed presence which had caused her to fall to the ground like that. And she hated the thought that Emily knew why she collapsed while they all just watched. She hoped that Shelly would be put away for a very long time and that Emily, when all this was over, gave no more thought to this despicable woman.

When the interview ended she and Crawley walked silently down the corridor together. He stared back down its familiar length as if memorising every inch of it. His face was drawn, his voice worn. She could hear a rasp in it as he spoke. 'What a sad mess. They've destroyed so many lives to save a sick little boy.' He shook his head sadly. 'There's no accounting for how far people will go to save a child.' He left her then and she watched him slowly amble away, his large shoulders slouching and looking heavier, his vitality seeming to have diminished.

The local evening news informed the viewers that a thirty-year-old woman had been arrested for the murder of Nina Barrows. Geraldine knew that when the story behind the killing broke, the residents of Bath would be deeply shocked. It was unsettling enough to hear of negligence and malpractice in the normal run-of-the-mill bad news. The story that was about to unfold would put the fear of god in them at the thought of ever step-ping into a hospital. She pitied the doctors and nurses out there now, who over the next day or so would be dealing with patients about to undergo surgery. They would probably insist on having a witness present in the theatre to ensure they left with every-thing they went in with. It was going to be an interesting few days, she was sure.

Geraldine hadn't been home since she'd packed her car boot with her finery in the hope of going to yesterday's wedding. She had dozed for an hour in a chair while waiting for a senior officer from the Romanian police to get back to her, and was relieved that he was fluent in English when she had spoken to him. He had managed, on the scant details she had sent him – a name and a photograph printed from the CCTV images – to discover that Sophia Trendafilova was from Ploieşti, a city some thirty-odd miles from Bucharest. She discovered that her only surviving relative was a grandmother, who sadly hadn't even thought her granddaughter was missing, because as far as she was concerned she was in England, and not expected back if she found work. Her monthly call to her grandmother wasn't due yet. She was seventeen years and eight months; she would have been eighteen in November. She was not nineteen, as Dalloway had believed her to be.

Geraldine had informed the inspector that she would keep him updated on any new developments, especially on the whereabouts of Sophia's body. Dalloway had refused to say where Sophia's body was, and Geraldine wondered if it was because of the shame of admitting that he had got rid of it in an incinerator.

Typing up the last few words of her report, she closed her laptop and readied herself to leave the office. She would call into the hospital and see Emily on her way home and then hopefully, finally, get to see her own family.

Her mobile vibrated on the desk. She didn't recognise the number and she answered it reluctantly. 'DI Sutton speaking.'

'PC Roberts, ma'am.'

Geraldine knew the voice; he was one of the two uniforms who had been with her at the Dalloways' house, the one who used his radio and nearly gave away their presence. 'How can I help you, PC Roberts?'

'I have a foreign woman here at the Dalloways' house. She is crying, and I'm not too sure what to do with her. She's got cases with her and is expecting to stay here.'

Geraldine's shoulders slumped; a further delay before going home was now inevitable. 'Keep her there and give her a cup of tea. I'll be along shortly.'

Emily ate the small pieces of toast cautiously, chewing slowly like Gems would. She was ravenous and could have gulped it down with two bites, but risked being sick and having to hold onto the wound in her side. It was the first solid food she had eaten in two days. Her last meal of cooked chicken seemed a lifetime ago. They had failed in their duties as hosts to feed her, she thought with dry humour. She would not be recommending them on TripAdvisor anytime soon. She sipped the lukewarm tea and over the rim of the cup saw a scruffy man, trying to look less scruffy with his dark grey hair combed over and an old suit jacket covering his collared T-shirt. Emily put down the tea as her father made his way to her bed.

'You look like you've been in the wars, girl,' was his first remark.

Emily's jaw had stiffened as she stared at the impossible sight of him standing there. She could not recollect the last time she had seen him anywhere but on a couch in their sitting room.

He spied a vacant chair at the bed beside her and dragged it over to sit down. In astonishment she saw him remove from his jacket pocket a small box of Maltesers. 'They were always your favourite when you were a kid.'

Emily gazed at him mutely. She had no idea what to say to him. Their conversations were always of few words, with her usually asking him whether he needed something to eat or fetched from the shop. She had no real idea what he was thinking or feeling. She couldn't recall any substantial conversation ever taking place between the two of them.

'Your mother was a bad mother for treating you the way she did, but I was a bad father for letting her. We're ignorant, you see, Emily. And you were always too bright for us. We didn't know how to handle you, and that's a fact. Zoe wasn't the same, you see. She was more like us. And if it weren't for you, she probably wouldn't have amounted to much.'

He looked her in the eye. 'Your mother resented you for that. Zoe loved you like you were her mother, and I reckon that you've mourned her loss like one.'

The tears rolled down her face and she used her hand to cover her trembling mouth.

'Don't be coming to the house anymore, girl, waiting on the likes of us. You don't need to do that no more.'

He stood up and leaned over the bed and awkwardly patted her on the shoulder. He turned to leave.

'Dad?'

He stared back at her and in his worn features she saw a resemblance to herself. 'Will you come and see me?'

He smiled. 'I might if I knew where you lived.'

Emily watched him slowly walk back down the ward. The man who had been her father all her life had just spoken to her as if she was his daughter. She was not so alone after all.

The woman was sitting on a garden bench, a mug in her hand, two suitcases at her side and her swollen feet resting on slipped-off white shoes. A cloth doll sat beside her. She introduced herself to Geraldine as Maria Vasile, before realising she had already spoken to the detective on the phone. Her first question was expected. Where were the Dalloways?

Geraldine sat with her for more than an hour, taking her through what had happened, letting her cry when needed. She questioned her carefully, but there was not much the woman could tell her other than the Dalloways were kind people who had two children, a son who was sick and a daughter she had grown to love. It seemed she knew nothing of what went on in the boy's room; it was only ever other carers who went in there. Her role was to mind Isobel and help out with housekeeping. Geraldine wondered how she was going to tell her that her journey was wasted and that any hope of seeing Isobel again was unlikely.

The activity going on around them showed that someone other than the police had taken charge of the Dalloways' property. A man was leading a horse into a trailer. Geraldine waved at him to let him know she was coming over. She left Maria on the bench, thinking she would ask PC Roberts to take her to a hotel, if that's what the woman wished, or even back to the airport to catch a flight home.

The man's face was similar to Rupert Dalloway's, though he looked older. Geraldine pulled out her ID and introduced herself.

'Henry Dalloway, Rupert Dalloway's brother.' he replied in a manner that suggested he didn't wish to converse, his hands busy closing the trailer door, his eyes fixed on the job he was doing.

'I've had permission to remove the horses, in case you were wondering.'

'I wasn't,' she said. 'I'm sorry for what's happened in your family.'

His shoulders stiffened and he bowed his head. 'My daughter has been charged with murder. My brother will go to prison. My nephew has died. A lot has happened to my family.'

'I really am sorry,' she offered again.

He ignored her and would have walked away but for the sound of a vehicle rolling across the gravel. They both turned to see the newcomer. Henry Dalloway's features marginally brightened. 'My wife. She's been to collect Isobel. She knows she won't be staying here, but we want to let her see her home is still here and that not everything has gone from her life. I haven't seen much of my brother's children over the years. Walter took all of his spare time, so Isobel probably sees us as strangers.'

The Range Rover pulled to a halt and as the passenger door opened they heard a squeal of delight. Henry Dalloway and Geraldine watched as the girl ran into the arms of the small woman, each holding onto the other fiercely. Maria reached for the doll on the bench and handed it to her. 'That's their housekeeper, isn't it?' he asked.

Geraldine nodded. 'Isobel's nanny. She's just returned to take charge of her again.'

Henry Dalloway stared at the sight of his small niece hanging onto the woman, the bond between them clear. He sighed and mumbled under his breath, 'I'm going to regret this,' before making his way to his wife, his niece and the woman who was her nanny. After a few minutes of talking, Geraldine saw Maria clasp her hands together and raise them as if in prayer and Isobel wrap her arms around her uncle's long legs. The wife, child and nanny got back into the Range Rover and Geraldine let out a thankful sigh.

Chapter Fifty

Emily was going home from the hospital, five days after her admission, with her few possessions and her one get well card, from Jerry Jarvis. He had offered to take her home, but she'd declined, telling him Geraldine would do it. Emily sensed he was hoping to become a bit more than a friend, but she wasn't ready for that. She still had too much going on in her head to allow anything else into her life just yet. She hoped he'd still be her friend, and was glad the police hadn't charged him with anything. His only crime had been to believe in her.

The nurse preparing her discharge removed the cannula from her hand and cut the name band from her wrist. She was free to go. Emily smiled goodbye and then stilled, feeling fear grip her insides. Dr Green was making his way towards her.

He was immaculately dressed and his manner was calm. 'I caught you just in time, it would seem, to say goodbye,' he said cordially.

Emily slowly relaxed. She held out a hand to shake his. She had something to say to him. She'd had time these last few days to think everything through. She was going to be impaired at every turn, because of what had been done to her. Every time she filled in a questionnaire she was going to have to tick the 'yes' box next to the question, 'Have you been sectioned under the Mental Health Act?' She was of sound body and mind, but she might as well have a criminal record.

'I'm truly sorry for what you've been through,' he said. 'Perhaps when some time has passed, we can talk about it?'

He saw her instant refusal and inclined his head politely.

'I read about your seahorses, Dr Green. I had time, lying here this week, and I learned that the seahorse is one of the deadliest predators of the sea.'

He raised his eyes in surprise. 'But don't forget that they are remarkable fathers.'

Emily watched him walk away and thought Dalloway was probably a remarkable father. A predator, who'd done everything in his power to save his son – and she, Sophia and Nina Barrows were all his prey.

Geraldine glanced around Emily's flat and felt no concern about leaving her there alone. She had discovered that Emily was a private young woman and was possibly relishing the moment she could shut her own front door and stand in silence, escaping the madness of the world outside for the safety of her own home.

She was sitting on the sofa, her finger twirling the short strands of her hair, her mind elsewhere.

'Was it Zoe's?' Geraldine asked. 'The necklace I put round your neck? Dalloway said it was important.'

Emily shook her head. 'No, it's mine, but Zoe gave it to me. We both have them. Yin and Yang. Mine fits hers. Zoe loved how they interlocked with one another. She said it was her and me. They form a circle when they're joined together. She had them inscribed.' Geraldine came and sat next to her, taking the pendant carefully in her hand. The chain was so short it only allowed the pendant to sit just below the hollow of Emily's throat. Her eyes fixed on the engraved word. 'Sister,' she said.

Emily frowned. She touched the pendant and her eyes opened wide. She reached behind her neck and undid the chain. She held it tightly and whispered, 'It's a different shape. Mine is the other way round.' Then her eyes went to Geraldine. 'It isn't mine. It's Zoe's.'

Chapter Fifty-One

It had taken a week to organise the visit to HMP Parc Prison and be granted permission to see one of its inmates. Geraldine had offered to come with her, but Emily had said she'd rather do this alone. She'd driven carefully to Bridgend in Wales, keeping her mind on the road and not on the visit ahead, and had parked in the large visitors' car park. In reception she produced her letter of invitation and her passport to prove who she was. She'd been made to stare into a camera for her photograph to be taken and was patted down by a female officer before stepping through an X-ray scanner and metal detector. She was pointed to where the lockers were and was asked to leave personal possessions in them, taking only cash and the key to her locker with her. Finally, she was sniffed by an Alsatian trained to detect drugs before being let through to the next holding bay. Mainly women and children were waiting in the large room, and she sensed the uncomfortable atmosphere. They were preparing themselves to see their incarcerated loved ones.

A door on the far side of the room was opening and an officer beckoned everyone forward. Emily followed the crowd and found herself outside staring at some of the innards of the prison, at the red-brick walls and high mesh fences, her eyes mainly fixed on the endless rolls of barbed wire at the tops of them. She saw a glimpse of blue sky before being taken into the visitors' hall.

At each white table sitting on a red chair was a man wearing a yellow sash. Blue chairs on the opposite side of each table were waiting to be sat in.

Emily waited for most of the visitors to sit down before letting her eyes travel across the room searching for him. He was staring at her, waiting for her to find him. She walked towards his table noticing the area had been set out like a canteen with vending machines on one side and a serving hatch on the other. A prison officer was standing at each corner of the room.

She sat down with trembling legs.

'You look well, Emily,' he said. 'Better than I feared.'

He seemed so out of place in the grey sweatshirt and yellow sash that Emily found it hard to look at him. Beneath the table she could see that he wore basic white trainers and grey tracksuit bottoms. An image of him in his tuxedo and bow tie on the night he came into his son's room filled her mind and she couldn't imagine when or if he would wear such clothes again. Out there he had been an eminent surgeon. Here, he was a prison number awaiting his sentence.

Emily opened the collar of her blouse and pulled free the two chains to show the two pendants she was wearing. Geraldine had found the other one when she searched the same drawer in which she had found the first necklace. In a drawer in his bathroom, she had taken Zoe's pendant without realising what she had discovered. She was only glad Geraldine had questioned her about it. The horror of discovering it alone, maybe while she was in bed that night, would have been even more distressing. She would have been alone knowing it was Zoe's.

'I knew the minute I saw you in that bed who you were. It was like looking at her. I'm so glad you have it,' he said. 'That you can finally know. I think I must have kept it for that reason.'

Her mouth trembled as she asked, 'Have you had it since she went missing?'

He nodded. 'I tried to make you stop looking for her.'

'How?' she asked, aghast. 'How could you possibly do that? By taking my mind off her? By making me think I was mad?'

'By writing you a letter,' he said quietly.

Her eyes rounded in astonishment. 'It was you. *You.*' She stared at him in shock. 'You were in my flat?'

He gave her a moment to let it sink in. 'I had her key. I had her mobile. Her messages showing me how she wrote. She always referred to you as Sis.'

'How could you?' she asked bitterly. 'How could you let me think for one minute that she was still alive?'

He glanced away and Emily banged the table. 'Don't look away from me. You don't have that right.'

He looked back at her and she saw sorrow in his eyes. 'I did it to give you some peace. I saw your room—'

'You touched her things!' Emily exclaimed, knowing it to be true. He had moved things about to make it seem as if Zoe had searched those bags.

'I had to convince you she'd been there. I'd hoped it would let you move on. There was no other agenda, Emily.'

She stared at him and felt no pity. He had destroyed her life. Let her be locked away. Knowing all along that her sister was dead. She wanted none of his paltry excuses.

'How did she die?'

He blinked and looked away.

'Aren't you going to answer me?'

She saw his chest heave as he silently shook his head.

She had only one more question to ask him.

'Where is she?'

He wiped a hand across his eyes and she saw they were wet. He cleared his throat.

'There's a stone wall on my property which stretches halfway down the hill. There's a row of trees beside it. You'll see a leafless, smaller tree among them – it stopped growing after . . . She's there. That's where you'll find her.'

On a day that was predicted to be warm the sun refused to come out and Phil Marsh, the senior crime scene investigator, pulled on a jumper before putting his arms back into his Tyvek suit and zipping it up. He felt a shiver run down his back and hoped he wasn't coming down with summer flu. He slung a chain around a root, one which was proving too stubborn to dig out with a spade and fork. He hooked the chain to the small orange digger and gave a thumbs-up to the driver. The satisfying snap was heard as it broke free, before it was dragged away.

The tree they were digging beneath was dying. The wood under the bark was brown and dry. So far they had cleared an area a foot deep and three metres square. He picked up the spade and fork and handed them to one of his colleagues as he took a breath to reassess the site and heard the sound of a dog barking. He stared up the hill and saw a police dog handler making her way down it, accompanied by an Alsatian on a leash. It was a cadaver dog, trained to smell corpses buried deep beneath the ground.

He didn't touch the dog. He stepped out of the way as its handler took the leash off. 'Go, Digby,' she said. He pranced back and forth across the place where they were digging. He circled the area, his nose sniffing the air and the ground and then coming into its centre, before lying down.

The dog handler grinned proudly. 'Good boy.' She glanced at Phil. 'Looks like you're in the right spot.'

Phil went over to pat the dog, but Digby was back up sniffing the air some more, moving away from the place they had dug. He scampered further down the hill, moving in between the trees and the drystone wall. He disappeared from sight and then they heard his loud bark. Following the trail, Phil went to find him. Behind a tree Digby lay on top of a mound of earth. The soil looked freshly dug. Slowly Phil trundled back up the slope, his expression telling the rest of the white-suited team their situation was about to change. He needed to bring half of them down to that mound of earth. They had two graves to dig now.

Twenty minutes into digging at the second site, the team unearthed the remains of a body from a shallow grave. Geraldine and Emily stood up from the bench they were sitting on as the senior crime investigator told them the news. Geraldine bade Emily stay at the top of the hill while she made her way with Phil to inspect the find. She was not excluding her, believing she had the right to be there, to know everything that was going on, but she wanted to protect Emily from unnecessary pain until she was sure of the findings. At a glance she knew it was not Zoe Jacobs. The small body was too short, and she suspected they had just found the remains of Sophia Trendafilova. She returned to Emily and sat with her and stared at the stunning views before them, happy to sit there quietly and wait.

'How did he know her? That's what I keep asking myself. How did she end up here? Did he bring her here? Secretly? Already dead? Or did something happen here?'

Geraldine glanced at her to show she was listening.

'Walter said my face looked strange. Smudgy. And at the time I thought it was because he was ill, his blood pressure causing his vision to blur. Isobel told me her daddy said I was asleep. She didn't believe him. And she didn't like it. Do you think it's possible his children met Zoe? That they thought I was her?' Emily stared at the green landscape and rolling hills. Geraldine heard the pain in her voice as she continued. 'I've asked myself the same question a hundred times. Was it an accident? Intentional? Did she suffer? Dalloway's the only one who knows the answer. You know I have to go back and see him. I have to find out how she died.'

Geraldine hoped she'd get answers. The next few months were going to be long and hard, waiting for trial dates to be set.

All four had been charged and denied bail. Meredith and Jemma were considered flight risks. Death resulting from assisting in an illegal operation was no lightweight crime. Jemma, Meredith and Dalloway had also been charged with conspiracy to murder, as it was believed from further interviews with Shelly that all three knew about the action Shelly was to take against Nina Barrows. It seemed that Shelly now had a jaundiced view of her uncle. Geraldine hoped Emily would stay strong. As the key witness, the prosecutors would rely on her.

Phil was halfway up the hill before Geraldine heard her name being called. She could tell by the slow wave of his hand raised in the air that they had found something. Preparing herself, she slowly walked towards him and then past him to stare down into the hole. They had uncovered a shape wrapped in a white sheet. The length suggested the shape was likely to be Zoe's body. She nodded to the senior crime scene investigator. 'Just the top of the head if possible,' and watched as another officer held a camera recording the whole thing as his boss leaned carefully over the grave and loosened a part of the cloth. She saw him pick out what looked like dead flowers and among them take up a small square of white card. He flipped it over and held it out for Geraldine to see. Two smiling faces stared back at her from a photo booth shot. They could have been twins. She stared back into the hole as Phil moved the cloth a little more and saw black hair.

She was startled when she heard Emily speak. 'Is it her?' she asked softly.

Geraldine turned to her. 'We think so.'

Tears rolled down Emily's cheeks. 'To think she has been here all this time. I climbed into a mortuary fridge to find her, and I wish I had. To have at least held her in my arms.'

Geraldine watched as Emily undid the chains from around her neck. Zoe's and her own. With trembling fingers she pressed the two pendants together to form a circle. Before Geraldine could stop her, she stepped forward and dropped them into the hole. They landed on the sheet and despite the fall they stayed together.

'I'm sorry for leaving you,' Emily softly called. 'But I'm with you now.'

Geraldine held Emily's hand as they stood side by side at her sister's grave.

'She died from a genetic heart condition.'

He stared at her in confusion.

'Sophia,' she stated. 'The post mortem revealed that to be the cause of death. Her mother died suddenly at the age of twenty-nine. There had been no cause of death given. Her father died of a heart attack three years ago. The pathologist found an abnormal thickening of the walls of her heart, which can result in sudden death at any age.' She looked at him sadly. 'You didn't kill her.'

'So you found her?' he said, clasping his hands, and she noticed the tremor in the long, tapered fingers. To someone who had healed so many, she wondered if he now viewed them as useless tools.

'How did Zoe die?' she asked.

If it was possible, Dalloway had aged a decade in the days since she had last seen him. In less than a week she had been granted permission to visit a second time. She knew that it was thanks to Geraldine. Special circumstances, Geraldine had said, when she told Emily it was arranged.

'Did you take her liver to give to Walter?'

He stared at her, horrified. 'Is that what you think?'

'Her post mortem is today, so I'll know soon enough, but I want you to tell me how she died. I want to hear it from you.'

He shut his eyes and gave a small shake of his head. Then he looked at her. 'I'll tell you the truth. Nothing but the truth. It was an accident.'

Chapter Fifty-Two

Zoe

The sun was warm on her face and she felt energised as she walked barefoot along the pathway. She had wanted to be out of the ward before Emily heard she was there, knowing that her sister would be angry with her for ending up at her workplace and embarrassing her in front of her work colleagues. Emily was a professional and took her work very seriously. Her younger sister's behaviour would be frowned upon.

Zoe wished sometimes that Emily would lighten up and let her hair down and not take things quite so seriously. Last night had only been a drunken night out to forget about all her worries, and she hadn't been arrested or got into a fight like some girls she knew. She had just drunk too much. Her loans were adding up and she could see no way of paying them off. She had failed her exams and doubted her ability to pass them next time. Those were reasons enough for anyone to go out and let off steam. And at the core of her worries was the real reason she had gone out and behaved so recklessly. She no longer wanted to be a nurse. She was not like Emily. She didn't have her drive or stamina. She tired more easily and wanted a nice job, maybe in a beauty salon or something like that, where she didn't have to worry all the time about making a mistake. If you painted someone's nails badly, you could wipe it off and start again. It was not the same pressure as dealing with sick people. She worried every time she touched a sick person that she was going to do it wrong and hurt them. And now she worried how she was going to tell Emily.

She had been lovely to her on the phone last night and told her that things would look better today and she was right, because Zoe had made her decision. She was going to hand in her notice and suspend her training.

Emily would have to accept that she had made up her mind, and if she could persuade her to help out just one last time with these money worries, she would pay her back double, because she would be earning a better wage. Then these worries would be nothing more than bad memories.

She smiled properly, feeling as if a weight had been lifted from her shoulders, and turned her head as a car pulled slowly alongside her.

She waved through the open car window at Mr Dalloway. So many people didn't seem to like him. They thought he was cold and aloof but Zoe thought he just looked sad. 'Hello, Mr Dalloway. Lovely morning.'

'Have we met?' he asked.

'Yes.' she answered gaily. 'You gave us a lecture, though please don't ask me what it was about.'

His lips twitched in amusement. 'And your reason for being in a hospital gown?'

'Drunk and disorderly. Wasting hospital time and using a precious bed to sleep it off. Guilty as charged, your honour.' She saluted him and was delighted when he chuckled. He had a nice face when it was not being serious. A bit like Emily's, she thought.

'Climb in,' he said. 'Before you get mistaken for a runaway patient. I'll drop you where you need to go.'

Zoe stepped round the bonnet to the passenger door, and as she did so, she felt a sharp stabbing in her right heel. 'Ouch!'

She sank back in the luxurious leather seat. It was the poshest car she had ever been in. There was blood oozing, and she quickly fretted that it would stain the foot mat.

'What have you done?' he asked.

'Trod in glass, I think.'

He tutted mildly, then handed her a navy handkerchief. 'Hold that to it. I'll look at it when we get you home.'

Even before he set the car in motion she had begun to tell him of her present plight, and some twenty minutes later she was still talking as she stared at her surroundings in amazement. His home was stunning.

'Oh dear, I talk too much, don't I? I bet you forgot to take me home.'

He laughed. 'You actually never said where you lived and I was so entertained I forgot to ask. My wife or I will drop you back after breakfast. I have to go back to the hospital to check on a patient I've just operated on. How's the foot?'

She held it up for inspection.

'It's barely bleeding. I've got some plasters indoors.'

Zoe suddenly felt shy and underdressed in the hospital gown. She reached down and put on her strappy high heels, using the handkerchief for a bandage round her foot, and pulling the long cardigan right round her to cover the gown. She hoped his wife was as nice as he was.

The front door opened as they approached it and an attractive red-haired woman and young girl were coming out.

The woman drew back in surprise, her eyes raking over Zoe, taking everything in from her cheap shoes and blue nail polish, to yesterday's smudged makeup and her short black hair. Zoe fixed her eyes on the child who was staring at her with the same intense gaze as the woman beside her. 'Hello,' she said, and was rewarded with a sweet smile.

Mr Dalloway seemed to ignore the uncomfortable silence and frosty stare the woman gave him. Instead, he introduced his family. 'Jemma, this is Zoe. Zoe, this is Jemma, my wife, and Isobel, my daughter. Zoe has somehow got glass in her foot,' he added, as if this was enough explanation for turning up with a stranger. The woman threw a withering look at her husband, took hold of the child's hand and moved her forward. 'We were waiting to hear your car. I shall be out for a while, Rupert. I'm not the only fucking doctor in this household. I need a break sometimes.'

He looked at her with a puzzled expression on his face. 'The shops won't even be open yet. It's Sunday.'

She smiled tightly. 'Well, we'll get breakfast somewhere then, won't we? It'll be nice to be out of the house for a while.'

'I want to stay with Daddy,' the child chanted loudly. 'Daddy. Daddy. Daddy.'

The woman cast her an impatient stare. 'In that case, you shall,' she said crossly, before marching in the direction of the car her husband had just got out of. 'You can use mine, if you have to go back out,' she shouted, before revving the engine and leaving a cloud of gravel dust in her haste to get away.

Zoe felt embarrassed at witnessing the domestic dispute and wished she hadn't been so foolish in coming here. The brief interlude of enjoyment was over.

Mr Dalloway led the way into his home and she followed. Isobel scampered through the house out of sight.

He frowned. 'She'll be on Jemma's iPad as soon as her mother's back is turned. Her behaviour of late—' He shook his head, despondently. 'Never mind. Come this way. Tea or coffee?' he asked pleasantly, as he led her into a huge kitchen. 'And I make a good scrambled egg when our housekeeper isn't here and for the moment she isn't. She will be at church, as she is at this time every Sunday, putting us lot to shame with her devotion.'

'Maybe I should go,' Zoe offered. 'I can get a taxi.'

'Nonsense,' he said. 'Never mind all that you heard. We're just going through a bit of a hard time. My wife's a doctor too, but she's minding our son at the moment.'

Zoe looked round for a second child.

'He's in bed,' Dalloway said, pointing at the ceiling.

'I'll make the tea,' Zoe suggested, feeling herself relax again. 'You make the eggs.'

In the kitchen they carried on talking and Dalloway turned to her. 'If I can help out with your money problem, I'd like to.'

Zoe felt herself redden. 'I didn't tell you about it to make you give me money,' she said in a hoity tone.

He smiled kindly and for a moment she wished he was her father. 'I know you didn't, Zoe. But I would be pleased to help you.'

She pointed a teaspoon at him. 'You know, if this country, like other countries, let us sell our blood, I'd have sold a good few pints by now. You know in the States you can get about fifty dollars for one pint. I'd only need to sell about six pints to sort my debt out.'

'More if you have a rare type blood group,' he said in a dead-pan tone.

'Really?' Her eyes brightened at the thought, and then she saw the look on his face.

'You're joking, aren't you?'

He stared at her mock sternly. 'You might get a free T-shirt or tickets to the cinema, though. Your information is dated. Imagine all the junkies who would be queuing up if that were the case.'

She gave a rueful shrug. 'Oh well, maybe I can sell something else. An arm, maybe? I have two,' she said impishly.

He chuckled. 'Look, if it makes you feel better I'll set up a payment plan and you can pay me back twenty pounds a month. How does that sound?'

She stared at him, astonished, then twirled on the spot, clapping her hands. 'That sounds like a great plan to me.' She looked at him, the mirth and silliness gone from her face. 'Thank you.'

He shrugged and turned back to whisking the eggs.

Zoe finished making the tea and then asked for directions to the bathroom.

He told her there was one halfway down the corridor from the front door. She found it and then instead of returning to the kitchen, she wandered through a stone archway into a room that would be big enough to hold a party for at least a hundred people. She saw the gallery and could not stop herself from climbing the stairs, her high heels clattering as she ran up them. She leaned over the balcony, imagining herself as Juliet, when she heard a small voice calling.

'Is that you, Daddy?'

She walked in the direction of the voice and through an open door saw a young boy in bed, his small body hooked up to a complicated-looking machine with blood running through its tubes.

'Hello,' she called softly so as not to alarm him.

He smiled shyly. 'Can you read me a story, please?'

Zoe smiled back. 'Of course.' She walked over to a low bookcase and knelt down to view the choices. 'Any particular one?' she asked.

'The Very Hungry Caterpillar.'

'I don't like that one,' Isobel said, and Zoe saw her sitting in a corner with an iPad held in her hands.

'We'll pick one you like after,' Zoe said to placate her. Isobel stormed out of the room and Zoe stared after her in surprise, hoping she hadn't upset her.

She was nearing the end of the story when Mr Dalloway found her. He was stood in the doorway, listening. 'Hello Walter,' he said. 'How's my boy today?'

Zoe felt unbearably sad. Though still a relatively inexperienced student nurse, she could tell that the child was seriously ill. She now understood why Mr Dalloway always looked so sad.

She got up from the boy's bed and made her way to the door.

'He'll eventually need a new liver,' said Mr Dalloway quietly.

Zoe stared at him in shock. Their conversations about her needing money and selling her blood were going through her head as she backed out onto the landing. Had he brought her to his home for a reason?

He must have seen something in her face, because he put a hand out towards her. 'Zoe, I'm not talking about you. I'm just saying it, that's all.'

She backed further away from him, feeling ridiculous, confused and embarrassed.

Of course he wasn't suggesting she be the donor, and now after this he probably wouldn't want to know her anymore. She'd had a sickening thought about him and he knew. She had spoiled their new friendship with her wild imagination. She turned and took flight and he called to her to stop running. She took the first step of the stairs fast, and before her other foot could find its partner she lost her balance in the high-heeled shoes. She teetered at the top of the stairs, seeing all the solid wood she would bounce off and the slab of stone at the bottom that would eventually break her fall. Then a hand touched the small of her back and she glanced back gratefully at her saviour, feeling the grip on her clothes. She trembled at the thought of how close she'd come to being seriously injured. Emily would have been so cross.

Chapter Fifty-Three

'It was an accident,' he repeated, as he came to the end of his tale. 'A tragic accident.' He looked wrung out. Emily stood up without a word and left him at the table. He stayed seated till a prison guard came to take him back to his cell.

Had he brought her to his home for a reason that day? He didn't think so. Had she planted the seed for what was to eventually grow? When he looked at her lying there, her young body hardly broken, her head touching one shoulder, the stem that kept her alive had simply snapped, he thought; how heartless death was to take a body that was in perfect order, because its weak point had broken under pressure. He saw her death as a betrayal of life and vowed he'd do everything to save his son. He owed it to her memory. A month after that terrible day, they thought their prayers had been answered. A possible match for Walter had been found; only to have their hopes dashed as further tests proved it wasn't.

When Walter started to get more ill, his unwillingness to give up on his son drove him to desperate measures. His patients were no longer just his patients. When they stepped into his consulting room and stared across the desk at him, telling him their ailments, his only thought would be: was today the day he found someone to save his son? He tested their blood without invitation, without conscience. It was his belief that if he could save Walter, Zoe would not have died in vain. That she mattered. If only to remind him how easy a life became a death. Dalloway felt tears blind him. In the end it was all hopeless. Everything had been in vain.

He could never tell Emily fully about that day. The secret was too painful to tell. The desperate call he made to Shelly – the only person he could think of to come and help him. She'd occupied Isobel and distracted Maria when she returned from church, sending her on errands she neither wanted nor needed. She'd taken Isobel for a walk, returning her with field-picked flowers clutched in her hand, wanting to give them to Zoe. Her eyes still looked shocked in her small white face. He'd taken them from her and said Zoe was asleep.

He wrapped her in a sheet, arranged the flowers around her head. He placed in her hand a small photo he had found in her purse of her and someone who looked like her.

She'd been a sweet young woman who had come into his home and for a short while chased the darkness away. Her visit changed his life for ever. Her death was a secret he could never reveal. Not even to his wife. She had seen Zoe visit their home, seen the news reporting her missing and yet she didn't confront him. She didn't say a word, and he knew then that she would do anything to save Walter. Even if it meant not knowing if her husband had anything to do with a young woman disappearing. When he found Sophia Trendafilova he wanted to get down on ber_ded knee, to give thanks for the gift she gave. But her gift came with a price he could never atone for.

She died trying to save his son.

Nina Barrows died because of his son.

Emily Jacobs suffered because of his son.

These deeds could not go unpunished. And nor too could Zoe's death. He would give anything to change that day. Her death, even though he tried to think it an accident, haunted him night and day. Isobel had stopped her falling. Her small hand had gripped her clothes. Then she'd looked at her father, and he'd seen a mutinous, calculating look in her stare, and in that final second, before he saw her small hand let go, her palm turn round, her hand at the ready, she smiled at him and then she pushed.

'She's sleeping,' he told her.

He lived every day knowing, seeing, exactly what his daughter had done. When she held his hand and touched his skin with the press of her small palm, when he looked down at her and she smiled, he felt his heart break at the secret he kept for her sake, and he saw something inside her was broken.

Zoe's death could not go unpunished. A sentence had to be served.

Acknowledgements

Writing is possibly the scariest job I've ever had and I am so grateful to have the opportunity to say a heartfelt thank you to you, The Reader, for helping me believe I could do it again. Your opinion matters!

A huge thank you to Sophie Orme and Jennie Rothwell, my editors at Bonnier Zaffre and the entire team for making this book the best it could be. Thank you for all the gentle pushes and enormous support you amazing team! Thanks to Joel Richardson for opening the first door.

Thank you to Rory Scarfe, my agent, for telling me I have at least twenty books in me. Your encouragement and belief does me the power of good.

A very special thank you to Miss Samantha Williams BSc MBBS FRCS (Gen Surg) Oncoplastic breast surgeon for your generous time and invaluable input and your intention to visit you know where . . . just to see if it were possible. Thank you so much! Any mistakes are of course mine.

Thank you to Michael Knight, my son-in-law, for pointing me in the right direction on how to hang out with the police (without being arrested). Thank you to PC Zoe Phillips for introducing me to the wonderful Sergeant Kurt Swallow. Thank you so much Kurt for not only reading my book and advising me on police matters, but also for the opportunity of riding along with the Fast Response Team! I am so grateful.

Thank you once again to Martyn Folks for keeping opinions honest.

Thanks to my sister, Bernie for taking time to read the first draft and still liking the story. Thanks to my three children Lorcan, Katherine and Alexandra and daughter-in-law Harriet for the endless chats on plot direction. Your imaginations gave me so many better paths to take – and some nightmares too. You know how scared I am of horror stories.

To my husband Mike, thank you for letting me just sit and be silent in my imaginative world, without noticing I stayed in my pyjamas all day every day.

To Darcie, Dolly and Arthur who light up my life and bring me back to the real world.

Lastly for you mum – hope they have a good library in heaven and you get to read this one too!

Note: If you visit Bath and should need to visit a hospital, you will find the care and service at the Royal United Hospital excellent. You may, however, not find The Windsor Bridge Hospital as you drive across the Windsor Bridge, sitting tall with its black glass windows looking down on the River Avon, but will agree it would be a perfect place to position this hospital. So who knows, maybe one day . . .

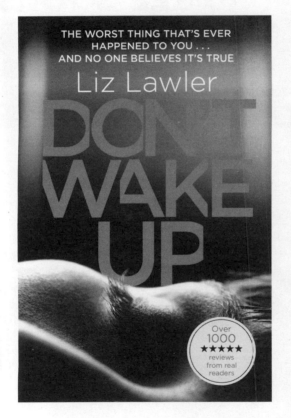

Want to read
NEW BOOKS
before anyone else?

Like getting
FREE BOOKS?

Enjoy sharing your
OPINIONS?

Discover
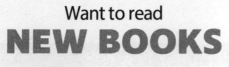
READERS FIRST
Read. Love. Share.

Sign up today to win your first free book:
readersfirst.co.uk